DUE
FEB 2020

DELETED

D0533235

Please return this book on or before the date shown above. To
renew go to www.essex.gov.uk/libraries, ring 0345 603 7628 or
go to any Essex library.

General

Essex County Council

a village affair

Julie Houston

HEAD
OF
ZEUS

First published in the United Kingdom in 2018 by Aria,
an imprint of Head of Zeus Ltd

This paperback edition first published in 2020 by Aria

9 7 5 3 1 2 4 6 8

A CIP catalogue record for this book is available from the British Library.

ISBN (PB) 9781838930639
ISBN (E) 9781788549806

Printed and bound in Great Britain by
CPI Group (UK) Ltd, Croydon CRO 4YY

Head of Zeus Ltd
First Floor East
5–8 Hardwick Street
London EC1R 4RG

WWW.HEADOFZEUS.COM

a village affair

1

How I Lost My Husband...

It was the first Saturday evening in September, the weekend before the long school summer holiday finally came to a close. Before we knew it, the nights would be drawing in and the supermarkets would be stocking up with the euphemistically termed 'Seasonal Goods', determined to be the first to roadblock both ends of each aisle with garishly purple octagonal tins of sweets. I leant forward to catch the light in the mirror and smiled at my reflection, accepting that the sales girl at the Charlotte Tilbury franchise in the newly opened John Lewis in Leeds had been right about the lip colour after all.

'Nice lipstick.' Mark stopped struggling with the ends of the black material, dropped a kiss onto my bare shoulder and lifted his starched-collared neck in my direction, a movement now almost automatic after eighteen years of marriage and the countless black-tie dos we'd attended together during this time. I reached both hands to his tie, deftly tied the fiddly bow and arranged the collar symmetrically before spraying myself with just two squirts of Jean-Louis Scherrer, the perfume that Mark never forgot to buy for me at the airport on his numerous business trips abroad.

I glanced around my cream-decorated bedroom, at the Jane Churchill curtains and matching cushions, at the neatly folded rose-pink and cream towels in their correct place in the immaculate en-suite. My eyes rested just for a moment on the three subtle pastels arranged neatly above our bed; gone were the tattered 'Ban the Bomb', Greenham Common and Led Zepp posters from my adolescence, arranged and stuck haphazardly with rusty drawing pins.

All was well.

At almost seventeen, Tom was more than of an age to be left at home to look after himself, although I wasn't so sure about his ability to babysit his fourteen-year-old sister. I frowned slightly and thought, not for the first time that evening, that maybe I should have asked Mark's mother to come over and stay. I knew the minute we were off in the taxi, which even now was idling in the drive, Tom would be back in his room, nose in his maths books, and Freya would have unsupervised access to her mobile, computer, TV and the cake tin. I hesitated for a split second longer but, hearing Mark shouting from the garden for me to get a move on, I grabbed my bag – another present from Mark – and told myself the truth: my kids were good kids, sensible, well-behaved and, while they might not spend huge amounts of time in each other's company, I knew when push came to shove they'd look out for each other and remember to lock doors and close curtains against the darkening September evening.

I smiled, congratulating myself on my life and achievements. I was with the husband I adored, who adored me right back; I loved my modern, bright and, let's face it, rather upmarket home in the village of Westenbury; I was realising my professional dream after only a couple of years back in the classroom after several years as a stay-at-home mum, and was about to start as deputy head at the much-revered Little Acorns Primary School just down the lane. And, right now, I was off to spend the evening with the three friends I loved most in all the world: Tina, Fi and Clare.

'You're looking lovely as usual, sweetie,' Tina said, pouring champagne for me and admiring the new black skimpy cocktail dress I was wearing in honour of this charity ball and auction. 'Mark been shopping for you again? You must have the only husband in Midhope who not only knows your size, but knows what will suit you and who isn't afraid to go into Bows and Belles to search for it.'

As she spoke I glanced up at Mark, who ran his fingers down my bare back while continuing his conversation with Simon, Tina's husband.

'Now,' Tina continued, polishing off her drink before reaching for the bottle and refilling her glass, 'we don't want to miss any of this auction. I've got my eye on the villa in Portugal that's up for grabs: one week next August. It sleeps fourteen – can you imagine? – so it'll be jolly expensive, but it comes with a personal chef...' Tina thrust the auction pamphlet into my hand. 'Look, Lot four... If we all club together it won't be too bad. What do you think...?'

'Sounds heaven.' I closed my eyes, imagining a week of hot sunshine and no cooking or clearing up into the bargain; being waited on hand and foot while drinking cocktails with my three best friends and our families. 'Will Clare come, do you think?'

'I don't see why not. She'd be able to bring her man of the moment. Whoever that might be...'

'*Should* we be bidding on something while Mark is the auctioneer?' I frowned. 'I mean, might it not be seen as bending the rules if the auction goes our way?'

'Oh, it'll be fine.' Tina dismissed my worries with a wave of her hand, which turned into a wave of welcome as Fi, Matthew and Clare made their way across the crowded bar to our table. 'Simon will bid for us. Anyway, it's who comes up with the best bid. Mark can't control that. We'll just have to make sure we urge Simon on to the bitter end... until we have victory.'

An hour had passed, the starter – a doughy, tepid mushroom vol-au-vent – had been served and, in some cases eaten with gusto; in most, attempted and left on the sides of plates. Fi and I, enjoying the champagne and Clare's tale involving her latest conquest – a traffic warden whom she took up to her office in order to avoid a parking ticket – had to be shushed by Tina as Mark took the auctioneer's stand and someone on the front table affected a drum roll with a couple of side plates on its wooden top.

'Ladies and Gentlemen, welcome to the 2017 Midhope Families in Need appeal. The majority of us here in this room will never understand what some families have to go through just to survive and stay together...' Mark paused theatrically and surveyed the room, smiling. '... So, dig deep in those pockets, refill your glasses and let's get going with the first ten lots in your booklet this evening.'

I felt tears threaten and swallowed hard. Mark had always been determined to put others first, but even so, it was ridiculous to be still so in love with one's husband after all these years. Fi and Clare were laughing at me: they knew how Mark and I felt about each other.

'Simon, are you ready?' As soon as the auction for Lot four – the villa in Portugal – was about to start, Tina shook Simon's arm none too gently and the white wine he'd been about to lift to his mouth spilt over both their hands. Tina glared at him. 'Look, I really want this. Do you want me to do it? Shall I bid...?'

Simon was very drunk.

He staggered to his feet with the auction pamphlet in one hand and, after stabilising himself by grabbing the loose folds of the starched white tablecloth, refilled his glass and immediately downed it in one.

'So, we come to Lot four. A really fabulous villa in Carvoeiro in Portugal…' The sound of Mark's steady, encouraging tone momentarily distracted my attention from Simon, who was now standing calmly to my left. Only his eyes, glittering almost manically, portrayed how much alcohol he'd consumed.

'We're up to £2,000. Come on, a fabulous villa for fourteen must be worth a lot more than this. Who'll give me £2,200?' Mark smiled at the guests in front of him. He wasn't going to hurry this; he knew he was on to a winner with this villa.

'Mr Auctioneer,' Simon shouted loudly and the whole room turned, surprised, towards our table '… Mr Mark *Fucking* Auctioneer. Tell you what. You stop shagging my wife, as you've been doing for the last… um, let me see… two years isn't it…? You stop *shagging* my wife and I'll give you however much you think *that's* worth…'

2

... And How I Found Him in the First Place

1998

'Mum, please don't tell me you're going like that.'
'Which bit don't you like?' Paula turned to the ancient, tarnished mirror that had hung in the exact same position over the mantelpiece for as long as I could remember, baring her teeth in a rictus smile.

'All of it, for heaven's sake. That hat looks like something from Oxfam.' I frowned, taking in my mother's bizarre wedding ensemble, and wishing once again the wish that I'd had ever since my first day at infants' school when I began to realise, with a five-year-old's desire to be the same as everyone else, that my mother was somehow different from other mothers. Paula's dreadlocked hair, pierced nose, flowing orange dress, and open sandals revealing grubby hennaed feet stood out starkly among the business suits, gym apparel, trendy jeans and snow-white shirts sported by my new class mates' parents and Miss Palmer herself.

'The hospice shop, actually,' my mother smiled beatifically. 'A bargain at £2.50 *and* I have the satisfaction of knowing that my purchase not only helps the planet by recycling someone else's unwanted goods, but also puts some money into something other than the capitalist shop owner's pocket.'

Oh God, did she ever give up?

'I just think you could have made a bit more of an effort for your only niece's wedding day.'

'Effort? *Effort?* Do you know how many charity shops I had to trail round in order to come up with matching items that wouldn't upset your auntie Linda's strict wedding colour scheme?'

'And you think what you're wearing *won't* annoy her?' I glanced once more at Mum's strange aubergine knitted dress, at the purple tights and offending purple floppy hat. 'At least let me put your hair up and try out a couple of my lipsticks on you; as a family member, she won't be able to hide you at the back out of the way, will she?'

'No time for that,' Mum said cheerfully. 'The taxi with your nan and granddad will be here in a minute. I think we both look pretty good, although...' she took an appraising look at the little peach-coloured dress and matching collarless jacket I'd spent too many Saturdays looking for, after being inspired by Carrie Bradshaw in *Sex and the City*, and on which I'd spent far too much of my newly qualified teacher's wage. '... I've a fabulous pair of dangly orange earrings that would liven up that outfit – give it a bit of colour...'

'Are we ready for the off?' My nan appeared at the open kitchen door, frowning up at the gathering dark clouds heading our way and tottering slightly on her new navy court shoes, bunions obviously giving her some gyp. 'Come on, our Sandra, let's be 'aving you. Your granddad's hoping he can have a quick one before the kick-off ...'

I grinned, loving Nan for her words. 'Letsby Avenue' and 'Our Sandra' – Nan had never been able to get used to my 'right weird' name of Cassandra Moonbeam – had been so often uttered over the years I reckoned they'd be engraved on her tombstone if she managed to avoid the willow casket and humanist service Mum had in mind for any of us popping our clogs before her.

Nan took my arm as we made our way down the garden steps to the beribboned wedding car waiting on the street. 'What *is* your mother wearing this time?' she tutted in a whisper. 'Our Linda and our Davina won't be happy. You'd have thought she'd have smartened herself up a bit, wouldn't you? I mean, it's not every day we have a right big do like this. Linda and Anthony have shelled out an absolute fortune for this wedding, you know. Mind you, Anthony can afford it...'

'Come on, Dot, get a move on,' Granddad Norman shouted through the open window of the wedding car. 'Stop telling tales or we'll be late.'

'Or *you* won't be able to sneak off to The Royal Oak, you mean. It's not the done thing, anyhow, calling for a pint before your granddaughter gets wed. Just behave yourself and wait for t'champagne to be served.'

'Hello, love. You look smashing.' Granddad leant over the front seat to hug me and I hugged him right back, breathing in the Old Spice aftershave he'd never veered away from wearing and which he regularly sloshed on with a heavy hand. He and Nan were such a big part of my life; the idea that, one day, they wouldn't be around was unthinkable.

'You look pretty good yourself,' I said. 'You scrub up well.'

Nan snorted. 'Had to send him back upstairs once he was dressed. He still had muck from the allotment under his nails. Shove up a bit, Paula,' she went on, inching her not insubstantial behind along the back seat. 'I can't breathe in this new corset. The woman in M&S said it was right, that it'd settle down a bit, but...' she took a deep breath, '... I think the next size up would have been better.'

'So, love, how's the job going? Still enjoying being in Derby? Got a boyfriend yet? Your cousin Davina's beaten you to it again.'

'She's welcome to it,' I said untruthfully at the same time as Mum tutted disparagingly. She didn't believe in marriage, especially when thousands of pounds were being forked out in order for a woman to enslave herself to some man who'd want his socks washing and his meat and two veg on the table at six every evening. 'And yes, I love Derby and I love the teaching. It's just what I've always wanted. I'm saving up to buy a house there, Granddad.'

'Property is theft,' Mum murmured mildly, glancing out at the street through a window of gathering and breaking raindrops.

'But "proper tea" isn't.' Granddad turned and winked at me, attempting to lighten any developing tension between Mum and myself, as had been his practice for as long as I could remember.

'You never told me this, Cassandra.' Mum now turned to face me, head on.

'Well, I don't tell you everything.'

'I don't think you tell me *anything*.' Mum's face, the bit that could be still seen under the floppy brim of the vintage purple hat, was momentarily sad and I felt a twinge of guilt. She was right: I rarely told her my plans.

'Hi, I'm Fiona, pleased to meet you. Friend or family?'

We'd been allowed, finally, to leave the interminable photo session outside the church where an unseasonably cold shower had left white streaks in over-the-top fake tans, and sent guests scurrying for umbrellas and waiting cars to head to the reception.

'Sorry?'

'Are you related to Davina or Luke?'

'I'm Davina's cousin. Mum and Linda are sisters.' I knew I was gaping at this rather large woman, who couldn't have been much older than me, easing herself into one of the twelve chairs decorated with jaunty pink and white balloons and chocolate-box bows in pink netting. They reminded me of the starched pink net tutus I'd dreamt of wearing in the ballet class I never got to go to. Mum was away at Greenham Common, if I remember rightly, and although Granddad had said he'd take me along to the village hall class, it never actually materialised. I knew I was being rude but I continued to stare at Fiona. She was hugely pregnant and blue. Literally. Blue lines, crosses and something that looked remarkably like the outline of a map of India were etched randomly on her face.

'Fell asleep before we set off,' she grimaced. 'I'm so knackered…' she rubbed her lower back in the way of all the pregnant women I'd ever met '… and the two-year-old found the blue felt marker pen. He also, little sod, decided to eat the green colouring I'd left out for the minute I had the energy to make his elf birthday cake and now he's shitting Martians. Oops sorry, shouldn't say shit at a wedding. Do you suppose the alcohol mafia will descend if I go for a glass of wine?'

'When's the baby due?'

'Last week.' Fiona rubbed her back once again. 'I've carted Van Gogh – obviously in his blue and green period – off to Matthew's mum so I'm free to go into labour as from this minute.'

A huge dark-haired giant of a man was in the process of finding his name on the table and once he did so he sat down heavily and looked at his watch. He must have been six-foot-four at least, and broad with it. His white shirt strained across his massive chest and he fiddled uncomfortably with the button at his neck.

'Matthew, my husband,' Fiona indicated with her glass of wine. 'He hates wearing a suit, collar and tie.'

'Doesn't he have to wear one for work?' I asked, smiling at the other guests on our table as they began to take their seats.

'The cattle might appreciate some sartorial elegance every now and again but getting cow shit out of his *overalls* is bad enough. Don't fancy trying to get it out of a pin-striped suit.' She laughed at the very idea.

'He's a farmer?'

'Yes. Adores everything about it. Farming's in his blood. I'm a city girl myself – from Leeds. Never understood the point of the countryside really.'

I laughed. 'So how do you know Luke?'

'Matthew and Luke were at school together. Known each other years.'

The rest of our table were settling themselves in, making introductions, taking off too-high heels and headache-inducing hats, and I suddenly felt a bit shy, wishing, as I so often did, that I had a partner of my own to pull out my chair and give me a knowing wink when it was time to go home.

A tall and very elegant blonde, wearing a hat almost as big as Mum's, sat herself on my left and immediately re-applied lipstick from a nifty little mirrored case she deftly flicked open. I made a note to buy one for myself. She offered a hand. 'Hi, I'm Tina. Davina said she was going to put any singletons together, and to look out for you.'

'Oh?' I had an awful feeling Davina must have told Tina to look after me in the same way Auntie Linda had always made a reluctant Davina include me in the many outings, parties and sleepovers arranged for her as the spoilt princess she undoubtedly was, and I could feel embarrassment rising.

'Yes, she thought you and I would get on. Davina and I are both in the same law firm in Leeds, at the very bottom of the slippery career pole.'

'Oh God,' Fiona sighed. 'What I'd give to be at the bottom of a slippery pole, inching my way up the career ladder instead of heading for another bout of displaying my bits and pieces to all and sundry.'

'What *did* you do before you became a mum?' I was curious. 'Can't you go back to it once you've had this baby?'

'Don't believe a word she says,' Matthew interrupted, laughing. 'Fiona was temping – spending her days filing other people's invoices as well as her nails – when I met her. She was more than happy to be whisked off to the country to play at "The Farmer Wants a Wife".'

'You continue to think that if you must,' Fiona said loftily. 'Once I've popped this one out I think I'm going to apply for a place at Leeds University. I quite fancy law...' She beamed across at Tina. 'You'll have to give me some tips.'

'Now, aren't all single girls promised a bonk of some sort at weddings?' Tina turned to survey the rest of the tables, straining her neck for a better view of any possible bonkers. 'Can't see any promising candidates at the moment...'

'What about the best man?' Fiona suggested, turning her bulk awkwardly in the general direction of the top table.

'Yes, have to admit, he's in the running. Although—' Tina broke off, ducking down in her seat. 'Sorry, I'm just trying to avoid that woman in the huge purple hat. She cornered me in the loo and asked me, if I was local, if I might be interested in joining her Astroshamanic workshop at some point next week.'

I closed my eyes and took a deep breath.

'Any bonking involved?' Fiona asked hopefully.

'Apparently, it's a practice that – hang on, what did she say – "involves a practitioner reaching altered states of consciousness in order to perceive and interact with a spirit world in order to channel these transcendental energies into this world."' Tina laughed. 'I told the purple hat that I'd already been known to lose consciousness after an interaction with spirits on a Friday night out in the middle of Leeds and to give me her card.'

'You got off lightly.' A devastatingly pretty girl dressed in yellow, whose pert behind had caught the attention of every male at our end of the hotel dining room, took the one remaining empty chair at the table. 'I've just spent fifteen minutes trying to escape from some guy determined to sell me Personal Breakdown Cover.'

'I could do with some of that,' Fiona sighed, massaging her bump. 'I think I'm on the point of a personal breakdown myself.' She began to laugh. 'I remember one of my first boyfriends, when I knew absolutely nothing about, you know, sex and all that goes with it, asking me about *mutual orgasm*...' She broke off, holding on to her bump as she continued to giggle. 'I was convinced he was trying to sell me some sort of insurance cover and I said,

"Oh, no, it's fine, thanks, I'm more than able to sort that kind of thing on my own."'

The girl in yellow laughed, downed her entire glass of champagne and grinned round the room at the rest of us. 'Hi, I'm Clare. I think I'm down for the singles table so I'm assuming that's all of us?' She raised her huge brown eyes questioningly and pushed an escaped strand of glossy chestnut hair behind one ear.

'Not me,' Fiona said. 'But this is Cassandra and Tina, and I think the chap next but one to Matthew is by himself.'

I took a closer look at the fair-haired man whom Fiona had pointed out and who was now deep in conversation with the girl on his left. He must have realised he was under scrutiny because he lifted his head and looked in our direction, meeting and holding my gaze until I felt myself redden.

'Would you like one of these?' I looked up from my place in the queue at the bar and saw that, close up, the man from down the bottom of the table was ticking even more of the boxes on my 'The Man I'm Going to Marry' list, first created at the age of eight and refined ever since. Tall, blue eyes, smiley face, no (visible) tattoos and wearing a suit. Tick, tick, tick, tick. And tick.

'Thanks.' I moved away from the post-speech scrum at the bar and followed him across the wooden dance floor, where the DJ was revving up to blast our ears with Eighties' favourites, towards an empty table at the back.

'I didn't realise you were Davina's cousin,' Mark smiled, pouring me a glass of champagne and managing to brush my hand with his own as he did so. When I didn't reply – couldn't reply because, in my nervousness at being alone with this man I'd spent the last two hours surreptitiously gazing at over the megalithic floral decorations, my ability to swallow appeared to have deserted me. I'd taken a ridiculously huge gulp of extremely gaseous champagne and now it appeared to have nowhere to go except into my lungs, which would result in it being spat out over Mark's morning-suit trousers or down my nose, which would surely be the end of a beautiful relationship before we'd even begun.

I managed to smile as well as one can smile with a mouthful of gas and liquid and hoped I appeared somewhat enigmatic as opposed to mentally deranged.

'Davina?' Mark tried again, obviously puzzled at my silence.

The enigmatic smile, slightly more manic, returned and Mark began to look worried.

'Are you OK? Can I get you a drink of water or something?'

Mustering all my strength, I willed my throat to open and swallowed the recalcitrant champagne. The resulting coughing fit and streaming eyes drew the attention of my nan who, seeing me struggling, bustled over and thumped me firmly on the back of my new and expensive little designer jacket.

'Are you all right, love?' Nan turned to Mark and said confidentially, 'Used to be a bit asthmatic when she were a little girl. If ever she got over-excited – Christmas, birthdays, a day out at Southport and the like – we had to watch her, you know.'

'Nan, I think I had one wheezy attack one Christmas,' I managed to splutter through another bout of choking. 'The drink's just gone down the wrong way, that's all.'

'Come and get some fresh air,' Mark smiled, standing and wrapping his jacket round my shoulders. Out of the corner of my eye I could see Fiona, Tina and Clare – who'd obviously bonded over the lemon tart – nudging each other and making surreptitious thumbs up signs in our direction.

The rain had finally stopped and quite a few of the guests were outside sharing a crafty fag or simply enjoying the cool summer evening breeze after the stuffiness of the hotel reception room.

Once outside, Mark led the way across the wet lawn to a dry-stone wall that separated the hotel grounds from a glorious wildflower meadow sporting cowslips, early purple orchids and the tiny blue flowers of leadwort.

'How do you know what they are?' Mark asked, impressed as I rattled off their names.

'My granddad. He doesn't believe in planting lupins and gladioli in his garden. Beyond his allotment there's a small field that no one seems to own and over the years he's thrown tons of wildflower seeds at it and now it's almost famous: "Norman's Meadow" it's called locally...'

'And you? What are *you* called locally?' Mark smiled down at me from his six-foot height and, as he reached out a hand and gently rubbed mascara from my cheek with the ball of his thumb, I felt such an unexpected lurch of anticipation and excitement that I was in danger of toppling over into the meadow and happily drowning in the sea of beckoning wildflowers.

Before I left home and Yorkshire for Derby I'd not clocked up a great deal of experience of men, and any dates I did have I'd made sure had finished at the bus stop in town: there was no way I was bringing anyone back to our house to meet Paula. Once away at university and now living in Derby, things had been a bit different and I'd had what I suppose was my fair share of men, but relationships had never lasted long. If I felt they weren't going anywhere – which in my book was finding a man who wanted the same things that Paula scoffed at and I craved: a mortgage, semi, two kids – I generally ditched them. 'I'm "Our Sandra" to my nan...' I took a deep breath, '... Cassandra Moonbeam to my mum. And Cassie to everyone else.'

'Well,' Mark said, smiling and bending his face to mine, 'I shall call you Cass, if that's OK with you?'

There was something wonderfully erotic about standing on this wet lawn, the sound from the hotel wedding party fading into the background while the heady scents of a summer evening invaded my senses.

I smiled right back. 'That's very OK,' I breathed, leaning into him. 'Very OK indeed.'

3

Could It Get Any Worse...?

The week before Easter, a couple of years before what would become known as 'the night of the auction' I was having a discussion with my class of eleven-year-olds as to whether Jesus knew he was actually going to die. We'd just introduced a brand-new RE syllabus and, rather than regurgitating the same old story with the accompanying pictures of Jesus on a donkey and the crowd waving palm leaves – or the actual palm *trees*, in a couple of cases where the illustrator had obviously been more intent on what was happening outside the window rather than the underlying theology – we were philosophically exploring the idea of *destiny* and whether Jesus could have done anything to change the path down which he was heading. He knew Peter was about to betray him (I'd been in the chorus of an amateur production of *Jesus Christ Superstar* a few months earlier and remember pointing a dramatic finger and singing to the somewhat bemused class, 'One of *you* will betray me, one of *you* will deny me...') so why the hell didn't he leg it while he had the chance?

Curled up in a foetal position on the sitting-room sofa in the early hours of the Sunday morning following my own betrayal at the hands of the twin Judases – namely my husband and my best friend – I ventured the same question to Clare who, together with Fiona, had brought me home after the auction and was refusing to leave me on my own. 'So, is this destiny?' I asked her as she passed me tea. I'd wanted gin, wine, the disgustingly cloying cherry brandy that Mark's mother kept buying for us at Christmas, anything alcoholic to numb the terrible pain that was coursing through every part of me but, apart from the half-bottle of wine the two of us had shared earlier, Clare had refused to let me have any, saying I'd only feel worse once its effects had worn off.

'Destiny? Is what destiny?'

'You know, the path I have to take in life. Was it all mapped out for me by God and whatever I did, this was his plan.'

'God's plan?' Clare snorted angrily. 'I rather think it was Mark and Tina's plan, don't you?'

'What I'm saying is, was there anything I could have done differently or is that irrelevant?'

'Cassie, I hardly think this bombshell is your fault, for heaven's sake. But, did you really have no idea? Two years?' She shook her head. 'I'm sure I'd know if the man I was with was sleeping with someone else.'

'Nope, not a clue.'

'You seem to be taking this remarkably calmly.' She peered over her mug of tea at me. 'I'd have expected you to be sobbing, tearing your hair out.'

'I think it's because I don't actually believe what's happened. It's this destiny thing: if we hadn't gone to the auction none of this would have come out. We'd have taken a different path.'

'Oh, bloody hell, Cassie, I'm sorry but that's just bollocks. Of course it would have come out. Probably Tina was hoping it would. You know she and Simon haven't been getting on for ages.'

'Two years, Clare. Two bloody years. My husband and my best friend have been having it off for two years.' I sat up suddenly. 'But when? Where? Hotels in Brighton? Cosy little weekends in Paris? I just don't get it.'

'Well, *you* might not get it, but they were obviously getting their fair share... Sorry, that wasn't funny.' Clare frowned. 'To answer your question, they both have fairly high-powered jobs that take them away a lot. Particularly to London. Weren't they always in London together, getting together for a drink after their meetings, staying overnight?'

'Well, yes, but it was all so innocent...'

'Obviously not. So, sweetie, what are you going to do?' Clare looked at her watch. 'It's after four, Cassie. You need to get some sleep. Show me to your spare room; there's no way I'm leaving you by yourself.'

*

'Where's Dad?' Freya, pouring enough chocolate Shreddies into a bowl to feed an army, looked up from the task, spilling cereal onto the kitchen floor as she did so. 'Bugger.' She bent to pick up the escaped squares and shoved them all into her mouth. 'Five-second rule,' she managed to say before drowning the Shreddies that had actually hit target in full-fat milk. At fourteen Freya was tiny – the smallest girl in her year at school – but she still managed to put away twice the amount of food in a day that I consumed in a week. How did one tell an adolescent girl that her father wasn't at his usual Sunday morning place at the kitchen table, eating bacon and eggs and toast and lime marmalade, because he'd been shagging her auntie Tina for the past few years and her mother had subsequently banished him from the house?

The banishing of my husband bit hadn't been quite as calm and stiff-upper-lip as I might pretend. There was no scenario such as you might find in a 1920s silent movie, where the heroine (me) holds one hand to a pale forehead and points to the door with the other while the baddie (Mark) falls to his knees, wringing his hands and pleading forgiveness, while the other baddie (bloody Tina) slinks off into the night like the she-snake she had suddenly become. *Au contraire.* In reality, it was like something off *The Jeremy Kyle Show*. After Simon's shouting out to Mark, there was a deathly silence as shocked, bemused and amused – I did hear a couple of drunken guffaws – faces turned as one in the direction of our table. Then, as the loud and totally unexpected crashing to the floor of a pile of plates being wheeled in for the main course broke the silence, all hell had let loose. Mark, deathly white, had left the auctioneer's stand, hurrying through the excited rubber-necking guests to get to me and, taking my arm, had tried to drag me with him out of the room. Simon pushed Mark away from me, took a swing at him, missed and, skidding on an escaped vol-au-vent, landed on the floor at Tina's feet.

'Get up, you fucking idiot,' Tina hissed in a voice so full of venom I would, forever after, name her Serpentina.

Mark, pleading with me to leave the room with him, had taken both my hands in his but I shook him off, whereupon Tina had thrust her Louis Vuitton over one shoulder, grabbed her drink with one hand, my husband with the other (*my* husband, Serpentina) and together they'd exited the hall.

'Had to be done,' Simon had mumbled from the depths of the floor. 'Sorry, Cassie, sorry to spoil your evening… sorry, everybody… just carry on as if nothing's happened. Don't suppose we'll be wanting that Portuguese villa now…'

Matthew had reached his big solid farmer's hands down and pulled Simon to his feet, dusting him off and holding him upright while both Clare and Fi had ushered me out of the emergency exit and into Fiona's car before driving me back home.

Shock is a funny thing. It can render one hysterical or, in my case, totally calm. I'd felt as if I were in a play, that some drama was being acted out around me in which I just happened to have a walk-on part. And now I'd walked offstage and back to the dressing room.

'Your mum has a bit of a headache – boring night, anyway – we've left the men to it...' Clare had executed her lines perfectly, shouting them up to my daughter as Freya leant over the stair banister, wondering why we were back so early.

'You all right, Mum?' Tom had appeared at Freya's side, his short fair hair askew from his habit of running a hand constantly through the front of it while grappling with maths and science problems set for those already at university.

'I'm fine, really. Go back to what you were doing. Clare, Fiona and I are going to have a drink here.' Amazing what lies come glibly out of your mouth in order to protect your kids.

'Did you two know?' I'd demanded, closing the sitting-room door behind us and turning to face these two women, with whom, along with Tina, I'd shared all my hopes and dreams, ups and downs since we'd bonded at Davina's wedding. Surely Fiona and particularly Clare, whose proud boast was that she had supercharged antennae that could detect exactly what men were up to – and with whom – must have known what was going on.

'Honest, Cassie, I had no idea, I promise.' Lovely reliable, motherly Fiona had been visibly distressed at the very idea that she might have been a party to this and worse, that I could even think her capable of such a thing.

'Clare?'

Clare had hesitated. 'God, it all falls into place now. How could I have been so thick? I guessed she was up to something: she and Simon haven't been right for years; we all know that. And she has dropped a couple of hints to me over the years that there was someone else in her life but who was totally unobtainable... but I'm as shocked as you, Cassie, about who the someone else was. I honestly had no idea. It never occurred to me.'

'I bet you encouraged her, didn't you?' I turned on Clare, venting my fury wherever I could. 'You've never been able to understand being with one man, have you? Does it never occur to you that when you're having sex with one of your married men that he's someone else's husband, someone's dad?'

'Cassie, don't take this out on me.' Clare was calm. 'I've never pretended to be anything other than I am. Just because I've never wanted a husband—'

'One of your own, you mean. You're quite happy to have someone else's.'

'Stop it, Cassie, that's not fair,' Fiona interrupted my rant, shaking her head at me.

Perfectly calm still, Clare added, 'Cassie, this isn't about me. It's about you, Mark and Tina and you need to sort it. I'm here for you, but please don't bring *my* personal life into this.'

'Clare's right, Cassie,' Fiona said. 'Look,' she added hopefully, 'it might even be one big mistake. Maybe Simon just got so drunk and accused Mark because... well, because...' She trailed off as Clare looked at her pityingly.

'The bitch. The snake.' I turned my anger away from Clare and back to the real perpetrator. 'One of my best friends,' I howled, 'and she's been sleeping with my husband all these years.' Red-hot fury was coursing through every vein. I could feel it creeping, running, surging through every artery, every sinew, every bit of skin and bone.

'I'm not sure there's been much sleeping,' Clare said wryly, but I wasn't listening.

Where were my car keys?

'Don't even think about it,' Clare said, obviously guessing my thoughts. 'You've had too much to drink, for a start. And where do you think you're going to go? Roam the streets until you find them? Look, it's more than likely that Mark will come back in an hour or two. He's going to have to face you.'

'I can't see him, well, *either* of them, going back to Tina and Simon's place,' Fiona said, taking my hand. 'Jack will be there, for a start. She's not going to suddenly arrive back at home with no Simon, and with Mark in his place. Jack might be a pretty laid-back seventeen-year-old, always plugged into his music, but I reckon even he would notice the difference. Come on, Cassie, take your jacket off and stop pacing the room. He'll come back home and then you'll have to... well, you'll have to have it out with him and see what he has to say. And then decide what you want to do.'

'Don't talk with your mouth full,' I now said automatically, but without much hope or even interest that Freya might change the habit of a lifetime. My daughter didn't appear overly bothered about the whereabouts of her absent father, being more interested in the front-page headlines screaming out the infidelity of some minor MP. God, was everybody at it? Contrary to Fiona's assumption that Mark would return last night, there had been no sight or sound of him: no text, no missed mobile call, no ringing of the house phone with gabbled apologies.

Fiona herself had left within an hour or so of bringing me home, but as Freya started on her third crumpet, dripping with butter and raspberry jam, I heard Fiona's voice outside the open kitchen window. 'Stick a couple of those in for me, Freya, I'm starving.

'How are you? Clare still here?' Fiona lowered her voice, mindful of Freya's presence. 'Bloody hell, Cassie, you look awful. Did you sleep at all?'

'She's upstairs having a shower, and no, not much.' My head throbbed, my eyes were gritty from lack of sleep as well as the protracted crying I'd eventually succumbed to once Clare had tucked me up in bed, and I felt sick. Sick to the very core of me. I glanced across at Freya who, plugged into her music, one foot tucked up underneath her backside, was still in last night's pyjamas and appeared to be at the breakfast table for the duration. 'Come on, let's go and take some coffee out into the garden.'

I loved our garden. While the inside of my house was immaculate, everything in its place, surfaces free of crumbs and mirrors smear-free, the garden was a different matter. I'd inherited Granddad Norman's way of gardening and the area to my left was a mass of colour from the wildflower border I'd cultivated over the years.

An abundance of species bloomed profusely, providing not only a display of which I was inordinately proud, but a rich source of nectar for the butterflies and other insects that were obsessively thrumming their paths around the flowers. On this beautiful early September morning, summer was stubbornly refusing any leeway to the autumn months ahead as Fiona and I made our way to a sunny spot at the bottom of the lawned area.

'Who's going to cut the grass?' I suddenly asked, starting to weep once more. 'I do the flowers and weeding and Mark cuts the lawn.' I paused, looking round at the soft green velvet on which Fiona and I were sitting. 'I don't even know how to pull the wotsit to start the mower. Or where to put the petrol.'

'Haven't you heard anything from him?'

'Nope. I honestly thought he'd have come back last night. You know, try to let himself in and slink upstairs to the spare room. I put the chain on so when he *did* appear I'd have to go down and let him in. Or not, as it turned out. Not a thing. Not a phone call, a text, nothing.'

'He'll be scared shitless.' This from Clare, who now hunkered down at our side with a tray of coffee, before handing a plate of crumpets to Fiona. 'Freya said these are for you.'

Fiona's eyes lit up. 'Yum... Actually, give me two minutes to do my exercise or I'll never get myself up if I've eaten.' She lay on her back and, hoisting her legs and white-jeaned backside in the air, turned her face fully towards us in order to carry on the conversation. 'Crapping himself, obviously.'

'What *are* you doing, Fi?'

'Got a sodding prolapse. My pelvic floor has been totally *vandalised* by carrying and giving birth to four huge children. I tell you, it looks like a damned road accident down below...'

'Too much information, Fi.' Clare visibly shuddered.

'... and I've done my research, googling fannies until the cows come home – and I've definitely got some sort of problem.'

'Can't you just have an operation and have it all hitched back up?' Clare asked, wincing. 'You can't be doing with your bits and pieces around your knees.'

'According to your mother...' Fi breathed out before pulling herself higher and directing herself towards me.

'My *mother*?'

'According to your mother,' Fi repeated patiently, 'this is a First World problem. I was chatting to her the other day in Lidl and she was telling me that African and Indian women don't have *their* collapsed wombs unceremoniously ripped out. There's more *walking wombless* around than you'd realise. Anyway, Paula says exercise, gentle dance movements, yoga and plenty of *rest*...'

'How about plenty of *sex*?' Clare asked hopefully. 'You know, push it all back up again?'

Fiona snorted, which is actually quite a difficult thing to do with one's legs virtually over one's shoulder. 'It's bloody sex that's got me in this state in the first place.' She suddenly swung her legs back earthwards and, face rather more puce than when she started, reached for a crumpet. 'Right, that's my little problem sorted – albeit temporarily.

We're here to support *you*, Cassie.' She took a huge bite from the crumpet and, with butter running down her chin, raised questioning eyebrows in my direction.

'I can't go to school tomorrow,' I suddenly said in a panic. 'I just can't. How the hell do I start a new job as deputy head; a new class, new colleagues? Oh shit, I'll have to take assemblies and I'll just want to cry. I can't do it.' I could hear myself talking louder and faster, ending in a strangled sob as I pictured myself in front of an expectant staff exchanging glances as I broke down in tears while helping the head, the rather terrifying Mrs Theobold, deliver new strategies. I'd been rehearsing all summer, talking to a row of cushions in my bedroom, excited at the thought of passing on up-to-the-minute government directives.

'I can't remember any of it,' I blubbed. 'I can't even remember how to take a register or teach the fucking chunking method of division...'

'Chunking method?' Clare stared at me. 'Sounds like a *Joy of Sex* position for fatties.'

'... Can't do it. I can't...'

'Get her a brown paper bag to breathe into,' Fi ordered, licking butter from her fingers. 'She's having a panic attack.'

'No, she's not.' Clare gently took both my hands. 'Come on, Cassie. You've had a terrible shock but it's quite probable Mark will be back later on. You'll need to talk to him, work out where you're both going, but meanwhile you have to turn up tomorrow, smile on your face, ready for the challenge.'

'Mum?' Tom was shouting from the kitchen, phone in hand. 'Phone for you.'

'That'll be Mark now,' Clare said. 'Be calm, be brave. Don't blub all over him.'

I ran up the garden, heart racing. I just wanted to hear Mark's voice. For him to tell me it all wasn't true.

'Mrs Beresford?'

Obviously not Mark then.

'Yes?'

'David Henderson here, Chair of Governors at Westenbury C of E, sorry, Little Acorns. Can't get used to the damned silly new name now that we've become an academy.' He coughed, cleared his throat. 'Bit of a problem, I'm afraid. Only just heard myself what happened last night...'

I closed my eyes. Shit, news travelled fast. Of course, a lovely little village school like Little Acorns would have no place for a deputy head who had been publicly shamed in front of half of Midhope.

'Mrs Beresford? Are you still there?'

'Yes, I'm here. I quite understand, Mr Henderson. Did Mrs Theobold ask you to ring me?'

'Well, hardly.' I could hear surprise in his voice.

'Right.' I didn't know what else to say. Thank God, I wouldn't have to go into school in the morning. I could stay in bed with the covers over my head and not have to face new staff, new parents and new children. I knew within a few weeks I'd be devastated: my dream job was no more. But at this moment I just felt profound relief.

'So how do you feel about it all?' David Henderson sounded cautious.

'To be honest, Mr Henderson, I'm going back to bed with a bottle of my mother-in-law's disgusting cherry brandy and I'm going to stay there until I'm very drunk and most probably passed out.'

'Right.' There was a long silence and then he said, 'Bit excessive that. I didn't realise you had become quite so fond of her.'

'Who? My mother-in-law?'

'Sorry?' Another pause. 'Mrs Theobold, the head? I think we're at cross purposes here, Cassandra.' David Henderson spoke slowly and gently. 'Mrs Theobold died of a massive heart attack last night. As from now, you're acting head of Little Acorns.'

4

She's Right Off My Christmas Card List...

At one a.m. on the Monday morning – the morning when I was apparently supposed to breeze into Little Acorns and take over at the helm, steering both staff and pupils in the direction demanded by the local authority, the governors and, more pertinently, bloody Ofsted, my husband slunk back home. I say 'slunk' but to be honest I didn't have a clue as to the speed or mode of his arrival, being dead to the world as a result of a couple of Fiona's little helpers.

Totally shattered from lack of sleep and the shock, as well as the bombshell of my sudden promotion, I was in a pretty catatonic state by the time Fiona and Clare left, late in the afternoon, to sort out their weeks ahead.

Clare, who was in the process of expanding her rather successful stag do business, Last Stagger, to incorporate hen dos, had been given a lift by Fiona to get her own car and laptop and, on her return, set herself up at my breakfast bar dealing with emails and the many enquiries for new business. Fiona, who believed any problem could be solved through food, and lots of it, found my pinny, ingredients in the fridge and freezer and set to rustling up a meal in order to have some semblance of normality for the kids. At least when Freya and Tom finally got around to realising this particular Sunday was shaping up to be rather different from the usual Sunday in the Beresford household, I had the excuse of being in shock and terror at suddenly finding myself head teacher instead of deputy. Having said that, while there might be a shepherd's pie in the oven, I still didn't know how I was going to explain Mark's absence.

Before Fiona left to feed her own brood, she'd nipped down to Sainsbury's, returning with an enormous chocolate cake, concealer and a pack of Nytol.

'The cake's for pud to stop your two talking,' she announced drily. 'If their mouths are full, they can't be asking too many questions. You'll need the concealer to cover up those red eyes in the morning and the Nytol...'

'I'm not taking sleeping tablets,' I protested. 'I don't believe in them...'

'They're just antihistamine,' Fiona said calmly. 'Far better that you actually get some sleep to face tomorrow than have another night like last night. You probably won't need them, you'll be so exhausted. I usually drop a couple when Matthew is snoring horrendously and doesn't respond to my clapping.'

'Clapping?' Clare looked up from her laptop, bemused. 'You *applaud* him for bloody snoring. God, I'd be *kicking* him, not encouraging him. Clapping?'

Fiona laughed. 'Honestly, it works. Try it next time one of your men happens to be a snorer. You just gently clap two or three times and they turn over and sleep without another sound. It doesn't always work.' Fiona started giggling. 'The other night I was so fed up with him I clapped really angrily – staccato – in his left ear, and he shot out of bed shouting, "What is it, what is it, wassamatter…?" fell over his bloody great size-fifteen boots – that I'm always telling him to shift from the bedroom – and landed in a naked heap on the carpet.' Fiona carried on chortling. 'Great entertainment,' she added.

'I think you need to get out more,' Clare said. 'Why don't you go into the spare room when the snorer from hell kicks off?'

'Haven't got one any more. Now that the girls are horrible adolescents and can't stand sharing a bedroom – or each other, come to that – Bea has purloined the spare room for herself. Moved all her stuff in there a couple of months ago and refuses to move.'

'I'd smack her bottom,' Clare said.

'Not when she's almost six foot and her hockey stick's a constant accessory, you wouldn't,' Fiona said mildly. 'Anyway, enough of my lot. How are you feeling now, Cassie?'

'Like I'm in a dream,' I shrugged. 'Totally not with it. Even if Mark hadn't done what he'd done, if he was here now with me instead of you two, I'd still be in a state about tomorrow.'

'But why?' Clare looked up again. 'I thought you *wanted* to be in charge?'

I took a deep breath, trying to calm myself as terrifying thoughts of the next day replaced incredulous thoughts of Mark's recalcitrant behaviour. 'I know you two – particularly you, Clare, not having any kids in the system – don't know much about what's going on in education at the moment, but being a deputy head in a primary school is totally different from being the head. I have a class of my own to teach, albeit on a slightly, and I emphasise the word *slightly*, reduced timetable. I'm given two afternoons off to perform my deputy's role.'

'Sounds much better now then,' Clare said, draining her cup of coffee. 'As head, you won't have a class to teach and you can shut yourself away in your office and swivel round on your chair, pressing those red and green lights that say, "Come In" or "Bugger Off".'

I actually laughed at that. 'You don't know the half. I'm still going to have to deal with my new class tomorrow; someone will have to teach them and I can't see David Henderson having sorted out any supply.'

'David Henderson.' Fiona whistled. 'I'm still amazed that the man they call "the Richard Branson of the North" is actually your Chair of Governors. What's he like? Rather attractive, isn't he?'

'*Rather?*' Clare snorted. '*Very*, you mean. He's gorgeous...'

'With a *very* attractive wife,' I smiled.

'Since when's that stopped Clare?' Fiona sniffed, giving me an anxious look. 'Look, Cassie, you can't do everything. You can't be expected to teach a class of thirty ten-year-olds and be deputy head and now head as well. What did David Henderson say? What's likely to happen?'

'Well, in cases like this, where the head is suddenly no more, if the deputy has been *in situ* for years then *they* will be acting head and another member of staff will be acting deputy until the post of head is advertised and filled. In my case, where I'm brand new, a new acting head is usually brought in from the authority. You know, someone who's been a deputy for years in their own school and is actively looking for a headship. They'll ship them in to take over temporarily.'

Clare looked disappointed. 'Oh, so you're not going to be head after all? Well, that's all your problems halved in one fell swoop. You just need to sort Mark out and you'll be back to square one, job done.'

'Clare!' Fiona frowned as she saw my face. 'I don't think it's quite as simple as that. You get back to sorting your rampant stags and don't be so damned flippant.'

I smiled at Fiona but realised my stomach was churning and I wanted to throw up. 'I'm sure they *will* bring someone in to take over as head but, according to David Henderson, it won't be tomorrow. He said he'd be on hand in the morning to help me. Shit,' I said, suddenly realising. 'I'm going to have to do a new-term, new-year, new-beginning assembly and I'll have to explain to the children that Mrs Theobold is dead. Or do I say she's with Jesus? No, I can't; what about the Muslim children? OK, Mrs Theobold is with Jesus or Mohammed – take your pick, kids.'

'Calm down,' Clare said as she realised panic was mounting in every fibre of my being once more. 'Sit yourself down, pen and paper in front of you, and we'll help you compose your very first assembly as head. How hard can it be?'

So, at one in the morning, when I was dead to the world courtesy of two of Fiona's Nytol and – I'll be honest here – despite Fiona and Clare's warning to the contrary, a rather large glass of Mark's favourite malt whisky, Mark came home.

He must have been in the house for a while, I realised afterwards, when some instinct had me shooting upright in bed, ears on stalks, heart pounding. At first, once awake from my drug-induced sleep, I thought there was someone standing over by the bedroom window and my poor heart went into overdrive. I could actually hear its rat-a-tat beating in my ears as I clutched the duvet cover. Relief washed over me as I realised the burglar/ghost was actually my Hobbs shift dress and jacket bought specially for my new role as deputy head and which, now upgraded to outfit for acting head – as well as cuckolded wife – were hanging above my newly polished navy court shoes ready to slip into in the morning.

A crash from somewhere below me had me out of bed and peeping over the banister. This was either a burglar or my husband. Mark's black shoes had been abandoned and left neatly as a pair at the bottom of the stairs. This was a first. Never in eighteen years of marriage had he deigned to take off his shoes: despite my nagging about bringing dirt and germs into the house, he'd cheerfully refused to remove them, saying we lived in a house not a Buddhist temple.

Mark was standing with his back to me over by the bureau in the sitting room, still dressed in the black trousers he'd been wearing for his role as auctioneer. His dinner jacket and tie were gone, and in their stead was a fawn sweater – obviously cashmere – that I didn't recognise. He was seemingly intent on searching for something in the top drawer of the bureau and occasional muttered oaths and 'Where the hell is it?' floated over his shoulder towards me. I realised I was shivering and wrapped my dressing gown tighter around me against the early autumn night air.

'What are you looking for, Mark?'

He started and turned, looking at me but not quite meeting my eye.

'Cass, I'm so sorry. I love you. I never wanted any of this to happen... never meant it to happen...'

'Hmm.' I was amazed how calm I sounded. Must have been the Nytol slowing me down. 'Two years is a hell of a long time to not mean *something* to happen. A drunken one off... a one-night stand with some floozie you met in a bar while you were away on one of your trips... I could probably get my head around that. These things do happen. You'd tell me and I'd probably sort of understand; you know, *why* it happened. But this? This, Mark…?'

Mark stepped towards me and I recoiled, hugging my arms around me, trying to stop my teeth chattering.

'I know, Cass, I know…'

'Just answer me one question, Mark. Why? Why have you done this to us? To me? With Tina, for God's sake, my best friend?' I stared at Mark. This was my husband but I didn't know him. He may as well have been the burglar I mistook him for.

'What do you want to do?'

'What do you mean, what do *I* want to do? What are you *doing* here? Sneaking in in the middle of the night. Were you about to sneak *out* again?'

'I don't know.' Mark's voice was low. 'I don't know. I think I'm having some sort of breakdown.'

I laughed at that. 'Oh, don't give me that, you wanker. You're as sane as I am. You'd have carried on this thing if Simon hadn't found out, wouldn't you?' I took a step towards him and, when he didn't reply, I hissed, 'My God, you would. Of course you would.' And then almost to myself, 'Why wouldn't you?'

'Cass…'

'So, are you in love with her? With Tina?'

'Don't…'

'Don't what?'

'Cass, I don't know what to do. It's different with her. Oh shit, what have I done?'

I did laugh at this. Laughed out loud, a dry, hollow sort of laugh I didn't recognise as my own. 'Is that a rhetorical question or do you want to know the answer?' It suddenly dawned on me what Mark was looking for in the bureau cupboard and I strode over, pushing him to one side. I pulled out the second drawer – I knew where everything was kept in this house: a place for everything and everything in its place – and immediately found it. 'Mine, Tom's, Freya's… Ah, here we are… yours.' I threw the burgundy-coloured passport at him.

He stooped to pick it up from where it had landed at his feet, but couldn't meet my eyes.

'Nice jumper,' I said. 'A gift from Tina?'

'Cass…'

'If you've got what you came for, I suggest you leave. I have an important day ahead of me tomorrow.' I stood as tall as I could, which, my being only a hair's breadth over five foot, has always proved slightly difficult.

'Oh, of course, your new job.'

'Actually, rather more than that now,' I snapped. 'But, of course, you weren't around to share my promotion with me.'

'Your promotion?' Mark frowned, and for the first time that night, looked directly at me. No way was I going to admit I was shit scared of what the morning would bring. If Serpentina could climb – slither – the slippery pole of success at her law firm, so could I in my new school.

'Yes, as from tomorrow I am head teacher of Little Acorns. As such, I need to get my sleep, and you, you…' I forcibly pushed Mark towards the door, '… *you* can take your cashmere sweater, your passport and your cheating self and take yourself back to Serpentina.'

Mark reached a hand out to me but I shrugged him off. 'I have *far* too much to do to think about throwing your stuff out on to the lawn,' I sniffed grandly. 'I suggest you make an appointment with my secretary at school as to when you can pick up the rest of your things.'

'What will you tell the kids?' Mark was ashen-faced but made no further attempt to touch me.

'I shall think of something that doesn't put you in *too* bad a light. My main concern is Tom and his A levels. The last thing he needs is to know his father is shagging his godmother.'

'Don't...'

'I already know.' Tom stood at the sitting-room door and Mark and I both turned in his direction, starting guiltily.

'Tom? What do you mean? *What* do you know?' I hurried over to him and searched his face, taking his hand.

'Bit of a relief really, Dad,' Tom laughed shortly. 'Now that Mum knows, I mean. I guessed she'd finally found out when all the troops were round on Saturday and Sunday... and you weren't. I've known for months. I saw you and Auntie Tina together – and I mean *together* – in The Frozen Knacker.'

'The Frozen Knacker?' I stared at Tom. 'Where on earth is that? Oh,' I said, as realisation dawned, 'you mean The Blue Ball? What were *you* doing in The Blue Ball?' I was momentarily taken aback that my sixteen-year-old son should have been hanging out in the rather remote pub out on the lonely stretch of the Pennines, towards Manchester.

Tom ignored my question. 'It's actually been really hard keeping this to myself, you two. I didn't want to be a party to these adult goings-on. I'm glad you know now, Mum, and I don't have to pretend anymore.' Tom spoke in a manner that belied his sixteen years, putting the two of us to shame. 'Now, if you don't mind, I have the first day of my A level course tomorrow so I suggest you go back to Auntie Tina, Dad, or make your mind up to stay here with Mum. And you, Mum…' Tom glanced towards the kitchen clock, before hoisting up his crumpled boxers with such an air of vulnerability I felt I'd have done anything for him not to have found out '… have got exactly four hours before you need to be up for your new job.'

'You heard the man,' I said calmly to Mark, ushering Tom back upstairs. 'Make sure you lock the door after you and post the key through the letter box. I'm assuming you won't be needing it any more. Oh, and one more thing: tell Serpentina she is, as from now, right off my Christmas card list.'

5

I Don't Want to Go to School...

Despite my lack of sleep the previous night – as well as the Nytol and Mark's best whisky – the four hours before dawn after Mark had left were spent in a half-sleep of strange dreams and waking moments, looking at the illuminated time beamed onto the bedroom ceiling by my persistently capable alarm clock. Around 4 a.m. I seriously considered getting up, emailing David Henderson that there had been a mistake, I couldn't possibly come in and be deputy head, never mind be in charge of the place, and thank you but he wouldn't be seeing me again. I must have dropped off around five and was startled awake, from what was now a pretty deep sleep, by intrusive birdsong. Not your actual birds tweeting (by September the avian chorus has usually packed up and buggered off somewhere else. Or just has nothing to sing about: I knew the feeling) but the wildly enthusiastic birdsong chirruping of my alarm clock.

I took the deepest breath possible, told myself I could do this, and headed for the shower. My bobbed blonde hair doesn't need a daily wash but it hadn't seen shampoo – had I actually had a shower since getting ready for the charity ball? – for a couple of days, and I went the whole hog, washing, conditioning, leg and armpit shaving, in an attempt to scrub away the last thirty-six hours.

Tom was already downstairs, stolidly munching his way through a bowl of cornflakes, one eye on the BBC *Breakfast* show and the other on a maths textbook. My son had always been emotionally self-contained, even as a little boy, so his calm demeanour wasn't unexpected.

'Would you rather I'd told you?' he asked as I sat opposite him at the kitchen table nursing a cup of black coffee. Food would have choked me but the coffee went some way to clearing my head.

Would I? Yes, of course I would. No teenager, especially one as outwardly impassive, even phlegmatic, as Tom, should have to keep such a secret to himself. I never knew what he was thinking. Never had. 'Oh, darling, of course you should have said something.'

'But at the time you were going for your interview, excited at the idea of being deputy at Westenbury. You'd have gone to pieces if I'd told you… Why have they changed its name to Little Acorns anyway? Don't you think it's a daft name for a primary school? Sounds more like a nursery to me.'

Living just a ten-minute walk away from the school itself, both Tom and Freya had been pupils there until passing the stiff entrance exam at eleven and leaving for one of the few remaining state-run grammar schools in the area.

'To be honest, Tom, I'm not overly sure about it all myself. It was already a *fait accompli* that it should change to academy status before I'd even applied for the job.' I frowned. 'I didn't even know C of E schools could actually change but apparently, as long as there is a church supplemental agreement with the Secretary of State and the diocese it's all OK.' I glanced across at Tom who, head back in his book, was obviously not overly interested in the status of his old primary school. 'You're just changing the subject, Tom. Not wanting to talk about Dad. It must have been awful for you. I'm really sorry. Oh, darling, was it all just before your GCSEs as well?'

I thought back to last April when I was so excited about getting an interview for the deputy headship. Tom must have known about Mark and Tina then. No wonder Mark had complained over the summer that Tom was moody, refusing to enter into any conversation with him, declining all Mark's invitations and, worst of all, adamant he wouldn't go on our family holiday to Devon as usual, saying he'd rather stay at home alone or, if necessary, with my mother or his great-grandfather, Norman.

'I'm starving.'

I gave Tom a warning look as Freya came into the kitchen. There was a time and place for everything and seven o'clock in the morning on the first day of term, when my daughter was about to be bollocked for her school uniform – or lack of it – was most definitely not it.

'Back upstairs, Freya and get that ghastly foundation off your face and that chipped black polish off your nails. And comb your hair so your fringe isn't hiding half your face.' I peered at my fourteen-year-old daughter through eyes that, despite a dosing of eye-drops, were still sore and scratchy from crying and lack of sleep. 'Is your hair darker than normal. It is, isn't it? What the hell have you done to it?'

Freya was, to the untrained eye, nonchalantly feeding crumpets into the toaster, but I knew from my daughter's stance she was alert and ready to backchat, if not flounce from the kitchen.

'Your hair, Freya?'

'Paula helped me dye it yesterday afternoon. You said I could go over and see her; you were so taken up with *The Fearbold* popping her clogs you didn't mind me having my tea with her.'

In the same way I'd been encouraged as a child to call her Paula, rather than 'Mummy' or 'Mum', my mother had refused to take on the handle of 'Gran' or – here Paula had visibly shuddered, declaring it to being equated to a piece of Indian bread – the dreadful title of 'Nan', and, as such, had always been known simply as Paula to Tom and Freya. *The Fearbold* was the name all the local kids, and even their parents, had dubbed Priscilla Theobold for as long as she'd ruled the roost at Westenbury C of E.

'For God's sake, Freya, school will send you home. I can really do without all this at the moment.' I could feel my voice beginning to rise and tried to speak calmly. I would kill my mother once I saw her but, for the moment, I issued the following directive. 'Crumpets down, make-up off, nail varnish off and your new school jumper on.' I looked closely at the garment in question. 'Why, in God's name, have you got your old one on? It's got holes in the sleeves...'

Tom raised his eyes from his book and stood up, taking his bowl and mug to the dishwasher. He was so like me in many ways: couldn't bear mess around him. 'She's an emo, Mum, you know that. She needs to have her thumbs through the holes in the sleeves.'

'Emo schemo,' I said crossly. 'Right, I'm off. I have a meeting with David Henderson at seven thirty. You *dare* to go to school looking like that, Freya, and you are in *big* trouble. Make sure she's dressed properly, Tom. Enjoy your first day at sixth-form college, darling... And you, Freya, make sure you've got your bus pass and money for lunch. And get that nail varnish off... *And* those ridiculous emo glasses I know you're going to put back on your face as soon as you're on the bus!'

I took another deep breath, slipped my new jacket over my new dress and picked up the lovely new, and very expensive, briefcase Mark had presented me with on the Saturday evening before we left for the auction.

Briefcase? Bollocks! This was going to be one brief case of being head teacher. I was off to resign before I'd even started.

*

The sun's rays, low in a brilliantly blue sky, heralding early September mornings and new academic years, blinded me on every corner as I drove, adding to my tension. I could have easily walked to Little Acorns, and was beginning to regret my decision not to do so. I'd spent much of the six-week break, after leaving my previous post, actually in school, planning the coming term, sorting my classroom, putting up displays, determined to be the best teacher possible to my new Year 5 class, in addition to being a superb deputy head. I'd had it all mapped out. I was up and running, everything in place, no stone unturned – until the walls came crashing down. I pulled into the school's car park. Not yet seven thirty and there were already several cars there.

I made my way down the corridor to my classroom, relieved to see it was looking as bright and welcoming as I remembered leaving it, took a deep breath and went to find David Henderson.

'Ah, Cassandra, you're here. Not the happiest of occasions...' David Henderson, Midhope's wealthiest entrepreneur, smiled and ushered me into Mrs Theobold's office. Her name, bold and determined, a personification of the woman herself, glared up at me from the huge leather-bound desk and I looked away.

'No. Look, Mr Henderson...'

'David, please. Come on, sit down, I've made us some coffee.'

'It's just—'

'It's just you think you can't do this? You want to run away, back home, ready to listen to Ken Bruce to see if you can beat whoever is on Pop Master this morning.' He smiled again and a tiny part of me began to relax.

'I'm a *Woman's Hour* girl myself.' I took a grateful gulp of the coffee David poured for me. 'Shit, that's hot.' I flushed as the invective slipped out. 'Sorry…'

David laughed. 'Don't worry, I used to hear much worse from *The Fearbold*, especially if she wasn't getting her own way with the governors. Used to terrify Ben Carey, the vicar of All Hallows, Westenbury. OK, as far as I can see, we *should* be getting an acting head in from the authority and you will just assume your position as deputy.' He paused, shaking his head slightly. 'Unfortunately, trouble-shooting primary heads, at the beginning of a brand-new school year, when Midhope Education Authority is not yet even open for business, are a bit thin on the ground. As I'm sure you're aware, as an academy, the school is now responsible for finding its own staff rather than relying on the authority, but I'm hoping they'll still be able to advise us on this. If the school had had its teacher-only days this week, instead of last, we'd have had a couple of days' grace. But, talking of Grace, I hope you don't think I've been presumptuous, but needs must, and I spoke to a very good friend of mine yesterday. She's prepared to come in and cover your class for a few days until we get sorted. She does have two young children at home, but she's been able to arrange childcare and should be in before the children here start arriving.'

'Oh gosh, that's a load off my mind,' I said gratefully. Why the hell was I going along with all this? Why wasn't I standing up saying, 'Woah, just a cotton-picking minute, Mr famous-businessman David Henderson. I'm off. I resign. Going home to Jenni Murray, my duvet and a bar of Cadbury's Dairy Milk?'

My stomach gave a loud rumble and I realised I'd not eaten a thing since the soggy mushroom vol-au-vent of Saturday night.

'Sorry,' I muttered again, embarrassed.

'Been too nervous to eat?' David grinned, and bent down, opening a drawer in front of him. 'Yep, thought as much.' He pulled out a huge and expensive-looking box of Hotel Chocolat biscuits, and pushed it towards me. 'Priscilla did have a predilection for chocolate. Come on, fill your boots, give yourself some energy. You're going to need it.'

'Mrs Beresford, could you have a quick word with Mrs Dawson, Rainbow's mummy?' Jean Barlow, the school secretary, popped her face round the head's door where I was still gathering myself before going down to my classroom to get things ready for this Grace woman.

'Yes, of course, show her in.' I smiled in what I hoped was confident, head teacher mode.

A short, nervous-looking woman around my own age, knocked and stepped into the office. 'Hello, er, Mrs Beresford? I *was* hoping to have a word with Mrs Theobold...' She hesitated. 'I mean I did mention it at the end of last term... but I've just heard...' Mrs Dawson blew her nose on a damp-looking tissue. 'Anyway, it's still carrying on...'

'What is? Is there a problem with Rainbow?' Giving thanks to the God of names for giving the child a damned silly name I was immediately able to remember, I smiled encouragingly.

'It's that Chantelle girl again,' she whispered crossly.

'Is it?'

Mrs Dawson nodded, but added nothing further.

'What is? What's Chantelle?'

'We had a problem with her all last year. Bullying our Rainbow. Demanding she bring summat in for her every day. It's started again, first day back. "I've got to take summat in for Chantelle." That's all our Rainbow will say.'

'And did Mrs Theobold have a word with Chantelle?'

'Well, she did, but Chantelle denied it all. She's *very* sly for a five-year-old.'

'Oh, Rainbow is so young?'

'Well, no, our Rainbow is six now. Chantelle's in a different class which meks it worse, really.'

'And is it money that she's demanding from Rainbow?' Golly what sort of school was this that had four-year-olds demanding money with menaces?

'Oh, I gets sick of it. Our Rainbow always nattering, "Mum, I've *got* to take summat for Chantelle." "What can I tek for Chantelle?" And she 'as a tantrum when I say she can't take my diamond engagement ring for Chantelle this morning. Well, Mrs Beresford, I'll leave it with you. I hope you can sort it better than Mrs Theobold – God bless her.'

Light was beginning to dawn. 'Does Rainbow sometimes bring the things back that she's taken for Chantelle?'

Mrs Dawson wiped her nose again. 'Well, that's the funny thing. I often find the stuff she's taken for her back in her bag.'

I smiled. If being a head was going to be as good fun as this, I was going to enjoy myself. I leant forward. 'Mrs Dawson, have you ever heard of Show and Tell?'

It wasn't. Good fun, that is. I dealt with at least five parents before nine fifteen, all of them wanting to tell me something about their child, whether it be a case of suspected chicken pox, a demand for Learning Support or an imminent divorce and could I possibly be the one to tell the child daddy wasn't coming home? (I couldn't, despite thinking I'd be getting some practice in for when I had to break similar news to Freya.)

I'd briefly met the supply teacher, Grace Stevenson, who assured me that, despite being out of the classroom for four years, she was ready to get stuck in. I had immediate misgivings: education and all that went with it had changed dramatically over that period of time, with new government directives being thrown at us on a daily basis. But I didn't have time to do much more than reassure her I was there if she needed me, thrust plans and documents into her hands and scuttle back to the office to practise the assembly Clare, Fiona and I had cobbled together sitting in the garden the previous morning. She looked almost as bemused as I felt.

*

I made the decision – my first, I realised, as head teacher – to leave assembling the troops until just before lunch, giving me more time to practise what I was going to say as well as open the myriad letters, emails and government directives that had amassed over the latter end of the summer break. Priscilla Theobold had just returned from a three-week round-the-Mediterranean cruise with, according to the gossip filtering out of the staff room at break time, a much younger lover, when she'd keeled over and died, hence the build-up of administrative stuff that needed sorting.

'Rome wasn't built in a day.'

'Sorry?' I looked up from the pile of paper that was beginning to spread out around the office chair like a snowstorm.

'What the mind can conceive, it can achieve.' Jean Barlow smiled sympathetically and handed me a mug of tea and a chocolate digestive. 'Just one step at a time, Mrs Beresford, and you'll be fine. Mrs Theobold used to dump most of this sort of stuff into the bin, unopened.'

'Really?' I looked up, slightly dazed. 'Oh, and please call me Cassie. I was Cassie when I was deputy... well, of course I still *am* deputy...' I trailed off. The last thing I wanted was the school secretary thinking I was being presumptuous.

Jean looked slightly shocked. 'Mrs Theobold always insisted on being called Mrs Theobold.' She paused. 'Now, at what point do you want to go over this little lot?' She wafted a pile of files in my direction. 'Last summer's SATs results.'

'Let me get my first assembly out of the way, Jean, and then we'll look at them together, shall we? I'm surprised they haven't already been gone through.'

'I know Karen Adams, being literacy coordinator, and Jessica Lane, maths coordinator, have already compiled statistics, but it was always Mrs Theobold's habit, on the first day of the new academic year, to use them to tell the staff where they were going wrong...'

'Or right, surely? We all need a bit of praise, don't you think?'

Jean smiled. 'Life doesn't give you things you can't handle, does it? Well, I'll leave them with you, then?'

'Absolutely.' I smiled with far more confidence than I felt, added the files to the tumescent pile already in the in-tray, and then watched as the whole lot slithered to the floor with a crash.

Shit.

Shoving escaped paper into what I hoped was its correct file, I hoisted the lot back onto the desk and set off down the corridor to introduce myself to each new class.

By the end of the afternoon I felt I'd been in charge at Little Acorns for ever. My very first assembly had gone well, apart from Karen Adams, the Year 3 teacher, looking bored stiff in between raising her eyebrows at another as I talked, and I'd floated down the corridor back to the office – probably the result of a surfeit of caffeine and Hotel Chocolat premium chocolate biscuits on an empty stomach as much as pride in a job well done – and began to think I could possibly *do* this. I could be head teacher, albeit for a few days until a new captain was brought in to save the sinking ship.

And then flashbacks to Simon outing Mark and Tina would suddenly take me unawares, and my heart would lurch and I'd have to dash and offload my nervous stomach once more in the tiny loo next to the head's office. But, on the whole, I held myself together, even to the point of adding another layer of lippy before heading back to yet more administrative tasks Jean insisted on finding for me. David Henderson, who'd apparently had a meeting in Manchester, had left fairly early in the day but returned by mid-afternoon. His presence, and the thought that really, as Chair of Governors, he was more in charge than I, had a calming effect on my whole being and we made good headway with a list of things that needed our immediate attention.

'You're doing fine,' he smiled, leaning back and stretching his arms above his head while stifling a yawn. 'You know, you were our outright choice for the job of deputy. There was only one other candidate who came anywhere near. I think Priscilla liked the idea of having a man as her second in command, but in the end your interview and presentation far outweighed your rival's boyish good looks.' David laughed and I smiled back. 'That's better,' he added, standing and reaching for his black pinstriped suit jacket. 'I've another meeting down in Midhope, or I'd stay on with you.' He yawned again. 'As Jean would say: tomorrow's another day. Go home and put your feet up and open a bottle of wine. Go and tell your husband you've survived.'

By five I was running on empty. I decided enough was enough and looked around for my new little linen jacket that I'd not seen since abandoning it after assembly. I retrieved what had now become a crumpled rag from under another pile of box files and headed for my classroom, in the hope Grace Stevenson might be still around for a quick chat. She wasn't.

'... her best friend, apparently. Can you imagine *that*? Bad enough your husband shagging some stranger, but your best *friend*... Two years, the other woman's husband shouted out to everybody there. And don't tell me any woman wouldn't know if it was her best friend. Course she must have known what was going on. Must be pretty thick if she didn't. My sister knows her vaguely – the other woman, I mean, not our new leader – Tina somebody... said it was all great entertainment...' Karen Adams' unmistakable nasal whine drifted malevolently through the open door of her classroom. How dare she discuss my business with all and sundry? I was about to go in and challenge her and whoever was in there with her when the sheer fury I was feeling suddenly changed direction and I knew it was the real perpetrator of my anguish I had to confront: Tina herself.

I let myself out of the main door, nodding in the direction of Stan, the caretaker, who was desultorily sweeping the hall floor as I did so, jumped into my car and headed straight for the centre of Midhope and Tina's office. Scalding molten lava was boiling through every bit of me, pulsating in a rampage of fury as I drove.

I pulled up in the car park of Holmes, Clavell and Dixon Solicitors and, not stopping to lock the car door, strode up the stairs to Tina's office.

'Where is she?' I yelled at a surprised Brian Holmes, Tina's senior partner.

'Hello, Cassie. Are you wanting Tina?'

'Too right I want the bitch. Where is she?' I looked round wildly, the red mist that had descended still in front of my eyes.

'Are you all right?' Brian jumped up from his chair, putting out a hand to calm me.

I shrugged it off and strode towards Tina's office. 'She's not here, Cassie. She's gone on the train to Leeds. Won't be back for ages yet.'

'Right. OK.' I marched back down the stairs, scrabbling in my bag as I descended to the main door and car park once more. My utter fury, as I snatched the lid from the gold-coloured tube, swivelled up the lipstick and scrawled:

MY HUSBAND, SERPENTINA, NOT YOURS!!!!!

in bright red, two-inch-high letters across the full length of Tina's white sporty BMW, only came to a halt when I realised the man in the black Jaguar F-type, looking absolutely stunned at my antics, was David Henderson.

6

Do You Want Me to Resign...?

The next morning, knowing this was going to be my last day as a head teacher – probably as a teacher in employment as well, come to that – I decided I might as well walk the ten minutes across the fields down to school to pick up my things and make my exit. When I'd finally arrived home from my little vandalising spree of the evening before, I'd not bothered to get in touch with my union rep. Instead, once I'd defrosted, and the three of us had eaten one of the many batches of lasagne, shepherd's pie and chilli I'd prudently prepared, cooked and frozen during the summer break, I headed for the sitting room.

Refusing to give houseroom to any thoughts of Mark and Tina, my new job or my recently developed hobby as a graffiti artist, I dispatched Freya to her room. I was still clinging to the fabrication, for Freya's benefit, that

Mark had been suddenly called down to London – as he so often was – but I knew I was going to have to tell my daughter the truth pretty soon. She wasn't stupid and was already asking questions.

Aided by a glass of red wine, a pack of Marks & Spencer's Percy Pigs and a rerun of *Peaky Blinders*, I managed an hour without breaking down in tears or further thoughts of violence apart from nodding appreciatively at Tom Hardy's character slitting a few throats that got in his way.

Once in bed, images of Tina with Mark danced before my closed eyelids. I pulled a pillow over my head in an attempt to obliterate and extinguish the pair of them together. The daft thing was that, had it been any other woman but Tina he'd been having an affair with, Tina would have been there with me, calling Mark every name under the sun as she stayed with me until I slept. She'd probably have moved in with me for a few days, letting me talk, pouring me gin.

How bloody ironic. My best friend. Why the fuck had she done this?

I hadn't just acquired a husband from Davina's momentous wedding do all those years before, I'd also found Tina. Being an only child – with just a cousin who had only ever resented, or at best grudgingly accepted, my presence – I could only ever dream of a huge extended family with a whole gang of exuberant loving siblings, aunts, uncles and cousins.

I used to write stories where the main character – a girl, always my age – was at the centre of a huge, functional family living in a rambling house by a meadow full of wildflowers. She had a rosy-cheeked mother who stayed at home and baked – but who could abandon, at the drop of a hat, her home-baked bread and scones, and, flinging off her pinny, donning an exquisite ball gown, sweeping up her hair into a smooth blonde chignon and, on the arm of the tall, handsome father, go off to some glamorous party, leaving my girl to be looked after by a *big sister*.

Oh, how I'd longed for this *big sister* who'd tell me stories about the fairies in the kitchen cupboard from her bed in the room we shared; who, as I got older, would whisper and talk to me about periods and take me shopping into town; would let me borrow her clothes and show me how to draw a straight black line on my eyelids.

Cupid's arrow had scored two direct hits on me during those hours at Davina's wedding because I fell in love twice. With Mark, obviously, but also with Tina. Three years older than me, she was the *big sister* I'd longed for and never had. I wasn't quite sure why Tina took me under her wing so robustly, certainly in the weeks and months after the wedding when she'd ring and arrange to meet me on the weekends I was home from Derby seeing Mark. It never, for one minute, occurred to me that it was Mark she was after rather than *my* friendship and, to be fair to Tina (*fair* to the bitch? Was I mad?) I honestly believe the love I had for her was reciprocated. Or she was a bloody good actress.

In the fifteen months that followed Davina's wedding, before Mark and I were married ourselves, I would spend my weekends with Mark in Leeds where he was living and working at the time. I'd drive up from my tiny brand-new one-bedroomed flat in Derby, leaving work and arriving in the centre of Leeds most Friday evenings.

It was such a wonderful time. I loved my teaching job in Derby, but adored my weekends in Leeds with Mark and Tina. Mark and I would start the weekend with a bottle of wine, sex, a pizza and then more sex. Saturday morning would usually be spent in bed and doing chores – I willingly cleaned Mark's flat for him – and then it was my time with Tina. We'd meet for a glass of wine either in Parkers Wine Bar or Len's Bar on York Place, stay for lunch and then head for the shops. Harvey Nicks had just opened its first branch outside London and we adored it, trying on the expensive shoes and designer dresses neither of us could afford on our newly qualified wages. We coveted one pair of scarlet Jimmy Choos so much that we made a pact, buying the pair between us and keeping the shoes on a two-week rota as well as on birthdays and special occasions before handing them over to the other for her turn. We never once fell out about them, but religiously polished and handed them over to the other as we'd agreed.

By the time Mark and I were engaged, Tina had taken up with Simon, whom we'd all met at Davina's wedding. She'd been out with him a couple of times but didn't appear all that keen on him and didn't see him at all for about nine months after that. Once Mark had proposed and we'd started looking for a house, and I'd relocated back to a teaching post in Midhope, Tina took up with Simon again and they became an item, marrying just a few months after Mark and I.

I'd asked Tina to be my bridesmaid and been hurt when she'd turned me down, laughing that I should have tiny tots to accompany me down the aisle, not someone three years older.

'But you'd be my matron of honour, like my *big sister*,' I'd argued, trying to get her to change her mind. She refused – probably the only issue on which we ever really disagreed.

Mark and I moved back to Midhope where our social life revolved around Clare and whichever man she was with that week, as well as spending time with Fi and Matthew. Once Tina and Simon also moved over to Midhope, the seven of us went everywhere and did everything together. I loved all my three 'sisters': Tina, Fi and Clare, but Tina, had a special place in my heart.

So, after another pretty restless night, once I'd sorted breakfast, found a lost pair of trainers in the linen basket, doled out money – Oh God, money: where was money going to come from once I was jobless and husbandless? – and left a note for Charlene, my cleaner, I slipped on my flatties, shoved my heels in my bag and set off down the fields towards school.

Just a week into September, autumn was already beginning to show off her colours, dressing the hedgerows in hues of yellow and carmine. Orangey-red rosehips, nestling in their toothed leaflets and ripe for picking, were already out in abundance, as were huge purple blackberries, clinging tenaciously to clumps of tangled and straggling brambles. Ted Jarvis, our local farmer, was already abroad on the huge plough.

Even though I had the feeling I was heading for the scaffold I began singing under my breath 'We plough the fields and scatter', a favourite at all primary schools.

Something was different. I came to a sudden halt as I realised I could go no further. The footpath, which had been trodden grassless by many a dog walker, rambler and schoolchild taking, like myself, a shortcut across the fields and through the hedgerows, had been rudely and abruptly terminated by ugly rolls of shiny, coiled barbed wire. Not the single or double rows of barbed wire the farmers sometimes laid in order to keep in cattle or sheep and through which walkers still persisted, catching hats or knickers as they did so, but malevolent coils of vicious-looking barbed metal more redolent of the Somme than the autumn fields of Westenbury. I retraced my steps, looking for a way through, but there was none. Tutting and glancing at my watch, I went forward once more, scanning the hedgerows for a possible way through. Again, there was none. Shit. I was going to have to go back home and get the car. I set off briskly back in the direction I'd come, dodging unpredictable hillocks that, with my current run of luck, would trip me up and sprain my ankle, and clumps of spitefully mischievous nettles that, now I was in a hurry, were just another damned obstacle to overcome.

Shit. Literally. The dry, crusted surface of the cowpat belied its viscous contents below. Up to my ankle in cow shit, I limped grimly home, uttering little mews of self-pity and frustration as I went.

'Do you want my resignation?'

'Do you want to tell me all about it?' David Henderson and I spoke as one as we simultaneously opened our car doors and stepped onto the tarmac. 'Come on.' He glanced at his watch, unsmiling. 'We have a good quarter of an hour before the first children start arriving.'

He quickly led the way into school, and I followed in his wake, visions of Anne Boleyn and her lost head swimming before my eyes. I suddenly realised, despite the fact that any imminent sacking would result in my not having to face a staff surely, by now, fully informed by Karen Adams of my disgrace, I wanted to fight my corner and stay.

David Henderson sat himself in Mrs Theobold's chair – not a good sign – and I was forced to stand in the same position, at the other side of the desk, where many a recalcitrant child had found themselves before. David was about to say something when, instead, he frowned, sniffing the air.

'Is there a bad smell in here? Drains, do you think?' He sniffed again, trying to pinpoint from which particular area the odour was emanating.

'Cow shit,' I said shortly. I was in no mood for niceties. 'Cow shit, I'm afraid. Some idiot has closed off the footpaths in the fields and I stepped in it. I've been home and rinsed my foot under the garden hose, but it's pretty tenacious stuff.' I raised my bare leg, my foot now shod in my replacement heels, and the noxious smell wafted up to my nostrils.

'Right. Look, Cassandra, what I caught you doing last night was an act of criminal damage. I did tell my wife, Mandy, who happens to be a magistrate, what you'd done, and it was her who said, if the complainant reported this, you would find yourself in court.'

'Well, if you don't tell anyone, I won't.' Fighting talk, Cassandra Moonbeam. I was impressed.

David actually smiled. 'Yes, but unless... Serpentina wasn't it...? unless this Serpentina is in the habit of running off with a multitude of husbands as well as your own – and I'm assuming, by your art work, that that's what she's done – then it's going to be pretty obvious who is the perpetrator.' He paused, looking straight at me. 'And if she wants to prosecute, I'm afraid you're snookered...'

'... Being reported in the *Midhope Examiner*,' I finished for him, 'and bringing Little Acorns into disrepute.'

'That's my worry, Cassandra. We have some pretty bolshy parents here, as I'm sure you've realised. The last thing we need is the local, and even the tabloids, getting wind of this.'

All the newly acquired fight went out of me and I sat on the one other chair in the room. 'OK, what do you want me to do? Resign?'

'Resign? Good God, no.' David looked astonished. 'You did such a brilliant job yesterday, stepping in to the breach, sorting parents. You'd have thought you'd been in charge for years.'

'You would?'

'Of course,' he smiled.

God, he was handsome when he smiled. Bit George Clooney really, I thought, taking in every aspect of his blue shirt, navy pin-striped suit, a full head of dark hair going grey at the temple, gorgeous brown eyes...

'... So, what do you reckon?'

'Sorry?' I brought myself back to Priscilla Theobold's office, rather than the log cabin with open fire in the snowy Welsh hills I'd transported both of us to, and felt myself redden.

'It's really just a matter of keeping this between us and hoping Serpentina doesn't report this to the police.'

'It's Tina. She's called Tina. She's – she *was* – my best friend and she's been my husband's mistress for the past two years.'

David stared at me. 'You poor thing. And you've just found out? And on top of all that, you've been thrown in at the deep end here?'

'Yep. That's about it in a nutshell.' I felt my bottom lip begin to wobble and looked out of the window, willing myself not to cry because of this rather gorgeous man's sympathy.

'Bloody hell, Cassandra, I'd have taken a stone to the side of the car if it had been me. Right, I'm assuming lipstick is removable so there'd be no permanent damage. And, at the end of the day you were simply leaving her a message spelling out the truth. No harassment, alarm or distress. Sorry, magistrate-speak again. Actually, she probably was alarmed but, compared to the distress she's put you through I don't think a bench would be overly sympathetic. Right. Forget what you did, Cassandra. Move on. You've more important things to consider than some philandering so-called best friend.' He shook his head. 'Jeez, best friend?'

I stood and David stood too, beckoning me over to the chair he'd just vacated. 'Yours, come on.'

'For how long? How far have we got with finding a replacement head?' I raised my eyebrows.

'Nowhere. Look, if you're happy to keep on for a few more days until the end of the week...? Myself and the other governors have a meeting with the Academy Trust this evening and we should be able to make some decisions. Now we're an academy, all decisions about employment and recruitment go through the Trust. It's quite possible there's a deputy in one of the Trust's other schools who's not only qualified but desperate to stretch their wings, as it were.'

'What about covering my class? Is Grace happy to continue? I feel awful I didn't have a chance to speak to her really, yesterday.'

David nodded. 'I spoke to her at home, last night. She's certainly happy to stay for the week. Let's take it a day at a time and I'll keep on trying.'

The rest of the day continued in a blur of activity. At lunchtime I held a staff meeting – at which Karen Adams lounged on her seat, doodling on a pad and refusing to take part unless there was a particularly contentious issue, when she rudely, and quite aggressively, overrode all of my suggestions before raising her eyebrows at whom I very quickly determined were her band of cronies.

I certainly wasn't going to throw my weight around at this stage but kept calm, going over with the staff new government directives that they'd have to take on board. I'd pored over these during the summer break in order to know what was up and coming, aware that it's often the job of the deputy to introduce such mandates. Safeguarding and Budget issues were always at the top of the list and, while I wasn't really up to speed on the state of the school's finances now that we were an academy, I was top of the class when it came to rules about keeping the kids, staff and school safe.

'Well done.' Grace Stevenson popped her head round the office door just before the end of lunch.

'Thanks, it's not easy trying to establish oneself.' I smiled wryly. 'Listen, have you got ten minutes?' Grace came in, closing the door behind her, but didn't sit down. 'How's it going? Thank you so much for stepping in like this. I really couldn't have taught my class as well as try to do all of this.' I indicated the desk that was overflowing with paper at the same time as a tapping came at the door.

Grace opened it and a little voice sobbed, 'Please can I see Miss Beery Ford?'

'It's *Mrs Beresford*. Do you think she wants to see *you*?'

'Mrs Atkinson said I had to come and tell Miss Berry Ford what I said at dinner time.' Six-year-old Robbie stood at the open door, his hand firmly grasped on the handle as if frightened to let it go.

I glanced across at Grace and mouthed, 'Mrs Atkinson? Who's Mrs Atkinson?'

Grace pulled a face and shrugged. 'No idea,' she mouthed back.

'Emily told Mrs Atkinson I said...'

Grace and I leant forward to catch what Robbie was trying to get out.

'... Emily told Mrs Atkinson I said that school dinners smell like your bum.'

Both Grace and I managed to compose our faces and look suitably shocked at such an appalling slight on the school meal system although I could tell, by the twitch of her mouth, Grace was desperate to laugh.

There was a long silence while both of us glared at the little mite and then, realising what he'd said was open to being misconstrued, Robbie added, in a panic, 'But not *your* bum, Miss Beery Ford. I didn't mean, *your* bum.'

'I'm so glad to hear your bottom is fragrant and not at all resembling stew and Spotted Dick,' Grace giggled after Robbie, suitably admonished, had scuttled away. 'I've really missed being at the chalk face,' she laughed, wiping her eyes with her finger, but then, grimacing slightly, added, 'apart from all this new stuff on Safeguarding: I mean, can I really not hug a child if he's fallen down or upset?' She shook her head in disbelief. 'Anyway, I have two kids at home, both under four – always demanding my hugs – and I can't possibly do this full time every week. One of the supply agencies or, now that you're an academy, the Academy Trust should be able to help out next week. Unless...' Grace looked at me hopefully. 'Look, I'd love to do a couple of days a week, a job share maybe? I'm probably jumping the gun here, but I did have a word with David. Anyway, I have a very good teacher friend, Harriet, who basically is in the same boat as me and would also like to get her hands dirty as it were... you know, job share a couple of days? Good supply is so hard to get, I know. Hat's a bit dizzy but she's pretty sound as a teacher. We used to work together over at Farsley. If you find you're actually going to be in charge here for a few weeks until a new head is appointed, we'd love to do a bit each. We could do two days each, which just leaves you a morning for yourself because Wednesday afternoon is covered with your class doing Games and French.'

I smiled. 'You seem to have it all worked out, but I'm not sure sharing a class at this stage would be a good idea.'

'Sorry, that does sound a bit presumptuous, doesn't it, but the offer's there if you want it. Harriet's twins and Jonty, my son, have just started at the Little Forest nursery school over where we live, and Harriet's previous mother's help has just returned from the Italian Alps and is desperate to get her hands on the kids again.'

'Doing a ski season or something was she, this mother's help?' I wasn't sure why I should be talking about someone I'd never met before, but Grace was so bubbly and interesting, I wanted to know more.

'Oh, no, no, nothing like that.' Grace laughed out loud. 'Lilian – we all call her Mrs Doubtfire – refused to come home with us. She fell for the chef in the chalet and had been shacked up with him ever since, but came back without him last month.'

'Handsome, was he?'

'Well, if you fancy seventy-year-olds – which, I have to say, I don't.'

'Seventy? A young nanny stayed out there with a seventy-year-old?'

Grace laughed again. 'Lilian's pushing seventy herself. She's got more energy than anyone I know and is desperate to be looking after the kids again. So, you see, it's all sorted. Harriet and I can leave our children for two days with Lilian. She's happy, the kids are happy and Harriet and I can re-join the world of work.'

I smiled at her enthusiasm. 'Leave it with me,' I said, as the outside bell for the end of lunch was heard from the playground. 'I'll talk to the governors and see what they want to do.'

We headed out, Grace down to my classroom and me to ensure the children were coming back into school in an orderly fashion. At the end of the corridor, before we went our separate ways, she turned and said, quietly, 'None of my business, I know, I'm only the hired help…'

I looked at her.

'… but just watch your back with some of the staff.' She turned, smiled at me and carried on walking.

*

Cassandra, any chance you can get over and see your granddad after school?

Paula had left a message on my mobile, but it was mid-afternoon before I had a chance to check my phone. Granddad Norman, now a ninety-one-year-old widower, my nan having died two years ago, still lived in the same house as they had in my childhood, the neatly compact terraced home on the edge of a small rural village just ten minutes' drive from where I now lived in Westenbury. Fiercely independent, he still managed all his own housework and shopping and, apart from Meals on Wheels serving him lunch twice a week and me taking round the odd casserole for his freezer, fed himself as well. Paula lived nearby, moving herself and me out of my grandparents' house into a small, rented two-bedroomed cottage when I was around two years old, and where she'd lived ever since. Having been there so long, she reckoned she had security of tenure and the house was, by rights – Paula's rights, at least – now her own and no one would ever be able to shift her.

Is he OK?

I texted back, knowing that, as much as I loved Granddad Norman, I didn't really have the time for a visit, no matter how fleeting, that evening. I still had to sit Freya down for a chat, but I knew I was putting it off, hoping Mark would get over this madness and come back, and I wouldn't have to put myself through the trauma of explaining where her dad was and what was going on.

He's upset

Paula texted straight back.

You know, because you're a teacher, he thinks you can
sort everything. Call round for five minutes this evening,
if you can.

I was just gathering my things together at the end of
the day and about to make a sneaky exit to go over to
Granddad Norman's when my door was pushed open
and a tiny woman, with an even more diminutive man in
tow, walked straight in.

'Oh? So, are *you* our Liam's new head teacher, then? I
remember *you* from the other school. Well, fancy *you* being
the head teacher.' The woman, all bleached-blonde hair and
tight jeans, looked me up and down for what seemed an age.

My heart sank. During the summer break the Simpson
family had been relocated to the small council estate in
Westenbury and once again their kids were now mine.

'Mr and Mrs Simpson?' I smiled sweetly. 'And Liam,
Demi, Chelsea and Rocky, too? You've all decided to
come and pay me a visit?'

All I needed was Kylie, who had constantly badmouthed
her way through my first class at my last school, and I'd
have a set. A set of Simpsons at the end of the day when
I was trying to make a quick getaway. Marvellous stuff.

'And Kylie as well,' I smiled through clenched teeth as
Kylie came through the door, skirt up to her knickers and
a chest that had expanded threefold in twelve months.

''Lo, Miss.' Kylie hitched herself up on to my desk, safe in the knowledge that she was no longer under my jurisdiction.

'How's High School, Kylie? Enjoying it?' I asked.

She moved her wad of gum to a new resting place in her mouth before replying.

''S'orright, I suppose. Not as good as it was when I were with you, at the other school, Miss.'

Blimey, she'd had a change of heart.

Glancing surreptitiously at my watch, I turned to Ma and Pa Simpson, who also seemed to have settled themselves for the duration.

'What can I do for you?' I asked, sending up a silent prayer that they weren't here to complain about something.

'We've just come to let you know that our Liam can go.'

Go? Go where? Had there been some school trip planned that I was unaware of?

'Go where?' I asked, genuinely puzzled.

'To that university place you was on about yesterday,' Mrs Simpson continued, her small, beady eyes and sharp nose reminding me of a terrier.

I really had no inkling as to where they were coming from, and it must have shown.

'Our Liam came home yesterday and said that *you'd* said he could go to that there university when he was old enough. We've just come to tell you we're really pleased with him and he can go. No one has ever been to university from our family, and we're behind you all the way. Any extra work you want to give him to make sure he gets there, well, we'll make sure he does it at home.'

Well, that would be a first. I don't think one piece of homework of Liam's had been returned when he'd been in my class last year. I racked my brains as to the actual conversation I'd had with him when I'd dropped into his class yesterday. It had gone something along the lines of, 'Liam, see what you can do when you try hard. You'll be off to university when you're eighteen if you carry on like this.' He'd given me his usual look which, roughly translated, said, 'Get a life, woman.' But obviously he'd taken it to heart.

In the certain knowledge that if I could just shake off the Simpsons I'd still be able to hotfoot it down to Granddad Norman's, I smiled sweetly at the whole gang.

'Great,' I concluded, moving towards the door and hoping they'd follow suit, 'I'll have a word with Liam's teacher, and we'll push from this end, and you pull from yours, and between us we'll start the ball rolling to get Liam to university. Mmm?'

'Don't worry, Miss,' Kylie said, jumping off my desk and going over to where eight-year-old Liam was standing, apparently distancing himself from procedures. 'I'll mek sure he gets in. If he wants to go out for footie practice, I won't let him out until I've checked he's done his homework.'

'Fantastic, Kylie,' I said heartily. 'I knew I could rely on you.'

'You see,' Kylie could be heard lecturing her parents as they left through the cloakroom, 'I told you she was really nice.'

Pleased that for once I'd not come to blows with one single member of the Simpson family but, instead, had sent them all on their way motivated and proud of themselves, I glanced once more at the office clock and, before anything or anyone else could detain me, made a dash for the door.

Ringing Tom to tell him to feed himself and Freya with the remains of last night's supper, I left school at five and drove along the country roads, avoiding the tea-time traffic, which was just beginning to build. It was a beautifully mellow September evening and I wound down the car window to let in the scents of early autumn. The morning's dew-laden lanes were now dusty and fat with heat, the leaves of the massive sycamores along the way already brushed with colour, while an abundance of plum and apple trees flaunted their bounty. We were so lucky, living here in the countryside, protected from the sprawling urbanisation of the industrial north by square miles of untouched greenbelt and farmland. For the ten minutes it took me to drive to my grandfather's, I managed to push all thoughts of Mark and Tina from my mind, relishing the landscape and its September sights and smells simply for themselves.

The kitchen door that opened onto Granddad's small garden was ajar and so, instead of making my way into the house, I looked across to the dry-stone wall that separated his vegetable patch from the fields beyond. Granddad Norman was there, leaning on his stick, and obviously taking in the scents and smells of his wildflower meadow in much the same way as I had on my journey here.

'Hi, Granddad,' I called, walking towards him. 'Are you OK?'

He turned towards me, the flat cap he assumed all year round, even on the hottest of days, atop his sparse white hair.

'What is it? What on earth's the matter?'

'It's t'fields, love. My lovely fields. They're going to build one huge, buggering estate, right here, right on me bloody doorstep. In t'wildflower meadows.'

7

Have They Got Three Backsides…?

'Come on, Granddad, I've made you some tea. Come and sit down and calm yourself. You really shouldn't be getting yourself into a state like this; it's not good for your blood pressure.' Granddad accepted the mug of strong tea I'd made him, but refused the chocolate biscuit or to move away from his sentry post, continuing to guard his beloved fields from the – so far – invisible enemy. 'Come on, tell me what you've heard. Who do you think's going to build here? They can't do that, you know. Not here. It's green belt.'

'That's just what I bloody said,' Granddad snorted. 'But, according to your auntie Linda, they can do what they want.'

'Who can?' I turned to the woman who was standing over at the wall gazing at the fields and realised I'd not seen Linda, my mum's older sister, for a couple of months.

When I was a little girl I'd loved to go to Auntie Linda and Uncle Anthony's house, watching *Fraggle Rock* on their huge colour TV while sitting on their capacious, squashy pink Dralon sofas; playing – when she allowed it – with my cousin Davina's Cabbage Patch dolls, Care Bears and her eye-watering My Little Pony collection. I'd coveted everything my cousin Davina had, but particularly the snowy white skating boots that accompanied her to Bradford's Silver Blades ice rink for her private lesson every Saturday afternoon. How I longed to chassé and spiral like Davina or, when she tired of ice-skating, and Saturday afternoons were taken up with the Midhope Junior Majorettes, don the plastic white boots, ra-ra skirt and flesh-coloured tights in order to twirl a baton over my head.

Born the same year as me, and, like me, an only child, Davina had every material thing going. Being taken from our little cottage at the end of a country lane, where Paula and I watched a tiny black-and-white TV on lumpy and leaking beanbags, to Auntie Linda's over-heated brand-new detached house on a modern estate was utter heaven to the eight-year-old me. Every time I went for a wee in their centrally heated downstairs loo with its swagged and tailed curtains, its pink shag-pile carpet in which one could bury one's toes, its pink, softly full rolls of real Andrex and the perfumed smelling disc in the toilet bowl that flushed beautiful blue bubbles, I felt pangs of pure envy. My reluctant return to our freezing, patchouli-smelling bathroom with the always-almost-empty roll of cheap white, scratchy loo paper inevitably rolled out of reach on the bargain-basement linoed floor, and always watched over by Che Guevara, had me swearing to myself I'd have every luxury Auntie Linda's house possessed once I was grown up and married to Torvill – or was it Dean? – skating off into the sunset to Ravel's 'Boléro'.

'Your auntie Linda knows the Bamforths.' He nodded in her direction and she walked towards us. She'd put on a bit of weight since I last saw her but the golfing gear, the pink lipstick, coral nails and dark bobbed hair were just the same. 'She plays golf with one of 'em.' Granddad sat down heavily on the wall, grimacing slightly as his stiff, arthritic hip made contact with the stone.

'Who's them? Who are the Bamforths?'

'You must know the Bamforth family? Made their brass out of engineering; gears and the like.'

'Oh, you mean *Samuel* Bamforth's, just outside Midhope?' Everyone in Midhope knew Samuel Bamforth's Engineering Company. Back in the sixties and seventies, school leavers from the local secondary moderns either went into the area's already struggling textile mills or, with a decent clutch of CSEs, became apprentice engineers at, or went into the offices of, the extremely successful Samuel Bamforth's, working there for the next forty years or more until retiring with the ubiquitous carriage clock or matching gardening tools for a newly acquired allotment.

'So, Samuel Bamforth's still alive?' I asked. 'He must be pretty ancient by now.'

'Don't be daft, lass.' Granddad Norman glared at me, his aching joints together with rumours about his precious meadow rendering him uncharacteristically sharp. 'Samuel Bamforth started th' engineering place last century. Edward Bamforth, who I reckon must be his... his, erm, his great-grandson, is behind all this building malarkey. Bamforths bought all the land round here years ago.'

'All of it? Which bits?'

'Never mind *bits*,' Granddad snapped. 'They bought *all* of it. Farmland, woodland, cottages – bought it from the duke of somebody's estate just after t'war. I suppose they had to put their brass into summat.'

'It'll be all right, Granddad. They'll never get planning permission. It's all green belt round here.'

'Well, I think they might, Cassie,' Linda said, wiping her shoe on the lawn. 'There's a lot of dirt up there, Dad.'

'It's not dirt, it's compost, rotting until it's just right for t'roses. Two great hosses came down t'lane a couple of weeks back and left me a present. Too great an opportunity to miss. It'll be just right in a week or so.'

'You shouldn't be lifting buckets of stuff at your age.' Linda frowned and swatted at a couple of flies that had followed her. 'Why don't you let Jason come and mow your lawn for you and see to your roses?'

'Who's Jason?' Granddad and I both looked at Linda.

'He comes over to do our garden. He works for Celia, Edward Bamforth's sister. It was her who recommended him. She was the one told me about the plans for their fields.'

Granddad snorted. 'I don't want nobody called *Jason* messing about wi' my roses. I bet he thinks he knows it all and charges you a fortune for a bit of a garden manicure.'

'Well, yes, he is rather expensive, but Celia says—'

'So, what does Celia say about Granddad's fields?' I interrupted, glancing at my watch. I had so much to do at home and the much-revered Jason's horticultural prowess didn't interest me. The wildflower meadows did.

'Well, according to your auntie Linda,' Granddad almost spat, 't'Government is telling councils they have to build more and more houses. Never mind it's green belt; people are desperate for houses. It has to be built on.'

'Absolutely.' Linda nodded in agreement, her shiny bob remaining curiously still. 'People have to live *somewhere*. And if all these immigrants and refugees we're insisting on letting in continue to *flood* in—'

'I know what *you're* talking about.' Paula said, walking up the path towards us, clutching a mug of tea. 'I could hear you from the house. Sorry, Linda,' she said lightly, holding up the mug, 'didn't realise you were here or I'd have made you one, too. Pot's not quite empty.' Paula leant against the sun-warmed wall, closing her eyes against the setting sun.

'Aye, well, nobbut else to talk about round here.' Granddad really was cross. 'How can anyone...' he picked up his stick and waved it in the direction of the cornflowers, poppies and white campion as well as a host of others I couldn't name or even recognise '... any *bugger* mow that lot down to build new houses? Nasty, tiny little boxes with three toilets – have they got three backsides? – but gardens smaller than a sodding postage stamp.'

'Dad, they haven't got planning permission yet,' Paula soothed. 'It'll probably all come to nothing.'

'Oh, I think you're wrong, Paula. Celia seems to think it's a *fait accompli*.' Linda smiled somewhat patronisingly. 'I mean, the Bamforths own virtually everything round here.'

'Well, the bloody Bamforths can stick their *fet* and their bloody *complee* right up their arses.' Granddad breathed heavily and all the fight seemed to go out of him. 'I'll be in me box by then, any road.'

'Well, that's no reason to give up a fight, if it comes to one, just because you'll be dead.'

'Mum, for heaven's sake.' I glared at Paula, who continued to calmly drink her tea.

'I hear you've some news of your own, Cassandra Moonbeam?' Paula turned in my direction, raising questioning, unplucked eyebrows over her mug.

'News?' My pulse raced. What had Paula heard?

'News travels fast in a small place like Midhope.'

'Are you having another baby, love?' Granddad looked at me hopefully. He loved children, but particularly new babies.

'Don't be ridiculous. I've just got a new job.'

'Oh, of course, you've started this new job of yours.' Linda scraped at some remaining horse muck on her golf shoes. 'Davina's been promoted, you know. I don't know how she does it. Two children, working full time and going off to London twice a week.'

'Not to mention the full-time cleaner, the au pair and the gardener,' Paula added drily. 'Give me a lift home, will you, Cassandra? I'm just going to do a few jobs for your granddad and then I'll be ready.' She collected the mugs and walked back down to the kitchen.

'We have to move on, you know, Cassie,' Linda smiled, draping a yellow Pringle sweater round her shoulders before giving her father a dry kiss on the cheek. 'We can't stand still. We are a global economy and the economy says houses have to be built.'

She'd obviously been reading the *Telegraph* in between eighteen holes and lunch with the girls. 'Not in Granddad Norman's meadow, Auntie Linda. I shall fight it every bit of the way.' I hugged Granddad and followed Paula into the house.

'Mark's got a mistress then?' Paula was angry. 'And for the last two years, Cassandra? I just can't believe you haven't told me what's been going on.'

'Shhh.' I shook my head warningly as we walked towards the car, not wanting Granddad to hear and upset him further. He'd followed me back down the path, stomping his way angrily towards the house, swiping at weeds as he went and the last thing I wanted was for him to know about Mark and me. 'Come on, I'll give you a lift home and tell you what's happened, although you seem to be pretty well informed already.'

'So how do you know? Who told you?' I'd parked up outside Mum's cottage, reversing down the narrow and pot-holed dusty lane.

'It's true then? Oh, Cassandra...'

'Mum, don't sympathise—' I felt the ever-present tears threaten and broke off, struggling to remain in control.

'Well, if it's publicly announced where Midhope's chattering classes are assembled, the whole bloody town will know by now. Dawn told me. Her daughter was there, apparently.' Dawn was one of Mum's yoga mates. 'Mind you, Dawn didn't know who it was Mark's supposed to have been sleeping with.' For all Paula's left-wing, free-love, let-it-all-hang-out idealism, she was strangely reticent about using the more basic words for what Mark and Tina had been up to.

'Shagging,' I said shortly. 'And Tina,' I added for good measure.

Paula stared at me. 'Tina? As in your best friend, Tina?'

'The very same,' I said grimly. 'Tom knows, but I'm going to have to tell Freya. Now. Tonight.'

'Do you want me to come with you? You know Freya and I have a special bond. She reminds me very much of myself at fourteen.'

God forbid. 'It's fine,' I said shortly. 'Actually, I think Mark might still come back…' While I might have made grand gestures a couple of nights ago telling Mark to get out and never come back, I desperately wanted him home.

'And you'd take him back?'

'… and then I wouldn't have to tell Freya anything. She'd be none the wiser.'

'Oh, for heaven's sake, Cassandra. What's the matter with you? Where's the strong woman I brought you up to be?'

'She rebelled against everything you tried to push down her throat,' I spat, as angry with my mother as with my errant husband.

'And don't I know it,' Paula said just as crossly. 'You had far more in common with your auntie Linda than with me.'

'Mum, you wouldn't even let me *call* you Mum. I had yoga, vegetarianism, veganism, transcendental meditation...' I counted each one off on my fingers, '...Ying, Yang, Greenham Common, Save the Whale, Led Zepp and Leonard bloody Cohen. Each time you discovered something new I had to be a part of it too. I wanted Pot Noodles and Angel Delight; a week in Majorca, Wham! and the A Team...'

Paula made a little snort and I didn't know if she was crying. She wasn't: she was laughing. 'You do exaggerate. I bought you the Wham! CD for your ninth birthday.'

'OK, I'll give you that one but, if you remember, my birthday party food was wholemeal bread and hummus and a solid brick of something or other for a birthday cake. What nine-year-old wants hummus, for heaven's sake?'

'Freya loves hummus.'

'Well, yes, I know that. Middle-class kids today love hummus and olives. But back then, we didn't. It was *weird* food, as Rebecca Warrington told everyone at school the next day.'

'Did she? Little bitch. Wait till I see her. She comes to me for an aromatherapy session every week.'

Did she? Rebecca Warrington? Blimey.

'We're getting off the point here, Cassandra,' Mum went on. 'Mark was always going to be the one to have an affair.'

'What? Right, that's it, Mum, get out of the car. I'm not discussing this with you any further. If that nosy parker Dawn, or Dawn's bloody daughter, hadn't told you, you'd have been none the wiser. Mark will be back. I'm certain of it. It just needs me to give him the word, maybe some marriage guidance *counselling*... You'd approve of *counselling*, wouldn't you, *Paula*?' I revved the engine as Paula quickly jumped out of the car, frightened, I think, I was going to drive off with her foot still in the door.

Yes, I was right. This whole debacle wasn't just Mark's fault: Serpentina had led him astray; I'd not noticed because I was so busy with my teaching and the children. Oh, I could see it all now. I just needed to see Mark, talk to him, tell him it was probably my fault as much as his. Let him come home, we'd talk, he'd swear to have nothing more to do with Tina and everything would be fine. I sped home along the country lanes and, as I pulled into Tower View Avenue, immediately saw Mark's shiny, elongated sports car he'd treated himself to when he hit forty last year sitting on the drive. When he'd brought it home, scattering unsuspecting pigeons as well as Mr and Mrs Craddock from number twelve as they walked back from picking up their pension, I'd laughed, teasing him that he obviously viewed it as a babe magnet. I wasn't smiling now, the bastard.

*

'Dad's upstairs.' Tom was standing in the kitchen methodically eating bread and Paula's home-made plum jam while staring out of the window at the growing dusk.

'Where's Freya?'

'Upstairs with Dad.'

'Oh, Tom, you've not told her, have you? About Auntie Tina?'

Tom just looked at me and shrugged.

Shit. I took the stairs two at a time and found both of them in our bedroom. Mark was filling suitcases with his shirts, sweaters, socks and pants. His suits, still on hangers, were neatly piled on the bed.

He stopped what he was doing as I walked in, but Freya continued to empty Mark's drawers, throwing the remaining socks into the furthest case with the same ease she scored goals at netball.

'Look, you don't have to do this,' I said, taking Mark's arm as he continued to empty the wardrobe of his things.

'Oh, yes, he does,' Freya snapped. 'I'm here to make sure he takes everything. That he doesn't have to come back from Auntie Tina's because he's forgotten some of his pants or his toothbrush.'

'Freya, go downstairs. Now. You're too young to understand.'

'Of course I understand.' Freya was a snarling bundle of fury. 'What am I supposed to say at school when my friends ask me where my dad is? He's gone off with my mum's best friend? My favourite auntie? My godmother?

Well, I tell you now, she can stick it when she sends me my next birthday present. What sort of godmother chooses expensive presents for me when all along she's ... you know... with my dad, for heaven's sake ...' Freya broke off, glaring at both of us.

'Freya. Now. Downstairs.' I yelled the words and she hurled a pair of ski gloves at Mark, catching him on his shoulder before storming out, eyes blazing.

'Look, Mark, we have to talk.'

His face was pale, its whiteness emphasising the huge black rings that had appeared under his eyes. He shook his head. 'I'm sorry, Cass, I don't know what to do. I've messed up.'

My heart gave a desperate little lurch of hope. 'Marriage guidance, a counsellor... I've been too bothered about the house being tidy... about the cushions on the chairs having to be vertical before we went to bed, about... about the toilet lid not being put down, about not having sex on the sofa because it'd flatten the feathers. It's probably my fault as much as yours.'

'Stop it, Cass, stop it. None of this is your fault.' He paused. 'Although, yes, you're right, you *were* constantly going on at me about the state of the sofa, the bloody toilet seat, taking my shoes off, the fucking cushions. The house is like a show house, not a home.'

I stared at him. 'You never said.'

'Well, that's just you. Always reacting against Paula's upbringing. It just gets a bit wearing.' Mark fastened his cases, refusing to look at me. 'Give me some time, Cass. I just need to find myself. I'll make sure money goes into your bank account every month. I need to work out what I want.'

And with that, he hauled the largest case off the bed and headed for the door.

8

Paula

1976

By 3.30 p.m. Paula knew that if she didn't leave the suffocating heat of the smoke-filled office she would explode. Go *Boom*, just like that, all over the millionth invoice she'd typed that day. The finished invoices – three copies of each – were piling up in her finished tray, but a surreptitious glance around the sweating office of Crosland, Crawshaw & Sons (Dyers and Spinners) confirmed she was miles behind the other typists with her workload.

Pushing back her chair, she stood and walked towards the female cloakroom at the end of the corridor. Anything to stretch her legs; anything to move on the bone-numbingly slow minutes until she could escape into the glorious July sunshine. Once there, Paula locked herself into a cubicle, laying her forehead against the white tiles, but even they were warm, absorbing the heat that was continuing, day after day, in this glorious summer.

Paula held her wrists under the cold tap, delaying the moment when she would have to return to the office, splashing tepid water up her arms and dabbing at her armpits laid bare beneath the flimsy purple top. Angela Cartwright, the office manager, disapproved of bare arms – and probably purple, too – but even she had arrived that morning in a sleeveless dress, shedding the ubiquitous fawn cardigan she always wore, by mid-morning.

Paula kept her hands under the water and gazed at her reflection in the fly-blown mirror. Her dark straight hair, unfashionably long in comparison to the short, angled wedges and the shaggy Farrah Fawcett Majors-style sported by the other office girls, needed a damned good cut according to Linda, Paula's older sister. Rowan loved her hair, winding it round his fingers and pulling her mouth towards him to be kissed.

Hell, she just had to escape. Get away from this mundane life of living at home, working in this godforsaken office…

'Your little visitor *again*?'

'Sorry?'

Angela Cartwright stood at the cloakroom door, arms folded. 'Paula, you spend more time in this cloakroom than at your desk. You're always in here. Now, either you have a chronic stomach upset, a bladder problem, or a permanent time of the month…' she paused, embarrassed '… any of which I suggest you take to your GP to sort. Mr Gregory keeps looking to see where you are.'

He would, Paula thought. He was always looking: dirty old man with his sweaty hands left too long on the girls' shoulders, his too-friendly, insinuating questions as to what they'd been *up* to the night before. 'Sorry, Angela, the heat, felt a bit queasy...'

Angela's eyes went involuntarily to Paula's stomach and Paula wanted to laugh. Did Old Carthorse really think she'd let herself get pregnant? Trapped by some man and have to stay forever in this northern backwater? Paula had a vision of the next forty years, typing bloody invoices until she retired. Not her. She was off. With Rowan, travelling once she'd saved up enough money. Morocco, Afghanistan, Australia – the whole bloody world. Just a few more months and she'd have enough money. Her Post Office savings were mounting. The thought, together with the knowledge that she'd planned a surprise for Rowan that coming evening, calmed her and she quickly dried her hands.

'Sorry, Angela, I'm feeling much better now. You know, we really should have some sort of air conditioning in the office. Workers' rights; Health and Safety and all that. Perhaps you should have a word with Mr Gregory. Get him to take it all the way up to Mr Crosland himself?'

Paula smiled beatifically at her line manager, patted Angela's arm and walked graciously past her, back to her desk.

'Where are you off?' Norman Rhodes lit a Player's Number 6 and drew in the first lungful of smoke, his appraising eyes following his younger daughter as she walked past him and up the path to the back gate.

'Out.'

'Well, I can see that. Out where? Out wi' that long-haired hippy again?'

'For heaven's sake, Dad, get your decade right. Hippies are a bit 1960s, don't you think?'

'I've no idea, love.' He paused, dragging on his cigarette once more before turning back to the spring onions he was planting. 'But aren't you a bit hot in that long dress? Our Linda went out wearing a nice little summer frock. Letting the air get to her legs.'

'God, Dad, you sound like Mr Gregory at work. He's always going on about our legs.' Paula tutted her disapproval, cross that her father was once again comparing her to Linda: the good girl, the sister who passed her eleven-plus, went to grammar school, Leeds University and who was, at this moment ensconced with Anthony Trinder and his parents, discussing the seating plan for her wedding three months hence. Three months away! Jesus, there could be a nuclear war before then, wipe them all out. Ha! So much for the damned seating plan then if the mushroom cloud went up. And how could anyone named Linda hook themselves up to someone called Anthony Trinder? Linda Trinder, for heaven's sake. Paula grinned to herself.

And what Linda, old Tommy Trinder and his parents – and her own parents, come to that – didn't know was that by the time Linda was walking down the aisle in Midhope Parish Church she, Paula, wouldn't be behind her, bringing up the rear in salmon satin. No way, José. She'd be in Amsterdam with Rowan, about to board the Magic Bus that would take them to Turkey and on to Afghanistan and maybe even India. Paula was a little hazy on the actual geography, despite it being her best subject at the dreadful local secondary modern she'd been allocated after failing the eleven-plus, but Rowan was planning it for both of them and all she had to do was ensure she had the money to fund it.

She knew her mum and dad would be furious – Linda perhaps less so – at her going AWOL just before the wedding, not to mention going off with a lad she wasn't even engaged to, but Rowan said they didn't want to leave it too long. The winter months could be harsh through that part of the world and they needed a clear run to get to India.

'What have you got in that basket?' Dot's head appeared at the open upstairs bathroom window where Maggy-from-number-ten was assisting in the four-monthly ritual of a home perm. Dot, an alien in pink curlers and white cotton wool ear protectors, leant out further, endangering not only herself but next door's curmudgeon of a ginger mog, who was basking in the evening heat directly underneath.

'Nothing.'

'What do you mean, nothing? It's not drugs in there, is it?'

'Mum, if I was into drugs I'd have hidden them in my knickers.'

'Shhh. Shut up, Paula, all t'street'll hear you.'

Maggy-from-number-ten appeared beside Dot, straining to see her neighbour's wayward daughter. 'What's she doing with that long purple dress on?' Paula heard her mutter. 'She'll be a bit warm in that thing, won't she?'

'So, what's in t'basket then, Paula? Don't you go leaving it anywhere. I'll need it for shopping tomorrow.'

'Cheese.' Paula shook the basket at Dot and Maggy.

'Cheese? I hope you haven't taken all of them Dairylea Triangles? I've just been on to t'corner shop for 'em. They're for your dad's pack-up tomorrow.'

'Brie. It's Brie. And olives and taramasalata...' Paula was proud of her purchases. She'd had to go into Midhope to the fancy new delicatessen at dinner time instead of eating her ham sandwich in the canteen with the rest of the girls from the office. The cheese had begun to hum a bit, festering in the heat under her desk all afternoon, but the Polish chap, who'd said no summer picnic was complete without a good piece of Brie, had told her it was best eaten runny. And, presumably smelly.

'What's taramasawotsit when it's at home?' Maggy-from-number-ten leant out even further from the bathroom window.

'Isn't it a spider, or one of them mucky dances they do somewhere foreign... you know, whirling around until they drop.'

'*Tarantula* and *tarantella*,' Paula tutted, heading once more for the gate.

Norman leant on his spade, flicked his cigarette butt in the same direction he'd thrown a foolhardy slug that had had the temerity to linger in his summer cabbage minutes earlier, and launched into verse quoting, verbatim, lines from a certain poem.

'Oh God, he's off again...' Dot retreated back into the bathroom, pulling Maggy with her.

'What's he on about?' Maggy's voice floated down the garden on the hot evening air, following Paula as she closed the gate behind her before taking the shortcut across Norman's Meadow towards the bus stop.

'Oh, it's his favourite poet,' came Dot's reply. 'Hilary Belloc or somebody. She's very good.'

9

Beginning to Survive...

Are you doing a Gloria?

My mobile, yapping like a Yorkshire Terrier, announced the arrival of a text. I'd thought the noise amusing when, six months ago, on directing Tom to find me a new text alert, he'd come up with the dog sound. Now it just bloody irritated me but I'd not had the time or the technical knowledge to change it to something rather more soothing, or at least in keeping with my new status as head of Little Acorns. Karen Adams, who'd pulled up at the same time as me on that Friday morning of the first week of term, glanced with a pained expression towards the yapping but sailed into school without so much as a good morning, leaving me alone to reply to the message from Clare.

Doing a Gloria???

Yep, a Gloria.

As in? Hunniford? Swanson? Sfood...?

Sfood?

Food, Gloria Sfood. Not had time for breakfast yet.

You're definitely doing a Gloria and surviving if you're thinking of food rather than your broken heart.

Ah good old Gloria Gaynor... Going into school. Will ring you in a minute.

I breathed deeply as, phone still in hand, I pushed open the head's office door with my knee and dumped briefcase, handbag plus a large plastic carrier bag onto the desk. This time last week I still had a husband, albeit a cheating bastard of a husband. Six days on, and not only was I husbandless but I was still in charge of Little Acorns. And had I survived? Well, if you call crawling into bed at the end of each day and alternatively sobbing and concocting lists of ways to torture Mark and Serpentina surviving, then I suppose I had.

I glanced at the clock. Five minutes, I told myself. Five minutes for a quick catch-up with Clare and then down to the business of the day. I had told the staff I was initiating a weekly Friday morning briefing session before school and, ignoring Karen Adams' pained expression and arched eyebrows, had suggested we meet at eight fifteen. I'd brought in muffins and croissants, my three cafetiéres and some good

Italian coffee as well as fresh orange juice for the non-coffee drinkers in order to soften the blow of yet another meeting when there was so much to do in the classrooms.

I closed the office door and reached for one of Priscilla's biscuits. I hadn't been able to face breakfast with the kids and was still needing three visits to the bathroom before setting off each morning, and Hotel Chocolat biscuits were all my stomach could, well, stomach at seven thirty in the morning. That and huge mugs of tea: I'd abandoned coffee as it made me jittery.

'Yes, I'm getting there,' I sighed, once I'd connected with Clare.

'Well done.'

'Apart from thinking of ways to torture and humiliate the pair of them.'

'I heard.' Clare chortled.

'What have you heard?'

'Tina told me what you'd done to her car.'

'Tina told you?'

'She came round.'

'She came round and you let her in? Whose side are you on?' I could feel my pulse racing and my stomach going into nervous spasms once more.

'Cassie,' Clare spoke my name calmly. 'Cassie, I'm not on anyone's side.'

'Well, you damned well should be.'

'Sorry, I don't do sides. Not since I was ten years old, at least.'

I fought my initial reaction to slam down the phone and burst into tears. Think of Gloria, I told myself. And your briefing session with the staff in the next half-hour. Red eyes and washed away mascara would give Karen bloody Adams the upper hand and I wasn't allowing her that.

'OK, OK. And are you going to tell me what she said? Is she going to let me have my husband back?'

'Cassie,' Clare said gently, 'I'm not ringing you for a gossip about what he said, she said. I'm ringing to see how you are. Now's not the right time for a dissection of what's gone on so far. Look, come out with me tomorrow night and we can chat.'

'Out? Out where?' The very thought of getting dolled up and going out filled me with dread. 'Why don't you come over to me and we can have a takeaway and a bottle of wine?'

'No, can't do that, sorry.' Clare was firm. 'I have to be in Leeds. I have my first hen party there and I need to see it's all going well. Fiona's coming with me. Look, I know the last thing you'll want to do is get your glad rags on and come with us but I think you need some adult company after a week of five-year-olds.'

'We do go up to eleven-year-olds here, you know.' I was still cross that she'd been talking with the enemy.

'Right, I'll take it that's a yes then? I'm working so I can't drink, but no reason you and Fiona can't enjoy yourselves.'

'Hang on, I haven't said yes yet... Hang on, Clare, there's someone at the door...'

'Get yourself round to Fiona's around seven tomorrow evening. Get your lippy on, girl.' And with that she hung up.

'Mrs Beresford, have you a moment?' Jean Barlow popped her head around the door. 'I know we have our *briefing*…' She breathed the word with reverence, adding, 'Golly, it's rather like working for MFI all of a sudden.'

'MFI?' I stared at Jean who continued to beam round the door at me. 'Oh, MI5, you mean?'

'Probably, dear. Now have you a minute to have a quick word with Mrs Miniauskiene?' Jean pronounced it 'Mini-Ow-Skinny', separating the syllables into digestible chunks, before mouthing, 'Although it's *never* a quick minute with that one,' at me as I walked over to the door.

'Plis, is Deimante. I needs quick minutes wis you, Mrs Head.'

'OK, come in, er, Diamante. What's the problem?'

'Is Deimante, not Diamante. I needs more works, plis. My man laids off from buildings. Alls we wants to do is toils and works and makes pounds. But my man, he on zero-hours contracts and we can't make our ends meeting. Is sitting at home in fronts of TVs and eatings McDonald's all days and getting big fats belly pot…'

'Hang on, Diamante—'

'Is *Deimante*…'

'I'm so sorry.' I felt myself redden, trying to get the poor woman's name correct. Deimante Miniauskiene was tiny, no more than four foot ten, but incredibly beautiful. I stared at the long curling black hair, at her very full mouth and dark eyes, which were now fixed on me.

'Deimante, I'm – at the moment – in charge of a school. I don't employ people round here.'

'No, no, Mrs Head, I already works for school.' She said it proudly, leaving the room for ten seconds before returning and brandishing a huge red and yellow lollipop almost as big as herself.

'Oh, I'm sorry,' I apologised again. 'I didn't realise you're Little Acorns' lollipop lady.'

'Sat's right. And I is very very good one. Not one childrens knocked over with cars or buses at all. "Gets back on that bloody pavements," I shouts if they tries to put even one leetle bits of toes into roads wisout my... wisout my...' Deimante screwed up her face in concentration, '... so say.' She beamed at me and then instantly frowned again. 'Sree month I is doing job and now I gets stress at Gatis – is my man – not having buildings jobs and I gets gyp 'ere...' She pointed to her head. 'Leetle pains in heads all time. So, now I sends Gatis – is my man – to pharmacy for pain pill and he comes back and says, "Deimante, you as pain in heads but you as to put pills up your..."' she paused, frowned. 'He say, "You as to put pills up your back bottom."'

'Right. OK. Are you sure?'

Deimante pulled a pack from her fluorescent yellow jacket, which should have been a giveaway to her occupation the minute she walked into the office. 'Look, see, *Anal gesic*. Am spending last two days putting them up here,' she hopped about a bit, indicating her bottom, 'buts gyp in head still there. So, needs more work to make pounds and not make stress and pain in heads.'

I looked surreptitiously at my watch. Briefing in the staff room in ten minutes and I hadn't even put the kettle on for coffee or found the glasses in which to pour the orange juice. Or looked at the notes I'd made last night. 'Look, Deimante, could you leave this with me? I have a feeling that the kitchen staff may need someone because one of the cooks went off a couple of days ago with a burst appendix?'

Deimante gathered her lollipop and was about to launch further, but I managed to usher her towards the door. 'Leave it with me,' I repeated. 'The children will be waiting on that pavement for you. Oh, and, Deimante, the pills? The pills definitely go down via your mouth with a lovely glass of water or cup of tea.'

'I knews it,' she tutted, swinging her lollipop onto her shoulder like one of the seven dwarves on his way to work, before heading down the corridor and the main entrance. 'I bloody knews it didn't go ups my back bottoms...'

The usual pre-school morning gossip and banter were in full swing in the staff room as I finally made my way down there, muffins and croissants still in their paper bags.

'So now, since last night, I've got this gorgeous new boyfriend,' Kimberley Crawford, the youngest member of staff, was saying as I walked in. 'Met him in Lidl when I was in there after school. Six foot tall, fab tattoos on both arms—'

'That was quick work. How did he ask you out? Over the baked beans?'

'Well, to be honest, he doesn't know he's my new boyfriend yet. It's a surprise...'

'... And, she says he's gone from weed and has started taking *Meerkat* now... Doesn't know what to do with him.'

'I think you mean *M-CAT*, Deirdre ...'

'... Loved the book. But not sure about that Russian character who kept popping up.'

'Which Russian character? There was no Russian in it, was there?'

'You know, wotsisname, er, Sonofabitch, he kept appearing but didn't really add to the plot...'

'OK, ladies, shall we start?' I realised I was very nervous. 'I've brought some goodies for us and Jean is bringing coffee once the kettle has boiled.'

'Oh, just had my breakfast,' Karen Adams drawled. 'You should have told us you were feeding us: I'd have left some room.'

'Ooh, lovely,' Grace Stevenson said, jumping up to help me. 'I can always eat a muffin.'

'Me, too,' Kath Beaumont nodded, reaching for a plate and a particularly large double chocolate chip specimen.

'We can see that,' Karen Adams mouthed at a couple of her mates, indicating with a nod of her head Kath's somewhat large backside.

'Do we all have a drink and something to eat?' I glanced across at Karen. 'Those of us who're indulging at any rate?' I noticed two of Karen's cronies – Sheila Wilson and Debs Stringer – about to help themselves to coffee and croissants, but a quick look from Karen had them sitting back in their seats empty-handed.

I took a deep breath and launched. 'I'm afraid I still don't know what's happening *re* my position here. The governors are trying to recruit an acting head from one of the other three schools in the academy trust but, according to David Henderson, they're a bit thin on the ground at the moment. I know there's one particular deputy head at Whitley Grange who would have jumped at gaining experience here but apparently she's off having a hip operation and won't be available for a term at least.' I glanced over at Grace. 'Obviously, you know that Grace has stepped into the breach this week, looking after my class, but she has two young children of her own at home. She has offered to do two days and knows someone who would be more than willing to do another two, leaving me to teach on the Wednesday morning—'

'Job shares are never a success,' Karen Adams interrupted, 'particularly in teaching. There's always one who doesn't do as much as the other, and when things go wrong they blame each other and things never get sorted out as they should.' She sniffed disparagingly and looked around the staff room for approval. She got it: several heads nodded in agreement.

'Well I can't agree with you there, Karen.' Grace took a final bite of her muffin and wiped her mouth on one of the napkins she'd found in a cupboard and distributed to those of us eating. 'While I've never actually been employed myself on a job-share basis, I know loads of teachers who have. And they're hugely successful. You usually get one of the pair who is brilliant at the science side or, like me, really good at all the arty stuff. The second half of the job share comes in midweek, fresh and with energy to do their two days and, the other goes off to recuperate.'

'Shouldn't be teaching if they need to recuperate after just two days,' Karen said rudely.

'I've already suggested a former colleague of mine who would love to work with me,' Grace went on, ignoring Karen. 'David Henderson knows both of us and of course wouldn't recommend—'

'Of course he knows the pair of you,' Karen said a sneer playing on her thin lips. 'David Henderson is your son's grandfather, and Harriet Westmoreland – I assume it's her you're planning to drag in with you – Harriet Westmoreland's husband is David Henderson's business partner. Talk about jobs for the girls!'

I looked across at Grace, who had gone slightly red in the face. I'd had no idea that Grace was actually related to our Chair of Governors and felt a bit put out neither she nor David Henderson had deigned to tell me.

'I hardly think my relationship with David Henderson is relevant either to you, Karen, or to my position here.' Grace spoke calmly but I could see she was cross. 'I have merely stepped in to help at David's request, and tried to come up with a solution, putting forward the name of a perfectly competent teacher who would be willing to job share with me. At the end of the day it's up to the governors and Cassie.'

Grace was absolutely right. It was now Friday and I needed a teacher in my Year 5 class on Monday morning.

Grace had already taught the whole of this first week, but I knew she wasn't willing or able to work full weeks from now on. I could, I supposed, trawl through the supply agencies in order to find a full-time temporary teacher but I was unlikely to get a better teacher than Grace Stevenson. According to David Henderson, Grace had been about to take up her own deputy headship when she discovered she was pregnant several years ago. Anyway, she'd been brilliant: competent and confident, with the class already in love with her, and I wanted her to stay. I made a decision. Wasn't that what heads did?

'Grace, before you go down to the class would you give me Harriet's contact details? I'll ring her myself as soon as we've finished here. And then could I have a meeting with you at lunchtime?'

Ignoring Karen Adams, who looked as if she'd swallowed a particularly bitter lemon, I turned to my agenda. 'I'd like to see all your planning on a weekly basis, please. Mrs Theobold and I had discussed this during the summer break and it was agreed that I would be in charge of this. I'm not asking to see all your short-term plans in detail at this stage, but it would be really helpful to have a single weekly sheet with a learning objective for each lesson. I'll make sure copies of these sheets are available to you by the end of the day and I would like them handed in to the office every Monday morning.' I held my breath, waiting for the backlash, the looks of disbelief, but none was forthcoming, apart from Karen Adams' folded arms and continued sour expression.

Instead, after the coffee cups were drunk, crumbs licked off fingers and bags and books gathered for the coming morning I overheard Kath Beaumont say to Grace, 'To be honest, Grace, Mrs Theobold let us get away with murder. She never looked at any of our plans – too busy schmoozing with the upmarket parents and those governors that she liked, or who thought she could do no wrong; it's actually quite nice to have a proper plan in place.'

I walked down to my office, a daft smile on my face.

'I hear you've asked Harriet Westmoreland in for a chat *re* working part time with Grace?' David Henderson appeared at the office door just as school was about to finish for the afternoon.

'Gosh, news travels fast round here.' I stood up from the desk, glancing at the clock on the wall that had apparently been there since the year dot. According to Jean, Mrs Theobold had been trying to throw it out for years, determined to replace it with 'something modern, electronic and that damned well keeps time' but I really loved the heavy oak Victorian clock with its soothing, steady tick. Loved the thought that it had been in place when the school was built – one of the first C of E village schools in the country. 'I need to be in the playground to see the kids off,' I said. 'Need to head off any parental problems at the pass, as it were.'

'And I need to speak to you,' David went on. 'And yes, news does travel fast in a small village like Westenbury.'

'Especially when the supply teachers I've set on are either your daughter-in-law or your business partner's wife?' I raised an eyebrow and David Henderson had the grace to look slightly shamefaced.

'Well, first, Grace is not my daughter-in-law; her son just happens to be my grandson. Secondly, I believe it was Grace who suggested Harriet, not me. You'll find they come as a pair. Always have done from being eleven when they were at school together.'

'But it will only be for a week or two and then I'll be back to taking my class myself?'

'That's what I need to talk to you about. As well as someone, apart from Harriet, who's insisted on coming in for a chat with us after school. Do you have time to stop and meet him? Apparently, he'd arranged it all with Priscilla, but she'd never said anything to me.'

'Why should she?' I realised that sounded a bit abrupt, rude even, and hurriedly added, 'I mean, I know governors basically run schools these days, but I'm sure Priscilla was more than happy to see people without one of you lot breathing down her neck all the time.' Oh shit, that sounded even ruder and I gave a nervous smile to soften the comment. I didn't want David Henderson to think I was getting cocky.

David laughed. 'You're finding your feet, Cassandra. Great. You'll be buying Hotel Chocolat biscuits next and putting your feet up on the desk.'

'I'm going to have to,' I grinned. 'I've eaten all of Priscilla's.'

*

I walked out onto the playground, stopping to chat to a granny here, an au pair there, a lone father who seemed a bit out of his depth amongst the chattering playground Mafia planning play dates for their kids, as well as nights out and dinner parties for themselves.

I waved across at Deimante, who had a gaggle of Year 6 boys up against the perimeter fence, her red and yellow lollipop almost severing their windpipes as she scanned the road for a break in the cars parking every which way and anywhere they could around the school. Hmm, Parental Parking needed to be on the next governors' meeting agenda, I reckoned, and then, chiding myself for my bossiness, picked up a toddler who, going AWOL from his frantically texting mother, was heading for the gate, and made my way back into school.

10

We'd Like to Build You a New School...

'Cassandra, this is Edward Bamforth. I don't know if you've met before?' David Henderson stood as I walked into the office, indicating one of the two men sitting opposite him. The younger of the two nodded and rose briefly to shake my hand before continuing to study the paper he held in his other, while the man introduced as Edward Bamforth walked across the room to greet me.

'Mrs Beresford, lovely to meet you. Now, this is a totally informal meeting: nothing will be noted or minuted and it's a chance for us to sit down together and air a few views.' He paused and nodded towards the younger man. 'This is my son, Xavier. Let me start by offering our congratulations on your new appointment, albeit under such sad circumstances. Tragic news about Priscilla: I did wonder if we shouldn't postpone this meeting, but Priscilla had been eager that we get together as soon as possible.'

I glanced across at David. If he knew what this meeting was about then he was giving nothing away, his face remaining impassive as I moved over to the one vacant chair. 'Jean's still here,' I said. 'I'll ask her if she'll bring us some tea.'

'Already done,' David said. 'She won't be long. And I've asked Ben Carey, the vicar of All Hallows Church, Westenbury, to be here too.' He frowned. 'I'm not sure where he is; he's notoriously late for every appointment.'

While we waited for Jean, David and Edward Bamforth continued their chat about someone both of them knew, and I had a minute to size up the latter as he sat, totally relaxed, in the chair opposite. He was, I guessed, much older than David Henderson – probably in his sixties – but, while both carried an air of privilege about them, Edward Bamforth appeared somewhat arrogant. Despite the warm September afternoon, both he and his son – who still hadn't said a word – were dressed formally in dark suits, white shirts and sober ties.

'Tea, anyone?' Jean trilled somewhat nervously as she knocked, came in and then attempted to push the piles of last summer's maths SATs papers to one side before placing a loaded tea tray of the school's best white china onto the desk. In her wake came a tall, bearded man whose dog collar announced his identity before David Henderson was able to introduce him. Jean smiled at us all and sang, in a top soprano, 'When your day seems topsy-turvy and as stormy as can be, there's nothing quite as tranquil as a nice hot cup of tea.'

We all stared at Jean who, now obviously somewhat embarrassed by the silence that had greeted her little ditty, had gone slightly pink.

'A good woman is like a cup of tea: the stronger the better.' David came to Jean's rescue and she smiled gratefully across at him and it suddenly dawned on me that our school secretary was slightly in love with him.

'And on the sixth day, when God created tea, he was well pleased,' Ben Carey laughed, and went to help Jean unload the tray.

The younger man frowned and looked bored but Edward Bamforth came back with, 'Never trust anyone who, when left alone with a tea cosy, doesn't put it on their head.'

I was just contemplating standing, one hand on my hip and the other outstretched, and singing, 'I'm a little teapot, short and stout, here's my handle, here's my spout...' when Xavier Bamforth looked across at us all and said, 'Do you think we could get on?'

Jean retreated, smiling coyly at both David and Edward as she went.

'Right, let's get down to business,' Edward said, stirring sugar into his tea before taking a sip and grimacing slightly. 'I'm sure you both know why we're here?'

I glanced across at David. 'No. Sorry. David?'

'I've a good idea,' he said shortly. 'Do you want to see if I'm right?'

'OK. I'll come straight to the point. The Bamforth

Estate wants to build you a brand-new school.' Edward Bamforth paused for effect. Xavier Bamforth said nothing.

'Really?' While I dislike intensely the phrase 'gobsmacked', that's all I could bring to mind to describe the impact of what Edward Bamforth had just said. 'Why?'

'You're a brand-new head teacher.'

'Hang on, I'm acting head for a few weeks until we find someone suitable.'

'You're a brand-new head,' Edward repeated smoothly. 'What better than a brand-new school to go with it?'

'So, is the Bamforth Estate a philanthropic charity then?' I asked shortly. I knew I was being a bit rude, confrontational even, but Granddad Norman's distress earlier this week because of this man and his desire to concrete over the surrounding area, had already put me on the defensive.

'No, Cassandra, the Bamforth Estate is a huge land-owning company. It owns the fields, the farms, much of the land around Westenbury...' David pushed his cup and saucer across the desk and leant back, folding his arms.

'The village of Westenbury itself, really,' Edward smiled. 'We own it all.'

'But not our little bit.' David smiled back, the smile not quite reaching his eyes. 'The Church owns the land Little Acorns is built on.'

'But we own *all* the fields, *all* the land that surrounds the school...'

'And you want *our* little bit of land because, without it, you can't access *your* huge amount of land to build the three thousand plus houses the Bamforth Estate has put forward the plans for to Midhope Council.'

'Well, I wouldn't put it as bluntly as that.'

'So how would you put it?' David asked.

'Three thousand houses? Hang on a minute,' I interrupted. 'First, it's all green belt round here. You can't build on that. The council wouldn't allow it.' I remembered the difficulty we'd had getting plans passed for our conservatory: because our garden on Tower View Avenue backs onto green belt land, the authority had taken a hell of a lot of persuading to let us encroach onto the edge of it. 'There's no way they're going to let you cover all the beautiful fields in concrete. The farmers won't let you either. They're not going to give up their farms to you.'

'We *own* the farms. We've already given notice to several of our tenant farmers.'

'Just like that?'

'You're implying we're throwing people onto the street.' Edward laughed shortly. 'The majority of the farms around here are tenanted, as they have been since the year dot. And most are only just scraping a living. Farming in the UK is going the same way as British Leyland, the coal mines and the woollen mills – down the drain.'

'Well, it will if you stick damned great houses on the farmland. *And* it's you lot that's upset my granddad.' I could feel myself going pink in the face.

'Your granddad?' Xavier Bamforth frowned once more and looked across at me, his dark eyes fixed on me as he tried to work out what my granddad had to do with his family.

'His field. Norman's Meadow.'

'Oh, Norman is your grandfather?' Edward said, surprised. 'Well, I'm sorry, Cassandra, your granddad might have adopted that field as his own, but it's ours. And people need houses. People have to live somewhere.'

'But not in my granddad's field…'

'*Our* field…'

'Look, this is getting us nowhere.' Xavier Bamforth looked at his watch. 'We need to tell you what the Estate is proposing. You might even like it.'

I folded my arms. 'OK, go ahead.' I was beginning to feel really angry that these men were in the school, trying to get me on their side. The Bamforths may have planned it as an informal, friendly meeting, but what they were mooting was anything but friendly.

'As David so rightly says, we need this land that the school is built on. I'm sure the Church would be very grateful for us to take an old building like this off its hands. At the end of the day it's ancient – Victorian.'

'Yes, and with a huge amount of history,' I tutted. 'Did you know that the original building here was one of the first Church schools ever built? Over a hundred and fifty years ago?'

'We would build a brand-new, up-to-the-minute, state-of-the-art school complete with computer suite and technology room.' Xavier was reading from his notes, as if only just realising what he and his father had on the cards.

I wavered slightly – a room for design technology and food technology would be heaven – but only for a second. 'I can almost guarantee any new school would be a concrete block with too-small classrooms and a flat roof that leaks. And I bet there'd be nowhere near as much land with it, if any. Here we have playing fields, a nature area; don't tell me you'd give up your precious land for wildlife.'

'We've already consulted the best architects and builders,' Edward Bamforth said smoothly. 'And what is the one thing parents want?'

'Besides happy well-rounded children in a country environment?'

'A car park. A decent car park to drop off their kids. You have the country lane alongside the front of the school here and you know as well as I do the problems with parking and the frayed tempers that go along with it every morning and evening.'

He had a point there. Dropping kids off at the school gates was a major headache for most schools in this country. It brought to mind my neighbours who had just moved to Houston, Texas with their kids, and Maureen writing to tell me how, every morning they waited in a line in their over-sized air-conditioned motors outside the school, handing over their offspring directly to the teachers who then ferried them straight into the air-conditioned schoolrooms. They thought it was marvellous. I thought it horrendous. I wanted kids to walk to school down country lanes, picking blackberries on their way, scraping their knees and being late as they chased each other into the yard. Blimey, I'd be having them bowling hoops along and carrying a hot potato for their dinner next.

'Mr Bamforth does raise a pertinent point about cars, you know, Cassandra. The lane right down to the vicarage is jammed every morning.' Ben Carey tapped his pen against his teeth. 'But that doesn't mean I'm agreeing with him about all this,' he added hastily as he saw my face.

'You'd be ripping out the very heart of the Westenbury community if you demolished this school. Parents send their children here *because* it's small. And we actually have a computer suite, thank you very much. This may be a Victorian building but don't forget the school had a huge refurbishment two years ago: we are bang up to date with our technology, albeit on a smaller scale than I would like. And,' I continued, now on a bit of a roll, 'once you take away the school from the village, others will follow. The baker will go, as will the organic butcher and the little hardware store where I go for a quick screw when I really need one...' Blimey, hark at you, Cassandra Moonbeam, I chided myself as all three men stared at me, wide-eyed and obviously impressed. You've been head for a week and you're acting as if you own the place. I suddenly realised that being rode roughshod over by Mark and Serpentina had brought out a fighting spirit in me. But I knew that at the end of the day, the governors and the Trust would be making decisions about Little Acorns' future. Not me.

'And,' David leant forward and spoke slowly, enunciating every word, 'I shall object to this whole development with every power I have; with every fibre of my being.'

I stole a glance at him. David's face was calm but set.

'Well, obviously you would,' Edward said just as calmly. 'With your place just across the fields from here, I wouldn't have expected anything other than your objection. What you *should* be thinking of is the people without homes – we will be building social housing as well as the more upmarket, five-bedroomed properties – and those children for whom a fabulous, brand-new, well-appointed school is their right. Nimbyism will reign supreme for the "haves" in this area. Try thinking about the "have nots" for a change, David.'

'You're absolutely right, Edward. The last thing I want is a sodding great soulless estate built right up to my garden wall. This is green belt, beautiful farmland that should remain untouched for generations to enjoy. Would *you*—'

'We're not talking about me, David,' Edward interrupted. 'But our plans *do* incorporate the fields around where I actually live…'

'And you will then sell up and go and live in your place down in the Cotswolds and your house in, where is it…? The South of France?'

That shut Edward Bamforth up for a second, but he soon came back fighting. 'You know, Priscilla was *very* much in favour of having a brand-new school built for her pupils.'

'It would have to be a jolly big school if you're planning

on three thousand extra houses in the area.' Ben Carey raised eyebrows and continued the rather irritating tapping of biro against his teeth.

'Absolutely,' Xavier smiled. 'It would be one of the biggest in Midhope.'

'And Priscilla was *more* than ready for the challenge,' Edward added. 'She would have *loved* being in charge of such a flagship school.'

I was beginning to understand the source of all those tins of luxury biscuits. And, maybe, the expensive bottles of wine I'd come across in the tall wooden cupboard in which Priscilla had kept her coat. I'd thought at first Priscilla Theobold had a secret drinking habit but, according to Jean, she rarely touched the stuff, just liked having it in the cupboard to take with her to any dinner parties she was invited to.

'I think you're forgetting that the school and the land belong to the Church.' Ben Carey sat up straight and stopped tapping his teeth.

'The land, obviously, but I believe, Mr Carey, that the Church has relinquished some of its rights over Westenbury C of E to the Trust?'

'Where does that leave us, Ben?' If the Trust was happy to get its paws on a brand-new school I wasn't sure what options we had.

'I'm not actually sure, Cassandra. At the end of the day I'm a vicar, not a politician or an education expert.'

'But would you be in favour of demolishing Little Acorns, Ben? Building a concrete box in the middle of a huge estate?'

Ben sighed and looked a bit shifty. 'I wouldn't personally, but I'm not convinced the parents and some of the other governors, particularly those who don't live round here, wouldn't jump at the opportunity for a brand-new, state-of-the-art school. You only have to mention computers, iPads, science equipment…'

'But the building is of historic importance,' David argued. 'I bet it's even listed. Actually, there you go: if it *is* listed they'll never get permission to knock it down. By flattening the school, they'd be flattening history.'

Edward Bamforth smiled somewhat smugly. 'Progress. We have to have it. Have to move on. You need to rid yourselves of your Luddite mentality, have vision, as we have.'

'Mr Bamforth, are you saying that without the Little Acorns site you wouldn't be able to go ahead with all your plans?' I asked.

'I'm not saying that at all, Cassandra,' he said smoothly. 'What I am saying is that we're determined to go ahead and build on the fields and we'll find a way. We have to. We're in the twenty-first century and need to move on. As landowners, we just can't keep up with the farmland. Do you know how many farmers have thrown in the towel in the last ten years? Those farmhouses and their accompanying barns are now houses for those wealthy enough to convert them. And David here, what did he do with Peter Broadbent's old farmhouse? He had no compunction in turning it into a successful restaurant. I'm sure you are aware of Clementine's, just down the road?'

'Of course. Everyone knows Clementine's. Clementine Ahern's daughter, Allegra, is a pupil here...'

'I do think we're getting off the point again,' Xavier Bamforth said, glancing at his watch once more and beginning to gather his papers.

'I think Clementine's is very much a case in point,' his father interjected. 'Progress. Moving on. And what we do intend, in return for planning permission from Midhope Council, is to build a super new leisure centre with ski slope, a cinema complex and a small shopping centre to serve the new houses.'

'You are joking!'

'What?'

'Not if I have anything to do with it!' David, Ben Carey and I spoke as one.

'This is the countryside,' I finally spluttered. 'What the hell do we need a ski slope for? And we have Meadowhall in Sheffield, the Trinity centre and the new John Lewis in Leeds a train journey away.'

'People want these things here, on their doorsteps. Not everyone has a car – although by the jammed-up lane outside the school every morning one might beg to differ.'

'Beg all you like, baby...' Oh heavens, had I just said that? I could feel myself blushing and David Henderson's look of astonishment which quickly turned to amusement. But this was not funny.

'We need to calm down a bit,' Edward Bamforth said. 'Look, we're obviously a long way from a solution, but I need to tell you, we are very serious. We've been contemplating selling the land around here for many years. Farmers don't want to buy it. If we don't develop, the fields will go to rack and ruin. Try and think of Titus Salt and the village of Saltaire he built for his workers. And George Cadbury who built Bournville with homes for twenty-three thousand people. Did the locals object when those great philanthropists built a community for their workers?'

'Those are totally different.' I almost laughed at the very idea of his comparison.

'Why?' Xavier Bamforth held my gaze. 'Why are they different?'

For the life of me, put on the spot, I couldn't think why it was OK for George Cadbury to build thousands of homes back in Victorian times, but certainly not bloody OK for Edward Bamforth and his family to build the same, right here and right now.

'Progress, Cassandra. The population is rising. Immigration is high.'

'As is *emigration*. And to be quite honest, if you're thinking of covering acres of beautiful green belt round here with dreadful shopping centres and... and ridiculous ski slopes then I'm going to be first on a plane out of here.'

'That is your opinion.' Edward Bamforth, I could see, was irritated by my constant counter arguments. 'You will find, particularly amongst young people round here who have nothing to do at the weekend, the general consensus is, bring it on.'

I turned to Xavier Bamforth, who had not said a great deal the whole of the time. He appeared incredibly deadpan, bored, almost, of the whole proceedings. He was around my age, I reckoned, with longish dark hair and very dark eyes. With a name like Xavier – as unlikely a Yorkshire handle as Lancashire Hot Pot – he must have foreign blood somewhere. The Bamforths, so far as I recalled Granddad Norman talking about this dynasty of an engineering family, were Midhope born and bred. The air of bored complacency Xavier exuded was marred only by the constant twisting of the gold band on his left hand. 'So, you're all for this as well, I suppose? You've not said much.'

'Absolutely.' He was succinct. 'I see no reason not to move forward. The plans have already been forwarded to Midhope Council and we want Little Acorns and the local community on board with us. It really would make life a lot easier.'

'I'm sure it would,' I snapped, suddenly very weary. 'As a local – forget my being acting head here – I would, like David here, oppose this all the way.' I had a sudden vision of Granddad Norman almost in tears at the very thought of the vandalising of the field behind his house. 'Particularly as you're planning to destroy Norman's Meadow.'

11

Do You Fancy a Stint as the Poison Dwarf?

Iknew I was shattered and emotionally drained, but when I was startled awake from a dream where I was having my legs waxed by the team effort of both Mark and Tina, I realised I must be in a pretty bad state of mind. Mark was yanking off strips of hot wax from one leg while Tina, enjoying every sadistic moment, was pushing red-hot needles into the other. 'Mine, now,' she was laughing gleefully. 'He's all mine.'

My head was buzzing. Literally. I opened one eye, trying to figure out whether I was having some sort of nervous breakdown, the buzzing in my ears symptomatic of the most traumatic week I'd ever been through.

The buzzing was getting louder and more insistent, shifting around but singularly monotone. I sat up, shook my head and peered through the dimness of an early September dawn. The work clothes I'd abandoned in a heap, after downing a couple of particularly huge gin and tonics before falling, almost comatose, into bed, stared up at me accusingly. My face felt dry, papery and very old, while my mouth was just as dry, but furred like a new Christmas slipper. I tried to locate the buzzing and, instead, recalled the conversation I'd had with myself as I fell beneath the duvet:

'Cassandra Moonbeam, get back out of this bed, take off your make-up, moisturise your face, clean your teeth, and hang up your clothes properly.'

'Fuck off, Cassandra Moonbeam.'

I really needed to get a grip. I didn't think I'd ever, in all of my adult life – even when I had new-born babies – gone to bed not having hung up clothes on their correct wooden hanger, replaced shoes in their proper shoe box and put used underwear in the laundry basket. I'd *definitely* never gone to bed in my makeup before. I switched on the bedside lamp, grimaced at the trail of mascara and foundation on my white Egyptian – 800 thread count – cotton pillowcase and then screamed out loud as I realised the buzzing was coming from a whole zoo-full of wasps crawling on, and flying above, the bed.

I leapt out of the bed, screaming and stubbing my big toe on the bedside cabinet for good measure, and looked on in horror at what must have been twenty wasps on the pillow while others, with an open invitation to join the party, buzzed and dive bombed like the Dam Busters, through the open bedroom window.

'Jesus, Mum, what's the matter?' Tom appeared at the bedroom door, his short fair hair tousled, his eyes full of sleep. 'Has something happened? Were you having a nightmare?'

'Wasps,' I yelled, grabbing him as I rushed for the door. 'Millions of them.'

'Slight exaggeration there. Having said that... Jesus!' He slammed the bedroom door behind us both and we stood on the landing, in the half-light, wavering as to what to do next. 'You'll have to get the council in.'

'On a Saturday morning at six a.m.? It's hard enough getting them to empty the dustbins on the right day; I can't see them coming over for a bedroom full of wasps. Ooh, and I've been stung.' I pulled my nightie up around my knees. 'Look, look at this lot.' I counted four red raised welts, each with a tiny white mark at its centre. 'Jesus, they hurt. Oh God, what if I have an anaphylactic shock? I feel a bit funny, a bit sick and dizzy...'

'That's probably the gin from last night,' Tom said drily. 'They were jolly big ones you downed.'

'You shouldn't have been watching.'

'What's going on?' Freya put her head round her bedroom door before joining us on the landing.

'Wasps,' I whispered. 'A whole mad gang of them.'

'A couple of wasps and you're both terrified?'

'A couple?' I whispered, affronted. 'There's a whole army moved in. Look at my legs.' I touched the tender areas that seemed to be swelling and pulsating more readily with every second that passed.

'Why are you whispering? They don't understand English, do they?'

'This is your father's fault,' I sniffed.

'Dad's fault? Why?' Freya looked baffled.

'Well, if he hadn't gone, *he'd* be dealing with them. He'd know what to do.'

'Are you a man or a mouse, Mum?' Freya tutted in the way only a fourteen-year-old forced out of her pit on a Saturday morning can tut. 'You're a head teacher, for heaven's sake. I bet if you'd been asked the question at your interview: "Mrs Beresford, you suddenly see that the wasps' nest that has been brought in for Chantelle is actually full of *live* wasps, reproducing at an alarming rate and heading towards the children in your care. How would you react?" you'd have an answer.'

I considered for just a moment. 'Have a shower, make a strong coffee and Google wasp murderers.' Oh, and while I'm about it, see if there's also a quick and discreet service for the murder of husbands found shagging one's best friend. I didn't vocalise this last bit, obviously, but just thinking about some sort of torture, if not actually doing away with the pair of them, made me feel slightly better as I headed for the shower, the coffee machine and Google.

Wayne the Wasp Man put in an appearance around ten. I'd very cautiously gone into the garden underneath my (note *my* – no longer *our*) open bedroom window and, seeing an ominously noisy black cloud, bid a hasty retreat back inside to wait for his arrival, telling the kids to keep all doors and windows shut: we were under siege.

'It's the heat, you see, darling,' Wayne said after an initial inspection of the enemy. 'It's been a very busy summer and I'm being called out to wasp nests every week, three or four a day on some days. And these aren't small nests.'

'Tell me about it,' I said, pouring him coffee. 'I've been stung four times. The little sods pounced on me in my own bed.'

'Well, I'm not surprised,' he grinned, looking me up and down somewhat lasciviously. 'Where's *Mr* Beresford then? Is there one?'

'Not at the moment,' I said shortly, realising that I was still assuming Mark would be back, this ridiculous thing with Tina over and done with once they'd lived together properly for a while.

Wayne looked me up and down again and I was glad I'd replaced my nightie with a pair of Tom's jeans and his 'MATHS MAKES ME PERSπRE' sweatshirt. Being a foot shorter than Tom, I realised I probably looked like a nerdy gnome but, deprived of all access to my wardrobe, I'd had to compromise my Saturday morning outfit.

'Well, your average wasp nest will have about eight thousand wasps in it,' Wayne went on proudly, as if personally responsible for the size and population of the average wasp nest. His eyes came to rest on the slogan across my chest, clocking, I was sure, that I was bra-less. 'But some of the *bigger* ones...' he leered at my bosom, '... have up to fifteen thousand in them. The problem you have at the moment is that they're still growing their colonies. Some of the hives I've had to deal with this week have split, with a new queen setting up a new colony nearby; if I'm called to one house, I'll be called to another nearby pretty soon.'

He was beginning to sound like David Attenborough on speed and I was glad when Freya thumped down the stairs demanding her netball kit.

'Netball kit? On a Saturday morning?'

'*Mum*, I'm off on the new season team-building weekend with Miss Lewis.'

Hell, I'd totally and utterly forgotten.

'… And then staying over at Gabby's tonight. You'd totally forgotten all about it, hadn't you?' Freya tutted accusingly, echoing my thoughts.

'Not at all,' I said loftily. 'Er, where is it exactly you need to be?'

Freya tutted again. 'At school in…' she looked at the kitchen clock '… an hour with a packed lunch and clean kit.' Freya looked around the kitchen as if expecting a pile of ham and beetroot sandwiches – her favourite at the moment – and a clean and beautifully ironed and folded netball kit to float miraculously around the kitchen before packing themselves into her waiting sports bag. As this was Tower View Avenue on a wasp-infested Saturday morning and not a set from a Disney film with an accompanying fairy godmother bent on turning the bowl of manky bananas into a packed lunch from the Ritz, I turned on my daughter.

'Freya, where *is* your netball kit?'

'I gave it to you to wash last night. You said you'd do it before you went to bed.'

Had I? I went into the utility where a sweaty pile of Freya's socks, aertex and slogan-emblazed hoodie gazed up at me just as accusingly as my own carelessly abandoned clothes had a couple of hours earlier. Shit. I shook out the garments, giving each a perfunctory sniff before grabbing the iron and board. They'd have to make do with a quick iron: no time to wash and dry them. If Mark were here, he'd be making sandwiches while I ironed. Correction. If Mark were here, I wouldn't have had the need for copious amounts of alcohol to blot out my despair, and the newly washed and ironed netball kit would already be sitting smugly in Freya's kitbag with a nutritious packed lunch ready and waiting in the fridge. Bastard. I shook the iron furiously at an imaginary Mark, yelling 'Bastard' just as Wayne the Wasp Man appeared once more.

'Hey, don't shoot the messenger, I'm only here to kill wasps.'

'Not you,' I snapped crossly. 'Freya, start getting the bread and ham out of the fridge yourself. You're not helpless.'

'There's nothing *in* the fridge,' she yelled back. 'Apart from half a bottle of gin and an empty bottle of tonic. What sort of mother are you?'

'*You're a tramp, a drunk and an unfit mother,*' Wayne the Wasp Man assured me while assuming a lazy Texan drawl. Freya and I both stared at him. 'You know,' he said, reverting to his normal Yorkshire vernacular, 'what JR said to Sue Ellen in *Dallas*?'

I turned back to the iron. 'You're far too young to

remember *Dallas*. My granddad Norman loved it – never missed an episode.'

'Well *of course* I missed the *original*; I bet I'm younger than you.' He peered at my puffy face and, embarrassed, I hid my newly acquired stress wrinkles in the ironing of Freya's tracksuit bottoms. 'However,' he went on proudly, 'I happen to be the founder member of the Midhope *Dallas* Club.'

'Freya, we'll grab a sandwich from Tesco on the way to school,' I shouted towards the kitchen. 'Go and get your overnight bag packed and ready. Don't forget your toothbrush and a clean pair of pants... The what?' I looked across at Wayne, who was leaning against the door finishing a second mug of coffee. 'The *Dallas* what...?'

'The Midhope *Dallas* Club. We meet once a month in one of the back rooms in the town hall. We're up to thirty members when we have a full complement.'

'Right.'

'Do you fancy it?'

'Fancy what?'

'*Dallas* in Midhope. We dress in the gear – you know Stetsons for men – and watch old episodes and discuss the roles. Sometimes we actually get hold of the scripts and act them out. *You* could wear a long blonde wig and come as the Poisoned Dwarf.' Wayne nodded towards Tom's jeans, which had come unrolled and were now trailing on the kitchen floor as I finished ironing Freya's kit.

'Right,' I said again. 'Look I'm going to have to go.

Got to get my daughter to the other side of Midhope. How much do I owe you?'

'I'll give you a ring then, shall I? I've got your number. See if you fancy coming to *Dallas*?'

Saturday afternoon and I was by myself in the house. Wayne the Wasp Man had finished murdering insects before I arrived back home, Tom had disappeared and Freya wouldn't be back until the following evening. I didn't know what to do with myself. I knew I should be gathering the piles of dirty laundry that had accumulated over the week, as well as running the hoover over the bedroom floor that still showed signs of broken bodies, legs and wings following Wayne's triumphant victory in the Battle of the Wasps. Instead, I decided to get to grips with the lawn mower and attack the grass.

It wasn't half as difficult as I'd imagined. Nursing just one broken fingernail, I was soon tootling along with the mower, enjoying the combined smell of petrol and grass and soothed by the horizontal stripes appearing in my wake. Once in a rhythmic stride, my mind reviewed the events of the past week. I felt as though I'd lived a whole extra life in the seven days just gone. As I walked and mowed, my mind wandered: from the different ways I could make myself so gorgeous Mark would have to come back begging forgiveness, to rehearsing calm – but cutting – responses to Karen Adams' constant undermining of my authority, and then on to mulling over the meeting with Edward and Xavier Bamforth the previous afternoon. The rolls of barbed wire I'd come across in the fields between Tower View Avenue and school, as well as the building plans already put forward for Norman's Meadow were, I realised, just the tip of the iceberg of the Bamforths' plans to take over the world. Well, Westenbury at least.

Westenbury's history was well documented. The best way, apparently, for William the Conqueror to undermine the militant rough necks Oop North was to apportion great rafts of land to his barons with the instructions that the land was theirs as long as they kept the local pesky peasants under control. Saxon manors were given over to William's supporters and one Gilbert De L'Ouest had the unenviable task of quashing any Saxon rebellion in these parts. The area soon became known as Westenbury, the manor house in which David Henderson and his wife now lived being built on the footprint of the original Saxon one. The village itself had grown and spread, and bits given, or sold off, to supporters of different monarchs. And then the Bamforths had come along in the fifties, buying much of the land and investing some of the huge profits their engineering company had made from its manufacture and provision of engines and gears needed for tanks and planes during the last war.

Now, it seemed, they were determined to make even more money by covering it all in concrete. And a bloody ski slope, for heaven's sake! I realised I'd speeded up my mowing as I became more and more incensed at the thought of Norman's Meadow being turned into something so, so *irrelevant* and so *ridiculous*, the lawn beginning to look decidedly scalped as I took out my fury over Mark's defection, as well as the Bamforths riding roughshod over the village, on the usually perfect lawn.

Lost in thought and the soothing repetitive hum, push and pull of the lawn mower, I didn't see Mark's mother until she was standing beside me, tottering on the leather court shoes she habitually wore whatever the occasion and waving her arms like some demented windmill in order to get my attention. Mark's mother, Mavis – or 'M to the power of 3' as Tom, ever the mathematician, had once dubbed her – was even shorter than me but a powerhouse of matriarchal intensity. She'd seen off Mark's father years ago to some strange condition that was rarely mentioned, and now spent her days dusting her ridiculously large collection of Lladró figures – the grinning girl on a swing was particularly mawkish – nodding in agreement with what she read in the *Express* and hoovering up the dysfunctional lives of soap characters as if she knew them personally.

By the look on her face I could see she now had her own personal soap to involve herself in, and I swore under my breath as I cut the power on the lawn mower.

'I've heard, Cassandra,' Mavis squawked. 'What's going on? What's happened to make Mark do such a thing? Mildred and Stanley next door have just been round to tell me...' She drew breath for three seconds, fanning the warm air around her before launching once more. 'And with that nice friend of yours, Tina?'

'Come and sit down, Mavis. You look a bit hot. I'll get you a glass of water.'

'Tea, dear, please. Yorkshire – none of those teas your mother drinks – milk and plenty of sugar; I need it for the shock.' Mavis followed me back into the house and sat in the kitchen, fanning herself with one of Tom's maths folders while we waited for the kettle to boil.

'I think it's Mark you should be asking, not me,' I said as I handed Mavis her tea.

'I've tried ringing him but he's not answering. I've been ringing for ages. Where is he?'

'With Tina, I presume.' Just saying those four little words made me want to cry.

'But what happened? Why? Why would he do such a thing? Had you been arguing?' Mavis put her head to one side like a little bird, her beady eyes searching my face for clues.

'Mavis, it's as much a shock to me as you.'

Mavis leant forward. 'Was it the sex, dear?'

'I'm sorry?'

Mavis sniffed. 'Men have different *needs* to women, I always found. Men, if they're not to stray, need their tea on the table every night and their… you know, their rights when they want them. We just have to put up with it.' She sniffed again. 'Mind you, my grandmother never did. She kept a claw hammer under her side of the bed, and any nonsense…' She trailed off.

'What…?' I giggled, but Mavis wasn't listening.

'This new job of yours, dear. Is it taking up too much time? Are you not home to give Mark his tea? I *never* worked, you know. My job was to look after the house and Barry's was to bring home the bacon.'

'Good job he wasn't Jewish then,' I muttered, but Mavis, humourless as always, simply frowned and carried on.

'It's all right having a cleaner to do your housework and buying meals from M&S, you know, but it's no substitute for the real thing. Maybe Mark was feeling in need of a home-made steak and kidney?'

'The only thing Mark was feeling was another woman, Mavis,' I snapped angrily. She was, I realised, blaming me for Mark's defection.

'Or a Battenburg cake? Mark could never get enough of my Battenburg,' she said smugly.

'Look, Mavis, I know this is a huge shock, but I'm hoping it will all right itself. And if it doesn't... well, I suppose I'll be seeing a solicitor.'

'Oh, not yet, not yet, Cassandra,' Mavis pleaded. 'Give it time to sort itself out. Mark will be back, I know he will. I know my son. He wouldn't intentionally hurt you or the children. And you know, there's never been any divorce in our family. It's not good, all this swapping of partners and sleeping around. Look what happened to Gail.'

'Gail?'

'In Coronation Street.'

'Look, I'm sorry, Mavis, I'm really not interested. I need to finish cutting the grass.'

'You shouldn't be having to do that. It's a man's job.' Mavis patted my arm sympathetically.

'I'm actually enjoying the exercise,' I smiled. 'Look,' I added, trying to get rid of her, but feeling guilty at doing so; she was Mark's mother after all, 'you try and contact Mark and find out what he's up to and then report back to me. I need all the help I can get.'

An hour later and sweating profusely with the exercise and the warm afternoon sunshine, I finally cut the engine on the mower just as a large silver car pulled into the drive. My heart lurched. Mark. And then lurched again as I realised the car was nothing like Mark's.

Simon, Tina's husband, walked slowly down from the drive, where he'd parked his car in a somewhat haphazard fashion, and across the garden towards me. Over the years, Mark and I had pinched more and more of the field onto which our house backed, extending the lawn and creating a vegetable garden. Even from the distance where I stood, almost in the field, waiting for Simon to join me, I could see he was upset.

Simon had rung me on numerous occasions over the past week, always apologising profusely for outing Mark and Tina but, by the end of the phone call, threatening the pair of them with every punishment and torture going before breaking down in tears. He'd never been my favourite person but, because he was Tina's husband, both Mark and I had put up with, rather than welcomed, him on all the social occasions we had come together for.

'I'm so sorry, Cassie, I'm so sorry...' Simon joined me where I was leaning against the fence. 'I shouldn't have done it, Cassie, shouldn't have done it. It would have all blown over.' Simon wiped his eyes beneath his Ray-bans.

I'd suddenly had enough of all this: this sense of guilt that *we'd* done something wrong. That because of *our* behaviour – whether it was me and the sodding ninety-degree-angled cushions or Simon and his nose-picking and bad breath: yes, he was guilty on both counts – we were the ones to blame.

'Bollocks, Simon. They were having an affair for two years. *Two years.* It wouldn't have blown over; it would have carried on. And do you know what, Simon, it probably actually hurts just as much that I've lost my best friend as well as my husband. Women shouldn't do this to one another. Best friends *certainly* shouldn't.'

'I know, I know, but I can't bear it, Cassie...'

'Well, at the moment, you'll just have to.' I felt as if I was talking to a naughty child. I'd spent hours I could ill afford on the phone during the past week, reassuring him, telling him it wasn't his fault, agreeing that if we just sat tight the whole thing would blow over and Mark and Tina would come back to their rightful owners. Simon took my hand and, as alcohol fumes wafted in my direction, I realised he'd been drinking. 'You shouldn't be driving, Simon.'

'Do you think I could stay here?'

'Here?' I had awful visions of him moving in, unpacking his suitcases, arranging his fancy leather brogues where Mark's trainers, until last week, had previously sat. You read all the time about the deserted partners of adulterous couples themselves getting together. I shuddered at the very thought.

'I could take you out for something to eat – we could walk into the village, have a couple of drinks; discuss our plan of action.'

'Plan of action?'

'You know, decide my next move on getting Tina back. And Mark, of course. I just don't want to be by myself at the moment.'

'Where's Jack?'

'He's seventeen. What seventeen-year-old wants to be in on a Saturday night with his dad?'

'How is he? Is he coping with it all?'

'Oh, *he's* fine. He's off out with his college mates. Plugged into his music, smoking dope, probably, and shagging birds. You know what boys are like.'

'I don't think you should just assume he's OK. I mean, on the surface, my two seem to have been pretty accepting of what's happened. Freya is putting all her energy into netball: I'd hate to be Goal Defence on any opposing team Freya's up against at the moment…' I laughed, attempting levity to lighten the tension I could sense as Simon talked about his son. '… She'll be taking out all her fury over Mark's defection on the opposition. And, of course, Tom has had the advantage – or disadvantage, I suppose – of knowing for months what's been going on.'

'Disadvantage, I suppose,' Simon said, taking my hand again.

I withdrew it from his rather sweaty one and folded my arms tightly across my chest. 'I'm still not sure what

Tom was doing over in The Blue Ball that night he saw the pair of them together.'

'Don't you? Really?'

I turned to look at Simon. He had a slight smile on his face and I realised I hadn't really liked him for years. If ever.

'Come on, Cassie.'

'Come on, what?'

'The Frozen Knacker? Why do you think Tina and Mark frequented it?'

'I've no idea. Presumably because it's so far out on the moors they knew there'd be no one there who'd see them together?'

Simon sighed, a rather unpleasant condescending little smirk on his pale face. 'The Blue Ball? The most notorious gay pub this side of Manchester? The only people who frequent it are couples having affairs, knowing there'll be none of their usual social circle there. And young gay men on the lookout for sex.'

12

Paula

1976

'**M**an,' Rowan complained as he descended the bus stairs and joined Paula on the pavement where she'd waited over half an hour for his arrival. 'I've just had to sit through fifteen minutes of the sodding Wurzels and "Combine Harvester". What is the matter with this fucking country that everyone, even the bus conductor, was singing along with the kids on the top deck?'

'Oh God, how awful. Why didn't you go downstairs; get out of their way?'

'I needed a smoke.' Rowan was irritable. 'Why've you dragged me all the way out here anyway? I've had to get two buses and they were both full of noisy kids and singing morons.'

'School holidays, I suppose,' Paula soothed, not wanting

Rowan's bad mood to spoil the surprise she'd planned. 'O levels're over and school's finished for the summer. Don't you remember how it felt when you knew you had six glorious weeks ahead of you and nothing to do except a bit of dusting, vaccing and washing up at home?'

Rowan wasn't to be placated. '*We* had eight or was it nine? And the minute term was over, I was on the plane and back home in Hong Kong. And the *last* thing I intended doing was hoovering, which is what I assume you mean by *vaccing*?' The son of a diplomat based in Hong Kong, Rowan had been at one of the North's minor public schools from the age of thirteen and, for all his left-wing posturing and socialist ideals, would often snidely bully Paula about her working-class upbringing and, what he assumed to be, her inferior education.

'Well, we won't be here for much longer,' Paula smiled, taking his hand. 'It was payday today and I put as much money as I possibly could into the Post Office. Just three or four more months and I'll have enough saved up for travelling. I can't wait to get out of this country either...'

Rowan took his hand from Paula's in order to light a thick, ready-made joint, but didn't offer her any. 'What's in the basket? It smells a bit...' Rowan screwed up his nose and took a deep drag on the smoke, filling his lungs before releasing it in a world-weary sigh.

'We're going for a picnic,' Paula said proudly.

'How bourgeois,' Rowan said, eyebrows raised. 'Pork pies and pickled onions?'

'Don't be daft. I've got Brie, tarasamalata, hummus and olives.' She offered the word *olives* with reverence, desperate for Rowan's approval.

'You do know Judas Priest are possibly doing a session at The Crypt tonight?'

'Judas Priest?' For a second Paula wavered. Next to Led Zepp, Judas Priest was her favourite band. 'At The Crypt? In Midhope? Never.'

'Yep. They've been playing Bradford and Leeds, and Brian knows their roadie.' The Crypt – a tiny one-room, dark and smoke-filled club, proudly trumpeted as Midhope's answer to Liverpool's Cavern – was run by Brian Mulligan, a squat, pugnacious electrician whose love of heavy rock had led him to convert what had once been Midhope Electricians' Union meeting room into a drinking club and venue for bands. Norman had banned both his daughters from going there as everyone knew it to be full of drugs, drug pushers and long-haired head bangers listening to loud music and getting high. The Crypt was as much off Linda's radar as Norman's, but Paula had been going since she was eighteen and, now that she was almost twenty-one, both she and Norman had given up any pretence that she'd never darkened its doors.

'I keep seeing this place from the top deck of the bus on my way home,' Paula said, putting all thought of Judas Priest on hold for another time and quickening her step. 'It's far too nice to be in a dark club on a gorgeous evening like this.'

'Good job I've not eaten then.' The joint had obviously

worked its magic and Rowan patted her purple-clad bottom before falling into step beside her.

'Shit, man, this is some place.' Paula had led the way around the perimeter of a huge, expertly-trimmed privet hedge until, stopping at the very end of its green and verdant length, she squeezed herself and her basket through a hole in the tangled bush before holding the limbs of the hedge apart, allowing Rowan to follow her through.

'Shit, that's tight,' Rowan complained, brushing leaves and dust from his black AC/DC T-shirt, and then, gazing around whistled. 'Bloody hell, is this your local park?'

Paula giggled. 'The park? Don't be a moron. Mind you, there is a tennis court somewhere over there. I saw that from the top of the bus, too.' She indicated vaguely with a wave of her hand before heading down an overgrown path, Rowan in her wake. 'They won't see us down here…'

'Who won't?' Rowan was beginning to sweat in the heat, beads of damp breaking out on his forehead. He wiped his face with the back of his hand and continued to walk, swatting at flies and high grass as he went.

'I've no idea. Somebody obviously lives here.'

'This is someone's garden? You can't just let yourself in and have a picnic on someone's private property.'

Paula turned and, smiling, quoted, '"Private property is already done away with for nine-tenths of the population; its existence for the few is solely due to its non-existence in the hands of those nine-tenths." Karl Marx said that,' she added proudly. She'd been to the library at the weekend;

it had been totally deserted, the rest of Midhope not wanting to be in a fusty library in the seemingly endless heat wave, and soon got chatting to the librarian who'd pointed her in the right direction to learn more about Capitalism and Marx. She was delighted she could show off what she'd learnt in front of Rowan.

'Yeah, right. Course. Well done... Have you got some wine in there?' He didn't offer to carry the basket for her, but continued to swear at the biting midges, sneezing occasionally as they walked.

'Right, we just need to get through here.' Paula hesitated as a red-lacquered bridge and a little oriental wooden house suddenly appeared before them, obviously a focal point of the whole garden. Camellias, azaleas and a Japanese apricot, its intense pink blossom long blown to the wind, dozed calmly in the breathless heat. 'Come on,' she whispered and, taking his hand, broke cover across the carefully raked gravel in front of them and raced for the cool, green copse of indigenous oaks, sycamores and beeches that had been spared by their Japanese interlopers.

'We're fine here,' Paula panted, pulling out a white starched tablecloth, together with a bottle of Blue Nun.

'How provincial.' Rowan pulled a face at her choice of wine, but nevertheless deftly pulled its cork and, settling himself back against a massive oak, downed half its warm contents in one go. 'Warm, too,' he added, finally holding the bottle out to Paula. 'Didn't you have any of those blue ice packs in your freezer? We couldn't do without them in Hong Kong.'

'Freezer?' Paula was momentarily puzzled. 'Oh, no, sorry, ours was on the blink; must have been the heat.' She didn't like to tell him that the nearest they had to a fridge was the cold stone sink in the cellar in which her mum kept the milk bottles once they'd been delivered every day by Jack, the whistling and limping milkman who'd been part of her life ever since she could remember. Together with the mesh-fronted meat safe – also doomed to exile in the cool, dark, musty-smelling depths of the cellar – and the huge metal bread bin, now dinted after she'd accidentally fallen over it and sent it crashing from its place at the top of the cellar steps one evening after an excess of Strongbow cider at The Crypt, these were as big a part of her home as Dot and Norman themselves.

Once the olives, hummus and taramasalata were eaten, the wine imbibed and the packet of McVities' chocolate digestives – pinched from the pantry before they'd had a chance to reach Dot's biscuit barrel – broken open and half of them also devoured, Rowan lit another joint and lay back in the long grass, pulling deeply on its pungent-smelling contents before handing it over to Paula. She didn't smoke cigarettes and usually found that, unable to inhale, cannabis had little effect on her. She drew in the smoke and immediately blew it out again, where it drifted on the warm evening air, mingling with the intoxicating vanilla scent of heliotrope and the unmistakable perfume of the white-blossomed nicotiana.

'Hey, don't waste it, man.' Rowan pulled deeply on the joint and, without warning, flung Paula onto her back, covering her mouth with his own, forcing the smoke into her lungs. 'Right, do it yourself now,' he grinned as she came up for air, coughing. 'That's it, slowly, let the shit do its magic.'

Already slightly tipsy from the wine and the sultry heat, Paula took another hit, inhaling and pulling the smoke into her lungs. A feeling of wild euphoria went through her and she broke off a chocolate digestive, slipping it into her mouth, tasting the chocolate, closing her eyes as her tongue and teeth met the crunchy sweetness of the biscuit. 'That is the most unbearably pleasurable thing in the world,' she sighed, reaching for the packet.

'I think you'll find this even more so,' Rowan grinned, delighted with the drug's effect on Paula. He lay her down gently on Dot's best tablecloth and, slowly unpopping the metal press studs of her dress, reached inside for the warm breast unhampered by any bra, holding it almost reverently in his hand before lowering his head to meet it with his mouth.

13

Escape from the Hoverers...

Mark had more often than not been away on Friday evenings, usually travelling home from London or Europe after a week there working. Or after, I now realised, making whoopy in some hotel with Serpentina. As such, Friday evenings followed a routine where, once I'd fed the kids, I'd make myself a much-looked-forward-to treat of cheese on toast, Branston pickle and a big glass of red wine in front of a *Poldark* catch-up to start my weekend.

On this Saturday evening, once I'd got rid of Slimeon – I'd rechristened him in the light of his insinuating comments about Tom – I headed for the kitchen, the fridge and the bread bin.

My usual Friday night treat, albeit carried over to a Saturday, tasted dry and totally unappetising, even with a glass of Mark's best Merlot, and I abandoned both and settled for some sensual pleasure with Captain Poldark. But, when the bastard abandoned Demelza and ended up in that whingeing milksop Elizabeth's bed, I threw the TV control across the room and rang Fi.

'Are you off to Leeds with Clare?'

'Yes, in about an hour's time. She's got her first Henotheism hen party in the middle of Leeds and wants to be on hand to make sure everything's going to plan. She's been with the hens most of the day already.'

'Right, I'm coming with you.'

'Are you? Are you sure?' Fi sounded doubtful. 'Are you up to it?'

'Up to it?'

'Well, I'm not sure a gaggle of women celebrating a forthcoming marriage is the best thing for you at the moment.'

'Neither's cheese on toast and Ross Poldark… Give me an hour and I'll come and pick you up.'

'You've lost weight,' Fi said, eyeing me up as I walked into her kitchen. 'If that's what it takes to lose this two stone –' Fi grabbed the flesh around her middle – 'then I'm going to have to encourage Matt to get his rocks off somewhere other than here.'

'Not funny, Fi.'

'No, you're right it wasn't. Sorry. That was crass.' Fiona sneezed and turned to give me a hug. 'Hell, the girls have been riding; they only have to bring their crops and hats into the house and I'm sneezing.'

'What on earth is that?' I looked at the narrow wire that appeared to be heading from Fi's shirt pocket before disappearing down the band of her jeans and into her crotch.

Fi grinned. 'I'm tasering my twat.'

I winced at the crude expression and Fi laughed again. 'You really are such a strait-laced girly, aren't you? If you lived here with us on the farm you'd see nature at its most basic, including Matthew up to his elbows in order to fertilise the girls.'

'The *girls*?'

'All right then, the cattle, the cows: our bread and butter.'

'Er, so what's this thing then?' I nodded towards Fi's nether regions.

'Marvellous little machine that does pelvic floor exercises for you. You know we women are meant to do them daily. Supposed to do wonders for you. I tell you, it gives me a thrill every time I plug myself in while I'm doing the washing up or ironing.' Fi pulled a red and white machine the size of a cigarette packet out of her shirt pocket, squinted at it before replacing it and then headed for the stairs. 'Give me two minutes until this programme has finished and I'll put on some lippy and be good to go.'

Once Fi had disappeared upstairs, I took a furtive look around at their huge farmhouse kitchen. Much as I adored Fi and Matt, I could never be in their house without wanting to have a good clean up. Ross, the farm's black and white collie, was stretched luxuriously on the ancient battered sofa. The previous Sunday's newspapers were abandoned on another chair while a plethora of rusting farm tools lay awaiting Matt's attention on the kitchen surfaces and in the otherwise empty glass fruit bowl. A decrepit tabby cat narrowed devilish eyes at me from its bed of unironed laundry in the garish tangerine plastic basket on the top of the cream Aga.

'Off you get, you damned thing. Go on.' Fiona, fully made up and looking particularly glamorous in tight jeans and a red low-cut top out of which spilt her ample breasts, reappeared in the kitchen, clapping her hands at the cat. 'God, it's like living in a zoo here. What I'd give for a smart flat in the city with not a dog or cat hair to be seen.'

I smiled. 'You married a farmer. What do you expect? Where *is* the farmer, anyway?'

'Come on, Cassie, you know what Matt's like. It's only seven o'clock. He won't be finished for another couple of hours.'

'And the boys?'

'Out helping him.'

'That's good then.'

'Is it? Why?' Fi looked puzzled.

'Keep them off the street.'

'Cassie, I'd *rather* the boys were out on a Saturday night enjoying themselves, having a beer, getting drunk, bringing home girls instead of muck-spreading with Matt.' She sighed. 'And when the three of them *are* actually inside they don't move from this kitchen. Every time I turn around, one of them is behind me, *hovering*.'

'Hovering?' I laughed, imagining Matt and the boys, all six-foot-four and built like brick shit houses, crowding round Fi.

'And if it's not the men, it's the dog. He knows he should be outside with the rest of the animals but, no, he slinks back in and *hovers* like the rest of them, waiting until I feed them all. Teatime is the worst – even the girls *hover*, blocking my way to the oven.'

'Next time they're behind you, just turn and hand the shepherd's pie, or whatever it is, to them and scarper.'

'I'd go to the bathroom, sit on the loo with *Hello!* magazine, but there's always someone in it.'

'You need an en suite.'

Fi snorted. 'In addition to the new tractor, slurry spreader, rotator and roller? Anyway, I tell you, Cassie, they're all in league, including the cats, to see who can corner me the most. I reckon they take bets to see who can get the closest without actually touching. I can literally hear them breathing down my neck.'

I laughed again. 'Maybe you could build a shed in the garden?'

'A shed? They'd *all* be in it demanding cups of tea and cake. *Hovering*'s an Olympic sport to them – the shed would just be them going international. And Matt's mother is as bad. She still thinks she's in charge of the kitchen even though she moved down the lane when we took over the tenancy. She *hovers* at least once a day, usually at mealtimes. Next time she puts her mug of tea just where I'm going to roll out pastry, I'm going to shout, "Checkmate" and hand her the rolling pin. Actually, do you know, she's gone really trendy since losing Matthew's dad and moving into that little flat. She told me the other day she'd bought herself a pair of NYPD jeans.'

'NYPD?' I laughed. 'New York Police Department?

'She meant DKNY,' Fi said, shaking her head. 'She's bonkers. One finger short of a KitKat. It comes from being a farmer's wife all those years. God knows how I'll end up.' Fi shook her head again, obviously lost in thought. 'So anyway,' she continued, 'you can see why I'd like my great oiks to leave home. I mean, they're twenty-two and twenty now. Shouldn't they be finding their own place to live? They just seem to adore the farm.'

'And you as well,' I said. 'The farm's in their blood; has been since they were tiny.'

'Well, their blood might just have to flow elsewhere.' Fiona sighed again.

'What do you mean?'

'You have to remember we don't actually own this place. Matt's family have been tenants for donkeys' years. I mean, literally hundreds.'

'Who are the landlords? Not the Bamforths?'

'How do you know about the Bamforths?' Fi was obviously surprised. 'Yes, they are, actually.'

'I know *all* about the Bamforths,' I said, picking up my keys. 'Come on, I'll tell you in the car. Where are we meeting Clare?'

*

'Fiona, have you ever thought that Tom might be, well, gay?' We'd parked the car in the Woodhouse Lane car park and were walking down to The Botanist on Boar Lane where we'd arranged to meet Clare.

'Your Tom?'

'Hmm.'

'I thought Tom was only interested in maths?'

'So did I.'

'What's suddenly made you think he might be gay?' Fiona turned to look at me as we walked round a group of scantily dressed young girls. Most of them appeared to be clad, on their top halves at least, in nothing but their bras, white flesh bulging unattractively around the Lycra holding them in, and I was momentarily grateful that Freya was going through her emo period and always covered head to toe in black.

The mild September evening, although still fairly early, had brought revellers onto the pavements, and Fi and I had to manoeuvre our way round them, our conversation constantly interrupted as we did so. A plethora of white and blue shirts swam before us, indicating that the football season was upon us and Leeds had been playing, obviously victoriously, at Elland Road.

'Cassie?'

'Hmm?'

'Why are you suddenly questioning Tom's sexuality?'

'Leeds, Le-eds...'

'Because of something Simon—'

Pontus Jansson's on our team, on our team

He's the best centre back you've ever seen. Ever seen...

Fi grabbed my arm and steered me round the chanting fans and into The Botanist. 'Come on, in here. Simon? Simon said so?'

'He came round this afternoon, and when I didn't play ball with him he took his bat home…'

'Whoa, hang on.' Fi pushed through the crowd at the bar searching for Clare. 'You're totally mixing your metaphors.'

'… and insinuated Tom was gay because he'd been in The Blue Ball. You know, where he saw Mark and Tina together six months ago?'

'So, does that mean if I happen to go to the pub I'm suddenly an alcoholic?' Fi had spotted Clare and was heading for her. 'Or if I happen to take the train once then I must be unable to drive…? Or if I go to The Frozen Knacker once, then I must be gay?'

'Who's gay?' Clare kissed us both and lifted her bag and coat from the two seats she'd been saving before pouring us both a glass of rosé from the bottle she was cradling in front of her. 'Come on, I can't keep my eye on these seats *and* my hens much longer. I'm going cross-eyed.'

'Simon's insinuating that because Tom was in The Blue Ball, months ago, he must be gay,' Fi said, downing half of her wine in one. 'God, that wine's good. Oh, I love crowds, bars and shops. I just love the city: not a sodding cow to be seen for miles.'

'I suppose because Tom's never had a girlfriend, I'm thinking Simon could be right,' I said. 'You know, he did have a tantrum once in the Trafford Centre, flinging himself on the floor because he wanted a Hoover.'

'Who did? Simon?'

'Tom, you fool. He was three and kept crying, "I want a *Hoover*, I want a *Hoooover*. Mummy, I want a *Hooooover* of my own."'

'Really?' Fi raised her eyebrows. 'Fair dos then, he's gay.'

'Oh, don't be ridiculous, the pair of you,' Clare said rather crossly. 'Firstly, you say Tom's never had a girlfriend. Well, has he ever had a *boyfriend*? And secondly, *if* he's gay, so what? Does it really matter who we fall in love with, just as long as we *experience* love?'

Fi and I both nodded enthusiastically in agreement – sometimes it just didn't do to argue with Clare – but I continued to worry as we stood with our drinks in the crowded bar, returning over and over again to Simon's insinuations. It was all right for Clare, who had no children of her own, being so cavalier about Tom's sexuality, but I was very aware of the jokes, the ribald laughter, the insinuations bandied to and fro about someone's gayness, of the kind of stupid cruelty it might expose him to. I sighed and tried to concentrate on being in Leeds on a girls' night out.

A very attractive, dark-skinned man, probably in his late thirties and wearing cut-off denims and a navy T-shirt, returned to what had obviously been his seat next to Clare. She moved her jacket from the seat and he sat down next to her but, if Clare knew him, she wasn't letting on and didn't attempt to introduce him to us.

'Oh, hell, they're on the move,' Clare sighed, indicating with her glass of rosé a gaggle of hens pushing their way through the crowd towards us. She glanced at her watch, looked towards the man and then stood up, scooping up jacket and bag and finishing her drink. 'You'll miss your train,' she said softly to him and, with a quick brushing of fingers, left him as he too rose to go.

'Who's that?' Fi asked curiously. 'Do you know him?'

'Oh, Fi...' Clare looked stricken, but then smiled and said, 'Look, I'm working. I need to be showing these women the bars where free drinks are all arranged for them. Come on.'

The three of us set off in hot pursuit of the hens as they crossed through the Trinity centre and up towards Greek Street, their pink rhinestoned cowboy hats marking them out like coloured flares in the darkening evening sky.

'Bugger, wrong hens,' Clare suddenly snapped, wheeling round and retracing her steps towards us before surveying the crowd in the manner of Captain Hornblower on the lookout for Napoleon and his gang.

'How do you know?' Fi panted as we crossed the road, trying to catch up with her. 'They were wearing pink hats.'

'As is just about every other hen party in Leeds,' Clare said grimly. 'Those we've been following were from Barnsley: Bev's Barnsley Babes it said on their pink sashes. Shit, I should have stuck to stag dos: at least *they* don't all dress the same.'

'Are you sure?' I giggled, as two distinct groups of men headed towards us, both dressed in various Village People guises.

Clare's eyes narrowed for a second. 'Who's organised your stag do?' she shouted towards one, done up as the Indian Chief. Being somewhat vertically challenged at around five-foot-five, as well as exceedingly drunk, he didn't quite carry off the stature or presence of Chief Sitting Bull. Holding on to his battered and moulting feathered headdress with one hand, he waved his bottle of Budweiser at us with the other and shouted back, 'Fuck knows. I was dragged in at the last minute to make up numbers.' He let go of his feathers, just for the time it took him to give us a quick, animated rendition of the first bars of 'YMCA', centred his headdress once more and ambled off after one of the Police Cops – I could see at least three – and the Construction Worker.

'There they are, up there,' Fi suddenly said. 'I recognise the one in the white skirt.'

'Skirt?' I said. 'It's a belt.'

'Pussy pelmet,' Fi wheezed, as we ran to catch Clare up.

'That is such a revolting expression, which does nothing for the emancipation of women...' I chided Fi, the pair of us puffing along side by side in Clare's wake like a couple of extras from *Thomas the Tank Engine*.

'Oh, and wearing pink cowboy hats, angel wings and furry handcuffs does?'

Clare was smiling widely at the group of hens she'd now brought to heel. The smile didn't quite reach her eyes, I noticed, and she looked suddenly tired. 'Right, ladies, drinks are waiting for you in here.' She nodded towards The Liquorist at the top of Greek Street, but none of them seemed to be taking much notice. They reminded me of a particularly noisy class of kids who wouldn't listen to instructions, but were determined to do their own thing. In a minute, I'd be clapping my hands, glaring at them, hands on hips saying, 'It's not *my* time you're wasting.'

'... So, the accountant says to me, "You run a beauty

therapist business, not a gardening landscape business, Kylie: you can't put a *lawn mower* through the books." So, I says to him, "You haven't seen some of the *bikini lines* I have to deal with, Mr Gale..."'

'... And all I wanted was a knight in shining armour. I mean, that's not too much to ask for, is it? A knight in shining armour? And what do I end up with? A sodding wanker in tinfoil...'

'... So, what they do is take fat... yes, fat, Maureen... from your backside and stick it in your boobs.'

'OK, ladies,' Fi suddenly yelled, getting the hen's attention. 'Are we ready to party?'

'We are that,' one of the older women cackled. She must have been the future bride's mother or perhaps mother-in-law. The other matron with her raised her eyes to the heavens, sighed deeply and rubbed at her varicose veins.

'Do you really need to be in charge of them like this?' I asked Clare. 'I mean, you're not planning on spending all your Saturday nights for the next ten years doing this? Herding women around bars in city centres?' I was beginning to feel depressed, unable to get images of Mark and Tina in little upmarket restaurants, holding hands across the table, out of my mind. I shook my head, determined not to be a party pooper. The last thing Clare needed was her first hen party complaining about the miserable woman following them round like some head teacher watching out for bad behaviour.

'God, no. Because this is the first one I've organised, I wanted to make sure all was going to plan. I've already escorted them on a coach trip to Lightwater Valley theme park this morning, and then come back into Leeds for afternoon teas.'

'Afternoon teas? Well, that sounds rather more upmarket,' I soothed.

Clare sighed. '*Afternoon Tease*, Cassie. I was locked away in some dive of a dark cellar at four p.m., watching male strippers as they fed the women cucumber – and I mean the whole damned cucumber – sandwiches and cream teas. You can imagine where most of the cream went. I've played Stick the Willy on the Man, and gone two rounds of the Dick Head Game, tossing the hoopla over a giant penis.' Clare sighed again. 'My idea for Henotheism was for managing rather more élite events. You know, a little wine tasting here, a personal shopper there, maybe the opera? And, to be fair, that's what I'm aiming for. I can't be doing with *this* every Saturday night. Maybe I should have trained to be a teacher like you. Do you think it's too late now?'

I laughed. 'Give over. You have a highly successful business with Last Stagger. It's just a matter of getting Henotheism off the ground in the same way. If you have to toss a few penises – oops, sorry, not a good choice of words – to begin with, then so be it. Anyway, you'd hate having to work for someone else, having to kowtow to school governors and Ofsted. And dealing, daily, with the school bully.'

'The school bully? Slap his backside and give him a taste of his own medicine.'

'Unfortunately, the school bully is my age and her backside is huge.'

For a second Clare took her eyes from the hens where Fi had abandoned her corralling of them and was, instead, sharing the bottles of mini-bar champagne being blatantly imbibed after being previously stashed discreetly away in Michael Kors and Hermès handbags.

'School bully? There's always one, Cassie. Let's get this lot inside and you can tell me all about it.'

'OK, as long as you tell me all about the guy you were exchanging glances and finger touches with in The Botanist.'

'Deal.' The pair of us headed for a couple of seats that had come free and sat down gratefully. We were, I realised ruefully, beginning to show our age.

14

I'd Like Sex with an Alligator...

'I want Sex with an Alligator.' By 10 p.m. Fi was having a ball, reliving her youth as an urban hipster as she joined in with the hens, downing more cocktails than I thought humanly possible without actually dying.

'Hey, Fiona love, I want sex with my old man but it's not about to happen any time in the foreseeable future. Last time I managed to get my leg over was the night of the Queen's Diamond Jubilee.' The hen, no spring chicken by any stretch of the imagination, must have been in her seventies – the learner bride's nan? – and laughed raucously at her own words, digging Fi in the chest for good measure.

'Never you mind, Beryl; have an Alligator instead.' Fi squinted at the menu in her hand, holding it from her face to read what was there. 'It's got raspberry liqueur, melon liqueur and the rest is Jägermeister. What's

Jägermeister? Cassie will know,' she added loudly. 'She's a head teacher knows everything.'

The hens in hearing distance all turned their heads to have a good look at me. 'That little thing?' Beryl said doubtfully. 'She can't be more than four-foot-ten.'

'Yes, but she knows *everything*.' Fi pronounced it 'everyshing', and I laughed at the slurring of her words. 'Jägermeister, Cassandra Moonbeam?' Fi shouted above the music. 'What the hell is Jägermeister?'

'Jaeger Master? I think it's like a headmaster but in charge of upmarket women's clothing,' I offered, laughing again as Fi winked at me.

'Ooh,' Beryl exclaimed, 'I've always liked a bit of Jaeger. Bought a lovely Jaeger frock for a wedding I went to twenty years ago. Good as new – comes out on special occasions.'

'Love those shoes,' the Bride's Matron of Honour was saying to the Bride's Mate from Work.

'Jimmy Choo,' the BMFW said proudly, pointing a rather pinched-looking toe in the general direction of the BMOH.

'Christian Louboutin,' one of the other hens joined in, raising her foot a good half-metre so that we could all see the red-lacquered sole – as well as her red pants – and almost falling over in the process.

'George at Asda,' Fi cackled, kicking off her ridiculously high heels and abandoning them on the bar. 'And bloody killing me. As well as doing my bits and pieces no favours.'

'What's up with our Kerry? What is it, love?' The mother of the bride – 'MOTB' picked out in rhinestones on the pink T-shirt – thrust her three-foot luminescent-pink inflatable penis with its accompanying testicles into my arms before pushing her way through the posse of hens to reach her daughter who appeared, suddenly, to be losing it.

'I feel sick, Mam,' she wailed. 'I think it must be something I've eaten.' She leant against the bar, flattening her angel wings, and holding her stomach.

'Or drunk,' Clare muttered, heading off to help the bride-to-be, whose face, despite the spray tan, had gone distinctly pale.

Left on my own, penis in one hand and glass of water in the other, I could only think of the phrase 'spare prick at a wedding', which seemed particularly apt. I stood to one side, the loud music drowning out any conversation, feeling incredibly lonely. I wanted and needed Mark at that moment, more than at any time since he'd gone.

Clare returned after fifteen minutes spent helping to wipe down and mop up the BTB, and sank gratefully onto the chair I'd managed to save for her – despite a couple of circling oldies giving me filthy looks – while keeping an eye on Fi, who was dancing with Beryl, the twin-willy deely bopper on her head flashing as she gyrated.

'So, how are you?' Clare leaned back, closing her eyes momentarily against the rest of the humanity in front of her. 'You don't seem too bad.'

'I can't believe it's only been a week since this all kicked off. It's been like a whole new other life. Suddenly I'm without a husband, in charge of a school and my son might be gay.'

Clare snorted. 'I think Simon's insinuation is the least of your worries. And if Tom is gay, so what? You'll sort it. He'll sort it.'

'You know, I suddenly realised this afternoon I really don't like Simon very much. I'm not sure I ever did.'

Clare smiled. 'Do you know, I'm with you there. He's supercilious one minute and ingratiating the next. I think we've all sort of put up with him because we love Tina.'

'So, you said you've seen Tina? She's been round?' I felt my insides begin to churn as they always did whenever Serpentina's name was mentioned, aggravated by Clare's present-tense expression of love for Tina. As far as I was concerned, any love for Tina should be firmly rooted in the past. 'What did she have to say for herself, the bitch? Has she had enough of my husband yet? Is she going to let me have him back?'

'Well, she wasn't entirely happy at your over-zealous decorating of her car.'

'Tough. The last thing I had in mind was her *happiness*. I'm not *happy* that she's pinched my husband.' I picked up my glass of water and slammed it back down on the table in disgust. God, I needed a proper drink.

'Do you not think that's rather an outmoded idea? You know, that people can be pinched? I mean, surely if you have no intention of going off with someone else in the first place, you don't give out any vibes.'

'Sorry, I don't get you.' I was feeling really cross that Clare appeared to be taking Tina's side.

'Come on, Cassie, you know exactly what I mean. If it hadn't been Tina it would probably have been someone else. Men, I've found, can be categorised into two...' She paused. 'Sorry, three: those who do, those who don't and those who would if they got the chance.'

When I just continued to glare silently at her, Clare went on hurriedly, 'Anyway, while Tina wasn't exactly jumping up and down with your art work, she said she'd have done just the same if the lipstick were in the other hand, as it were. And, I'm not sure I should be telling you this, don't know if this makes the whole thing better or worse...'

'Oh Jesus, she's not pregnant? Please don't say she's pregnant.' My heart joined in with my rolling and pitching stomach. I took a deep breath, wiping my sweaty palms on my jeans.

Clare actually laughed at that. 'Pregnant? Tina? Don't be daft. She hated every bit of being pregnant as well as the first few months at home with Jack as a baby. No, she said that basically she's always loved Mark.'

My head came up in shock. 'Tina has *always* loved Mark? My best friend, the friend I saw as the sister I never had, has always loved my husband? This is surreal, Clare. Totally and utterly bloody surreal.'

Clare shook her head. 'Tell me about it. She sat down in my kitchen and told me, from the minute she saw Mark...'

'At Davina's wedding...'

'... at Davina's wedding, she wanted him for herself.'

'But she encouraged *me*. I can see her now, sitting down with Fi and giving me the thumbs up as Mark bought me that first drink and put his jacket round my shoulders before we went outside.'

Clare shrugged. 'She said that basically you got there first and she couldn't really jump up and knock him off you before claiming him for herself. She said no man has ever affected her in the way Mark did, from the moment she glanced across the table at him at that wedding.'

An awful thought suddenly occurred to me. 'So, are you telling me that Tina has never really wanted me for a friend? That she only became my closest friend as the best way to be near to Mark?'

'Gosh no, Cassie, you mustn't think that.' Clare was visibly distressed. 'We all fell a little bit in love with you at Davina's wedding. You were so, so...'

'So what?' I stared at Clare. 'What was I?'

'Sweet and vulnerable and shy and—'

'Sweet? Oh, great. If that's supposed to be a compliment, then forget it.'

'All right, not sweet. You just seemed all alone, abandoned on the singles table with the rest of us when you should have been Davina's bridesmaid. Or at least on the top table. You were family, for heaven's sake. And you had no dad. I remember asking you where your parents were. And you just said, "I've no idea where my father is – unless he's still trying to find himself in Morocco – and my mother is the Purple Hat over there." And then we all felt horribly guilty because we'd been laughing about your mum. And you sat there really uptight, your face pale and pinched, and told us you were planning to buy a house in Derby and we just got the impression that you were sort of running away from home. That you'd rather still be living here in Midhope, but that you somehow needed to prove yourself.'

'That's bollocks. You're making me out to be some sort of Orphan Annie. I loved my job in Derby, was more than happy to buy my flat there...'

'But even happier to come back to Midhope and settle down with Mark.' It was a statement rather than a question.

'Well, yes, I suppose so.'

'And being married to Mark, well, you sort of blossomed, Cassie. You were still pretty uptight about your mother; still totally over the top about everything being neat and tidy, but that tight, nervous look went from your face. You'd got what you wanted.'

'And Tina hadn't?'

'She got the consolation prize with Simon. Once she saw Mark only had eyes for you, she made a play for Simon at the wedding and the rest is history.'

I laughed shortly. 'As are Simon and I.'

'What?'

'History.'

'Well, if it makes you feel any better, after Tina had got off the train from Leeds the other day – the day you decorated her car, I mean – she walked up from the station to the office with a new client she was wooing. Apparently, they'd been on the train from Leeds together talking business, and Tina suggested the client walk up to the office with her so she could then give them a lift home...'

'Oh, good, I'm glad he saw her for what she is.'

'A *she* actually – why do we assume clients in business are men? Anyway, *she* was a woman whose husband had just left her for his secretary. What a cliché.'

'Nearly as bad as going off with your best friend's husband.'

'Anyway, you scored a bull's-eye. Tina said, once she saw the car with its lipsticked message, the woman had a strop and she's not heard from her since. She's refusing to deal with her.'

'Yes!' I waved my willy in the air, catching one of the hen's crumpled silver wings as I did so.

'Bitterness doesn't become you, Cassie.' Clare took my arm but I shrugged her off.

'Neither does being lied to, cheated on and generally being made a fool of.'

Clare sighed. 'I know, I know. What's happened's really terrible. I can only begin to imagine how you must be feeling. That's why—' She stopped abruptly.

'That's why what?' I glanced at her and when she didn't continue I looked at her more closely. 'What, Clare?'

'I've fallen in love, Cassie. Big time.' Clare raised her eyes and gazed straight at me and I saw just how tired and strained she looked.

'You're always falling in love, Clare,' I laughed. 'There's a new man every week with you.'

'Cassie, I've *never* been in love.'

'But...' I stopped what I was saying and stared at her. Clare's eyes were full of unshed tears. I'd never, in all the years I'd known Clare, seen her cry. Or Tina, come to that. While Fi and I could sob for Britain – and generally did – both Clare and Tina always remained steadfastly dry-eyed even when watching the most tear-jerking films. Or even at Tina's father's funeral, where the three of us had sat behind Tina and Simon, her mother and three brothers and their wives. Fi and I had gone through a pack of tissues, but Tina had remained stoically emotionless. I conceded, at the time, *I* was probably crying for the now almost mythical Man in Morocco rather than Tina's dad.

'I've had more than my share of men...'

I nodded in agreement and then ducked as one of the hen's willy deely boppers flew through the air onto the glass-topped table in front of us. I put it on my head for safe-keeping. The hens were now being entertained by a party of stags dressed from head to toe in pinkishly transparent plastic bags tied in neat bows atop their heads, beer-flushed faces peering from cut-out holes. I stared, trying to catch Fi's eye, but she was in full flow, explaining animatedly to the now seemingly recovered BTB that she must nip any *hovering* in the bud from day one if she was to have a long and happy marriage.

'Condoms,' Clare said, following my eyes.

'Sorry?'

'Stags, dressed as condoms.'

'Right. OK.' I turned back to Clare, giving her my full attention. 'But you've never wanted to fall in love with one man, Clare.'

'No. But only because I never have. Never understood this need other women seem to have to spend the rest of their lives with just one man.' Clare wiped her eyes crossly with the back of her hand and waved away the tissue I proffered from my bag.

'The man in The Botanist?'

Clare nodded.

'So, that's lovely, isn't it? What's the problem? He looked very gorgeous. And very single: no woman out with him on a Saturday evening…?'

'I rescued him,' Clare smiled.

'From what? A mad dog? Muggers? Himself?'

'From the stag do he was part of.'

'Right, OK. How come?'

'He was the stag. It was *his* stag do.'

I stared at Clare. 'Oh shit, he's about to get married?'

'Yep. The one man I know is the man for me and I can't have him.'

I frowned. 'But, Clare, I hate to remind you of this, but *most* of your men you can't have. You do tend to have a thing for married, unobtainable men.'

'But I've *never* wanted to *keep* one for myself before. I'm more than happy to have a bit of a fling and then hand them back to their wives. No harm done.'

'Well, that's a moot point, Clare; you know what I think of your dalliances. So, how did you rescue him?'

Clare sighed. 'It was on Thursday evening. I was just about to put my feet up with a glass of wine and watch a catch-up of *Broken*. I've always had a thing about Sean Bean. Mind you, he's looking a bit old now…'

'Get back to your story, Clare.'

'Anyway, I'd only been sitting down five minutes when I heard a knock at the back door. So, I go to open it and there's a man shivering on the doorstep.'

'Shivering? Why was he shivering? We've been having a late summer heatwave.'

'He was stark-bollock naked apart from the tiniest of thongs and bandages.'

'A woman's thong?'

'Yep. And wrapped in bandages.'

'Bandages? Why bandages?'

'Presumably because they were a bunch of doctors from some hospital in Sheffield, and I'd say he was shivering more from shock than the cold. He'd fallen over, because his ankles were tied with a ball-and-chain thingy, and his head was bleeding.'

'How come he was in *your* backyard? Did you know him previously?'

'Not at all. I knew his mates because I'd organised the stag do. They weren't your usual condom-wearing stags: they were much older, for a start, and professional – as I say, mainly hospital doctors. I'd worked over the phone, and also face to face in the office, with his best man, and together we'd planned that just eight of them should start off here in Midhope with canapés and champagne at the new wine bar down East Street and then a meal at George's restaurant and spend the night in The Mucky Duck before flying out from Leeds Bradford airport to Prague. I did tell him Prague was a bit passé, that everybody did it, and suggested Le Touquet as being rather more in keeping with their professional status. But he wasn't having any of it – wanted the whole traditional stag do with strippers and pole dancers.' Clare sighed, looking weary. 'I mean, I pride myself on being rather more upmarket than other stag-do organisations – you know, champagne rather than beer; culture rather than blow-jobs from arresting women police officers.' Clare nodded towards her hens, a couple of whom were now simulating energetic and inaccurate sex with the condom-disguised stags, and sighed deeply once more. 'I appear to be going steadily downmarket at the moment.'

'So why did the groom-to-be end up on your doorstep?'

'Panic. He'd really not wanted a stag do unless it was very low key. He'd only agreed to it as long as he had some control over it, and no strippers or pole dancers or being tied up in cling film was involved. They'd called into the office on Thursday afternoon on the way to The Mucky Duck and I could tell then he really was pretty uptight about the whole thing. Probably didn't help that he'd been in theatre all morning and was tired...'

This was all a bit of a strange tale. 'So, he didn't go back to The Mucky Duck and re-join the party then?'

'To be honest, I did tell him I was off duty, that there was no way I wanted him in my backyard. Then I relented: I couldn't just turn him out into the street in that condition so I let him in and bathed his head – he had a deep cut and it was bleeding quite badly. I actually thought he might need a stitch but he had a good look at it in the bathroom mirror and assured me it didn't warrant one. And then he slept.'

'What, you just let a strange man into your house to sleep?' I was quite shocked.

'Yep.' Clare was slightly on the defensive. 'I reckon they'd spiked his drink with something.'

'Doctors spiking drinks? Doctors wouldn't do that, surely?'

'Sometimes, Cassandra, you really are incredibly naïve. Doctors, remember, have access to any number of weird drugs.'

'Sorry, I don't believe that. Doctors just wouldn't do that.'

Clare was impatient. 'Whatever, Cass, he was out of it. The plan for Thursday night had been to get him to the hotel, strip him, wrap him in bandages, handcuff his legs and then time him to see how long it took him to make his way from the hotel garden and back to his room. Totally puerile stuff. Anyway, their little jape came to nothing because he decided to have the last laugh by disappearing.'

I pulled a face. 'Oh God, his mates must have been so worried when they lost him. You can just see the headlines in the local paper can't you: SHEFFIELD DOCTORS IN NAKED STAG DO ROMP. I bet they looked everywhere for him.'

Clare laughed too and relaxed somewhat as she carried on with her story. 'He managed to find a taxi that was prepared to take him, but he didn't know the area so just asked for my place. He remembered seeing The Four Feathers pub and the church, and the next minute he was banging on my door. I had to pay the taxi driver, of course. By the time I got him inside he was pretty cross: thought it was me that had suggested and organised the whole ridiculous prank.'

'Don't you think he overreacted a bit? I mean, this is the sort of thing that *happens* on a stag do. Maybe he should have just gone along with it and enjoyed two days in Prague.'

Clare glanced across at the hens, who seemed to be getting a bit restless. 'I think I'm going to have to move them on to the nightclub soon,' she frowned. 'God, I can't bear the thought of several more hours of this.'

'Oh, don't leave it like this,' I exclaimed. 'I want to know what happened next.'

'Well, he said he wasn't hanging around to find out if Prague would be any better. He'd never really wanted a stag do in the first place.'

'Bit of a party pooper. All this had been arranged for him and then he decides to go AWOL.'

'Do you blame him? I certainly don't. Anyway,' Clare went on, 'he obviously had no phone on him so he used mine to ring The Mucky Duck and passed on a message that he was fine and the rest of the stags should go to Prague without him.'

'Really? How on earth is he going to face them back at work?'

'Cassie, he was absolutely exhausted. He'd been in theatre all day operating on a little boy who'd been in some hit-and-run accident in Sheffield.'

'Oh, the poor thing!'

'Yes, but even worse, just before they set off he'd called onto the ward to see how he was doing. He'd died. He was only five years old. Just started school and he'd *died*.'

'But why did he stay with *you*? Where was his fiancée? Couldn't you have got in touch with her and asked her to come and pick him up?'

Clare shook her head. 'On her own hen do: New York, apparently. So, there I was, at home, with a strange man so I just put him to bed in the spare room. He was desperately upset he hadn't managed to save the child, mortified that he'd gone AWOL, leaving his own party, but equally determined that he wasn't re-joining it to go to Prague.'

I looked at my watch and then across at Fi, who was in the middle of some sort of drinking game with Beryl and two more hens. 'I'm going to try and get Fi home in the next few minutes. Just tell me what happened yesterday. How come you've fallen in love with him?'

'There's just something about him. Yesterday he was totally apologetic that he'd ruined the party, but couldn't bear to go back to an empty flat or the hospital. So, he sat in the garden all day and just reread books he'd loved as a child and I happened to have loved and kept too. He started on *The Water Babies* before breakfast and then went on to *The Famous Five*. I was busy in the office but kept running down to the garden to make sure he was OK. He was either sleeping in the sun or reading. Last night, Cassie, I made us spaghetti and we just talked and talked and talked. I have never felt such an affinity with another human being before.'

'Did you sleep with him, Clare?'

'No, Cassie, I didn't.' Clare was cross. 'He needed a friend, not a lover: he has one of those at home. I eventually managed to get hold of James, the best man, and very diplomatically suggested that Rageh was not in a good place.'

'*Reggie?* Sounds like an old man, or an East End mobster.'

'Clare tutted. 'Rageh. His parents are originally from Somalia. Doesn't really get the laddish British stag culture. He said he tried to get involved, tried to find the party spirit, but it just wasn't in him.'

'I want to go home,' I said, hoisting my willy over one shoulder and adjusting my twin willy deely bopper. 'I've really had enough.'

'Snap,' Clare said grimly. 'But, unfortunately *I've* another lifetime to spend with these women. I'm not sure how you're going to extricate Fi from this lot...'

We both looked over to the bar where Fi and the hens were still entertaining and, in turn, being entertained by the now somewhat bedraggled condoms. Fi didn't look as if she was anywhere near ready to leave.

I made my way over and, in an attempt at jollity, slapped the tall dark-haired man blocking my path to Fi and the now extremely raucous hens, over the head with my three-foot, day-glow penis.

The man and the very attractive brunette to whom he was attached, both turned crossly as I interrupted their tête-à-tête with a willy and a manic smile.

Great stuff. I'd just executed Actual Bodily Harm with a Giant Todger on Xavier Bamforth. The very thing to finish off my evening from hell.

15

Paula

1976

'You putting on a bit of weight?' Dot narrowed her eyes and looked directly at Paula's stomach before holding her younger daughter's gaze.

Paula looked away first, taking time over the cutting of her slice of toast and marmalade into four neat pieces. 'Summer seems to be over,' she said, deliberately changing the subject. 'I'm glad – I've had enough of the heat.'

'Paula, I'm talking to you. Don't ignore me with chitchat about the damned weather.' Dot opened and emptied the green and orange Brook Bond tea packet into the caddy, manoeuvring off the little orange dividend stamp before licking and sticking it into her divvy book.

Paula reached across the tablecloth for the tea packet, searching for the picture card between the wrappers as she'd done all her life. Ridiculously, she still got a slight thrill in being the one to extract it after years of competition with Linda as to who should get to the giveaway card first. Linda, Paula now thought somewhat sourly, was two months into married life and queening it in her brand-new detached up on the Copper Beech estate. Not that there appeared to be any copper beeches up there: just a mass of houses and bungalows in a monochromatic beige fake stone.

Play Better Soccer. Well, that was no good to man or beast. Paula twisted the card and flicked it across the table where it came to a halt by Norman's finished breakfast plate. The discarded bacon fat and white gristle from Norman's favourite black pudding made her stomach heave and she quickly looked away.

Dot poured tea for both of them before sitting down heavily across from Paula. 'I reckon, Paula, there's a lot more in there…' she indicated Paula's middle '… than has gone in through your mouth.' Embarrassment made Dot's words cruder than had been her intention and she reddened but still held Paula's gaze.

Paula didn't say anything but, aware of her mother's scrutiny, buried her face in the steam rising from the green Beryl Ware cup.

'Paula? Your dad's upstairs in the lav with his newspaper. He'll be there for another five minutes at least. Are you going to talk to me or what?'

'What do you want to know?' Paula's head came up, defiant, and she glared at Dot.

'I want to know if you've been up to something you shouldn't.'

'Yes, Mum. I'm pregnant. Are you satisfied now? You've been staring at me for days...'

'Oh my God, Paula. You stupid girl. And who is he? The lad, I mean? Is he going to wed you?'

'For heaven's sake, Mum, it's 1976, not the Dark Ages. I'm assuming you're not going to throw me out and tell me never to darken your door ever again.'

'Shhh,' Dot hissed, 'your dad'll hear.' She hurried to close the kitchen door that led upstairs, knocking over the milk jug as she did so. 'Damn, now look what you've made me do.' Dot snatched Paula's toast-crumbed plate, shoving it under the spreading wet stain in order to protect the oak veneered table.

'He'll have to know sometime.' Paula felt defeated; didn't know what else to say.

'What will Maggy-from-number-ten say? What will our Linda think? And the Trinders? What will *they* think when they know their new daughter-in-law's unmarried sister is in the family way?' Dot frowned furiously. 'I can see Mrs Trinder now, pulling that face, like she's been sucking lemons. You know, like she did when she saw the sausage rolls at the reception.'

'Mum, I don't give a damn about the bloody Trinders, Maggy *or* Linda. And, I don't give a *shit* about sodding sausage rolls.'

'Paula,' Dot raised her voice and glared. 'There's no need to swear. I just don't know where we went wrong with you.'

Paula stood up. 'Oh, for God's, sake, Mum, I've heard it all before.'

'But look at you! It's not normal, Paula, to not brush your hair and to wear all them long dark clothes.' Dot paused. 'So, who is he, Paula? Will he marry you, accept his responsibility?'

Highly unlikely, Paula thought, seeing as how not only did Rowan have no idea that she was up the duff but, more importantly, she had no idea where the bastard had gone. Up the creek without a paddle, as Norman always used to say whenever he came home with news that one of the girls where he worked, at the fishmonger's in Midhope's inside market, had gone and got herself pregnant. Well, he'd be saying it about his younger daughter now.

Bloody stupid thing to say anyway: 'got herself pregnant', Paula thought as she stomped upstairs away from her mother's probing and went to lay down in her room. Nobody gets *themselves* pregnant unless they're the Virgin Mary.

Paula suddenly felt very tired. Turning over on to her side, she switched on the tiny transistor she'd been given for her fourteenth birthday and it crackled into life, Ed Stewart's jocular voice tinnily celebrating the fact that Pussycat's 'Mississippi' had finally managed to knock 'Dancing Queen' from the number one slot after Abba's tenacious hold on it for the past six weeks. 'Thank God for that,' Paula muttered, but none the less continued to fiddle with the control in an attempt to find something less banal. When *The Sunday Service* invited all those tuned in to pray, she threw the radio across her bed, slipped under the pink candlewick bedspread and, curled up in a foetal position, tried to figure out what to do.

It had all been going so well the night of the picnic. Rowan, she knew, had been impressed with the Brie and taramasalata. Of course, living in Hong Kong for most of his life, apart from his days at boarding school where, he'd assured her, the food was 'total shit, man' he was used to such exotic fare.

It couldn't have been more perfect. He'd made love to her as if he really loved her, stroking her hair, kissing every bit of her until she was almost pleading for more. She knew she'd had too much alcohol – half a bottle of wine had gone straight to her head – and combining that with the unaccustomed joint had made her head spin.

In that small back bedroom, huddled under her candlewick bedspread, Paula clenched her fists and went over, yet again, what happened next.

'Hey, you're some chick, Paula,' Rowan had said, smiling down at her. 'I'll really miss you. You know?'

Paula had struggled up from her supine position on Dot's tablecloth, lifting Rowan's arm that had grown heavy across her waist and stared down at him. 'What do you mean, you'll miss me? I'm not going anywhere. I can see you tomorrow. Any day.'

'No, man, *I'm* going. I need to split. I've had enough.'

Paula felt panic rise. 'Enough of what?'

Rowan shrugged. 'This. All this.' He'd waved vaguely with his arm. 'All getting a bit heavy…'

'But I'm coming with you, Rowan. You said...'

When he didn't reply, but simply stroked her arm, she went on: 'Look, give me a week. I can give in my notice at work. I've some holiday money owing. And then, then I'll ask my sister to lend me the rest. You said, Rowan, you *said*...'

Rowan stood up and stretched before stamping out the joint beneath his foot. 'Don't want to start a fire here,' he said. 'Come on, man, your coming out East with me was all a bit of a dream. I never promised anything...'

'Yes, you bloody well did.' Paula felt tears well and brushed them away angrily with her hand. 'I'm all ready to give up my job and come travelling with you. I want to see India, Thailand...'

Rowan prised Paula's fingers away from his arm before removing bits of dead grass and brushwood from his jeans. 'Look, I need to go, Paula. I need to be somewhere later on. Come on, I'll give you a hand with this lot.' He bent down to pack the picnic basket but she slapped his hand away and started to do it herself. 'Tell you what, Paula, I've got your phone number...'

'Of course you've got my sodding phone number.'

'... I'll ring you in a couple of weeks from wherever I am. We can sort something then.' Paula had looked up into Rowan's face as he'd had the damned nerve to quote, '"To gain that which is worth having, it may be necessary to lose everything else." The immortal words of Keir Hardie, Paula. Come on, I'll go ahead first and once you've got your shit together you can join me...'

Paula had sat back down on the rug as Rowan set off for the hole in the hedge and the bus back into town. He turned when he realised she wasn't following. 'Come on, we shouldn't be in here anyway. It's someone's garden.'

When she stayed sitting where she was in the same position under the tree, he shrugged and started walking once more. 'Too heavy,' he muttered, the words floating backwards in the warm, headily-scented midsummer night air.

'I've got some pride,' she'd said to his departing back. 'And it wasn't bloody Keir Hardie who said that – it was Bernadette Devlin.'

She must have fallen asleep – she'd been feeling desperately tired lately, almost unable to stay awake at work in the stuffy office as the long hot summer had eventually burned itself out like a forgotten fire – but opened her eyes as she felt the springs of her mattress depress.

Norman was sitting on the edge of her bed, looking down at her.

'God, Dad, you made me jump, just sitting there. What's the matter with you?' Norman hadn't stepped foot in her and Linda's shared bedroom after they'd hit their teens, and it seemed strange to have him sitting there now.

'Your mum's just told me.'

'Right. I supposed she would. But don't you start having a go at me as well. I've had enough with Mum giving me the third degree.'

'Come on, Paula. How did you expect her to react? Say well done, how bloody clever of you?' When she didn't say anything, but tried to pull the covers over her head in order to shut out his hurt face, he said, 'You're not the first, Paula, and you won't be the last. I've seen it all afore, during the war. There were dozens of lasses left holding the baby – literally – when their men were killed or went back to wherever they came from in the first place. You'll just have to get on with it.'

'But I don't want a baby, Dad. I want to go travelling. I don't want to stop round here and have to keep on working in that bloody awful office.'

'So, does this lad of yours know? You've not mentioned him for a while.'

'He's gone back to his parents in Hong Kong,' Paula said. 'But I'm sure if he knew about this – that I'm, you know – I'm sure he'd come back and help me.' Since the evening of the picnic, exactly eleven weeks and three days ago now, Paula had begun to build a story in her head even she was beginning to believe. That he'd gone home to his parents and that, if he only knew what state he'd left her in, he'd be back like a shot. Maybe even take her to Hong Kong with him. They'd have a quiet wedding arranged by his diplomat father and he'd help them find a little apartment where she'd have the baby and maybe they'd then go off travelling together, the baby snuggled into Rowan's chest in one of those baby papoose things everyone seemed to have these days.

'Aye, well, you'll just have to see what happens. That's all you can do.' And with that Norman had stood, shaken his head and followed his nose down to the kitchen where Dot's Sunday roast beef was already beginning to make its weekly complaint at being cooked almost to cremation.

16

What Doesn't Kill You Makes You Stronger...

By the beginning of October, the reality of being a deserted wife and single mum to two teenagers had set in. I hadn't heard much at all from Mark: he'd transferred generous amounts of money into our joint account, which would more than enable me to carry on paying the mortgage and bills, but I'd heard nothing about whether he wanted a divorce or if he regretted doing what he did. Clare informed me that the pair of them were renting one of the modern mill conversion apartments over in Eastfirth, a large village about six miles away, but even knowing that, I prayed nightly that he would soon return, that he was going through some mid-life crisis and would realise what he'd done and come home. I was certainly ready to take him back with open arms.

My life basically consisted of two things: Little Acorns, and running the house and kids, with the school taking up most of my energies. In an effort to forget my personal situation I completely immersed myself in its running, sorting kids, parents, teachers, governors, and not forgetting a Lithuanian lollipop lady and a secretary who, now that they both knew of my situation, appeared to make it their combined purpose in life to bring me tea, cake and wise words of comfort.

'What doesn't murders you, Mrs Head, will only makes you keep fit,' Deimante announced one Monday morning before school started.

'Sorry?'

'Jeans she tells me sis and I sink very, very good sing. Very wise lady, Jeans...' Deimante nodded her head in agreement with herself as the Wise Woman of Westenbury herself walked into the office.

'What doesn't kill you makes you stronger,' Jean corrected, beaming at her protégée. 'Very good, Deimante. Now, what have you got there?'

'*Skilandis*. Very good breakfast. You needs feeding up, Mrs Head. Big shock of your mans leaving yous for best friend. Yous getting sin...'

God, did everyone know of my situation? And getting sin? I'd certainly not had any sin for the past month.

'Sin?'

'Yes, sin.' Deimante grabbed my arm and gave it a good feel. 'Too sin. Needs good meals. No lovers ever wants makes sex wis you wis sin arms. Now *skilandis* will sets you up for day. Betters than biscuits of chocolate. Fulls of goodness. Come on, eats, eats...'

A large slice of pig's stomach stuffed with minced meat

and matured (and for some time if the smell and texture had anything to do with it) was put into my hand while Jean and Deimante stood over me like a couple of doting mother hens, urging me to eat and not relenting until I'd had several bites of what I can only describe as smoked sweaty sock.

'Gosh, that's salty,' I gasped, looking round for the bottle of Evian I usually had to hand.

'*Gira*, you needs *gira*, Mrs Head. Here.' Deimante rummaged through her huge carrier bag and produced a two-litre plastic Coca-Cola bottle of very dark sticky-looking liquid and poured a substantial amount into my empty coffee cup. 'Sis nots Cokes,' she shook her head vehemently. 'Not rotting tooths. Now drinks, drinks up…'

'It's really quite delicious, Cassandra,' Jean encouraged. 'Made from fermented rye bread.'

'Fermented?' I asked, sniffing the contents suspiciously. 'Are you sure it's not alcoholic?'

'No, no.' Jean shook her head vigorously. 'Apparently full of Vitamin B. I've had mine already.'

'Bums ups,' Deimante grinned. 'Is freshly made last month.'

I took a sip and it really *was* delicious with a sweet, yet tangy yeast taste. It was a bit like drinking molten brown bread and I finished the cup, slaking my thirst before wiping my mouth on the back of my hand.

'Are you sure there's no alcohol in this?' I asked as a rather familiar warm glow began to spread through my whole body.

'Just goes wis flows like Jean say,' Deimante admonished as she gathered up the remains of her booty and I finally managed to usher the pair of them out of the office in order to start the day properly.

'Only dead fish go with the flow,' I muttered to myself as I closed the door, but then immediately opened it again as I spotted Karen Adams walking into school.

'Ah, Karen, do you have a minute?' I pounced.

'Can it wait?' she said, unsmiling. 'I've got rather a lot to do before the children arrive.'

'I insist,' I replied, rather too gaily for a damp Monday morning. 'I'm not going to take no for an answer. Come on. In. Now.'

'Sorry?' She looked at me with the same suspicion I'd given the cup of *gira* ten minutes earlier, but followed me into the office where I sat down leaving her to stand in front of my desk. I'd once read in *Cosmo* that's how bosses get the upper hand.

'Now, you might not like what I'm going to say, but I'm going to say it anyway. You and I have to work together, and I've gone along with your decidedly snide comments, as well as your determined efforts to undermine me at every turn, for the last month. It's up to you, Karen. You can carry on like this, making life unpleasant for me as well as the two new supply staff, or you can try changing your tune: accept I'm going to be in charge until a permanent head is found to take over – which could be at half term, Christmas, summer. No one knows when it will be.' I paused for breath and then launched once more. 'So, until then, I would appreciate your co-operation in working with me for the good of the school. Oh, and Karen, I should be grateful if any gossip you hear about my personal life is kept to yourself. I'm sure you get my drift?'

Karen opened and closed her mouth a couple of times, rather like a landed fish gasping for air, but then she gave me a look of utter disdain, wheeled round and left the office.

I burped discreetly and, catching sight of myself in the office mirror, apologised to my reflection and set off to find Harriet Westmoreland, the new supply teacher who worked Mondays and Tuesdays, and whom I was beginning to like enormously.

By break time I had a pounding head and was feeling hung over. Wait until I saw that Deimante. Having said that, I didn't regret my little alcohol-fuelled confrontation with Karen Adams – one I probably would have had only in my imagination had it not been for the *gira*-induced Dutch – Lithuanian? – courage. And Deimante was right: I had lost weight. Being only five foot tall and with a love of good food as well as a tendency to bake – and then eat – I had gone from my wedding day size eight to what was probably no more than a ten, just before the break-up. Mark had teased me, taking hold of the new flesh around my waist and backside and calling me a little dumpling but assuring me he loved it all because it was mine. I should have taken heed: Tina is tall, very slim and extremely elegant. Maybe that's why Mark went for her. Well, he'd have nothing to get hold of now.

I took a couple of paracetamols, covered the reception class for an hour while Kath Beaumont dashed off to the dentist, and gave thanks that I'd not had to prepare assembly because we were having a visit from the RNIB to talk to the children about how they could help raise money for blind people. I always enjoyed these little talks. It meant I didn't have to do much apart from introduce the speaker, give a vote of thanks at the end and basically sit back and let someone else take over for a while. The session this morning was particularly good, as we had four visitors: the charity fundraiser, a partially sighted man who showed the children the latest gadgets for helping blind people and, drawing oohs and awws from everyone including the staff, a trainee Labrador puppy and her foster mother. The children were totally in love with Sidney the puppy, particularly when he let himself down by leaving a puddle on the hall floor.

All was going well, apart from the occasional dagger winging its way in my direction from Karen Adams, when Beau Baxter, a usually rather quiet five-year-old, put his hand up.

'My daddy's going blind,' he shouted down the hall to the fundraiser, his bottom lip trembling. Two hundred heads swivelled in his direction.

Oh shit.

'Oh?' the fundraiser said, giving me a panicked, *you're the head teacher, you sort it* glance 'Really?'

'My mummy was talking to my auntie Bea last night on the phone and she said Daddy was going to go blind.'

'You're really going to have to help Daddy then.' The fundraiser was floundering.

'Well, we've got a new au pair to help as well. She's very pretty.'

'Right, OK, that will be a help, won't it, then?'

'Yes,' he lisped, sadly. 'Mummy told Auntie Bea that Daddy is going to go blind if his right hand gets any more exercise now that the new au pair has come to help.'

Harriet Westmoreland, sitting on my right, hurriedly turned a snort of laughter into a cough as I quickly jumped in to rescue the fundraiser whose reddening face was doing nothing to help her problem acne.

'Now, do we have any more questions, children?' I trilled, Joyce Grenfell-style. 'About Sidney, the lovely dog, maybe…?'

The rain that had been threatening all weekend arrived with a vengeance and, by 5 p.m., after a wet break and lunchtime when the kids had been cooped up, annoying and pecking at each other like battery hens, together with the usual after-school staff meeting, I was longing for a soak in a bath and an early night.

'I'm assuming you're going to be at tonight's meeting?' Harriet asked as we walked together across the playground to the car park.

'Meeting?' My heart sank.

'About the new development? The Bamforths are holding a public meeting in Westenbury village hall. I thought you'd want to be there – I hear it could affect Little Acorns?'

My heart sank further. 'Gosh, I'm glad you reminded me. I'd totally forgotten. Of course I need to be there.' I looked at my watch. 'I'm going to have to get a move on: I promised I'd pick up my mother and grandfather. My granddad Norman is going to be devastated by this. They're planning a huge estate in the wildflower meadow behind his house.'

Harriet looked at me. 'Your granddad isn't the Norman who actually made the wildflower meadow, is he?'

I nodded. 'Yes, and he's ninety-one now and seems to have given up the will to live because of all this.'

'Gosh, he's quite famous: I remember reading an article about him in the local paper. I often used to take my older kids down there in the summer when the flowers were in full bloom. We've had loads of picnics in that meadow.'

I smiled. 'So have we. But you don't live over here in Westenbury. Would any development affect you?'

'If I didn't go to the meeting to give my support that would be a bit of "I'm all right, Jack." I mean, the Bamforths don't actually own the fields around where we live but, if they do get planning permission to build on their land, I can't see how the local authority can turn down others round here who might decide to jump on the bandwagon. Anyway, Lilian, my nanny, rents a cottage on the Bamforth Estate and I said I'd go along with her. She's pretty upset about it all, as you can imagine. And to be honest, it's a bit of a night out.' She laughed. 'Nick's at home at the moment, for a change. He can put the kids to bed.'

'I can't believe I'd forgotten the meeting was tonight – I mean, I've already had a phone conversation with David

Henderson about it today. God, how awful if I'd got in the bath with a glass of wine as I was planning to do.'

'I forget things all the time,' Harriet laughed. 'It comes with having five kids – it addles your brain.'

'So, what's my excuse? I've only got two.'

'Do you really need to ask?' Harriet laughed again, but this time with a modicum of sympathy.

I rummaged in my bag for my car keys, which I'd forgotten I'd left for safekeeping in the office drawer. 'See, look, I've forgotten my damned keys now. Shit, I hope the caretaker hasn't locked up.'

Harriet glanced back towards the school entrance. 'Quick, Stan's just going into school.'

'OK, you two. It's going to have to be a takeaway for supper. I'm out again in an hour.'

'Takeaway again?' Freya dragged herself away from *Hollyoaks* long enough to air her disapproval. 'We're going to turn into takeaways. It's not good for a teenager to eat junk food, you know. Paula said.'

'Yes, well, Paula isn't the oracle on teenage dietary habits.'

'Oh, I think she is.'

I ground my teeth. 'Curry then, or a bowl of cornflakes? Your choice?'

'Curry, if you insist.'

'I don't. As I say, up to you.'

'Well, you need to eat,' Freya said, without looking up from the TV. 'Paula and I were only saying the other day that you're too thin.'

'What are you now? My mother?'

'Well, Paula is.'

'That's debatable,' I muttered, hunting for the takeaway menu and phone number. I always used to know exactly where it was: a place for everything…

With fifteen minutes to go before I left, Freya suddenly announced she was coming with me.

'You need to get changed then,' I said, eyeing her studded dog collar and oversized holey hoody.

'I am changed,' she said in some surprise. 'Which is more than can be said for you.' She looked my black work suit up and down before raising her – black heavily kohled – eyes at me.

'You can't go like that,' I said. 'I'm representing the school.'

'Yes, and I'm representing Great-Granddad. Oh, and you'd better see this…'

'What? What is it?' I looked suspiciously at the crumpled letter Freya produced from her school bag. The envelope had very obviously been opened and resealed – badly.

'It says you have to sign it to say you've seen it. Good job I opened it first or I wouldn't have known.'

'Known what?' I looked at her.

'Known you had to sign it,' she said patiently, as if talking to one of my five-year-olds.

'Oh, for heaven's sake, Freya, I can do without this right now. "*If Freya continues in this vein,*" I read, "*I will have no alternative but to exclude her for a period of time...*" I carried on down the page. 'A protest?' I glared at her. 'What protest? What were you protesting about?'

Freya fiddled with her My Chemical Romance badge (I thought they'd disbanded years ago) but then said defiantly, 'School dinners. There's not enough nutritional value in them.'

'I thought turkey twizzlers were banned.'

'I'm sure they were, but there's still not enough vegetables. The veg we have is tinned sweetcorn or almost brown, mushy broccoli. The cooks even call spaghetti hoops a veg. And the vegetarian choice is usually just pizza or a baked potato and so...'

'And so?'

'And so, because no one would listen to us, despite politely asking for a meeting with our head of year...'

'You surely have some sort of school council to which you can take your grievances? Go through the proper channels?'

'Mum,' Freya sighed, 'I *am* the school council.'

'What, just you?'

'I'm the Year 10 rep. I knew you weren't listening when I told you I'd been voted in.'

'I'm sorry, darling, I have had rather a lot on my mind lately.' What a dreadful mother I was to forget. 'I can't believe that the school would think it an exclusion issue because of your request for a bit of fresh cabbage.' I looked at the letter more closely while Freya looked decidedly shifty.

'Hang on, Freya. A sit-down protest in the yard? A refusal to come into lessons until your demands were met? Inciting others to protest?'

'It was only RE. Not much of a lesson,' she said sulkily.

'Encouraging male students to wear skirts as part of a gender-equality protest,' I read. 'For heaven's sake, Freya, there are hundreds of kids who'd love a place at a state grammar school like yours. The head won't think twice about booting you out, especially as you very rarely do your homework and insist on wearing as much of this emo stuff as you can get away with on your uniform.'

'Mum,' Freya said patiently, 'I'm the mainstay of the first seven netball team. They need me.'

'Yes, well, Theresa May thought that as well.'

'Theresa May played netball? I didn't know that.'

'Now you're being deliberately obtuse.' I looked at my watch. I'd had enough of trying to bring up teens single-handed. 'Wait there. No, don't. Ring Paula on your mobile and tell her I'm running late.'

I went into the sitting room, but Tom was in there, watching TV. I ran upstairs, closed the bathroom door and, with heart pounding, rang Mark. Why on earth was I nervous about ringing my own husband? *My* husband, Serpentina...

Mark answered immediately. 'Cass, I'm so glad you've rung.'

I was put on the back foot immediately. 'Are you? Why?' Hope surged through me. Mark must have just needed me to ring him for him to come home.

'Well, I don't see why we can't be friends. I know what I did was awful for you, pretty unforgivable, but we're all adults, and Tina and I really want to be there for you.'

'You moron. You pillock. You... you ridiculous wanker.' I was seething, a red-hot mist descending as I shouted down the phone. I slammed it down and then immediately picked it up again and hit redial.

'Cass...'

'Mark, I'd like you to sort out your children.' I spat out each word, like a volley of bullets.

'The children? What's wrong with the children? Are they OK?' I felt a modicum of satisfaction that there was a sense of panic in his response.

'I'd like you to know there is a big possibility that your son is gay and your daughter is a revolutionary and about to be expelled.' There, that should rattle the complacent wanker's cage.

There was a long silence and then Mark said, very calmly, 'Cass, I've known for months that Tom is very probably gay.'

'What? And you never said? Never thought to discuss it with me?'

'Cass, how could I tell you I'd seen Tom in The Blue Ball? You'd have wanted to know what I was doing there, who I was with, why I was in a gay pub...'

I shook my head in disbelief. 'So, Tom saw you with Tina and couldn't say anything because he was with another boy and you saw Tom and couldn't say anything because you were being an adulterous bastard?'

Mark didn't contradict me. Instead he said, 'It really isn't the end of the world, Cass.'

'Oh, don't be so bloody condescending as well as being a lying cheat. And what about your daughter? What about Freya?'

Mark had the audacity to give a little, what can only be called paternal, laugh. 'Freya? What did you expect? She's Paula's granddaughter!'

17

Whose Village Is It, Anyway...?

The village hall in Westenbury is situated between Little Acorns School and the main village pub, The Jolly Sailor.

'I can manage,' Granddad was saying crossly. 'I'm not an invalid. Just pass me my stick, Freya, and I'll be fine.'

The car park, usually empty of an evening unless the Brownies or Zumba class were *in situ*, was surprisingly full and, once inside, we had to search for seats. 'I knew we were going to be late,' Granddad grumbled. 'All the best seats at the front have gone.'

'Over here,' Harriet Westmoreland waved from the second row back. 'We've saved you some seats.'

'Brilliant, thanks,' I mouthed back, and ushered my lot forwards.

Edward and Xavier Bamforth were already sitting at a trestle table up on the stage where, previously, I remembered fondly, a six-year-old Freya, dressed in cute yellow PVC mac and wellies had sung and danced a rendition of 'There's a Worm at the Bottom of the Garden' in the only concert I'd ever managed to get her to perform at. She'd been a bit of a revolutionary even then, producing two real live worms from her mac pocket and shaking them at the audience as the other tots shook imaginary worms and lisped '... *and his name is Wigg-er-ly Woo.*'

'Our Linda and Davina are here,' Granddad said, pleased. 'Why aren't we sitting with them?' He started heading down the hall towards them.

'There's no seats left down there, Granddad,' I said, hurriedly steering him to the left-hand side where Harriet had placed bags and cardigans on the wooden chairs. I suddenly realised it was a bit like being at a wedding and, instead of 'bride or groom?' it was 'for or against?' Linda and Davina, together with Anthony and some others, were sitting firmly in the 'for' camp. As was Karen Adams. My heart sank: I could really do without her there.

'Snap!' Ben Carey, the vicar of All Hallows said as Freya sat down next to him. He fingered his dog collar, eyeing her studded one, and she laughed out loud with him. To Ben's right sat David Henderson and a very beautiful blonde I assumed to be David's wife.

'Cassandra, this is Mandy, my wife.' David smiled vaguely but his eyes were scanning the room, obviously intent on working out just who was for the Bamforths' plan and who was not.

'Hello, Cassandra,' Mandy Henderson said coolly. 'I've heard a lot about you.'

I reddened slightly, remembering she was a magistrate and knew of my little infraction in causing 'Criminal Damage' to Serpentina's car. All I needed was for her to say something about it and for Freya to find out what I'd done, and I'd have absolutely no bargaining power when it came to Freya's own – less artistic – protest. I'd already heard Freya proudly telling Paula what she'd been up to at school and, despite my glaring at Paula through my mirror as the pair of them sat and whispered in the back seat of the car, Paula had praised rather than condemned Freya's sit-in at school.

I glanced at the stage where, in front of a very professional-looking display showing a huge map of Westenbury and its neighbouring villages, the enemy was already seated and ready for action. Edward Bamforth was talking intently to the woman on his right – apparently a secretary taking notes – while Xavier Bamforth was sitting somewhat moodily to his father's left, reading from some papers in front of him. He suddenly looked up and in my direction, holding my gaze for several seconds before looking away.

People were still making their way in and more chairs had to be ferried from side rooms into the main hall while several groups were left standing, leaning against the shiny terracotta-coloured walls, their pints of lager and glasses of wine presumably transported from The Jolly Sailor across the road.

Edward Bamforth lifted the glass of water to his

mouth, put it firmly back on the table and then stood.

'A big thank you to everyone for coming along this evening...'

'Can't hear you at the back; speak up.'

'Is that better?' Edward adjusted the tinny-looking microphone in front of him and, as high-pitched buzzing static flooded the hall, Granddad Norman winced theatrically and twiddled with his hearing aid.

'Tonight, I want to share with you all a marvellous opportunity to build and develop this village of ours...' Edward started.

'*Ours?* We were under the impression it was *yours*?' I glanced round and saw Wayne the Wasp Murderer leaning against the wall, enjoying both his pint of lager as well as heckling Edward Bamforth. 'If it's *our* village, then you can keep your thieving hands off it.'

'Sit down, give the man a chance.' This from the 'for' contingent.

'You may not know this,' Edward started speaking once more, 'but under a government consultation launched two years ago, rules have been changed to allow local councils to allocate small-scale sites in the green belt specifically for starter homes.' There was silence from the gathered audience as Edward warmed to his theme. 'We have fantastic plans for the whole of this area. Times are changing, people want new houses, new leisure facilities...'

'I'll tell you what we want round here, well, in Midhope any road...' A tall lugubrious-looking figure dressed in black stood and faced the stage. 'John Clarke of Clarke and Sons, Funeral Directors. Never mind your fancy ideas for shops and a ski slope, what we need is a new crematorium in this town. Have you been to the old one, Mr Bamforth?'

'Er, not recently.' Edward Bamforth seemed lost for words. He laughed. 'I do try and avoid it if I can.'

'You agree to his plans for Westenbury, Mr Clarke,' Wayne the Wasp Murderer yelled, 'and he'll promise you a new one. A *crème de la crem*, as it were…'

Hoots of laughter filled the hall. I glanced at Xavier Bamforth, who appeared to be biting down on a smile. He was rather handsome when he smiled. Dark hair, dark eyes. I'd always been a fair hair, blue-eyed sort of girl myself. Mark came instantly to mind but, for the first time in four weeks, my stomach didn't lurch with sorrow and longing for him. Pillock, I thought to myself comfortably, and continued to stare at Xavier Bamforth.

'Old people used to poke me at weddings and say, "It'll be your turn next,"' Paula was whispering to Freya and Harriet. 'So, I used to poke old people at funerals and say the same thing back to them.' The three of them cackled and several heads turned and glared with the accompanying 'Shhh.'

'I think, Mr Bamforth, you've not done your research well enough.' I hadn't seen Matt and Fiona sitting several rows behind us and Matthew now stood, everyone turning in his direction. 'Matthew Richardson, tenant farmer on one of the Bamforth farms on the other side of Westenbury. My family has been farming this land since 1630: I've checked the date today – been doing a bit of historical research as it were.'

'And are you making a living, Matthew?' Edward Bamforth asked, attempting familiarity with his tenant.

'Yes, as much as any tenanted farmer can. But any expansion we may have envisaged, any new equipment we may have considered buying, we've had to put on hold knowing this damned silly idea of yours is hanging over my sons and me. I want to be able to pass on my farm to my children as my ancestors have passed it down the line to me.'

Matthew, a naturally fairly shy man paused and looked at Fi. She squeezed his hand and he turned back to the Bamforths. 'Mr Bamforth, this is *our* land. OK, you may own the acres round here after your family bought it – what, seventy years or so ago, just after the war? But *you* don't own its life, its very heart, and you never can or will. The farmers who, three hundred and sixty-five days a year, tread its soil, know the depth of its streams, the foundations of its actual farms and the birds in its hedgerows; these are the people who really own your estate.'

I turned and caught Fi's eye and she pressed her hand to her heart, and winked at me. She may have been affecting nonchalance, but I saw her blow her nose on the tissue she fished out of her cardigan sleeve. I don't think I'd ever heard the usually shy, and sometimes even taciturn Matthew speak so many words all in one go.

'But, Matthew, surely, with the perpetual uncertainties in farming such as climate change, farmers are in the unenviable position of not actually knowing what their future might be?' Edward reached behind him for some notes he'd obviously brought with him and said, 'As it is, the whole farming industry is propped up by subsidies. The report by Informa Agribusiness Intelligence estimates that without subsidies ninety per cent of farms could collapse and land prices could crash. The Government has promised to provide subsidies only in the short term. Beyond that it has promised *nothing…*' He peered over his glasses at Matthew. 'The ball's in your court, Matthew.'

Matthew snorted disparagingly. 'You're reading out statistics meant to frighten us. But folk who have been working this land for generations believe in farming and we know it's viable.' He looked around the hall and, counting on his fingers, said, 'There are one, two, three, four other farmers here in exactly the same position as me and you are going to destroy us, our families and our histories…'

'Shame on you,' a woman shouted from the middle of the hall towards the Bamforths and Matthew sat down heavily, Fi patting his arm.

Because of my own worries over the past month, I realised I'd not really thought about anyone else. I'd not had much time for Fiona and felt ashamed of myself. 'Sorry, really sorry,' I mouthed and she nodded. Although Clare rang or texted me every couple of days to see how *I* was coping, to ask how *I* was feeling, I'd no idea, I realised guiltily, how she was now feeling about her rescued stag. What a dreadful friend I was.

Lost in thought, I didn't see the elderly woman next to Harriet stand and face the rest of the people in the hall.

'Lilian Brennan,' she said quietly in a mesmerising Irish lilt. 'Sure, and I'm not from round here originally, as you can probably tell...'

'Speak up, can't hear you,' Karen Adams shouted rudely from the front. 'Anyway, shouldn't we be hearing what Mr Bamforth has to say – listen to his plans – rather than everyone piling in with negative comments?' She stood and glared in our direction but whether the hostility was aimed at me or Lilian I wasn't quite sure.

'Who's that?' Freya whispered.

'The dreaded Karen Adams,' I whispered back. 'You know, one of my staff at school.'

'Oh, is that her? What's *she* got to do with all this? Does she live in the village?'

'No, she doesn't. Shhh, listen...'

'I may be from another country,' Lilian was saying, 'but I've lived on the outskirts of Westenbury – in Netherbridge – for several years now and I settled here because it reminds me of home.'

'Another bloody immigrant,' a bald-headed man with an incredibly red face sitting across from us spoke too loudly to his wife, and then glared at me, sniffing defiantly as he realised I'd overheard.

'This village is a little oasis,' Lilian went on. 'Do we really want to be covered in concrete? Just another urbanised part of Midhope town itself? I rent my cottage from the Bamforth Estate but, even if I were lucky enough to own it outright and so be in a position to block the Bamforths' path, as it were, I'd still be here, fighting for the countryside. And I urge you all to do the same, regardless of where you live.'

'I bet if you were fifty years younger you'd be talking a different tale,' Baldy across the aisle shouted. 'Not being a skier, you won't be interested in a dry ski slope round here.'

'I can assure the... gentleman to my right...' Lilian spoke with feeling and I wanted to laugh because I was convinced she'd been listening to Prime Minister's Question Time on the radio and was about to say '*I can assure the honourable gentleman*'. '... I can assure the gentleman to my right,' she repeated, 'I am a superb skier, having just spent the last nine months in Cortina d'Ampezzo where I skied black runs daily.'

'Maybe you should have stayed there then and allow the kids rounds here to have a ski slope themselves.'

Freya, who had become increasingly fidgety as Lilian fought her battle, suddenly shot up out of her seat.

'Freya...' I put a warning hand on her sleeve but she shook me off.

'And *I* can assure the *gentleman*,' Freya looked at him with some disdain, 'who implied that all fourteen-year-olds want this damned silly ski slope, that I *am* fifty years younger than the last speaker and the very last thing I want round here is a dry ski slope.'

'You'd hang yourself skiing with that thing round your neck,' someone yelled, but was immediately turned on.

'Sshh, let her finish, let her have her say...'

'This is a beautiful place to live,' Freya continued. 'We have Meadowhall in Sheffield, if we want to shop. But you build on the land round here and you'll no longer have Norman's Meadow. We have the new Trinity centre in Leeds as well as the Trafford Centre in Manchester, both right on our doorsteps. How much shopping can a person do?'

'I don't think you've seen our latest plans, Miss…?' Edward Bamforth interrupted.

'*Ms* Beresford. Freya Beresford, but Freya will do.' I saw Karen Adams turn to look at me, and then say something obviously disparaging to the man with her.

'Freya, it's so good to have the future generation not only interested, but confident enough to get up and speak. We've totally abandoned the idea of a shopping centre. It would only have been a very small one anyway, but we agree with you – there are far too many shopping areas around here.'

'Oh.' For a moment Freya was nonplussed, but then came back fighting. 'But the ski slope stays?'

'Well, that's why we're here, to get the residents' views,' Edward said smoothly. 'And to outline some plans; no one has given us the opportunity yet—'

'But you don't deny you want to build three thousand houses on green belt?'

'Freya, you are very young. When you are older and want to get on the housing ladder, you'll be really grateful for our house-building programme.'

'Please don't patronise me, Mr Bamforth.'

'Freya…' I tugged warningly at her arm but she ignored me.

'I'd just like to ask one question and then I'll sit down and let someone else speak.'

'Thank the Lord for that,' Baldy muttered, and I gave him a filthy look.

'Do you deny, Mr Bamforth, that the idea of a ski slope has been put in place in order to bribe the local authority into granting planning permission on your land – our beautiful green belt land – for three thousand houses?'

'I really don't like the word *bribe*, young lady, and I'd like it retracted.' Edward Bamforth was getting angry. 'What we're doing is offering an exciting opportunity to develop the area, to build much-needed houses for this and for future – *your future* – generations on farmland that is becoming increasingly unviable in today's economic climate. If the community is with us, we will build a fabulous school for the new trust, combining Westenbury High and its three feeder schools into one big, community school.'

As heads nodded in agreement and murmurs of assent filled the hall, Edward Bamforth visibly relaxed and, ignoring Freya, who was now left awkwardly standing, asked for the lights in the hall to be dimmed as he and Xavier took it in turns to run through plans outlined in a slick, twenty minute PowerPoint presentation.

'Well done, lass.' Granddad Norman patted Freya's hand while Paula kissed her cheek and carefully replaced her emo fringe over her left eye.

'I'm very proud of you, darling,' I whispered. And I really was.

Xavier Bamforth, obviously skilled at presenting, spoke crisply and concisely, and soon had the majority of the audience eating out of his hand. The long round of applause he received was started and kept going by the elfin brunette who'd given my penis – not *literally* mine, but you get my drift – such a withering look in The Liquorist in Leeds, the night of the hen party. 'Well done, darling,' she mouthed at Xavier. 'You were marvellous.'

I nudged Harriet. 'Who's the brunette clapping like someone demented in a television audience?'

Harriet laughed. 'She *is* a bit over the top, isn't she? That's Ophelia Bamforth, Xavier's wife. Gorgeous, isn't she?'

For some reason, I suddenly felt terribly deflated. I gathered my bag, leaflets and various members of my family.

'Come on,' I said, trying to be jolly. 'Let's get the little revolutionary home. She'll never be up for school in the morning, otherwise.'

18

I Owe You One, God...

I was forty. Half my life gone already. I lay in bed on the following Sunday morning, taking stock of my life so far.

Mark had always said he'd been planning a great surprise for me for my big birthday back in April, and that I'd never guess what it was. Well, he'd been spot on there: ten out of ten for originality, Mark darling. April and my big birthday had come and gone and, he'd put off the much-lauded surprise until the summer break, and then, because I was so busy preparing for my new deputy headship, postponed it again until the October half-term holiday, which was now just a week away. I wonder what he *has* planned, I mused, as I pulled up the duvet over my head and decided I deserved another half-hour in my pit. A cruise? A trip to the Aurora Borealis? Or to that ice hotel up in the Arctic Circle? Was October too early for that? I did hope it hadn't been that: I hate being cold. God, can you imagine going to bed on ice? The very thought made me chilly, and I stretched out my legs searching for the hot-water bottle I'd started taking to bed to replace Mark's warm feet. Daft bint, I chastised myself, I was going nowhere with anyone. Let alone my husband whose biggest surprise had been to bugger off with my best friend.

Sod that for a game of soldiers. I sat up in bed and grabbed my iPad.

I searched around on the Internet until I found just what I wanted: Clementine's, just down the road from here. I'd met Clementine herself several times, her daughter being a pupil at Little Acorns. Under David Henderson's patronage, she'd built up a national reputation in a very short time and there was always a waiting list for her very select fine-dining restaurant, and her cookery school classes were booked as soon as they were advertised.

Bugger. Everything completely booked for months ahead. I'd suddenly had the brilliant idea of taking Fi and Clare out to thank them for all their friendship over the years.

There must be a way. I decided I'd get up, have a shower and, after breakfast, wander down the lane to see what turning up in person might achieve.

Tom was already up, squirting brown sauce into a pile of bacon sandwiches and, for once, reading the Sunday papers rather than deciphering exponentials and logarithms. To my utter shame, I'd still not talked to him about his – oh God, what did I call it? His sexuality? His preferences? Every time I'd been about to take the plunge, Freya had walked in on us or the phone had rung or he'd been so involved in a textbook he'd given me a murderous look for even daring to disturb him. Basically, I'd lost my bottle, asking him if he fancied a cup of tea and a brownie rather than if he fancied boys.

I made myself a coffee and sat down with him. The kitchen table, I saw, needed a good wipe, the milk bottle was on the table and the sauce bottle lid gunged up, but I made a big effort to ignore these and concentrate on my son instead. Bent over the 'Business and Money' section, his exposed neck between his short hair and sweatshirt appeared so vulnerable I wanted, needed, to plant a kiss there.

Tom looked up from the paper, surprised. 'What's up?'

'Nothing. Can't I kiss my son if I want?'

'Sure.' He went back to his paper but, realising I was still intent on getting his attention, he put the paper back down on the table and turned to me. 'OK, what is it?'

'I was just wondering how you are? I've been pretty well wrapped up in myself since... well, you know...'

'Since Dad did the dirty? Understandable.'

'I know I keep asking you, but has Dad been in touch with you? You won't upset me by telling me.'

Tom shook his head. 'He's texted me a few times. You know, to ask about college, to tell me he's put money into my account. To ask if I want a beer...'

'A beer? Since when have you been drinking beer? And since when has Dad been encouraging you?'

Tom gave a sound something between a laugh and obvious exasperation. 'Mum, for heaven's sake, I'm seventeen…'

'Only just. I saw Dad sent you a card.'

'I wasn't hiding it, Mum. I just didn't want to flaunt it. And no, it didn't say "from Dad and Tina" …'

I knew that; I'd had a jolly good look at it in his bedroom.

'… And I know you'll have had a jolly good look at it in my bedroom…'

Blimey, was the boy psychic?

'… so, pointless trying to say he hadn't sent me one.'

'Well, I hope he was generous with his birthday money?'

Tom looked slightly embarrassed. 'He was actually. He put five hundred pounds into my account.'

'What? That's ridiculous. Why did he give you so much?'

Tom shrugged. 'Driving lessons. That was the plan, if you remember, to have driving lessons for my seventeenth birthday.'

Oh God, of course. 'I'm so sorry, Tom, *I* should have been organising them for you. How about we get some booked in for half term next week?'

'Well, I'm away for half of it.'

'Away?'

'The maths taster thing at Cambridge?'

'Oh, gosh, yes.' My heart dropped. With Freya being chosen for some national netball training course in Newcastle, it meant I'd be spending quite a bit of the break alone, instead of swanning off with Mark on my surprise half-term treat. I needed to be upbeat about this. Here were my children being selected for two top national events and I was just feeling miserable.

'Tom...?'

'Hmm?'

'You know the evening you saw Dad with Auntie Tina and you realised what was going on?'

Tom looked wary. 'Yes?'

'Well, why were *you* there?'

'Why not?'

I felt my heart begin to thump. I took a deep breath. 'Tom, The Blue Ball out on the Manchester Road is a gay pub.' He didn't say anything, but looked down at the table and began peeling the gunge off the sauce bottle. 'Tom?'

'What?'

'Dad *saw* you there that night.'

'Oh.' Tom's neck went very pink and, as he rolled the solidified sauce gunge into a ball and flicked it across the table, I noticed how his fingernails were bitten down almost to the quick.

Well, here goes, I might as well bite the bullet. 'Do you think *you* might be gay, Tom? I mean, if you are, that's fine, it's not a problem, no one minds about these things these days...'

'Oh, for heaven's sake, Mum, you'll be telling me next your *best friend* is gay.' Tom was cross.

'I'm sorry, darling, I'm just worried for you.'

'Oh, so you *do* think being gay is a problem? All that stuff about it not being a problem is just... is just bollocks.'

'Darling, if you're gay I'd rather know...'

'Mum, I *don't* know. All right?' Tom suddenly got up from the table, pushing away his chair with such force it nearly fell backwards. 'I'm off to do some work. OK?'

I knew better than to make an awkward situation worse with Tom by harping on; leaving him to cool down was a far better strategy. So with Tom's anger still ringing in my ears, I donned my trainers and walked the fifteen minutes across the fields to Clementine's. It had rained a lot the previous week and the ground was sodden, the grass long. The fields, I conceded, were beginning to look unkempt as if, with the uncertainty of their future, no one could be bothered with them. A couple of the dry-stone walls had lost some of their stones and, whereas before, the farmers would have been out almost immediately to build them back up, rearranging the pieces in the way that only those with the knowledge and experience of these structures could, the stones now lay forlorn on the fields like extracted teeth, leaving gaping holes in the wall. Granddad Norman always loved dry-stone walls, had always pointed them out to me when I was a little girl on one of our walks to gather blackberries or elderflowers for his home-made wine. He'd explained a wall's load-bearing façade of interlocking stones, stroking its rough side almost reverentially and always picking up fallen stones, easing them back home like the final piece of a difficult jigsaw puzzle. I knew that if the wall lost a stone it was a bit like a dropped stitch when knitting:

ignore the lost stitch and you'd soon have a big hole. The farmers, it occurred to me on this dull and misty October Sunday morning, as I climbed stiles and wished I'd put on wellingtons instead of my now soaked trainers, had seemingly abandoned their knitting.

At ten o'clock on a Sunday morning, the reception area of Clementine's appeared deserted, the only sound the rather jolly cacophony of church bells belting out from nearby All Hallows, Westenbury ringing to call its flock to order. I was just about to ring my own bell for attention when I heard laughter coming from what I presumed was the kitchen area. A door opened and out came a little woman enveloped in a huge white pinny, flour up her arms and smudges of the same on her nose. She started when she saw me and then laughed when I said I was after a table for the coming week. She soon gave me short thrift, telling me in no uncertain terms that tables at Clementine's were like gold dust and the earliest available one was at least six weeks into the future and did I want to book that? Deflated, I shook my head, and was about to leave, when Clementine Ahern herself came down the stairs that led into the reception area.

'Oh, Mrs Beresford? You're out and about early.' Clementine's chef was heavily pregnant with her second child, her tunic strained across her abdomen, and she smoothed an escaped tendril of dark hair behind her ears as she spoke. 'Has Betty here, been able to help you?'

'I've just been telling her, she'll have to get with the rest of them in the queue – we're fully booked until Christmas.'

'Betty, back to the kitchen,' Clementine ordered. 'Go on, I'll sort Mrs Beresford.'

Betty sniffed, raised her eyebrows and made her way back from where she'd just come. Once the door had closed behind the woman, Clementine turned back to me.

'Sorry about that: Betty's been with me almost since I started and she does like to lord it a bit over us lesser mortals. Sorry I wasn't around when you arrived: I don't seem to be able to stop peeing at the moment – oops, sorry, too much information from the cook; it'll put you off eating with us.' She grinned. 'Are you wanting to book a table?'

'Well, I was, but I looked online, saw you had nothing available so thought I'd actually have a walk down here myself and double-check in person. It was silly really...'

Clementine frowned. 'Sorry, no, Betty was right when she said we're fully booked up.' She turned to a large leather-bound book behind the reception desk and spent a good minute turning pages. 'Honestly, there's nothing until January.'

'January? Goodness, it's only October.'

'I know, but with Christmas just around the corner...'

'Oh, don't remind me.' Any thoughts of Christmas had been resolutely squashed: how were we going to spend Christmas Day without Mark?

'Oh well...' I turned to go, pulling on my gloves, conscious that my wet trainers were making me feel even more miserable.

'Was it a special occasion?'

'Well, only that it was my big birthday six months ago and I've not yet really celebrated.'

'I bet you've been too busy with your new job. I have to say, Mrs Beresford, Allegra absolutely loves you. She comes home after one of your assemblies and relates the whole thing back to us. She had us in stitches telling us the balloon story…'

'Really? How lovely.' I could feel myself go pink with pleasure.

'Yes, and we sat through a retelling of "Pandora's Box" last week and now know *all* about the International Space station. We have to go out every night and wait for it to go over. "Mrs Beresford says, and she knows *all* about it…"' Clementine affected a child's bossy voice, '"… that it's more *punctual* than the number 457 bus into Midhope."'

I laughed. 'Well at least someone's listening to my ramblings.'

Clementine smiled. 'Seriously, I think you're doing a great job. Don't get me wrong, I really liked Mrs Theobold, but the kids were a bit frightened of her. They didn't call her *The Fearbold* for nothing.'

I smiled somewhat wryly. 'Maybe that's what a good head teacher should command.'

'What? Fear? No, sorry not with you there.' Clementine smiled again and rubbed her abdomen. 'Ow, little footballer in here, I reckon… Anyway, I had meant to call in to school and just say how happy Allegra is with you. Sorry you've ended up coming to me rather than me to you.' She glanced at my wet feet. 'Have you walked? I didn't realise you were local?'

'Yes, I've always lived round here. My own kids were under *The Fearbold's* rule.'

'So, I assume you know what's going on with the Bamforth Estate then?' Clementine frowned. 'We just can't let them put three thousand houses onto these wonderful fields.'

'Well, if they get their way, your kids will have a brand-new community school to go to.'

'Sorry, not interested. I don't want a through-school where children just go to one school from four to eighteen. I know it's the new way of thinking, but I like small, village schools. Little Acorns – sorry, bloody daft name for a primary school – is perfect as it is.'

'I doubt it. It'll be Westenbury Community Trust School, or some such name. Right, I need to go. I'm sure you're really busy.'

'Very. Oh God, need to pee again. Look, lovely to meet you in the flesh as it were. Both Rafe, my husband, and I are totally against any new development so I'm sure our paths will be crossing if there's a fight about the school and the land ahead.'

'Well,' I said, '*I'm* not going to take it lying down. I'm really not.'

Walking back home past All Hallows, Westenbury, I made the sudden decision to join the service. This was my church, my community, after all. Feeling slightly ashamed that, although the church was just a fifteen-minute walk away from Tower View Avenue, I'd only ever been one of the 'Christmas Eve and Easter Sunday'-type brethren and could count on one hand the number of times I'd actually sat through a Sunday service.

Ben Carey, the vicar, was in full flow as I opened the ancient wooden door and crept into a pew on the very back row. There were several of my pupils in the congregation and they'd turned to look as the door creaked and then gone a bit pink as they saw their head teacher, dressed in old Barbour and trainers, sitting self-consciously at the back.

I smiled, but bent my head, hoping not to attract any more attention.

'We all have our ups and downs,' Ben was saying, 'and some of these are much, much worse than others.'

Tell me about it, Ben.

'But when we go through bad times and we recover from them, we should celebrate that we got through it. No matter how bad it may seem, there's always something beautiful that you can find.'

Really? I was feeling pretty bad, sitting in that church, but raised my head and looked around. Come on, God, help me out here: I'm forty; my husband's left me; I've lost my best friend; my son is struggling with his sexuality; my village is about to be covered in concrete. Oh, and my wonderful idea of taking out my friends for dinner has been scuppered. I closed my eyes and tried to be positive.

The next minute I felt a movement by my side and a little hand was put into mine. Surprised, I opened my eyes and looked to my left. Matilda Hogarth, one of my three-year-olds in nursery, sat there holding my hand and smiling up at me, her sturdy little legs, encased in their Sunday-best white tights and shiny red shoes, swinging from the pew.

'I love my school,' she whispered solemnly, gazing up at me. 'And I love you too.'

The sun chose that minute to shine through the stained-glass window to my left and the aisle and my pew were decorated with kaleidoscopic lozenges of light.

'Thanks, God,' I said, silently, smiling down at Matilda and squeezing her hand. 'I owe you one.'

19

Thou Shalt Go to the Restaurant...

God continued to be on my side. On the Monday morning, just before school started, the guardian angel of mid-week restaurant tables had appeared to me in a telephone call: 'Lo, blessed of all women. Rejoice for thou art highly favoured. Thou shalt go to Clementine's after all.'

OK, in actuality, Clementine Ahern had rung me. 'Mrs Beresford? We've had a cancellation for Thursday evening. Would you like the table?'

'Gosh, yes. Yes, please.' I did a little on-the-spot dance.

'The only problem is that it's a table for six and sort of around a corner by itself, and I think you wanted it just for three? It's no great problem, we can bring in a smaller table...'

'That's really kind. I mean, you could have sold it to a party of six, I bet.'

'Well, yes, we could. But I'd like you to have it. Seven o'clock? Is that OK?'

'Super.' I'd already checked with Clare and Fi, once I returned from church the day before, that they were free during the week and said I'd go ahead and book somewhere probably down in Midhope town centre. This was much, much better and I began to feel really excited about not only eating at Clementine's but being able to show Clare and Fi just how much I appreciated their loyalty and friendship. There hadn't been a week gone by when one of them hadn't rung to see how I was. *Really* how I was.

'Good things come to those who wait,' Jean smiled, when I popped into her office on the way to morning assembly and told her my good luck. 'We had to wait seven months for a table there. I was nearer my *next* birthday by the time I celebrated my last.'

I was on a bit of a high and my planned assembly, which had involved nursery rhyme characters doing good deeds – think All the King's Horses and all the King's Men trying to put the Fat One back together again – necessarily went off at a bit of a tangent when I realised, on questioning them, that the vast majority of the kids had no real knowledge of any nursery rhyme characters apart from Little Miss Muffet and that spider.

'Right, children,' I said, 'shall we see if the *teachers* can do any better?' And they certainly could. The kids turned, open-mouthed as Kath Beaumont knew who rode to Banbury Cross, Debs Stringer recited 'Ding Dong Dell' and Sheila Wilson knew it was Doctor Foster on his way to Gloucester as well as who was running through the town in his nightgown. Harriet Westmoreland actually sang the whole of 'The Big Ship Sails Through the Alley, Alley O', the kids riotously joining in with '*on the last day of September.*'

Karen Adams didn't. 'We'll never settle them after this,' she muttered to Kimberley Crawford as she marched her eight-year-olds out of the hall, fingers planted firmly on their lips.

'Congratulations,' Harriet whispered as she led her own class back to their room. 'Must be the only time I've heard cocks, pussies *and* willies all put in an appearance in a Monday morning assembly.'

'New connotations,' I laughed. '"Ride a Cock Horse", "Ding Dong Dell, Pussy's in the Well", and "Wee Willy Winky" were total innocents when I was a child. I'd like every kid to be as au fait with them as we were.'

'Right, Mrs Beresford.' Stan the caretaker appeared at the door of my office just as the children had returned to their classes after the lunchbreak. He seemed uncharacteristically hesitant. Shy even. 'Do you want to come and take a look at my goolies?' When I just stared at him, he went on hurriedly. 'It's OK, love, I've not shown them to the kiddies yet.'

Yet? Heaven forfend.

'If you come with me down to the cellar, I'll let you give 'em the once over before you decide if you want them or not. They might not be the size you had in mind.'

Pushing seventy, Stan was sandy-haired, balding and not that much taller than I am. He'd been at Little Acorns for ever and should probably have been put out to grass years ago. He was a walking medical textbook, full of real and imaginary complaints – his most vocal complaints being about his wife, Vera – and his 'rheumatics' were the stuff of legend on which he would expound endlessly to anyone unlucky enough to be cornered by him.

'Erm... Stan...' I continued to stare at him, my face red.

'Come on, I've not had me dinner yet and the missus won't be too happy if she knows I'm showing you 'em at all. She's a bit funny like that, doesn't like me showing off my pride and joy, if you get my meaning...?' He headed off down the corridor, glancing back occasionally to see that I was following him, until he stopped at the huge bolted wooden door that led down by way of a stone staircase to the cellars. In Victorian times, Mrs Theobold had informed me on my initial visit to the school, the boiler and great piles of coke to feed it had filled the cellar, but though now its cavernous space was mainly used for storage, I'd never actually ventured down there.

Stan drew back the bolts and we descended the flight of stairs. 'Er, just keep that door open, Stan, will you?' I muttered as I followed him down. 'Where are the lights?'

Stan tutted and shook his head. 'You'll get a much better feel of 'em if I don't actually put the lights on,' he said and then stood aside so that I went in front of him.

'A feel...?' I was about to turn and make a sharp exit back up the steps and then I saw Stan's goolies. 'Oh, my goodness, Stan. Look at these. What beauties!

These are wonderful...' I stood, speechless, as my eyes became accustomed to the gloom and feasted upon myriad ghouls and ghosts, wafting gracefully from the ceiling, iridescent with some sort of luminous paint. They weren't a bit frightening, but were smiley, friendly, Hallowe'en characters that the kids would love. There must have been ten or more Casper the Friendly Ghosts and a whole family of Allan Ahlberg's *Funnybones* characters – I knew the younger children had already been treated to a performance of Big Skeleton, Little Skeleton and Dog Skeleton by a travelling theatre last term and loved the books – and big orange and silver smiling pumpkin faces.

'Do you like them?' Stan asked shyly. 'The missus said I should grow up and stop wasting my time.'

'I can't believe you've spent your spare time creating these for us!' I said in delight. 'The kids will love them for our Hallowe'en day. You're very talented, Stan.'

'Aye, well, I always wanted to go to art school, but well, you know how it is...' He trailed off. 'So, if you're happy with them, if you think they're not too big, I can get them hung up in the hall over the weekend. They won't glow as well as down here, of course, but once we turn the lights out up there, they won't be too bad.'

'Stan,' I smiled, 'they're the best goolies I've ever had the good fortune to come across.'

My euphoria at getting a table for the three of us lasted all the way to Thursday evening.

'Whoah, you're a bit done up,' Freya whistled as she looked up from her laptop when I called in to her bedroom to say goodnight. 'Are you sure you're only meeting Auntie Clare and Auntie Fi?' She smirked. 'I bet you're on your way to meet Wayne the Wasp Murderer, aren't you? Having a night of passion with a bit of a sting in the tail?' She guffawed, looking me up and down. 'You could do worse, you know. At least we wouldn't have to worry about another wasp invasion... and it would show Dad you're still up for it.'

'Up for it? What a revolting expression.' I peered over Freya's shoulder at her screen. 'What *are* you doing?'

'Paula and I are organising a demonstration against the Bamforth development, in Norman's Meadow. I'm just trying to create some posters and flyers.'

'Oh, right... Well done. Can't I be part of it?' I felt a bit left out that the pair of them were getting on with it without consulting me.

Freya looked at me and frowned. 'Do you think you should? As the local head teacher, wouldn't it be politicising your position? Shouldn't you be neutral?'

It was my turn to look at Freya. Here she was, at just fourteen, so full of idealism and using fancy words; I was sure, at her age, I hadn't a clue what politicising even meant. At fourteen, my thoughts would all have been on Kevin Costner in *Robin Hood Prince of Thieves*. As well as the knowledge, with Freddie Mercury dying, that I'd *never* be able to have sex because I'd be *bound* to catch Aids.

'Of course I can get involved,' I said. 'I went to the meeting the other evening, didn't I?'

'Well, yes,' she said. 'But you weren't putting forward any *views*, were you? It was just a public information meeting. What *we're* planning, Paula and me...'

'Paula and I...'

Freya tutted. 'What Paula and *I* are planning, might be too controversial for someone in your position.'

'Oh...'

'Are you ready, Mum?' Tom shouted from the bottom of the stairs. 'I'll walk down with you and then you won't have to drive and you can have a drink.'

I leaned over the banister. 'In these shoes?'

Tom waved my wellies at me. 'Come on, put these on and put your heels in your bag. You can get a taxi back.'

It was the first time since I'd broached the 'g' word with Tom the previous Sunday that he'd spoken more than a couple of muttered words at me.

It was a beautiful evening, cold but clear, an incredible full, Hunter's moon following us down the lane as we walked. Neither of us said a thing for the first few hundred yards.

'Look, Tom,' I eventually managed. 'I'm really sorry about what I said to you last Sunday morning. It has nothing to do with me and it was crass and inappropriate for me to ask you.'

Tom didn't say anything for a while. 'Mum, I don't know what I am. I don't seem to be able to join in with all the lads at college when they keep going on about... about, you know... girls and things. I mean, I really like girls. I actually prefer their company to the lads. But...

but I don't *fancy* them. I've tried. I've tried to think about them in... you know, in *that* way...'

I could feel Tom's embarrassment and knew why he'd offered to walk me down the lane. He'd wanted to talk but without my seeing his face as he spoke.

'Tom, darling, you're very young. There's loads of time to start fancying girls and things...'

'Now you're patronising me.'

'If I am, I really don't mean to. I just want to be here for you; to listen if and when you need to talk.'

'The thing is... the thing is...' Tom stopped, unable to go on. 'OK, the thing is I do really like someone...'

'And he's male?' I asked gently.

Tom breathed deeply, and picked up his pace. 'Yes.'

'And you were with him at The Blue Ball when Dad saw you?'

'Yes.'

'How old is he, Tom?'

'My age; well a year older. He's in his second year of A levels.'

I breathed a sigh of relief.

'So, do you see him often? Where do you meet up with him?'

'He's part of the crowd I hang around with. You know, Jenny's friends?' Jenny and Tom had been friends from being six at Little Acorns and, even though they'd gone to different schools at the age of eleven, had continued to be so. She was as much a part of Tom's life as Freya's netball gang were a part of hers.

'Jenny got us together. She thought we'd have a lot in common...'

'Right, OK. And so, you are, er, *together* then?'

'The thing is—' Tom stopped abruptly as Clare and Fi fell out of a taxi and shouted at us from across the road.

'Cassie, yoo-hoo we're here,' Fi shouted. 'Come on, we've already had a drink at Clare's place. You're one down...'

'Two down, actually,' Clare said, hugging Tom. 'How's my favourite seventeen-year-old? You get more gorgeous every time I see you. Must be all that algebra.'

Tom grinned. 'Enjoy yourselves. Don't forget, Mum has to work tomorrow... Oh my God, Auntie Clare. What have you done to your face?'

Tom and I both stared at Clare, who had, despite an obvious attempt to cover it with concealer and foundation, a beautifully defined black eye.

'Oh, it's nothing,' she smiled. 'The ironing board fell off its hook on the back of the door and I was under it.'

'Really?' Tom peered at her through the dark. 'You must have one hell of an ironing board.'

'Come on.' Fi was impatient. 'I don't want to miss one second of this treat.'

Clementine's, until a couple of years previously, had been a country house – one of the few round here, along with David Henderson's manor house across the fields, *not* part of the Bamforth Estate. The gardens, where Clementine held private parties in the open air when the weather was good, stretched down to a tennis court and a quaint summerhouse, which apparently, for an exorbitant fee, was available for loved-up couples to be waited on, pampered and treated to the delicacies on which Clementine's had built its reputation.

Clare, who had done her research, explained all this as we were shown into the Orangery by a young waiter dressed in black jeans and black T-shirt emblazoned with the Clementine's logo in orange. Just a handful of tables were laid for dinner. It was all perfect: relaxed, not stuffy; inviting, yet not overwhelming.

'I've been so excited about this,' Fi said, gazing round the Orangery. 'How on earth did you get a table at such short notice?'

'I'm not sure, actually. Apparently, Allegra, Clementine's daughter, loves being at Little Acorns and that gave me a few Brownie points. There was a cancellation – and here we are.' I turned to Clare who, despite the black eye, was looking radiant. 'So, what *really* happened to your face?'

'What really happened? I told you – the ironing board fell on me.' She paused as our waiter appeared with a bottle of Moët. 'Gosh, champers as well, Cass? Actually, let me get this.'

'From Clementine,' the waiter grinned. 'For your birthday.'

I was beginning to feel a bit of a fake. After all, my birthday had been six months previously. But to hell with it, I'd not really celebrated it at the time. 'My birthday was actually quite a while ago.'

'I know – Clementine said.'

I suddenly had the feeling that Clementine must know all about Mark leaving me for Tina. I guess I was still a topic of gossip in the village.

Fi stroked the waiter's arm in such a way that, had it been a man stroking the female equivalent, he'd have been thrown out for being a dirty old man. 'And we get such a lovely young man to wait on us too.' She peered at his name badge. 'Patrick. Thanks, Patrick…'

Clare grinned. 'Stop flirting with the children, Fi…'

'OK, as long as you tell us who smacked you.' Fi took a long drink of her champagne. 'God, that's bliss. If I had my way – and the money – I'd drink champagne like this every day. So, come on, Clare, that's no ironing board black eye.'

'Well, Last Stagger has probably had it.'

Fi and I stared at her. 'What do you mean? What's happened?'

'Well, would you let *your* fiancé have a stag do arranged by a woman who nicks the stags into the bargain?' Clare pulled a wry face and emptied her glass of champagne. She poured another. 'I'm going to be splashed all over the Sunday papers.'

'Oh, Clare. She found out? How?'

'Rageh told her.' Clare looked at both of us. 'He stopped the wedding.'

'But the stag do was over six weeks ago. Shouldn't they have been married by now?'

Clare smiled. 'Gone are the days when men go out on their stag do the night before the wedding. You know, they used to turn up at the church stinking of booze and with a hangover. Nowadays, stag and hen dos are very often months ahead of the actual wedding, especially when a trip abroad's included.'

'But that poor girl… Oh, Clare. How could you?'

'I didn't, Cassie.'

'Didn't what?'

'I refused to have anything to do with him. I know you don't believe me. Once he'd gone back to Sheffield, after you saw him in The Botanist in Leeds with me, I wouldn't answer his calls. For once in my life, I really tried to do the right thing. I knew – well *you* obviously know, Cassie – how *I'd* feel if I'd been just about to marry him and then he'd fallen in love with someone else.'

We stopped talking as Patrick the waiter arrived with a sage shortbread and goat's cheese *amuse-bouche*.

'Utter heaven,' Fi murmured, closing her eyes in ecstasy. 'Go on, Clare,' she said through another mouthful. 'Get to the black eye. I assume that's the bride-to-be's work?'

Clare nodded ruefully. 'For the last six weeks, Rageh has texted me, emailed me, arrived back on my doorstep...'

'Fully clothed this time, I hope?' Fi said drily.

'I don't know,' Clare said seriously. 'I didn't see him. I knew he was there, but I refused to go down. He left a note.'

'And?'

'He said he'd broken off his engagement. He'd known it wasn't right even before he met me. That's one of the reasons he didn't want a stag do: the whole thing seemed like a farce to him.'

'So?'

'So, I still didn't get in touch with him. I didn't want to be responsible for breaking up a marriage even before it began. I can't tell you how hard it's been. I needed to know that even if he couldn't have me, he wouldn't go back to her.'

'And he hasn't?' I looked at Clare's animated face and knew the answer.

'No. He arrived in the office on Monday just as I was locking up. Said that even if I wasn't interested in him, I'd done him a favour by giving him the strength to break off the relationship and if I really *wasn't* interested, he was going to leave the area.'

'So, what happened then?' Fiona's eyes were wide. 'Did he grab you and carry you upstairs?'

Clare laughed ruefully. 'Well, to be honest, that's probably what would have happened. Unfortunately, an ex-fiancée got in the way.'

'Oh, my goodness...' My hand flew to my mouth.

'She'd followed him in the car.'

'Really? Down the A629 and the M1?' Fi was doubtful. 'I've never understood those films where someone is following someone. Surely, they'd recognise the car and the driver? Or, if they were keeping their distance, they'd lose it. I know I tried to follow Matt once to some farm in Sherburn-in-Elmet to look at some heifers. Got totally lost: ended up in Harrogate...'

I giggled. 'For God's sake, Fi, let her finish.'

Clare grimaced. 'She walked into the office, saw him kissing me, thumped him and smacked me. I don't blame her a bit.'

'No, neither do I,' I said. 'I'd have probably killed you.'

'I love him,' Clare said simply. 'He's not slept at his flat for three days. I've never, ever, felt like this about any man. I'm sorry, I know what I've done is awful...'

'You've fallen in love,' Fi said gently. 'It had to happen one day.'

Patrick laid our starters in front of us. All three of us had gone for the hot-smoked salmon and celeriac remoulade, served in exquisite dainty portions and with the primary effect of making us stop talking.

'Well, she's gone to the Sunday papers, determined to get her revenge by ruining my business. There were a couple of reporters round yesterday and a photographer taking photos of the outside of the office. No one's going to touch Last Stagger after this. Anyway, enough of me. This is *your* celebration, Cassie. Cheers.' Clare leaned over to kiss me, then held her glass to mine.

'This is divine, isn't it?' I put down my knife and fork with some reluctance.

We were all silent for a minute as we took in the exquisite food. Every sense – taste, smell and texture – was highlighted in turn as we ate.

After a while I said, 'Fi?'

'Hmm?'

'Did you love Matt with that all-consuming love Clare has just described for Rageh?'

'Did I? Or do I?'

'Both.'

Fi laughed. 'I must have done to leave my life in Leeds for a ramshackle farmhouse in the sticks and a load of cow shit.' She paused. 'And do I, still? Well, when he's not bloody *hovering* with the rest of the menagerie I live with, well, yes. I adore the great lump.'

Clare frowned at Fi. 'Sorry, Fi, I know *I've* just been going on and on about Rageh – and I promise, that's it for now – but the last thing Cassie wants to hear, especially on her birthday celebration, is us going on about love.'

'No, really, I want to know,' I smiled, starting on the bottle of Sauvignon Blanc Clare had ordered. 'Fi, tell me what it was like when you met Matt.'

She looked puzzled. 'What do you mean?'

'How did you feel?'

'As though my whole body had turned inside out. I didn't want to sleep because reality was even better than any dream.'

'Gosh, that's poetic,' Clare laughed.

'She asked,' Fi said seriously.

'What about you and Mark?' Clare asked, stroking my hand. 'Are you able to talk about it? Quite understand if you aren't.'

I frowned. 'You see, hearing you two... oh, it doesn't matter... really...'

'What? Is it too painful? Oh, this is silly, stop it,' Clare ordered. 'Tell us a joke instead, Fi.'

I frowned. 'No, really.' I took a long drink of the deliciously cold wine and, emboldened by it, said, 'I've never felt it.'

Clare and Fi both looked up and stopped eating. 'What? Felt what?'

I screwed up my face. 'You know, that butterflies-in-your-stomach thing.'

'Yes, you did,' Clare said, gently. 'With Mark, you did. You might hate him for what he's done now – and who can blame you – but you mustn't lose sight of what you both felt for each other all these years.'

I took a deep breath. 'I loved him; I wanted him to be the father of my children. I wanted a detached house like my cousin, Davina. I wanted tidy drawers, and coat hangers that held one dress rather than four tops and two pairs of trousers scrunched up underneath. He ticked all the boxes.' I laughed. 'You know I had a notebook from being eight years old, for heaven's sake, with *The Man I'm Going to Marry* written in there in my very best handwriting. Even then I had written down: tall, blue eyes, smiley face, no tattoos and wearing a suit. Tick, tick, tick, tick. And tick.' I laughed again, but sadly. 'Mark ticked all the boxes,' I took a deep breath, 'but never once have my insides turned inside out; never once did I want to slide down the wall.'

'Slide down the wall?' Clare laughed.

'A girl I lived with at college once came back home and literally slid down the wall...'

'Too much gin?'

'... slid down the wall with lust and love. She couldn't stand up.'

Fi and Clare both nodded, obviously in empathy with that almost-forgotten flatmate's gymnastics.

'Would I have wanted to marry Mark if he hadn't been able to give me what I'd aspired to all the years I was growing up with Paula?' I asked. 'I mean, if he'd lived in the cottage next to ours and didn't have a white-collar job and a smart car, would I have felt the same way about him?' I shook my head, ashamed at my own thoughts. Had I married Mark because I felt he could give me what I yearned for and not because of who he was? 'And,' I said sadly, 'you know, never once was I willing to give Mark up, like you insisted on giving up Rageh, Clare, because you loved him more than you loved yourself.'

20

If Mary Kingsley Could Do It, So Can I...

'So, Cassie, half term coming up. What are you going to do with it?' We'd got to the pudding stage where you're far too full to actually eat any dessert but, because it's a set three-course meal, you'd be daft not to.

'Talking of desserts,' I said, 'one of my kids wrote this week: "And Jesus wandered for forty days in the *dessert*..."'

'The Black Forest?' Fi quipped idly. 'I always remember Rosie doing some homework about the water cycle and she wrote: "The raindrops join together and so become *lager* before falling from the sky..."' She laughed again. 'That'd be all right, wouldn't it?'

'I reckon you need to get away for a week,' Clare said. 'Stop thinking about kids and school for a while. I'm assuming you're carrying on as acting head after the break?'

'Yes, it would seem so. David Henderson has asked me if I'm OK to keep going until Christmas.'

'And are you?'

'Definitely. I love it. I'll really resent it when they advertise for a proper head and someone comes to take my place.'

'Can't you just tell them you'll carry on? If they're happy with you, what's the problem?'

'Oh, it's all got to be done properly. You know: advertised, short-listed, references, presentations, interviews.'

'Well, you'd apply, wouldn't you? You'd walk it, surely? The staff like you, don't they?'

'Most of them, I think. Just the dreadful Karen Adams who seems to have it in for me.'

'You do know that I know her?' Fi said. 'I didn't realise it, but her husband's a second cousin of Matt's. He's a developer – he'll be after any building contract he can get. He'll be working hand in glove with the Bamforths, I reckon.'

'Oh really? Well, that explains a lot. She and her husband were at the Bamforth Estate presentation the other night... Oh, hang on, there are two of my staff here now.'

I pushed my chair back and stood up as Harriet and Grace popped their heads round the Orangery door. 'Hello, you two, are you treating yourselves as well?'

'In a way,' Harriet smiled. 'Clem's our mate so we've come round for a drink and nibbles in the kitchen. We do it once a month – Clem is usually so busy, we come to her rather than her coming out with us. And occasionally, if she's very busy, we help out doing a bit of waitressing.'

'Come and join us in here,' I said. 'We're at the pudding and coffee stage. We can shift round a bit.' Fi and Clare were already moving their chairs. 'Has Clementine finished in the kitchen?'

'I think so, but she might not want us to intrude,' Grace said.

'Actually,' Clare said, 'I'd really like to meet her. I've been thinking of popping in to see if I can sort something for my hens.'

'Your hens?' Grace frowned. 'As in free-range eggs and chickens, you mean?'

Clare laughed. 'No, I organise hen parties... well I *did*.'

'You *do*,' I said firmly. I turned to Harriet and Grace who were still standing in the doorway. 'Clare has two companies, one called Henotheism and one called Last Stagger. Look, I'd really like it if the three of you would join us. Go and have a word with Clementine.'

'It's Cassie's big birthday celebration. And she's your boss, so you have to do as she says,' Fi laughed. 'Come on, let's order another bottle of wine.'

Ten minutes later and the six of us were in full flow. Clementine had changed out of her working gear and, because the table was away from the rest of the diners, was happy to sit with us.

'Sarah, my mother, is in charge of the kitchen tonight,' she said as she took the weight off her feet, 'so I'm allowed some time off.'

'How will Edward Bamforth's plans affect you, Clementine?' I asked.

'Oh, don't mention that man's name in here,' she tutted. 'Rafe, my husband, is furious about what he's proposing. We all are.'

'Well, my daughter and my mother are planning a demonstration in Norman's Meadow after half term. Knowing my mother, she'll probably be trying to get in touch with that chap that became famous for demonstrating against the Newbury Bypass. She spent some time with him back in – when was it? I was away at university, so it must have been in the mid-1990s.'

'Swampy,' Clare said. 'Wasn't he called Swampy? Did you know David Cameron's mother was the magistrate that convicted him at one point?'

'Oh?' Clem was really interested. 'Gosh, that would be good if your mother could get hold of *him*. It would really get us some publicity and persuade the council not to give planning permission for all this building they're after.'

'Don't be so sure that everyone's against the plans,' I said. 'A lot of people are really for the Trust building a huge new school. And a dry ski slope would bring new jobs and tourism to the area. It's what people want – progress.'

'But not in *my* back yard, Cassie,' Clem smiled. 'I'm afraid I'm as guilty as the next woman of Nimbyism.'

'Are you sure you'd not rather be by yourselves?' Clementine asked fifteen minutes later as Patrick brought in our puddings. 'We can away back to the kitchen now we've put the world to rights, and leave you in peace.'

'Not at all,' Fi said. 'We're just trying to persuade Cassie to take a holiday next week instead of going into school, as she invariably will do.'

'That's what head teachers do,' I protested. 'Anyway, where would I go?'

Pudding was just as delicious as the rest of the meal. While Fi, Clare and I sighed greedily over the hot chocolate fondant with Westenbury blackberry and thyme ice cream, a honey and lemon mess and a burnt-apple soufflé, Clementine and the other two drank tea and nibbled at a cheese board Clem sent to the kitchen for.

'So, Cassie, a holiday?' Fi said, once she'd finished her pudding. 'You need one.'

'God, Fi, you're like a dog with a bone.' I snapped. 'Look, I may have enough money to jet off somewhere at the moment, but who's to say Mark won't suddenly stop putting money into my account? You hear about separated couples arguing so much over money that the majority of it goes to the solicitors and they end up with nothing.' I shivered slightly. My biggest nightmare was losing the security I'd gained through marrying Mark. I didn't want to go back to living in a run-down, damp, rented cottage like the one I'd grown up in.

'So, what's happening about solicitors?' Clare asked. 'Did you make an appointment with that guy I suggested?'

I frowned at Clare and shook my head slightly. This was the last thing I wanted to be discussing at my birthday celebration, but particularly in front of members of my staff and one of my pupil's mother. 'No, not yet. I've been too busy, you know that.'

The truth was I'd totally avoided any of the next practical steps with regard to separation and divorce. I didn't want to be divorced from Mark. I was still hoping he would come back. Paula and Clare had both urged me to protect my position *re* finances, the house and of course the kids, but the children were, I reckoned, old enough to make their own minds up about seeing Mark and where they wanted to live. And, in a nutshell, they didn't want to see Mark because of what he'd done to me, and because going to stay with their father for the weekend would mean staying with Tina, too. I'd suggested they meet him for lunch – they were too old to be doing the weekend trip to the zoo thing or having a Happy Meal at McDonald's – and, while Freya had agreed to meet up with him as long as he wasn't with Tina, Tom just didn't appear interested at the moment. While I knew it wasn't very noble of me, I was secretly pleased that they both appeared to be getting on with their lives without him. And of course they wanted to live at home. With me.

'A holiday then, Cassie?' Fi wasn't going to let it go.

'Where do you suggest I go?' I sighed.

'Take your two to – oh, I don't know – Greece or somewhere. It'll still be warm down in the south. Crete, maybe?'

'Tom's off to Cambridge on some maths taster course and Freya is on a netball course in Newcastle.'

'Well, take your mother.'

'Paula?' I was horrified at the very thought. 'If I go off anywhere, I need her here to look after Freya once she's home mid-week. Anyway,' I said crossly, 'I'm more than capable of sorting myself out.'

'Do it then,' Fi said.

'I will,' I retorted, crossly.

And I did.

So that's why, two days later, ridiculously early on the Saturday morning, I found myself shivering on Midhope train station awaiting the first trans-Pennine train to Manchester airport. I'd been up since 3 a.m., the taxi had tooted its arrival at three thirty, and now, at 4 a.m., I was beginning to wonder what the hell I was doing, all by myself, on the way to Mexico. I must be mad. I'd only booked it to prove to Fi and Clare that I could. I was considering creeping back home and holing up with a sun lamp and several family-sized packs of nachos when the airport train pulled up in front of me and I was on my way.

I slept for most of the ten-hour flight to Cancún, waking only to eat a plastic lunch and watch fifteen minutes of some children's Ninja Turtles film.

Feeling dishevelled, and suddenly very homesick, I waited for my lone case, heaving it off the carousel with the other luggage retrievers and then headed towards the transfer coaches.

It was raining. Warm rain, I concede, but still wet. The sort that frizzes up your hair and has you running for hair balm and a pair of GHDs. Bugger, I'd left mine on the kitchen table where'd I'd put them so as not to forget them.

'I didn't think it rained in Mexico,' the Mancunian sitting behind me shouted to the rep, Sadie, who was just about to launch into rep-speak.

'Well, not very often,' Sadie smiled. The smile didn't quite reach her heavily mascaraed eyes. She bent to scratch a sturdy leg beneath her American Tan tights.

'It's hurricane season,' someone from down the back of the coach shouted. 'What d'you expect?'

Hurricane season? Oh shit, of course. In my excitement to get away from it all, I'd totally and utterly forgotten Hurricane Irma had hit this part of the world back in early September. No wonder there had been rooms available at such short notice. I wiped condensation from the inside of the coach window and glanced nervously out at trees bending forty-five degrees.

'Hi, everybody, I'm Sadie and I'm your lady...'

Maybe I should have gone on that Lake District coach trip after all. The weather and the rep-speak would have been no different and I could have saved a fortune and caught a train home if it all got too much. Homesickness, loneliness and a sudden longing for Tom, Freya, Granddad Norman and even Paula came over me. It's just a week I told myself: Clare always goes off by herself and loves being able to do just what she wants to do without thinking of anyone else. I tried desperately to think of single women: pioneers, adventurers who'd not thought twice about setting off for foreign climes by themselves.

There was Mary Kingsley, who'd gone to Africa with a small amount of luggage and collecting cases for samples, and a phrase book with such helpful phrases as 'Get up, you lazy scamps!' Mind you, she died of typhoid fever and never came home. And who was that woman who'd climbed Mount Coropuna in Peru and stuck a sign at the summit demanding 'Votes For Women'? Annie Smith Peck, that was it. And then there was Gertrude Bell, who'd gone to the Alps and spent two days clinging to the rock face on a rope when she was caught in an avalanche. I shook my head in disbelief at her antics as the coach driver jumped on board and started the engine. I'd never got further than two feet up the rope in the gym at Mount View Comprehensive.

Just a week, Cassandra Moonbeam, and you'll be back on this coach and heading home, tanned, rested, well read and up for the rest of the term in front of you.

'You need to be aware of mosquitoes,' Sadie, our lady, was saying. 'The Zika virus is in Mexico and October is officially the rainy season...'

Oh, great stuff. Had I remembered my sou'wester and umbrella?

'... which does mean more mosquitoes than in the summer months and you should be prepared. We can supply you with all the preparations you will need to keep yourself safe. I'll be walking down the coach in a moment and I strongly suggest you stock up with them if you haven't got them already. Better safe than sorry.'

I closed my eyes, massaged my aching head, lay back in my seat and thought of England.

Three hours later and I was the last one still on the coach, every other passenger's hotel being called in turn as we pulled into seemingly endless forecourts, the driver jumping out to drag out luggage before jumping back into the driver's seat and setting off once again. Travel sickness was beginning to feature alongside homesickness as Sadie the rep, Jorge the coach driver and Cassandra Moonbeam, the miserable intrepid traveller, sped along wet roads to their final destination.

A strong wind was whipping and twisting hotel signage, metal chains bashing ominously against the hotel stonework as the coach pulled out of the long drive, leaving me and my little red case alone in the wind and the rain.

'Welcome, welcome. Mrs Beresford? We wondered where you were.' A particularly attractive tall man in white uniform rushed out with an umbrella and ushered me into the reception area. 'I think you were put on the wrong coach. Never mind, let's get you sorted, give you a drink and take you to your room. I'm Cristiano and anything you require, you just ask.'

'Is it going to rain all week?' I asked petulantly, sounding like the whingeing Brit I invariably was.

'It's October. It might rain a little bit every day, but still warm. Better than your October weather, I would think. Now, have a drink and then I'll find your personal concierge.'

My what? Cristiano handed me a fruit punch and, thirsty, I downed it in one. Golly, it had a bit of a kick to it. I looked around at the reception area which, almost deserted at this time of day, was light and airy and filled with both the traditional rattan-type Caribbean furniture as well as luxurious cream sofas stuffed with cushions. I couldn't resist: I sank into one and closed my eyes. The drink must have been stronger than I thought.

I could spend the week here, I reckoned. One of these sofas, more of that fruit punch and a good book and I wouldn't care about the rain...

'*Hola?* Mrs Beresford?'

I jumped guiltily, realising I'd nodded off, and tried to get to my feet, but the cushions sucked me back into their depths like quicksand, my arms and legs encased in travel-crumpled clothes flailing like some rudely disturbed insect.

'Mrs Beresford, I am Julio, your personal concierge. Would you like a hand?' Julio reached down for me and pulled me to my feet. 'You have had a long journey. You are tired.' He smiled. 'You need lunch...'

'Lunch? I think I had that around eight hours ago, watching Ninja Turtles.'

'Sorry?'

'I think I'm a bit jet-lagged. I thought it was bedtime.'

Julio smiled. 'You can go to bed if you want. Or you can go and eat. There is always somewhere to eat. At any time of day,' he added proudly. 'Now, I am here for you all week. I take you to your room now? You're OK to do that?'

I rubbed my eyes. They felt gritty and, when I caught sight of myself in one of the huge mirrors that lined the reception walls, I was glad there were no other guests around. My hair, with the long journey, rain and humidity, was a rather luxurious bird's nest; the trousers and warm jacket I'd chosen to combat the cold of an English October morning were creased and crumpled and my face pale. I looked old, knackered and very, very provincial.

Two tall, incredibly slim girls walked past wearing, despite the rain, emerald-green bikinis only just concealing tanned, lithe bodies under matching transparent cover-ups.

I wanted to go home.

Julio led the way and I followed, back out into the warm rain towards a motorised buggy. 'There's always one available for you, if you don't want to walk,' he said solicitously.

Oh God, did I look so knackered? I looked around for my trusty little red case. Had I left it on the coach?

'My case...?'

'In your room, waiting for you, Mrs Beresford.' He smiled, seeing my panic. 'All will be well. I think you are very stressed, no? You've been having a hard time in the UK? Well, we are here for you. But...' he sighed, 'your travel company has overbooked. You were very last minute. I'm afraid your room is no longer available.'

'What? Well, that's all I damned well need. I knew it was all too good to be true.' I burst into tears. 'I should have gone to Blackpool,' I blubbed. 'Hot and cold water in every room, a view of the sea and free entry up the Tower...'

'*Lo siento.* Sorry, sorry. I am so sorry, Mrs Beresford.' Julio looked aghast. 'I tease you. The room you booked and paid for is not there. So, we upgrade you to our very best suite. Here we are, look...'

The buggy came to a stop, skidding slightly in a puddle of warm rainwater. Julio took my arm, manoeuvring me round the puddle and gently moving me forward. I reckon if he'd had a cloak he'd have whipped it off and laid it down for me to walk over *à la* Walter Raleigh. He pressed me forward through the gardens, which I began to realise were the most beautiful I'd ever seen, the heady scent of rain-washed exotic flowers overpowering all my other senses as I stopped briefly to breathe it all in.

'Come.' Having unintentionally upset me, Julio was obviously desperate to make amends. He took a little navy-blue key card with 'Premier Suite' emblazoned in gold on it, opened the door and led me in.

'Here we are, Mrs Beresford. I think this make you feel better. Yes?'

I took in the huge king-sized bed, the pile of fluffy white towels, the enormous en-suite bathroom with walk-in shower, white robes and slippers. I gazed out of the window at the sea directly below, at the bottle of champagne, cold in its bucket of ice and the bowl of exotic fresh fruit.

I didn't say anything for a few seconds.

'OK, now? All is well?' Julio beamed.

I burst into tears once more.

21

Heaven, I'm in Heaven...

Idon't think I realised quite just how the events of the last two months had affected me. I had put *everything* into my new job: up before six most mornings to sort out my own kids with their breakfast and other daily needs before arriving at school at seven to deal with other people's. And then not going to bed much before midnight as I sorted admin I had to bring home with me. Many a night I'd fallen asleep at the computer, glasses falling off my nose, head lurching towards the keyboard, mouth dribbling as I struggled with some new government directive I'd need to pass on to the staff the following day. It had only been eight weeks since Mark had left me for Tina and yet it seemed like a lifetime ago. That other me: the contented – let's face it, smug – teacher in her white middle-class oasis of pointy cushions and Dettoxed kitchen and bathrooms, totally sure of her man and with her well-behaved, well-brought up kids, was almost totally gone. I needed to take a good long look at myself to see what was left.

I didn't leave my hotel room for the rest of that first day. By the time Julio had departed, leaving instructions on how to find the all-inclusive restaurants, bars and wellness spa – which I promptly forgot – it was mid-afternoon. It was still pouring down outside, rain lashing against my balcony window, the wind howling such a gale that I quickly closed it again when I attempted to get a better look at my view. I texted the kids, Paula, Clare and Fi to tell them all I'd arrived, found a socket to recharge my phone, and then decided to switch it off for some total peace and quiet. After stripping off my grubby travelling clothes, I kicked them into a corner and, with the huge Jacuzzi filling up nicely, opened the bottle of champagne.

I lowered myself into the bubbles, drank half a glass of fizz and then, lying back, took stock of my good luck, suddenly finding a big daft smile on my face. The last-minute room I'd grabbed had been a standard pool view, all-inclusive and more than adequate for my week of doing nothing. This upgrade was an absolute bonus.

By early evening I'd unpacked, polished off another couple of glasses of champagne, investigated the mini bar and ordered food from room service. I didn't quite feel up to making my way down to one of the restaurants, sitting by myself, nose in Kindle, while other diners tried to work out why I was there alone, or attempted to make conversation with me. Besides, I was enjoying the very unusual situation of my *being* all alone: no one at all in the world really knowing exactly where I was. Apart from Julio, of course. I was beginning to feel a little embarrassed, ashamed even, of my tears and rants about Blackpool and its bloody Tower. I began to giggle as I recalled Julio's face, and poured myself more champagne.

I switched my phone back on and it immediately started barking the arrival of texts. I really must get Tom to change its tone to something more fitting, I mused idly. One in the morning, back in the UK: I did hope neither Freya nor Tom was still awake in their respective Newcastle and Cambridge beds. The texts had been sent earlier and both kids said they'd arrived, the food and weather were dreadful, but Freya had already scored a number of goals during training and Tom had cracked some maths code before anyone else on his course. What clever children I had. I could never work out where Tom's maths ability had come from, although Granddad Norman had said he'd been a bit of a hotshot with trigonometry during his advanced training as a conscript at the beginning of the war, before being sent over to France.

Reassured that my kids were safe and happy, I felt the champagne, wonderful food and jet lag beginning to work their magic and I was just falling asleep once more when the barking dog announced another text. Cursing that I'd not switched the phone off, I reached for it and squinted in the dark at the message.

I've just heard you've gone to Mexico all by yourself. Not like you!! Keep yourself safe, Cass, and watch out for strange men. Wish I was there with you. Mark

What? I sat up in bed and read and reread the text. What was Mark trying to say? Was he missing me? Did he want to come back home? I had to switch on the light and get out of bed to calm myself, my heart doing a samba in my chest.

It was another couple of hours before I eventually slept.

I was awoken by a cacophony of birdsong outside my window. At least I think it was birdsong: the calling was so loud, so insistent it could have been cicadas, or even monkeys. You wouldn't get *this* in Blackpool, I told myself happily.

It was only 6 a.m. and still dark outside, but it sounded as if the whole forest was coming alive. It had stopped raining completely and, apart from a few dark clouds on the horizon, the sky was clear. In front of me the sea was calm, as far as I could hear. I hugged myself in delight: I was both beside the sea and actually on the edge of the Mexican rainforest. Wrapping one of the huge towelling robes around myself, I went further out onto the balcony, sitting down on one of the sun loungers just to take it all in. The air was fragrant with the scent of flowers and wet foliage. I gazed for a long time, fascinated, as the dark sky lightened into pink, which then morphed into oranges and then reds while the sea itself, reflecting every carmine shade, seemed to be on fire.

I finally allowed myself to revisit Mark's text. Was I feeling so wonderfully alive because of the message implied in the words? Mark wished he were here with me. Presumably not with Tina, then. Unless he was after a threesome, the pillock. Ha! What would Serpentina think of *that*?

With the early morning sunshine now warm on my whole body, I made my way down to a beach bar for breakfast. Mark would have loved the full range of cooked breakfast, I thought wistfully, filling his plate with the scrambled eggs and bacon – his favourite Sunday morning treat after a week at work – and relishing the good, strong coffee. After ordering food, I took out my phone and, unable to resist, read and reread the text message he'd sent the night before. What *did* he mean? Should I text him back and say I *also* wished he was here in Mexico with me? I did seem to recall, in my previous life as a smug married duo, being in hotels with Mark and, seeing what I assumed to be sad singletons, nose in a newspaper or book propped up against the salt and pepper, feeling ever so slightly superior. Oh, sod it, I thought. My single status had nothing to do with anyone else. I looked around almost defiantly, slathered butter and jam onto a flaky, buttery croissant and opened my Kindle.

I was pleased to see, once I surfaced from my thriller – which wasn't overly thrilling – in order to pour more coffee, that on further inspection there were several tables of same-sex couples and I wondered idly if the pairs were lovers or just mates away on holiday together. Two men, deep in conversation over their breakfast, were particularly good-looking – very fanciable, in fact – and

I hurriedly buried my nose back into my Kindle as one, realising he was under scrutiny, smiled in my direction. I didn't think I was up for flirting across the coffee pots just yet. I took a couple of quick photos of the breakfast feast and view of the beach from my table, sending them by text to Tom, Freya, Clare and Fi, and then, determinedly avoiding reading Mark's message once more, switched off my phone and headed for the beach and sunshine.

And so I spent the day and the following days in heaven, swimming, sunbathing and reading, eating delicious food and drinking the all-inclusive cocktails. I walked on the beach, was pampered and cosseted in the spa and gazed in wonder at the giant iguanas and pelicans that roamed the verdant grounds of the hotel.

By my fourth day there I was fully into the routine of it all. In the evenings, after a day on the beach, I would shower and walk to one of the many bars, admiring the spectacular sunsets over a Mojito before going into dinner. At first, I'd been nervous of walking into the restaurants by myself. On the first evening the waiter had asked 'One? Just for one? A table for one?' very loudly and, humiliated at my lack of friends or husband, I'd almost turned and gone back to my room and ordered room service. But instead I'd smiled serenely and replied, just as loudly, 'Just me; a table for one, please.' After that it had got easier and by the third evening I'd even relinquished my book in order to take in the wonderful ambience as I feasted on the view from the terrace dining room as well as the incredible food. OK, I drank too much, but it was there, all laid on for me, and it helped me relax and even enjoy my own company.

On that fourth evening, I'd just finished a rather glorious chocolate mousse and was feeling replete when I noticed the two men I'd seen at breakfast on my first morning there. They were sitting around the corner from me and as I turned to find the waiter in order to ask for more water, the taller of the two, the one who'd smiled at me, raised a glass. I raised my glass of wine back, not really knowing what else to do. I wasn't used to strange men raising glasses of wine at me and couldn't for the life of me think what the protocol was when one actually did so.

'Come and join us?' The tall smiley one appeared at my side. 'You look a bit lonely by yourself.'

'I can assure you I'm not,' I said rather stiffly. Then I relented and smiled. 'Well, maybe a little...'

'We've just ordered coffee and a liqueur. Come and sit with us and we'll order one for you as well.'

I was totally relieved when I realised Ritchie and Julian were together in every sense of the word and could relax and enjoy their company without trying to work out whether either of them fancied me, or what might happen next if I'd fancied one of them.

Julian, the taller guy, was, I'd guessed, quite a bit older than me and this was confirmed when they told me they were out in Mexico to celebrate Julian's fiftieth birthday. Ritchie was nearer my own age and both were vets who lived near Manchester.

'Were you on my flight?' I asked. 'You weren't on my coach transfer. Mind you, *no one* else from that flight was. I was bundled onto the wrong coach, apparently, and the hotel was about to send out a search party in the rain to find me.' I laughed ruefully. That awful coach journey now seemed years ago.

'We certainly saw you on the flight,' Julian smiled. 'We were sat almost across from you and started taking bets as to whether you'd ever wake up. You were obviously in need of a jolly good sleep.'

'We dubbed you Little Orphan Annie,' Ritchie joined in. 'You seemed so little and alone.'

'And now you feel you have to adopt me?' I smiled back at them. 'You really don't, you know. I'm learning to be by myself...' I paused. 'Actually, beginning to learn to love myself as well.'

'We all need to love ourselves,' Ritchie laughed, handing me the Cointreau and coffee I'd ordered. 'Rule number one: no one will love you until you learn to love yourself.'

And so these two lovely men became my mates, in much the same way as if Fi and Clare had been in Mexico with me. I was conscious that they were a couple on a romantic holiday in this rather wonderful hotel and didn't want to be a gooseberry, but they constantly assured me they'd been together far too long to spend the time holding hands and smooching like love-sick turtle doves, and that I must join them whenever being by myself wasn't what I wanted any more.

And for most of the time it was. To be by myself, I mean. With very little to do but lie in the sun all day – the heavens opened most days but only for half an hour at the most and usually before breakfast or after dinner – I soon acquired a rather lovely tan. My hair, which I'd not had the time or inclination to do anything with since Mark had left, had grown long and rather messy while the sun now lightened it from gold to silver. Looking in the mirror before joining Ritchie and Julian for drinks and dinner one evening, I smiled at my reflection. New freckles had appeared on my nose, my hair – newly washed and simply towelled-dry rather than straightened into submission by the left-at-home GHDs – fell onto my shoulders and the white dress Clare had brought round for me the night before I left, assuring me that, yes, it would fit me, showed off my newly slim figure and tan. A slick of bright pink lipstick and I was ready for anything.

The three of us drank rather a lot that evening, moving from pre-dinner cocktails onto wine at dinner and then back to the piano bar for a sedate nightcap. I was about to say my goodnight, relishing finishing the thriller – which had actually turned out rather thrilling after all – in bed.

'No, don't go to bed,' Julian protested. 'Come on, it's karaoke evening over in the Cholula bar. Ritchie hates karaoke and will never come with me.'

'I love karaoke,' I beamed, 'although I've never dared to get up and sing.'

'We can sing something together,' he grinned. 'Come on. I can be Marvin *Gaye*...' he pouted '... and you can be Tammi Terrell.'

'Who?'

'Tammi Terrell. You know: "*The wo… rld is ju… st a great big on… ion …*" Julian took my hand, singing the words in a high falsetto.

I laughed. 'Sorry, before my time.'

'And mine.' Ritchie grimaced, downing his glass of Kahlúa in one. 'Oh God, come on then if we really have to.'

While not the world's best singer, I could hold a tune and, shored up with several glasses of Kahlúa myself, Julian and I went for it. There was quite a crowd gathered but Julian was actually a really good vocalist and together we sang 'Islands in the Stream' moving on to 'Don't Go Breaking My Heart' and finished with Patti La Belle and Michael McDonald's 'On My Own'.

This last duet made me think of Mark and I suddenly wanted to cry. Jumping up, I went over to the DJ, scanned the song list and, before I lost my nerve, booked a solo spot. I could do this, I told myself. I was a head teacher, for heaven's sake; I could do *anything*.

'What are you going to sing?' Julian laughed as I downed two more Kahlúas. 'Do you want me to join you?'

'Only a *woman* can go for this one,' I said tipsily. 'Only a very *strong* woman…'

Ten minutes later and I was back up on the stage. I gave it all I'd got, I really did. I saw Ritchie wincing and Julian doubled over with laughter, but I went for it. I *was* Gloria. I *was* that woman. I'd just got to the best bits about crumbling, about laying down and dying when, as if in some sort of slow-motion dream, my eyes met another pair and locked with them. I crumbled. I could have lay down and died. Literally.

What the fucking hell was Xavier Bamforth doing in this bar, in this hotel, in this *country*?

22

Is That a Frigate I See Before Me…?

'Are you all right, lovely?' Julian came up to the stage as soon as Gloria and I had belted out our last note. To be honest, Gloria did the belting while I petered out, stumbling over the words and notes as the crowd in the bar smiled in sympathy.

'I'm fine,' I pulled a face. 'Just very embarrassed.'

'You were fine to begin with.'

'Well, I don't know about that. I think I need a drink.'

Julian handed me a glass of water. 'What happened? You suddenly looked as if you'd seen a ghost.'

'Not a ghost. Just someone from home.'

'From home? From Midhope? Here?' Julian stared at me. 'Oh, Cassandra Moonbeam, not your husband? He hasn't followed you here and come to claim you back, leaving Serpentina to slither back into her pit from whence she came?'

I'd told Julian and Ritchie the whole story of Mark's defection, and their favourite game was now thinking up new and evil tortures for the pair of them. We'd gone from forcing tacos up their nostrils to super-gluing Mark's willy to his stomach and on to rubbing both of them all over with sandpaper before soaking them in a bath of lemon juice.

'No, someone from home I don't really like,' I muttered, keeping my head down as I spoke. 'I'm so embarrassed. Mortified, in fact. The time before last when he saw me I was wrapped around a giant penis...' I looked round to where Xavier Bamforth was now sitting a few tables away, ordering a drink from one of the waiters. 'Look, I'm going to have to go over and speak to him. I'll see you both in the morning.'

'Early, remember.' Ritchie kissed me goodnight.

'Early?'

'We need to be in the hotel lobby at six.'

'Oh, gosh, yes. The boat trip. I'll just go and have a word with the guy over there and then I'm off.' The three of us turned, as one, to Xavier and he raised his glass. What was it with men and raising glasses? Oh God, now he'd know we'd all been talking about him.

'Are you stalking me?' I asked as I sat down opposite him. 'First, you're in my office, then in Leeds, then at the meeting in the village hall and now you're here, for heaven's sake.'

'Erm, I think I could ask *you* the same question,' he said drily.

I shook my head. 'I bet *I* was here first.' I realised I must sound childish and tried to find my head teacher head. It seemed to have disappeared along with Gloria Gaynor. 'So, Mr Bamforth, are you on holiday?'

Xavier looked at me as if I was daft. Or drunk. I think very probably I was both.

'That would appear to be the general idea,' he finally said, not smiling. 'One does tend to be on holiday when one finds oneself in a five-star hotel in Mexico.'

'You could be working,' I sniffed. 'Selling your engineering stuff – or whatever it is you Bamforths make – to the Mexican government.'

'Really?'

'You don't appear to be in a very holiday mood,' I said.

'As opposed to you, who obviously are. So, are those two your roadies?'

'Sorry?'

'Roadies? Backing group? Promoters? I'm assuming you spend your half-term breaks moonlighting as a Gloria Gaynor tribute act.'

I laughed. 'I was pretty crap, wasn't I? But I *was* OK until I spotted you.'

He actually smiled at that. 'No, you weren't. I should stick to the day job if I were you.'

'So, where's your wife? Did she hear me sing and make a hasty retreat?'

'My wife is tucked up in bed, I should imagine. Whose bed that is, is anyone's guess.'

'Right.' I didn't quite know what to say to that.

Xavier drained his glass. 'Sorry, I need to go to bed myself: I'm booked on some trip to some island in the morning.'

'Isla Contoy?'

'Er, I think so. And the other one?'

'Isla Contoy and Isla Mujeres? Six a.m. at reception?'

'I believe so.' Xavier actually smiled. 'I thought I ought to see some sights while I'm here.'

'You don't sound overly enthusiastic.'

'My mother booked this whole damned Mexican trip for me. She saw it advertised in the *Midhope Examiner* and booked it all before I could argue. I was suddenly at Manchester airport, passport in hand.'

'She obviously thought you were in need of it.'

'She obviously did.' He stood up. 'Goodnight, Mrs Beresford. Sleep well.'

By six the next morning I was up and ready for the off. Ritchie and Julian had suggested we all needed a bit of cultural activity rather than the sybaritic eating, drinking and sunbathing lifestyle we were getting used to on a daily basis.

'Do you not think, on a boat trip, we'll be doing just that but in a different location?' I'd asked somewhat doubtfully.

'Exploration is all important,' Julian had replied loftily. 'It broadens the mind.'

Xavier Bamforth was already in reception speaking on his phone. He nodded at me but carried on what appeared to be a rather heated argument with someone.

By six fifteen Julian, Ritchie, Xavier and myself had been joined by two American couples from the hotel and were being herded onto a small minibus that would take us down to the port and to our boat.

'I do hope we're not going to be made to follow a group leader with an orange flag on an umbrella,' Ritchie was grumbling. 'We had enough of that in Venice when we were there.'

'I doubt it,' I said. 'Cristiano told me we're picking up two other couples from the next hotel and then it's straight onto the boat and off to Isla Contoy.'

Once the twelve of us were on board with a welcome from the captain and his two staff as well as introductions, and 'Ooh, isn't this lovely?' all round, we bagged spaces on the deck or in the shade according to whether we were sun worshippers or not, and the boat's engine throbbed and we were off.

Xavier, I ascertained from his tan, must actually have been here quite a few days before me. He immediately stripped off down to rather brief white shorts, lay down on the deck and, with a straw hat over his face, went immediately to sleep.

'Come on, lovey,' Julian called over to me. 'We've saved you a place here between us.' He patted the area next to him and I walked across, feeling my way carefully as the swell from the sea rocked the boat, catching me off balance.

'Nice swimsuit,' Ritchie whistled as I stripped off my shorts and T-shirt and hunted for my sunglasses.

'It's not mine,' I smiled.

'Well, it's certainly not *mine*,' Julian quipped. 'Ooh, but I wish it were. I think it would really suit me.'

'Cut it out, Julian,' Ritchie said, slightly crossly. 'So, Cassie, if it's not yours, whose is it?'

'I have a glamorous friend called Clare who came over with a caseload of very upmarket stuff for me to borrow. If she hadn't, I'm afraid I'd be wearing my baggy old Primark bikinis that actually need throwing out. I never thought her stuff would fit me. Pre-Mark going they certainly wouldn't.'

'So, darling, he's done you a bit of a favour then in buggering off with Serpentina,' Julian smiled. 'Every cloud and all that.'

'Listen, you two, can I ask you something?' I hesitated, not sure if what I was going to ask was an intrusion.

Ritchie smiled. 'When did we realise we were gay? That's the usual one.'

'The very one, I'm afraid. Not very original, am I? The thing is, my son, Tom, is quite possibly gay. I mean, he's seventeen. Would he know by now?'

'Well, Julian didn't. He was married for fifteen years, has two kids...'

'I *always* knew,' Julian drawled. 'It was just easier in life to not go with being gay. My parents would have been horrified at the time. They find it even stranger now that I've been married, but there you go. Besides, I loved my wife. I still do. I just don't really like having sex with women.' He laughed and stroked my arm.

'And you, Ritchie?' I asked.

'Probably in my adolescence when all the boys in the class were boasting about how far they'd gone with girls. I never wanted to, really. I liked girls. In fact, I preferred their company. Just didn't fancy them. I used to hang out with them, go along to Boyzone concerts with the girls in my class and all the time I was having fantasies about Shane Lynch.'

'Ritchie, you still do,' Julian tutted. 'I've had to compete with Shane Lynch ever since I met you. So, Cassandra, does that help?'

'It does actually. What Ritchie's just said is almost identical to what Tom said to me the other night.'

'Cassie, if he is, he is. It's no big deal. Just be there for him and try not to judge.'

We hugged the coast for several miles, marvelling at the expanse of rainforest and lush palm trees. We'd been promised sea turtles and double-crested cormorants but none had as yet put in an appearance.

'Isn't that a frigate over there?' Xavier suddenly appeared at our side with binoculars.

'A frigate? Where?' We all shaded our eyes, searching the horizon for warships.

'Mexico isn't at war with anyone, is she?' I asked, slightly nervously.

'Only Donald Trump, as far as I know,' Julian said. 'So, where is it then, Xav? This frigate? I can't see it.'

'There, look.' Xavier was quite animated, waving his free arm towards the sky while continuing to peer through his binoculars.

Julian, Ritchie and I all looked at each other and I began to giggle.

'I hate to tell you this, mate,' Julian said, 'but that ain't no warship. That's a bloody great bird. A big one, I admit, but not really to be confused with a warship.'

'Yes,' Xavier said excitedly. 'The magnificent frigate bird. It's a male. Look at that magnificent red pouch. It inflates during the mating season to attract a female. They're a bit of a dying breed now. We're very lucky to see one.'

As the boat pulled away from the coastline and out into deeper water, clouds were starting to roll in and I felt drops of rain. The boat began to lurch and I sat down hurriedly. Five minutes later I knew I was going to throw up.

'Are you all right, Cassie?' Ritchie looked across at me as I sat up and then attempted to stand. 'You've gone very pale.'

'White, actually,' Julian frowned. 'Oops. Somebody get the sick bucket.'

To anyone who has never been carsick or seasick, the feeling is almost impossible to explain. It's one of the worst feelings in the world: a cross between homesickness, dizziness, nausea and being totally out of control. I lurched to the side of the boat, my legs jelly, and clung onto the rails with cold, clammy hands. Salty water sprayed up into my face and I knew I just had to get off the boat. Stop the world, somebody, I need to get off.

'Would you like to lie down in the cabin?' the captain asked solicitously as he came up beside me.

'No, I want to die.' I muttered. 'Just let me die.'

Xavier came up on my other side. 'It affects my mother like this. Did you not know you get seasick?'

'I've never *been* on a boat before,' I managed to say, before I pushed Xavier out of the way and heaved over the side.

'It's not going to go away,' he said. 'The weather looks set to deteriorate. We need to get you off.'

'Oh, please. Just get me off. Find me a helicopter. Winch me off...'

Thirty minutes later and we were back where we started. I'd hugged the rail all the way back, throwing up so many times until I was just throwing up the water that Xavier made me drink between each bout of retching.

'Just leave me here,' I said to the others, totally embarrassed. 'I'll get a taxi back to the hotel once I feel better. Please, go. I really don't want to spoil your day.'

'You shouldn't stay by yourself,' Xavier said. 'Look, I've sailed loads of times; I'm not really bothered about setting off again. I've seen my frigatebird now; that's all that matters. Come on, let's get you onto terra firma and see if a flat Coke will help.'

Shivering, even through the humidity, I pulled on my shorts and T-shirt, and on legs of jelly walked off the boat and onto the solid ground of the dock side.

'I still feel as if I'm on board,' I said. 'Everything's going up and down.'

Xavier laughed. 'It will for a while. I need coffee. Come on.'

*

Within ten minutes, in a rather upmarket little café on the port, I began to feel better although I was left with an intense need to lie down and sleep. 'I used to feel like this in the back seat of Granddad Norman's old Austin,' I said. 'On one trip to Devon we had to stop so many times, Granddad said we might as well turn round and go back home.'

'Ah, Granddad Norman.'

'You know my granddad?' I looked in surprise at Xavier.

'I know his meadow.'

'Oh, of course you do. Tell me something, how is it that a man who obviously enjoys nature – I mean you were really into that frigatebird – how can you be happy to concrete fields over and kill all that wildlife and plant life?'

'Cassie, I've never said I was happy to do it.' Xavier had the grace to look embarrassed.

I looked at him. 'I'm sure you did. Why would you be wanting all this development if you're not happy to do it?'

'Something's got to be done with all these acres of land. They're just not sustainable as they are. Farmers don't want to farm.'

'I think you'll find they do.' I was thinking of Matthew and Fiona. While Fi might moan and groan about being a farmer's wife, the last thing she'd want is for Matthew to lose the tenancy. 'My friend Fi's husband would be happy to extend his acreage. And he's got two strapping great sons who're ready to have farms of their own. There are loads of people around Westenbury who'd be more than happy to work on the farms if they could only expand.'

Xavier didn't say anything, but signalled, instead, for the waiter to bring more coffee. 'People need houses…'

I stared at him. 'Is your aim to get as much money as you can so that you can have a huge house and not ever have to work again? And so that your children have an inheritance?'

'I don't have any children.'

'Well, there's still time. And when you do, what better inheritance for them than beautiful greenbelt fields instead of lots of money that they will only spend on fast cars, Hermès handbags and oh, I don't know, big houses and and PlayStations.'

'PlayStations?' Xavier began to laugh.

'That's all *my* kids ever wanted. A PlayStation each.'

'And did they get one?'

'One to share, eventually. Damned things rot the brain.'

Xavier smiled but there was such sadness in his eyes. I was taken aback.

'What is it? What's the matter?'

'Ophelia, my wife, has gone.'

'Gone? Gone where? She was with you when I bumped into you in Leeds, wasn't she? The little brunette? And at the meeting?'

'Ophelia's been coming and going for *years*. One minute she wants to go and live back in London where we used to live before I came back to work with Dad at Bamforths. Then she wants to live in South Africa or Dubai. Next, she's come up with an idea for a new business that she wants me to fund: she soon tires of that. We still have a tiny flat in London where she spends much of her time hanging out with her friends, but she wants a huge house, preferably in Hampstead. And a place in Spain. She hates the North, hates living in the sticks. So you see, Ophelia is desperate for us to build on the land because it means I get lots of money and she can have all the stuff she craves.'

'Oh.' I didn't know what else to say.

'Oh, indeed.'

'She sounds a bit, you know, a bit spoilt...?'

'Incredibly. But, not my problem anymore.' He gave a wintry smile. 'There comes a time when enough is enough. When you have to get out of the whole toxic situation.'

'You must be feeling pretty bad.' I studied Xavier's face, inscrutable behind the designer sunglasses, as he ran a tanned hand through his thick dark hair.

'Yes, you could say that.' He hesitated. 'But what on earth is the point of a relationship where your wife is staying with you for what she can gain materially? I should have finished it properly a long time ago.'

'But you love her.' It was a statement rather than a question and Xavier didn't answer.

'When my mother knew I'd finally finished with Ophelia she bundled me off on holiday out here. She's a bit like a tiger with a cub, is my mother. There was no arguing with her. I did consider holing up in Manchester for a week rather than getting on the plane.' He laughed. 'But I did want to see the frigatebird.'

'So, now that you don't need huge amounts of money in order to keep your wife from straying, where does that leave the fields and the planned building?'

Xavier smiled. 'Cassandra, at the moment I really don't give a fuck one way or the other. I'm tired of the whole thing.' He leaned forward. 'Good, you've got a lot more colour now. Are you feeling a bit better?'

'I feel fine now. Just totally mortified. Thank you for looking after me. It's very kind.'

'Not at all.' He hesitated and then said, almost shyly, 'Would you have dinner with me tonight?'

23

And Then I Slid Down the Wall and onto the Floor...

Why on earth are you shaving your legs, scrubbing between your toes and generally slathering yourself in every body lotion and perfume known to woman? This was the question I kept asking myself as I went through the fairly limited wardrobe I'd brought to Mexico with me, feverishly dismissing most with a flick of my hand.

It's not as if this is a date, I told myself crossly. *You've got to eat tonight in the hotel; he's got to eat tonight in the hotel.* So why not together? But why then, when Ritchie texted me to ask if I was joining him and Julian for dinner, did I not invite them along as well?

I couldn't wear the lovely white dress I'd worn the previous evening. It would forever remind anyone present of '*Tonight, Matthew, I'm going to be Gloria Gaynor...*'

I grabbed my credit card and, tutting at my ridiculousness, ran down to the lobby where a number of expensive boutiques were based. The interiors were air-conditioned but basically empty, their clothes and jewellery being far too expensive for mere mortals like myself to consider.

I saw it straight away. A simple, but extravagantly expensive, shocking-pink little number. Not my size. Bugger. I picked it up and held it against me, caressing the cotton fabric.

'Try it on,' the assistant smiled. 'It's your colour: goes beautifully with your blonde hair and tan.'

'But, unfortunately, not my size. It'll be far too small.'

'No, really, your size. Here...' She pulled back the curtain and urged me in to the changing room giving encouraging little smiles as she did so.

It was heaven in a dress: totally plain, strappy and fitted like a glove.

I winced when I saw the price and took the dress off, pulled my shorts back on and returned it to the assistant.

'You have to have it,' she said, aghast. 'It was born for you.'

'*Made* for me,' I laughed. 'Unfortunately, far too expensive.'

'But you have to have it. Look, I take twenty per cent off. It shouldn't be in the sale but you are so tiny I don't think anyone else will get into it.'

'I'll have it.' Feeling horribly guilty, but horribly excited, the precious thing was wrapped and it was mine, *all* mine.

*

'So, Mrs Beresford, how come you're here in Mexico all by yourself?' Xavier handed me a mint-laden Mojito and smiled.

'Same reason as you, I guess.'

'What, my mother bullied *you* into coming as well?'

I laughed. 'My friend Fi was the instigator. She saw the same travel page in the local paper and within two days I'd booked, packed and was on the train to the airport.'

'And *Mr* Beresford?'

'I'm amazed you haven't had the lowdown on the sudden ending of my marriage.'

Xavier looked surprised. 'Why should I?'

'It ended very publicly, and, as a new head teacher, I very quickly became the subject of the gossip in Westenbury and, quite probably, Midhope as well.'

'Oh? Do you want to talk about it?'

'Do you know, I don't think I do.' And I didn't. Two months on and I'd had enough of telling the story.

I looked at Xavier, taking in the very dark hair and olive skin which, after a week in the sun, had turned a deep mahogany, now emphasised by the beautiful crisp white shirt he'd chosen to wear. 'What about you? You must be feeling pretty raw still?'

'I think when a relationship has limped along as mine has with Ophelia; when it involves periods of intense remission where you feel it's all going to be OK after all…'

'And then it isn't OK and it falls apart again?'

He smiled. 'No, it never is OK. A toxic relationship never succeeds in the end. You both tell each other it will work this time, but it doesn't. The same problems just raise their ugly heads once more; they never go away. I'm probably as much to blame as Ophelia…'

'Oh, don't blame yourself,' I said, almost cheerfully. 'I told myself it must have been my fault that Mark ran off with my best friend, that it must be something that I'd been unable to give him that made him try to find it with her. But, that's all bollocks. I think now, in hindsight, he probably totally got off on the drama and danger of it all.'

'A bit like James Bond?'

We both laughed. 'I hadn't thought of it like that, but yes, I think you're probably right. Anything to titivate his mundane existence of a job, a wife and two kids.'

'He'd have been better taking up skydiving or robbing banks,' Xavier laughed again.

The picture of sensible Mark, in striped sweater and balaclava, toting a SWAG bag while holding up the balding manager of the one remaining branch of a certain bank in Westenbury village, made me giggle. Or maybe it was the Mojito, but once I'd started I couldn't stop.

'That's wonderful,' Xavier grinned, as I wiped my eyes. 'What is?'

'You, laughing like that. On the occasions I've seen you, you've looked so uptight and totally unapproachable. A real crosspatch, even with a giant penis over one shoulder.'

I started to giggle again. 'Gosh, strong stuff this Mojito; I think I'd better have another…'

Xavier and I spent the next two hours ensconced at a corner table on the terrace of the Italian restaurant facing the Caribbean coastline. The food, several courses of quite tiny portions, was just perfect: I could enjoy the incredible flavours without the fear that my new pink dress might split at the seams.

'I'm assuming you've lived in Midhope all your life?' I asked, in between mouthfuls of a delicious Italian Tiramisu. 'I mean, most people in Midhope know of the Bamforths, probably because they, or someone in their family, have worked in one of your factories.' I thought for a moment. 'I'm not sure that Granddad Norman didn't work at Bamforths at one point, before he set up his own stall selling fish down in the market hall.'

'Possibly. I wouldn't know. Really, apart from some of the school holidays, I haven't spent much time in the North. Dad's lived there all his life, of course, but Mum is French so after the age of eight, when I wasn't away at school in the South, I was often *avec mon grandpère et ma grandmère à Paris.*'

'Ah, hence the name Xavier? It did seem a bit exotic for Midhope.'

He laughed. 'If Dad had had his way I'd have been George or William, but Mum insisted.'

'You were eight when you were sent away to school? That's child cruelty. Weren't you horribly homesick?'

'To begin with, yes, but that's the way it was. The pair of us – myself and my sister, Amelie – were sent away at an early age in the same way that my dad had been. And to the same school as my dad. Family tradition and all that.'

'Didn't your mum object? I would never have allowed *my* kids to be sent away from me – at *eight.*'

'She did at the time. I remember her crying for weeks before I went, arguing with my dad that I was too young; throwing a few things at him, if I remember rightly. As I said, she's always been a bit of a tiger, but the Bamforths are a forceful lot and my grandmother, particularly, was a matriarch you didn't cross. And then, after school, I was at university in Bath and then I worked in the City for quite a few years. After that, Dad wanted me back up North to start taking over the reins. I'd actually had enough of the stress of London, so the idea of coming back to my roots was one I welcomed.'

'And Ophelia?'

'She was very reluctant to move north. She eventually agreed to the move because the idea of being able to afford a much larger house, rather than the flat we were living in, was quite inviting to begin with. I think she had the idea she was going to be lady of the manor, workers doffing their hats to her while she kicked a few northern peasants into submission.' Xavier laughed. 'She'd obviously been reading too much D. H. Lawrence. The workers at Bamforths are the last people to try to keep down. We've had to deal with a lot of union stuff over the past two years, the union leaders constantly insisting on negotiating with us on whatever is being suggested to keep the company abreast of competition in a global market.'

'As is only right,' I smiled, echoes of my mother suddenly appearing out of the blue.

'Absolutely. I have no problem with workers' rights. Unfortunately, the constant battle we seem to have does get in the way of progress at times. Dad's fear is we may not be able to compete for ever.'

'Ah, hence the selling off of some of the Bamforth Estate? And the planned building on the rest?' I was beginning to understand Edward Bamforth's motives.

Xavier nodded. 'Yes. Dad won't actually admit to it, but if he can make a great deal of money by putting houses on the estate, that will be the time to sell up at the factory, too. He can retire on the proceeds and play golf for the rest of his life.'

'Why doesn't he just sell the factory and retire on what he makes there? Then he can leave the fields as they were and we'd all be happy?' This seemed perfectly logical to me as I scraped my plate of chocolate and sat back, replete.

Xavier sighed. 'Does anyone want engineering companies these days? I'm not sure anyone would want to part with the kind of money Dad would want for the factory. He's a stubborn bugger – always has been – and he'd rather sell off the estate where he knows there's a good deal *more* money to be had.'

'And that's what Ophelia's hoping for, too?' I remembered the very gorgeous brunette who'd clapped so encouragingly after Xavier had put forward the Bamforth Estate's plans at the meeting. As his wife, she stood to share a good deal of the profits of any sale of the estate.

'Yes, we all know exactly what Ophelia is after.' Xavier smiled. 'And *with* me, or *not*, she'll make sure she gets what she feels she is owed.'

I looked at Xavier, at his tanned fingers with their very clean nails wrapped around the stem of his wine glass; at his very dark hair and beautiful brown eyes, no longer sad, but smiling at me across the table. I felt myself flush slightly as he poured more wine, his fingers somehow making contact with my hand as he did so. Was that a deliberate move on his part or wishful thinking on mine?

'Just off to the loo,' I squeaked.

'I'm not going anywhere,' he said.

I examined my face in the marble-edged mirror as I dried my hands with one of the white fluffy hand towels before discarding it in the basket to my side. My beautiful pink dress, despite sitting for the past few hours, still clung in all the right places. I added a slick of lipstick, a squirt of Jean-Louis Scherrer, took a deep breath and headed back to the table.

'Would you like to get some fresh air?' Xavier was standing, screwing up his napkin before abandoning it at the place he'd been sitting.

We walked along the beach in silence as I tried to work out why my heart was beating more quickly than it should: I'd either drunk too much, was incredibly unfit or was about to have a heart attack. I took off my heels – ridiculous trying to walk on sand in heels – and the cool sand quieted the fluttering of my pulse for a while.

'Cassie...?' Xavier stopped suddenly, turning in my direction, bringing me to a halt.

'Hmm?'

'Thank you for today.' He put a warm hand on my arm and stroked it lightly, and yet with such expertise, my pulse raced once more.

'Thank *you*.' Oh God, I didn't know what to say or do. I only knew that if he didn't kiss me I would die, right there and then, crumbling into a messy heap on that Mexican beach.

Xavier brought his face down to my upturned one and, very slowly, oh so incredibly slowly, kissed the corner of my mouth. And then, encouraged by my response, moved his mouth to my open one and kissed me softly. Without thinking, I reached for the back of his head, burying my fingers in his thick, dark hair while my toes scrunched the sand beneath my feet.

Back in my hotel room, I texted both Clare and Fi with the same message:

> For the first time in my life, my legs won't hold me up and I have just slid down the wall and onto the floor.

24

Avoid the Hairy, Toilet-Brush Ones…

Ilanded back at Manchester airport on a cold and dank Sunday morning. October had morphed into November in my week's absence, and I could see through the huge windows as I exited the Nothing to Declare channel, that the new month was already living up to its reputation as Mr Miserable.

I thought back to all the holidays to Spain and the Canaries, to Majorca and Minorca that Mark and I had, over the years, taken with the kids. Tired and quarrelsome after a night flight, or one that had been delayed for hours, I always hoped for some sort of welcome in Arrivals. Even though I'd *known* there was no one waiting to pick us up at the airport – that there was no *need* for anyone to pick us up as our car was in fact waiting for us where we'd left it a week earlier – even though I always *knew* that, there was always that little *frisson* of hope that there might be someone standing and smiling, holding up a piece of paper with

WELCOME HOME, MR AND MRS BERESFORD
AND FAMILY.

Daft really.

I stopped to adjust my watch back to UK time. Six a.m. and nowhere near being light. There were very few passengers around at this time in the morning, and those there were appeared lost and slightly bedraggled. A couple of cleaners were cleaning the floor, manoeuvring their long-handled dust sweepers around chairs and tables in a desultory manner, with the distinct lack of energy and enthusiasm that suggested they'd already been at it for hours. I looked up, eyes scanning for directions to the train station, and there he was, leaning against a post on the periphery of the waiting taxi drivers, friends and relatives.

'Oh, gosh, what on earth are *you* doing here?'

'I needed to see if you were real, that you were as I remembered...' He looked at me with those devastating brown eyes and grinned.

I laughed, pulse revved up several notches. Thank goodness I'd cleaned my teeth with one of those disposable toothbrushes just before landing. 'Oh, how lovely!'

'... and, to be honest, I'm also catching a flight to Copenhagen in...' he looked at his watch '... three hours' time.'

'Ah, *not* just here for me then?'

'Well, I could have gone straight to Departures, but I checked your time of arrival, set off a little earlier and thought I'd welcome you back.' Xavier held up a piece of white A4 paper on which was written:

WELCOME HOME, MRS BERESFORD.

'You remembered.' I laughed out loud.

'How could I forget that you've always aspired to being met at the airport with a card with your name written on it? Come on, I'll buy you a quick cup of coffee and then you need to get your train. You'll be wanting to get home to see your kids.'

'So, you've been back from Mexico just two days and you're having to set off again?' I asked as we sat with a coffee each. I tasted mine: it was bitter and tasteless, nothing like the wonderful coffee I'd been used to every morning in Mexico.

Xavier grimaced, both at his own coffee and the fact he was having to set off once more. 'Yes, last thing I want, really, but a company just outside Copenhagen is interested in buying from us. And then Dad wants me to go on to Brussels. I thought I'd hire a car and drive down to see *ma grandmère à Paris*. I've not seen her for six months and she's having a bit of a strop about it. So, I'll be away until the end of the week.' He took my hand. 'I want to see you, Cassandra, as soon as I'm back in the UK. What do you think?'

I grinned across at him and stroked his hand with my thumb. 'I think, yes please, Mr Bamforth. That would be very acceptable.'

*

All the way back home, on the hour's journey from the airport back into Midhope, crossing the Pennines from Lancashire, through Marsden, Slaithwaite and into Midhope, I sat with a ridiculous grin on my face. I couldn't read my book; skimmed through, without a great deal of interest, the messages that had accumulated during the last twelve hours or so it had taken me to get home from Mexico, and, instead, just thought of Xavier. I went through all the images in my mind, from the moment I'd first seen him, aloof and uninterested in my office; to his raised eyebrows when he saw me in Leeds accompanied by my giant penis; to his looking after me as I threw up on the boat; to that kiss on the beach...

And then I was at the station and Clare was there with Freya, helping me with my case and both hugging me as if I'd been away for years instead of a week.

'Wow, you look fabulous,' Clare said. 'Look at that tan. And your hair's great. Much more natural; suits you like that.' She looked again and grinned. 'You don't half scrub up well.'

'Even after a twelve-hour flight?' I laughed.

'Absolutely. Something, or...' she lowered her voice '... *somebody* has done you some good.'

'Shhh,' I glanced over at Freya who, declaring herself starving, had stopped to buy a giant cookie from the newsagent booth. 'Tell you all about it, later. How's Rageh?'

A big smile lit up Clare's face. 'Rageh is ...' she sighed, '... Rageh is the best thing that ever happened to me. He's working – been called in to an emergency – but he'll be over this evening.'

'No more black eyes?'

'Another visit from her, plus phone calls and rather unpleasant texts… and this.' Clare handed me a copy of one of the Sunday rags – folded and folded again at the relevant article – as we got into her car.

I read the whole article, which, although it didn't put Clare herself, as the owner of Last Stagger, in a particularly good light, only mentioned the name of her business twice. The photographs of Clare, Rageh and the girlfriend were grainy and didn't give a great deal away.

'I actually think I've got away with it fairly lightly,' Clare said. 'What do you reckon?'

I nodded. 'It's not as if it's front-page stuff, is it? It is actually hidden quite well at page…' I peered at the top of the page at where the newspaper was folded '… seventy-five. It might even get Last Stagger some free advertising. What about the hospital, though? How will Rageh's boss and the hospital administrators view it? I mean, he is a children's doctor after all? Might they not think it a bit sleazy, all this?'

'Let me see it,' Freya demanded from the back seat. I handed her the newspaper, knowing it was pointless not to. She'd only Google it, and read it at home if I refused.

Clare bit her lip. 'That's my worry. We'll just have to wait and see if they get hold of the story. They might not think it's a problem. We just don't know at the moment.'

'Well, it wasn't exactly his fault, was it?' Freya tutted through a mouthful of cookie. 'I mean, good on him not to be part of the whole ridiculous male-bonding shebang. *I'd* never marry anyone who thinks it good fun to dress up as a condom and spend time drinking and vomiting it all up in the gutter. Mind you, I'm sure I'll never shackle myself to any man: I think the whole idea of marriage is an outmoded...'

'Right, OK, Freya, we hear you.' Clare and I turned and grinned at my daughter. 'Come on, let's get home; I've missed you and Tom. I hope the house is still standing.'

It was, but drowning in a plethora of homemade banners and flyers that were either still sticky from wet paint or in the process of being created, Freya's printer regurgitating paper from her bedroom as if there were no tomorrow. Paula was sitting at my kitchen table, her face furrowed in concentration as she carefully applied red and green paint to the pencil lines already written on the huge piece of card in front of her.

'Hang on, Cassandra, just let me finish this,' she shouted over her shoulder, 'and then I'll be with you. Green for the countryside, you see,' she went on 'and red for danger.' A pile of dirty dishes tottered precariously on the kitchen units, waiting, presumably, for the dishwasher to be emptied and refilled. One of the electric hobs was sticky with something I couldn't quite make out, while a pan, bearing the remains of someone's scrambled egg, sat carelessly to one side of the other. The bin, stuffed to its limit, was now fighting back, spewing out an empty packet of cornflakes, a banana skin and a dangerous-looking tin of baked beans from its smeared metal jaws. Every inch of the kitchen granite was covered in an eclectic mix of toast crumbs, card, flyers, string, sticky jars of honey and jam and dirty pants.

'Those pants should be in the utility, Freya,' Paula now said, seeing my face and, in doing so apparently condoning the rest of the stuff gathered unceremoniously on my granite. 'I said I'd put the machine on if you got all your dirty washing together.' She wiped her paint-splattered hands on her jeans and, moving the still-wet poster further onto the kitchen table, stood up and came over to give me a hug. 'Welcome home; you look great. And your hair's grown – I always said you should let it have its own way instead of ruining it with those straighteners all the time. Right, what do you think of this lot?' Paula indicated, with her hand, the finished banners that were stacking up against one of the chairs.

'I'll leave you to it,' Clare grinned. 'I've got a ton of work I need to get on with before Rageh comes over. And it looks like *you're* going to be busy too.'

'Right,' I said faintly, speaking for the first time since I'd come into the kitchen. 'You *do* seem to be getting sorted. This is all for Saturday, is it?'

'Yes,' Freya said proudly. 'We're meeting in Norman's Meadow, then marching around the village and back to the meadow for speeches. I'm press secretary and I've been in touch with the *Midhope Examiner* and I've been tweeting—'

'Hang on, you're not fifteen yet. You *can't* tweet...'

'Paula set up a Save Norman's Meadow account and I'm managing it. We've got loads of followers already including... da-dah...' Freya imitated a drum roll, '... Harry Kennedy.'

'Who?'

Freya tutted impatiently. 'Harry *Kennedy*? He's in Second Coming and he's famous. He went to our school. You *know*. Anyway, his grandmother lives in one of the Bamforth Estate's cottages, very near Granddad Norman. He's following us and I've tweeted him and asked him to come on Saturday.'

'Right. Well, good luck with that, darling. Where's Tom, by the way?'

'Still in bed,' Paula said. 'He was out late last night.' She looked at me meaningfully while Freya was bent over one of the posters. 'He's met some new friends at college, hasn't he? He brought one home yesterday. Nice kid. They had a pizza together.'

'Oh, yes,' I said airily, determined that Paula shouldn't think she was telling me something I didn't know already. 'Lovely kid, you're right.'

We left it at that.

By mid-afternoon, I felt restless. I'd unpacked and set the washing machine going, cleaned up after a week with Paula in charge, done a shop and even made a chicken casserole. I knew my restlessness came from a heart-lurching need to see Xavier again, to relive that kiss on the beach, to just be with him...

With Paula and Freya still stuck into organising their protest meeting up at Norman's Meadow, I offered to do a spot of leafleting around Westenbury village and the villages beyond that were also going to be affected by the Bamforth Estate's plans.

With wonderful images of Xavier in my head, and Freya's leaflets in a rucksack over my shoulder, I strode out across the fields and through the woods until I reached Littleford, one of our neighbouring villages.

After the heat and humidity of Mexico, I actually relished the cold fresh air. I chatted to a few friendly people and worked up quite a sweat posting the flyers, at manic speed, through an amazingly diverse set of letter boxes. Why bother with a gym membership when you could walk, bend and stretch like this for free?

Walking down one particular front path, I saw a Jack Russell at the window of the house and, while I should have known better than to deliver through that particular letter box, I went for it. The next thing I knew, the bloody thing had my finger in its jaws and wouldn't let go. Thank God, I was wearing gloves, and leather ones at that, but Jesus, this was embarrassing. Here I was, Westenbury's new head teacher, stuck to a letter box in the certain knowledge that my finger was about to lose all contact with my hand.

With one final yank, I managed to retrieve my finger from the slavering beast's jaws, leaving my leather glove behind. A bit shell-shocked, I walked, gloveless, both tittering and crying down the rest of the estate.

Back at the house, Paula, Tom and Freya enjoyed my retelling of the story – with somewhat over-the-top dramatic actions – immensely, but once in bed I developed rabies, tetanus and gangrene, interspersed with an uncontrollable urge to titter with an even more uncontrollable desire to have a very naked and tanned Xavier in the bed with me, all of which was not conducive to a good night's sleep. I woke tired and bad-tempered, and nearly rang school to say I wasn't well.

I didn't.

My second half term as head teacher.

Even after a long flight, jet lag and a day spent wiping, hoovering, washing and disinfecting, not to mention ten rounds with a Jack Russell, I was more than ready to begin the new session at school. I'd spent a lot of the flight back from Cancún planning the weeks ahead and was looking forward to getting stuck in once more.

'Right, we've got squirrels.'

I stared at Stan the caretaker, who'd pounced on me as soon as I opened the main door.

'Squirrels?' I'd heard of nits, lice and even crabs but *squirrels*? 'What do you mean?' I frowned.

'Time of year, Mrs Beresford. Come on, I'll show you.'

I walked behind Stan into the hall and followed the direction of his pointing finger. I squinted up at the ceiling but could see nothing. 'What am I looking at?'

'Little buggers have got into the roof space where it's warm. They've started eating the ceiling.'

'Eating it?' I glanced across at Stan. 'I thought squirrels ate *nuts*?' I smiled.

'Not a laughing matter, Mrs Beresford,' Stan admonished me. 'If that hole up there gets any bigger you'll need a new ceiling and the kiddies won't be able to eat their dinner in here. Health and Safety and all that.'

'Oh crikey, what does a new ceiling in an old Victorian school cost these days?' Gone were the days when the local authority shelled out for repairs. We were on our own. Or, at least, the Trust was.

'I've already rung Rentokil,' Stan said importantly as a tiny flurry of plaster flakes drifted down towards us. 'They'll be here later this afternoon.'

'Not until then? Is the ceiling safe? It's not going to fall in on us, is it?'

'Oh goodness me, no. The squirrels come in most years.' Stan rubbed his chin. 'Think of it as their winter holiday home. Mind you, I've never known 'em start *eating* the place before.'

'Well, let's keep this to ourselves. I don't want the children to know.'

'Mrs Head, you looks wonderfuls.' Deimante followed me into my office as soon as I'd opened the door and hung up my coat. 'Hairs good, should keep its longs like that. Too shorts before for goods-looking lady like you. Now, I mights be leetle bits late sis afternoons...'

'Oh? Well, I do need to know if you're not going to be out on the lane, Deimante. If you'd leave your lollipop where we know where it is, then I'm sure one of us can pop out to patrol the traffic at three thirty.' I actually quite fancied jumping out into the road with a lollipop.

Deimante leant over my desk and whispered confidentially. 'I goes for Samiri Exam.'

'Right. OK. Samiri Exam?'

'*Taip*. Yes, is correct.'

'So, is this an exam for a new job? We'd hate to lose you.'

'Lose me?' Deimante frowned. 'Nots getting lost. Very very goods at directions...'

'Yes, I know you are. Oh, I know...' Light suddenly dawned. 'Is the Samiri Exam the test that you have to take in order to become a British citizen? You'll have to answer questions such as: "What is the name of the admiral who died in a sea battle and can now be seen on a monument in Trafalgar Square in London?"'

'Sat's easy,' Deimante scoffed. 'Is Nelson. And Drake was bossy of Armadas...'

'Oh, you'll have no problem.' I beamed as if she were one of my pupils about to take her SATs tests.

'No, Mrs Heads, you don't gets it. Samiri Exam.' Deimante was getting impatient. 'S A M I R I.' She enunciated each letter crossly.

I glanced at the clock. I had a meeting with David Henderson in five minutes. 'That's fine, you go for it,' I said, having no idea what she was going for.

Deimante grabbed her lollipop from where it was leaning against the chair and, sitting down, leaned back, legs apart and proceeded to use it in what I can only describe as a rather lifelike simulation of penetrative sex, just as David Henderson and Edward Bamforth walked in.

'Samiri Test?' Deimante panted. 'Yes?'

'Smear test perhaps?' David said, eyebrows raised.

'Oh, *smear* test. Right, got you now. Absolutely, Deimante, take as long as you need for it.'

She straightened her clothing, pulled down her luminous vest before shaking her head in despair at David. 'What a dickheads she is,' she laughed affectionately, before heading for the office door.

'I'm sorry, I wasn't expecting you as well, Mr Bamforth.' The very idea that Xavier's father was in my office had me hot under the collar. Had he told his father he'd been with me in Mexico?

'Yes, sorry, last-minute thing really. Just thought I'd pop in on my way to work. Bumped into David in the car park.' He paused, looking me up and down. 'You look as if you've seen some sun. Been anywhere nice?'

'Er, Mexico,' I said, blushing.

'Really? Xavier was there last week as well. Must be the place to go.'

'Mustn't it?' I squeaked. 'Now, can David help as well or did you just want to see me?'

'Just wanted a word about the plans, you know? I'm not sure we got off to a very good start at the meeting here at school and then...' Edward paused, '... and then at the general meeting in the village hall I think I came to blows with your daughter. It wasn't my intention to fight with a little girl.'

I laughed. 'She may be a *little* girl, but she's nearly fifteen, she's feisty and she's on a mission.'

'And that's why I'm here. I believe she's planning some sort of protest this weekend?'

'Oh, news travels fast.'

'It does when it's plastered all over the *Midhope Examiner*. Lefty rag, that one.'

'Oh, brilliant,' I said proudly. 'She and my mother have been organising it all week.'

'To be held in Norman's Meadow?'

'Yes, right there in Norman's Meadow.'

'Well, Mrs Beresford, as I'm sure I reminded you a while ago, Norman's Meadow *isn't* Norman's, but *ours* – part of the Bamforth Estate. I suggest that any protest that is being held on those meadows will involve trespass on the part of your daughter. And your mother. I would also suggest that, as head teacher here, you really should remain neutral.'

'Oh? Why?'

Edward didn't seem to have an answer to this. 'Well,' he said, after a while, 'you have a position here. You have clout. It may be seen as abuse of that position – you know, politicising your headship…'

'I'm willing to risk that. I will be there, Mr Bamforth, supporting my daughter, my mother, the tenants, villagers and farmers of Westenbury. And… and… Harry Kennedy.'

'Who?' Both Edward and David Henderson stared at me.

I tutted. 'Harry Kennedy? You *know*, the kid from round here who won *The X Factor*? I think, if you have Harry Kennedy in Norman's Meadow, you'll have the national press as well as the local rag in attendance. Maybe even *Look North*.'

'I'll remind you once again, Mrs Beresford, your involvement in organising some protest on the Bamforth

Estate will not only look poor for your position as head teacher, but will involve trespass.'

'And as *I* said, Mr Bamforth, I'm willing to risk that.' Blimey, I was getting cockier with each week that passed. Where had Cassandra Beresford, doormat and cuckolded wife, gone? 'Now, can I help you with anything else? I do have a school to run…'

Once Edward Bamforth had left, I turned to David Henderson. 'We've got squirrels.'

'Have we? Friendly ones?' He smiled in my direction.

'Up in the roof. According to Stan they're eating the ceiling.'

David frowned. 'Not good.' He lowered his voice. 'I'm glad you didn't mention it while Edward Bamforth was here,' he said conspiratorially. 'He'd have loved that, wouldn't he? The school falling apart and him just the man to build us a new one.'

'Absolutely. Someone's coming out once the children have left this afternoon to look at it.'

'Good, we don't want parents getting wind of this. Not a word to anyone. Right? We'll get the little varmints sorted once the kids have left this afternoon and no one will be any the wiser.'

'Exactly,' I nodded. David and I looked at each other and together said, 'Mum's the word.'

And we'd have been fine, no one *would* have been any the wiser, had one particularly bold – and one can only assume hungry – squirrel not had the misfortune to fancy a particularly large piece of loose plaster, miss his step and plummet from the ceiling, landing neatly and squarely into Mikey McArthur's lunchtime chocolate pudding and pink sauce.

I was crossing the hall at the time, admonishing those with elbows on the table or handling their roast potato like a lollipop, and saw the whole scene before my own eyes. Mikey, for once stunned into silence, eyed the equally stunned squirrel for a few seconds before, totally traumatised, he shot out of his seat, sending pudding – and squirrel – onto the floor.

Mrs Atkinson, the dinner supervisor, who habitually jack-booted her way round the dining room, rounded on Mikey but, when she saw the pink-sauce-covered squirrel, screamed loudly, backing away as it staggered in her direction like some Hallowe'en zombie. The squirrel suddenly stopped, mid stagger, sat up on its haunches and, obviously perking up, proceeded to eat the chocolate pudding and sauce that had stuck to its paws. There were a few seconds of silence before the rest of the children – some craning their necks, some out of their seats, and some screaming and shouting – joined in the general hullabaloo. Tufty stared cheekily at the kids before shooting underneath the tables and chairs and out of the door and to freedom.

Keep this under wraps? Not a chance in hell.

By early Friday evening the whole of the garage was piled high with banners nailed onto wooden posts, boxes of flyers and balloons printed with the words:

JUST SAY NO!

Paula drove round in her old Fiesta – she rarely brought it out, preferring to walk and take the bus in order to save money and the planet – and Tom and I helped her and Freya load the boot and back seat with the banners. There was:

CENTURIES TO MATURE, MINUTES TO DESTROY

as well as:

DON'T HAVE THE DEATH OF YOUR VILLAGE ON YOUR HANDS

and:

THEIR CASH, YOUR CONSCIENCE

Dressed in her best emo gear, Freya had decided to spend the night at Paula's after the pair of them had cooked food round at Granddad Norman's. 'We need to be at the battlefield at the crack of dawn,' she announced. 'And we need to make sure Granddad Norman is up, ready and dressed for it. I mean, he is the main event, after all.'

I laughed. 'Granddad is always up early. Anyway, I thought Harry Wotsit was the big attraction?'

Freya sighed. 'Oh, wouldn't it be wonderful if he made an appearance? He ought to, seeing his granny's home is at stake. Paula is hoping Swampy is going to come, too.'

'Really?' I turned to my mother who was struggling with the logistics of the final banner.

'Absolutely,' she puffed. 'He and I go back a long way. He said he'd put in an appearance if I sent him the train fare.'

'Oh, Paula, you didn't? And where have you got the money for this lot?'

Paula looked defiant. 'I have savings, and Granddad Norman has contributed some.'

'Forget that,' I said. 'Whatever the pair of you've spent, I'll reimburse you. Don't forget you did some babysitting last week – I owe you for that.'

'Whatever,' Paula said dismissively. 'If I'm out of pocket, and out on the street, I know where to find you. You are coming tomorrow, aren't you, Cassandra Moonbeam?'

'Oh, absolutely. I'm looking forward to it.'

As the pair of them drove off, Paula's exhaust rattling, Tom appeared at the front door. 'I'm off out, Mum. I'll be back late.' And before I could ask any more, he was off, running for the bus into Midhope.

I was dying to see Xavier. He'd texted once during the week to say he was in Paris and eating *escargots* with *grandmère*. It had all sounded highly exotic and I was loath to say I was in Westenbury eating sausage and mash with my two kids. I bet Ophelia didn't eat sausage and mash. Or ketchup. I did hope she hadn't flown out to Paris to surprise him.

I was contemplating my Friday night treat of cheese on toast and a glass of red wine when my phone barked the arrival of a text.

Xavier? I grabbed the phone.

Mark.

Are you home? I do hope you had a good time. We did always plan a trip to the Caribbean together, didn't we?

Yes we did, you pillock. Probably at the same time you were planning little cosy trips to London with Tina. Ha! I texted back.

Fabulous, thank you, Mark. I didn't realise how much I would enjoy my own company. Thailand, I think next. Enjoy your weekend.

There, that would show him.

The dog barked again. I really would have to change that damned canine to something a little more soothing.

Xavier! My heart lurched as I feverishly read his text.

Are you at home? Could I pop round to see you?

Could he? I'd quite possibly die if he didn't.

Yes of course. That would be lovely. Everyone else is out.

OK, I'll be there in twenty minutes.

Twenty minutes to frenziedly pull off my work clothes, shower, rub moisturiser into every bit of me – tan was looking good – pull on jeans; pull them off and try on a skirt; pull the jeans back on again; try them with a white shirt, a pink shirt, a navy sweater, back to the white shirt... buttons fastened? Definitely not. Three unfastened and I was begging for it; one and I looked like a headmistress. You are a bloody headmistress, Cassie. Two buttons, then. Shoes? Sandals? It's bloody November, Cassie. I went for a pair of soft suede ankle boots and stood at the mirror. Too much makeup? Not enough? Red lipstick? No, pink with the tan...

By the time the bell went downstairs I was a gibbering wreck and had to count to ten before I went down. I opened the door.

'Hi, you,' Xavier smiled, kissing my cheek oh so softly. 'I've really missed you.'

25

Hunt the Lemon...

'**P**resent for you,' Xavier smiled as I led him through to the kitchen to find glasses and pour the wine I'd remembered to shove in the fridge before my mad dash upstairs.

Chocolates? French perfume? Champagne?

'Aren't you going to open it?' He sounded disappointed.

'Yes, yes, of course.' I said, and then laughed as I pulled out a CD of Gloria Gaynor's greatest hits, and a string of those French bonbons that kids bring back from France. I was so faint with longing for him to kiss me that I couldn't put them back in their bag, and left them on the kitchen table so that he wouldn't see my hands shaking.

'Cassie?'

'Yes?'

'I don't know what you've done to me, but I've spent a week unable to get you out of my mind.'

'Oh, crikey,' I squeaked and then, realising I probably sounded like a fifth former from *Malory Towers*, I made an effort to calm down. 'I mean, how lovely. And in Paris, too, with all the distractions on offer there?'

Xavier laughed. 'I'm not sure my grandmother is that much of a distraction. I'd rather have been here seeing you. She usually gives me earache about my life, about my lack of children, about Ophelia.'

I was curious. 'Did you never want children?'

'I'd have loved children,' Xavier said sadly. 'Ophelia seemed keen to begin with, but then she kept making excuses – you know, the flat was too small in London; she didn't want to bring up children in Yorkshire as she didn't know the area; she was in the middle of yet another business venture. All a bit too late now...'

'Well, you can borrow mine,' I said. And then, because it sounded awfully forward and presumptuous, I said, 'I mean—'

He laughed. 'I know what you mean, don't worry.' He came over to where I was standing against the fridge and took my glass from my hand. 'Cassie, if I don't kiss you, I'll go mad.'

The smooth, cold surface of the fridge behind my back was a distinct contrast to his warm mouth that started at my lips and was now forming moist shapes on my neck and shoulders while making its way towards the remaining fastened buttons of my shirt. Thank God, I hadn't buttoned up to the neck, was my one thought: I don't think I could have prolonged the suspense. I pulled his jersey over his head and started unfastening a few buttons of my own. Heavens, he smelt good. I buried my nose into his smooth brown chest, breathing in his scent as he unbuttoned my shirt cuffs and slowly pulled my shirt from my shoulders.

The fridge chose that moment to bounce into life, throbbing rhythmically beneath me. Every sense was aroused as Xavier took a mouthful of cold wine and, with an open mouth, passed it between my own lips before reaching behind me, unfastening my bra and pressing me back against the cold vibrating fridge…

'Hi, Cassandra Moonbeam, it's only me.' Paula's voice drifted down the hall and disappeared into the sitting room at the other end of the house.

Without thinking, Xavier stuffed my bra into his trouser pocket and pulled his sweater over his unbuttoned shirt before smoothing his hair and sitting himself down nonchalantly at the table with his glass of wine. I shot into the utility with my shirt, closed the door behind me and frantically did up buttons, before running fingers through my mussed-up hair.

'Oh…' I heard Paula say as she opened the kitchen door and saw Xavier.

'Hi, I'm Xavier Bamforth.' I heard his chair push back as he stood. 'Cassie's just gone to find a … er, a lemon…' He laughed. 'Apparently she discovered a taste for gin and tonic in Mexico.'

I looked round desperately for a lemon in the vegetable rack at the back of the utility room and then, clutching a very poor withered specimen as if it were the Holy Grail, opened the door, a bright smile on my face.

'Oh, Mum, I didn't hear you... This is Xavier Bamforth. Funnily enough, we ended up at the same hotel in Mexico. He's just, er, just brought back a CD he borrowed while we were there.'

'Oh, right. Hi, Xavier.' Paula seemed even more on edge than we were. 'I just called back for the megaphone.'

'The megaphone?' Xavier and I looked at her.

'Yes, I borrowed a megaphone for tomorrow and left it here somewhere. I thought it was down in the sitting room but I couldn't see it there. It's probably in the garage.'

Xavier looked at his watch. 'I'm going to have to go, Cassie. I promised I'd have dinner with my father.' He turned to Paula and said, by way of explanation, 'I've been in Europe all week – Denmark and Paris – and I need to report back.'

'Er, right.' Paula didn't seem to know what to say and I glanced across at her, trying to work out what was wrong with her. 'So, are you Edward Bamforth's son, then?'

'Yes,' Xavier said cheerfully. 'The enemy, I'm afraid.' He glanced at his watch once more and drained his glass of wine. 'Thanks for the drink, Cassie. Bye, Paula, nice to meet you.'

I followed him out, both of us giggling like naughty children. 'I am an adult, for heaven's sake,' I laughed, 'and a totally free agent. I was sure Freya was with her.'

'Come and have dinner with me tomorrow,' he smiled. 'I'm not a bad cook and we can finish what we started... that is, if you want?'

'Yes, please,' I said as he kissed me, leaving me in no doubt as to what was at the end of the finishing line the following evening, and left.

Still giggling, I went back into the kitchen and threw the manky old lemon I still had in my hand into the bin.

'Xavier Bamforth?' Paula said. She was sitting at the kitchen table, her back towards me.

'Yes.'

'Cassandra, he had a *bra* hanging out of his trouser pocket.'

'Don't worry,' I giggled. 'It was mine, not his.'

'So, are you seeing him?'

'Mum, I am madly, truly deeply in love with Xavier Bamforth. I've never felt like this before. I've truly never been in love before. It's heaven. It's bliss. Give me some more wine… I need to celebrate…'

'Cassandra, you can't be.'

'What, because of Mark? After what Mark's done, I can do anything I want. I am a totally free agent.'

'No, really, Cassandra, you can't be.'

I poured myself more wine. 'Oh, you mean I'm sleeping with the enemy…'

Paula swivelled round in my direction. 'And *are* you sleeping with him?'

'I certainly intend to be by tomorrow evening,' I said, beaming at her.

'Cassandra, you can't.'

'Mum, I *can* and I *will*.'

'No, Cassandra, you *can't*.'

I looked at her white face. 'What is it? Why can't I?'

She looked directly at me. 'Because, Cassandra,' she said slowly, 'I've got a horrible feeling that Xavier Bamforth is your brother.'

26

Explain Yourself, Paula…

'What the fuck are you talking about, Paula? What do you mean, he could be my *brother*?' I glared at Paula. What the hell was she up to now?

Paula appeared not to know quite what to do. She stood up, sat down and then stood up again. 'Look, I need to get back to Granddad and Freya. I only popped out for the megaphone. They'll wonder where I've got to.'

'What? Paula, you are going to sit down and tell me what the hell you are on about. Let me ring Freya and tell her you're just helping me with something here and you'll be a while.'

Once I'd returned to the kitchen, Paula was pacing the floor like a caged animal. I put the kettle on and made the ginseng tea Paula always drank and poured myself more wine before we sat at the table.

'Explain yourself. You can't just come out with a

comment like that and then expect to leave without telling me what you mean.'

'Yes, you're right.' Paula had regained some of her colour, but she was still in a state of anxiety. 'I'd been seeing Rowan for a few months...'

'My father, Rowan? Rowan who left you to go to Morocco?'

Paula nodded. 'It was like this, you see, Cassandra...'

27

Paula

1976

'I've got some pride,' she'd said to Rowan's departing back. 'And it wasn't bloody Keir Hardie who said that – it was Bernadette Devlin.'

Paula sat on her mother's tablecloth for another good ten minutes hoping Rowan would come back, hoping he'd tell her he'd been joking and of course they were going to go off travelling together.

Paula lay there in the sultry heat of that hot July evening for a bit longer, not quite knowing what to do. She felt spaced out, knew she was a little drunk, maybe a little stoned. Never having smoked pot before, she *liked* the idea of being stoned. Rowan was often stoned, she realised. She should have got stoned with him before: it felt sophisticated, worldly, less provincial, less this

damned town that she appeared to be stuck in. Well, sod
Rowan. She didn't need *him* to go travelling. Lots of girls
went off by themselves. She could get a job in London,
maybe. Earn more money than at bloody Crosland,
Crawshaw & Sons. But where would she live in London?
How did you go about finding a flat, a job?

It was getting darker: not the black of a winter night,
but a subtle, hazy dusk that would take over for only a
few hours before the hot sun would break through once
more in this amazing, wonderful summer of 1976 that
people would talk about, and then reminisce over, in the
same way they'd know exactly where they were when
Kennedy was shot and Elvis died.

Paula couldn't bear the thought of the next day and
the day after that, having to sit in that damned office with
Janet on one side discussing how much stuff she'd now
accumulated in her bottom drawer in case Alan actually
asked her to get engaged. While Alison at the desk to her
right, waved her own tiny solitaire pointedly across her
at Janet before solicitously asking, after every weekend,
'Any news?'

Paula glanced at her watch. It was nearly ten o'clock.
She sat up and started to gather the remains of the picnic.
Wine – lucky it wasn't red – had spilt on Dot's white
starched tablecloth and a couple of grass stains and
ash from the joint they'd shared stared out accusingly
down one of its sides. She sighed, knowing she'd have to
secrete the cloth upstairs and get to work with the OMO
in the bath before her mother saw it and started asking
questions.

When she'd gathered everything up, retrieved the empty wine bottle from behind one tree and had a pee behind another, Paula headed for the Japanese garden and the hole in the hedge. Except, in the gathering dark, it all appeared a bit different and she realised she'd lost her bearings. Must be more stoned than she thought, she giggled to herself, tripping over a stone that suddenly appeared in her path.

'*What did you do last night, Janet?*'

'*I got engaged. You, Paula?*'

'*Stoned, I got stoned, Janet, and had sex in someone's garden...*'

She giggled again and then stopped suddenly as she realised someone was watching her progress from his seat on the decking of the summerhouse.

Rowan? Had he waited for her, after all?

'Can I help you? You do know this is our garden, you're on our property...?'

'Oh, property is theft,' Paula said, more bravely than she felt. 'I only borrowed it for a while.'

He laughed at that and Paula, peering through the half-light, was relieved to see he was a boy, probably around her own age, rather than an older man. 'Not in my back yard, you don't, you cheeky thing.'

She laughed with him: it *was* a bloody cheeky thing to do, after all, to creep into someone's garden and have a picnic there. And get stoned and have sex as well, she reminded herself. Blimey, her mother would have an absolute fit if she knew what she'd been up to.

'Just thought I'd have a little wander,' she apologised. 'It's such a beautiful evening and I didn't think anyone would mind.'

'We could have you arrested for trespass.'

'Well, yes, I suppose you could. But you'd have to go back up to the house to phone the police, by which time I'd be gone.' Paula sniffed the air. 'And the police would then come and arrest you for smoking weed.' She realised the path she was taking was heading totally in the wrong direction and she turned, thankful to see the outline of the hedge to her left. 'See you.' She shifted the picnic basket to her other hand and set off once more.

'Do you want a drink?' The boy held up a bottle and a glass. 'I've only one glass, but you can share it.'

Paula hesitated. She didn't want to go home. Her mum and dad would still be up, demanding to know what she'd been doing. 'OK, thanks.' She turned once more and walked up the steps towards the boy.

He shifted over so that she could share the wooden sun bed and the one glass of wine and then passed her the joint.

What the hell: why not? She was no longer a novice – she knew how to do this now. Paula took a deep drag on the joint, closing her eyes as she inhaled the acrid smoke.

'Careful,' he warned. 'It's strong stuff, that.'

She inhaled again, wanting to block out the fact that Rowan had left her: he wasn't coming back; he didn't want her to go off with him after all.

Paula turned to look at the boy. 'So, do you live in that big house, up there?'

'No, I'm just the gardener. I live here in the garden.' His voice, cultured, educated, was not that of a gardener from Midhope.

'Like Bill and Ben?' she laughed.

He laughed with her and she looked more closely at him. He was very good-looking, she thought, tipsily. Not her type really, but lovely eyes. Were they blue? She peered even more closely. 'Are they blue?'

'Are what blue?'

'Your eyes?'

'They were last time I looked in the mirror.'

'Hmm. So, what are you doing down here, all by yourself?'

'Having a drink…' he waved the bottle once more, '… and getting away from the dinner party my parents are having at the house.'

'Oh, so *not* Bill or Ben then?'

'One of them, I reckon.' He smiled and took the joint from her, inhaling and filling his own lungs.

'So, *Bill*, what do you do? I've not seen you round here before.'

'I've just finished at Bristol University. I've come back *oop north* – as they say round here – to start work with my father.'

'And are you happy about that? Do you want to stay round here?' Paula couldn't imagine why anyone would want to come back of their own accord, once they'd managed to leave, and she peered at him once more to gauge his reaction.

Bill shrugged. 'I've been away from here, first at school and then at university, since I was eight. I know the boys I was at prep school with before I went away to boarding school. Most of them are still round here:

Old Midhope families who've owned, and still do own, the textile mills and the engineering companies. There are loads of them; they always make their way back to where they started from.'

'Right.' Paula was beginning to feel very floaty: she couldn't decide if she was totally miserable or a strong, independent woman who could do anything she wanted. A bit of both really.

'I'm off to Paris next week. Going to stay with some friends of my parents for a month before I start work here. I'm really looking forward to that. I love Paris.'

Paula felt sudden tears well. Oh, to have a family that had friends in *Paris*, for heaven's sake. As far as she knew, Dot and Norman had never been to France – except for Norman being part of the D-Day landings during the war – never mind have friends there. She wiped the tears away with the back of her hand.

'Hey, come on,' Bill said kindly. 'What is it? What's the matter?' He took Paula's hand and stroked it gently.

'I'm just feeling a bit lost and alone.' She sniffed loudly, wiping her eyes on her long purple cheesecloth skirt.

Bill laughed again. 'Well, what do you expect, wandering round someone else's garden at night all by yourself?'

He moved nearer to her, slipped his arm around her shoulders and pulled her to him. While she'd convinced herself that Rowan had smelt wonderful, in reality, she now admitted to herself, he'd only ever smelt slightly feral and unwashed, while this boy gave off a fresh, clean scent: some sort of lemony aftershave; and his hair, short, blond and springy, smelt as if he'd just got out of the shower. He very likely had. 'Have a good cry; grass can do that to you,' he said into her hair. 'You really shouldn't have any more.'

Paula didn't like to tell him she'd been getting stoned all evening. It was lovely just lying there in the warm evening air, the night-scented stocks, jasmine and honeysuckle mixing their thuriferous perfume with the clean scents of this boy. She leant into him further, feeling the heat from his body.

'I think I'd like to kiss you,' she said dreamily.

'By all means do,' he laughed. 'You're very different, but very gorgeous.'

Paula turned and met his mouth with hers. He tasted of toothpaste, wine and pot, a heady combination of clean living and rebellion. He teased her with his fingers and his tongue until she knew she was going to go all the way with him because she wanted to, and because she could. And while Rowan might not want her, this boy obviously did. At one point he stopped, looked down at her and said, 'Are you sure about this. I don't want to take advantage of someone who is out of their head.'

'I can assure you, I can just as easily get up, walk through that hedge and make my way home. Or, I can stay here and finish what we've started. I don't usually do this sort of thing, but from now on I'm a liberated woman and am going to do whatever feels good.'

And so she did.

28

Blame It on the Heat...

'So, who the hell was he, then, Mum? And what's he got to do with Xavier?' I just stared at my mother after she'd talked solidly for the past half an hour, relating the events of that hot evening back in 1976 when she'd gone into someone's garden and, by the sound of it, had sex with some stranger who now appeared to be my father.

'I *knew* he lived there – was the son of the owner.'

'And?' I wanted to shake Paula, make her get to the point.

'Well it's *obvious* who he was, for heaven's sake.'

'Is it?'

Paula tutted. 'Edward Bamforth. Who do you think I've been going on about?'

I actually laughed. 'What? You're trying to tell me Edward Bamforth is my *father*?'

Paula looked sheepish. 'Possibly... Probably...'

'Well, make your damned mind up, Paula. He either is or he isn't. And if he is, well, you've just bloody well ruined my life once again.'

Paula sighed, and twisted the many bangles up her arm, a sure sign she was distressed. 'Cassandra, like all sensible girls I was on the pill. I couldn't get pregnant, or so I thought. I was nearly twenty-one and madly in love with Rowan. He was the first boy I'd ever slept with.' She stopped and glared at me. 'You know, this isn't easy, Cassandra, talking like this. I am your mother, after all.'

'All right, Mum, I'm sorry. Just tell me what happened next.'

'When I woke up the next day I was so ashamed of what had happened, as well as utterly miserable that Rowan had gone, I couldn't go into work. I stayed in bed all day, unable to face the world, and though your nan knew I wasn't really ill she understood there was something wrong and she played along with it and brought me nice things to drink and let me sleep.'

'Nan would. She was very kind under all that brusqueness.'

'I made plans that day. I was going to save up as much as I could and then set off travelling by myself. When I found out I was pregnant, I was devastated. Why the pill hadn't worked, I've no idea. Maybe I missed a couple – I was never very good at remembering to take it.'

'So, it's just as likely I'm Rowan's as much as I am Edward Bamforth's?'

'I convinced myself you *were* Rowan's. We'd been, you know, sleeping together for a couple of months. It was just a one-off with Edward Bamforth. I *wanted* the baby to be Rowan's. I thought if I were able to tell him that I was pregnant, he'd come back and stand by me.'

'You never thought about a termination then?'

Paula looked at me. 'Yes, constantly. But Granddad Norman persuaded me not to. Said he'd known girls during the war who'd had backstreet abortions and who'd been maimed for life.'

'But it was 1976, Paula. People had legal terminations all the time.'

'I know. Part of me hung on to the hope that once Rowan knew, he'd come back for me and we'd go and live in Hong Kong or somewhere.' She shook her head. 'I was a fairly immature twenty-year-old.'

'You're not helping me out here, Paula,' I tutted. 'Which one of them *is* my father?'

'Well, if I tell you that Rowan had red hair...'

'Really?' I was surprised. 'You've never told me that before.'

'Just think about it, Cassandra. I've got very dark hair and brown eyes and Rowan had beautiful auburn hair and brown eyes. You're blonde and blue-eyed.'

I tried to picture Edward Bamforth. 'Edward Bamforth's grey and balding.'

Paula smiled. 'But at twenty-one he had blond hair and blue eyes.'

My stomach was churning and there was a pounding at my temples. 'But if Edward Bamforth *is* my father, then

Xavier is my half-brother.' I started to cry, huge tears rolling down my face. 'It's not fair, Mum, it's not *fair*.'

Paula stroked my hair as I buried my head in my arms on the table and wept.

'I'm so sorry, Cassandra, but I had to tell you. You know you can't have any sort of, well, sexual relationship with Xavier. It's not right.'

'But if you hadn't told me all this, I'd never have known. Everything would have been OK.' I was crying into my shirtsleeve turning the white cotton transparent with my tears.

'Yes, but *I'd* have known,' Paula pleaded. 'Can't you see that?'

I lifted my head. 'So, does Edward Bamforth have any clue he may have fathered a child that night? Did you go and tell him?'

'Well, for the first few years, I'd no real idea. I tried to pretend it hadn't really happened. I mean…' Paula was embarrassed. 'Look, I'd done something I was terribly ashamed of. I'd … I'd slept with two different men within an hour of each other. And in someone else's backyard. All these years later, I still can't think about it without feeling utterly guilty, and yes, totally ashamed. How could I admit to it? Cassandra, this is the first time I've told *anyone*. Can you imagine telling your *nan* what I'd been up to?'

'Well, no…'

'You have to understand, Cassandra, I *still* don't really know. And I *might* have actually gone and spoken to him, told him he was possibly your father. He was a nice guy; I liked him. He rang for a taxi to take me home that night.'

'Oh, big of him.'

'Cassandra, he didn't force himself on me, if that's what you're thinking. From what I remember – and it *is* forty years ago, for heaven's sake – I instigated it. Needed to prove to myself that someone wanted me after Rowan abandoned me...' Paula stood up and refilled the kettle and then looked at the clock. 'I'm going to have to get back. Freya will wonder what on earth's happened to me.'

'Text her and say we're sorting something and you'll be back in half an hour,' I pleaded. I didn't want to be alone, didn't want to go to bed with this new knowledge hammering in my brain.

Paula sat down with her tea. 'As I say, I *might* have plucked up the courage to go down to the house and have a word with him at some point, but funnily enough your nan did a bit of cleaning there around that time for Mrs Bamforth. Do you remember when your nan used to have quite a few cleaning jobs? Anyway, Mrs Bamforth's daily was a friend of Nan's and when she had some sort of fall, Nan stood in for her. It was only for a few weeks and it'd be about the time Nan found out I was pregnant. I can see her now, sitting at the kitchen table with that damned great brown teapot in its tea cosy. Do you remember it?'

I nodded.

'"Well," she said, "it's not just you that's got yourself into trouble, Paula. Edward Bamforth's got some nice girl in France pregnant. There's a right how's-your-father going on down at that big house: Mrs B crying, Mr B shouting and that young Edward slamming doors and saying he's not getting married." After that, I really couldn't introduce him to the idea that he *might possibly* have fathered another child at almost the same time.'

'You were a rampant lot in the seventies, weren't you?' I said almost bitterly.

'I blame it all on that hot summer of 1976,' Paula said vaguely. 'If it had rained you wouldn't be here.'

'Thanks for that,' I muttered. 'Well, you must have come across him since. Does he know who you are?'

'No. I saw him in town once, but he moves in different circles. And once he was married, he lived right the other side of Midhope, over towards Colneborough. I never saw him again. It was forty years ago, Cassandra. When I saw him chairing the meeting the other week, I wouldn't have had a clue it *was* him. It was a one-off and all in the past.'

'Xavier's mother *is* French.' I said. 'He's just been staying with his grandmother in Paris.' I broke off as I heard a key in the door. For a split second, I thought it might be Xavier returning.

'What's up?' Tom walked into the kitchen and looked at us both, frowning as he saw me with a tear-stained face once more. 'Is it Dad? What's he done now?'

'No, darling, it's not your father this time. I wish to goodness it was.'

After a week of typically morose, damp November weather, the Saturday morning promised a respite from the mist and rain – perfect for the Norman's Meadow protest. Tom, who had sat with me after Paula had finally gone around 10 p.m. and listened while I told him all about Xavier, as well as Paula's revelations, was up early and brought me tea in bed.

'Right, Mum, you're not going to cry today,' Tom warned sitting on my bed. 'You can give me a driving lesson and we'll drive over to Granddad's and see what's happening. You do know Freya's been on Twitter and Instagram saying Harry Kennedy's going to be there?'

'What, saying he's definitely going to be there, not that he *might* be there? Oh lordy, she's going to get lynched...'

While I was in the shower, my mind went over and over what Paula had revealed the previous evening. Once she'd left I'd been very tempted to ring Xavier there and then and tell him, but how do you tell the man who's still got your bra in his trouser pocket that he might be your brother? And what about his poor mother, knowing that her husband of forty years has a love child? It really wasn't a nice feeling to think I was the result of three stoned kids getting carried away in a huge garden.

I'd always wondered about my father, of course, who he was, where he was, why he didn't live with us like other dads. It was always my cousin, Davina's, final insult in any childhood argument: 'Well, *you* don't even have a daddy.' At first, when I was really small, Paula told me Daddy was an explorer and couldn't live with us as he was off exploring new places. I remember learning about Columbus at school (Paula had tutted when I said we were doing Voyages of Discovery, asking whether the native Americans hadn't *realised* who they were until some little Italian had come along, *discovered* them and plundered their resources) and shouting out that my daddy was out in the world discovering new places, too. It had given me some credence with the other kids in the class who regularly scoffed at Paula's dreadlocks, piercings and flowing dresses.

I stepped out of the shower, drying myself on one of the huge fluffy cream towels I insisted on having in the bathrooms. It had been years before I realised towels were meant to be big, soft and bouncy, not cheap, scratchy affairs that remained wet and slightly odorous from having nowhere to dry in between use. By the time I was in my early teens and knew about sex, I quickly worked out that my mother had got herself pregnant and my father had done a runner. Rowan in Morocco took over from Daddy the Explorer and, fairly uninterested, I'd put him to one side and got on with my life.

I'd cried enough over Mark, I told myself severely as I felt tears threaten once more. I really didn't want to start all over again with Xavier. But it was very tempting to get back into my pyjamas and curl up on the sofa with hot chocolate and the remote control. You are a strong woman I reminded myself. I looked in the mirror. Slim, tanned and with long blonde hair into the bargain: well at least I looked OK. Sort yourself, girl: get out there and support your daughter, mother and grandfather. I found a pair of jeans I'd bought and never been able to get into before, added a cream cashmere polo jumper, flat brown leather boots and my shearling jacket and went downstairs to find Tom.

*

'My goodness, look at this lot. Do you want me to park the car?' Tom had driven the fifteen minutes or so to Granddad Norman's but my usual parking place down the lane was already occupied.

''S OK,' Tom breathed. 'I can do it. He reversed the car, manoeuvring it into a tiny space in front of a brand-new Mini.

'Stop, Tom, STOP.' There was a gentle bump as the car's back end made contact with the front of the Mini and a woman immediately jumped out of the driver's seat.

'Shit.' I jumped out myself and walked to where the woman was examining her car.

'I'm *so* sorry,' I gushed. 'Tom's learning.'

She smiled. 'It's fine, really, no damage at all. I've been there myself when Harry was learning to drive. *He* wrote off a brand-new Porsche when I was sitting with him.'

'Oops.' I glanced at the boy sitting in the passenger seat, looking out at Tom and grinning.

'Aren't you Cassandra Rhodes?' the woman asked, peering more closely at me.

'Well, I was. Cassandra Beresford now.' I looked at her. 'Oh, Nicola Foreman?'

'Nicola Kennedy now. Heavens, I've not seen you since junior school.'

'Kennedy? Oh gosh, is that Harry Kennedy? Is he your son?'

'Yes, we're just deciding whether to go round to my mother's house or go straight to Norman's Meadow. I seem to remember you and me playing in there when I came round to visit her.'

I smiled. 'You're right, I'd forgotten all about that. I think you were the only person I did play with round here. There weren't many other children.'

'Harry's feeling a bit nervous about speaking but he wants to help.'

Harry got out of the car and shook both Tom's and my hand. He was older than Tom, probably around nineteen, but Tom appeared to remember him from school.

'We're going to walk up through the playing field at the side of the meadow,' Nicola said. 'Do walk with us and we can catch up. Gosh, can't believe it's been over thirty years since I last saw you.'

We set off, Tom and Harry behind us chatting non-stop as if they'd known each other for ever, and made our way up the lane, climbing over one of the broken dry-stone walls and into the field that had been used by local football teams as long as I could remember.

'I used to love coming and watching the footballers,' Nicola grinned. 'Great place for getting off with the lads when you're in your teens.'

'Really?' I'd obviously missed out somewhere.

'Ooh, yes. The only reason I didn't put up too much objection whenever I was dragged to see my granny, who also lived along here, on a Saturday and Sunday. I just offered to take her mangy old dog for a walk up the fields.'

I laughed and then stopped. 'Oh, my goodness, look at that cow.' A small black and white Friesian was ambling curiously towards the touchline, scattering the small crowd of spectators. 'You see, this is what's so brilliant about these fields,' I laughed again. 'You wouldn't get a cow coming to watch a game anywhere else. And where are the locals going to play if the Bamforths get their way? I assume this field is owned by them, too?'

Nicola nodded.

'Never mind the *foreplay*,' one of the crowd was shouting in exasperation. 'Bloody well *shoot*...'

'Bring on the sub...' another yelled.

'Never mind the sub,' another laughed. 'Bring on the bloody cow...'

There was a collective groan as the home team let in a goal. 'It wasn't my bloody fault,' the goalie protested, looking our way as the four of us walked behind the nets and towards Norman's Meadow. 'I'm sure that's Harry Kennedy over there...'

'Yah, you gay twat,' his team-mates jeered, but nevertheless stopped to gawp, too.

Would Tom be followed, wherever he went, with homophobic insults once people were aware of his sexual orientation? I glanced back at my son. He was animated, perfectly at ease with the little superstar that Harry Kennedy had become since Second Coming had won *The X Factor* two years previously.

'Come and join us once your game is over,' Nicola shouted at the staring faces. 'It's your playing field you'll lose if you don't fight for it.'

If I hadn't been feeling so dreadful about Paula's revelation I would have enjoyed every minute of the protest organised by the NMLA (Norman's Meadow Liberation Army). Harry Kennedy's presence had brought out teenage girls in their droves and, while they themselves might not have had much influence on trying to stop the Bamforths building on the fields, their accompanying mothers, who were just as star-struck as their daughters, certainly had. Petitions were signed, balloons released and speeches made. Paula kicked off, then Freya and then Granddad Norman got up, leaning on his stick and breathing heavily as he lifted the megaphone with his free hand. He was wearing his war medals on his chest and he'd replaced his usual flat cap with his purple British Legion one.

For the first time, as Granddad Norman spoke, haltingly at first but then with some gusto, I began to realise where Paula's fighting spirit, her constant railing against inequality and what she saw as the pernicious destruction of the planet, had come from.

'I fought the Germans,' Granddad shouted. 'I don't like war: war's a dreadful thing, but it were a necessity. This too, is a just fight. There is no *reason* to build on these meadows. People need houses, of course they do, but not in your backyard and not in my backyard. Not here. There are brownfield sites just begging to be built on away from t'countryside…' His voice faltered, seemingly overcome with emotion, and Freya joined him on the makeshift stage she and Paula had cobbled together with packing cases and – I saw – my filched kitchen steps.

A pair of arms went around me and for one hopeful moment I thought it might be Xavier. Why would the enemy be here, you stupid woman? I chided myself.

'They're good,' Clare smiled, kissing me. 'Matt's going to say something soon... Oh my goodness, look, Harry Gration from *Look North*. They've obviously got wind of Harry Kennedy being here... Oh, sorry, this is Rageh...'

The tall, dark man holding Clare's hand grinned at me. 'Hi, you must be very proud of all your family. What fighters they are. Brilliant.'

I smiled back. 'You're right, I'm really proud. If there's something worth fighting for then...'

'... it's worth fighting for?' Rageh finished. He was smiling down at Clare from his six-foot height with such love and adoration I almost felt like crying with envy.

'He's lovely, Clare,' I whispered. 'Really lovely.'

'I know.' She squeezed my hand with her free one. 'I love him. Simple as that. I love him.'

Matt was standing by the packing boxes, Fi at his side. Freya and Paula helped Granddad Norman down the makeshift steps before handing Matt the megaphone. He spoke for a good five minutes, obviously very nervous to begin with, but then his passion for the fields, for farming and for the way of life in the Westenbury area came through.

'This is our village,' he said. 'It's been our village for hundreds of years. The church has been here for many *hundreds* of years. The village school...' Matt glanced over in my direction and smiled, '... is one of the oldest church schools in the country. Do *not* believe the Bamforths when they tell you the land is untenable: I know of at least two young farmers, at present still up at Askham Bryan agricultural college, as well as my own two sons, who are eager to get their hands on farmland of their own around here, should the opportunity be there.' Matt paused, not through emotion but, I could tell, through a burning anger. 'That opportunity will *not* be there for them if you people here don't protest against the planned destruction of these beautiful fields. If you want a ridiculous ski slope instead of flowers and fresh air then do nothing. If you want farming round here to disappear, then do nothing. If you want your little ones to have to travel to a huge community academy instead of being educated like they have for years in small classes in a small caring school – then do nothing...'

There was a round of applause and cheering.

'... But if, like me, you want to see the area stay as it is, to be farmed and looked after as it should be, for your kids to walk to school...'

More applause.

'... then fight this. Sign the petition, speak to your local MP – he's over there – and let the council know you don't *want* this in your backyard. You won't *allow* this in your backyard...'

Harriet and Grace, and an ensemble of small children all clutching the brightly coloured balloons, were standing to one side of the platform with David and Mandy Henderson and I waved across at them. Fi helped Matt down as the crowd cheered, hugging him and wiping her eyes as she did so.

David, a beautiful little dark-haired girl with Down's syndrome clutching one of his hands, patted Matt on the shoulder and then made to take his place on the platform.

Grace tried to take the little girl from him but she refused to let go of David's hand and, instead, he took the hand of the little boy at Grace's side and led the two children up the steps.

'Where's Swampy?' someone shouted. 'I thought *he* was coming to lie down and protest?'

David grinned. ''Fraid not,' he shouted through the megaphone. 'You've got the home-grown protesters instead. These two here are my grandchildren. It's *their* future I care about. I want them to be able to run through Norman's Meadow...'

'But *you're* not home grown, David Henderson,' the same man interrupted. 'You're a bloody southerner. Coming up here and lording it over us; living in your big house. What do *you* know about not being able to get on the housing ladder because there aren't houses being built? And don't tell me your grandchildren will be going to school locally. They'll be off to some posh boarding school.'

'They most certainly will *not*,' Grace turned, shouting. 'I teach at Little Acorns – best school I've ever taught in, with a *superb* head teacher, and those two there...' she inclined her head towards her children, '... will, if I can get them in there – if the Bamforths don't knock the place down first – be attending there and then on to the local high school.' Grace was angry.

'That school needs knocking down,' a different voice shouted. 'Giving it a daft new name doesn't modernise it. It's full of vermin. A squirrel fell out of the ceiling and into our Mikey's dinner the other day. Edward Bamforth would build a brand-new school for our kids where squirrels don't land in your dinner.'

'D'you hear that, Mr Henderson?' the first man continued. 'We want progress round here: new houses, a modern school where there's dinners without squirrel on the menu.' Hoots of laughter went up from that part of the crowd.

'Let him speak,' one of the football dads yelled towards the heckler. 'You're frightening the kiddies.'

'I'm just saying...'

'Well, shut it, mate, and let the man have his say.'

'I can assure you, as Chair of Governors, I was fully aware that squirrels had made their annual pilgrimage into the school roof, and can also put your minds at rest that the incident was dealt with immediately. The hall was out of bounds for the rest of the day and experts removed the squirrels and mended the very slight damage to the ceiling. It's a rural school: we should give thanks for the wildlife in our midst. Now then...'

As David Henderson spoke, urging the locals to sign the petition and to attend other meetings being planned, I looked round. Harry Kennedy, waiting nervously to get up and speak, was still with Tom, standing close to my son and occasionally smiling across at him while a whole gang of teenaged girls and their mothers hovered. I continued to scan the crowd. Clementine Ahern had arrived with Allegra, her daughter, and a dark-haired man I assumed to be her husband. They walked over to join Harriet, Grace and Mandy and the two men standing with them, presumably Harriet and Grace's husbands.

Clare had also made her way towards them, introducing Rageh to the other couples, laughing and joking and listening to David, and then to Harry Kennedy speak. Couples. That was it: they were all couples.

I don't think I'd ever, even in the weeks after Mark had gone, felt so alone.

29

So, He's Good at His Times Tables...?

Later that evening I keyed in the postcode Xavier had texted me and set off for his house and the promised food. Clementine had asked me to join them for a quick impromptu victory gathering at Clementine's before she ushered in her first customers of the evening, but I managed to make my excuses and left them all to it. Tom and Harry seemed joined at the hip – much to Freya's chagrin – and Tom was given a lift by Harry and his mum down to the restaurant.

'I'll see Granddad's OK,' I'd said to Paula. 'As one of the main organisers of the NMLA, you've been invited down there, too. Could you give Freya a lift down and tell her she's got to stay with you again tonight? I'll stay here with Granddad; make sure he has something to eat.'

'So, why aren't *you* coming, Cassandra Moonbeam?' Paula had looked at me intently.

'Because I'm going to have supper with Xavier.' I looked back at my mother, daring her to question my decision.

'Just be careful, Cassandra…'

'*And* it's all couples. I'm a bit short of another half.'

Following the Satnav instructions, I indicated left and followed the lane down until I was ordered by the bossy woman to turn a sharp left and I'd have reached my destination. The evening was clear, the black sky starlit and illuminated by a silvery moon sailing by on the left, and I peered through my windscreen to see where I was going. I pulled up outside the only house at the bottom of the lane and exited, pulling my bag, wine and flowers after me. I felt sick with nerves. How on earth was I going to tell this gorgeous man I'd fallen in love with that he was quite possibly my brother?

Xavier was at the door before I knocked. 'Hi, I heard the car. Come on in, it's far too cold to be out there. Flowers? For me? How lovely. Now, food won't be long. I do hope you like lamb…?' Xavier seemed almost as nervous as I was. He turned to look at me and smiled. 'I just needed to see you're as I remembered.' He bent to kiss me on the cheek, unwinding my woollen scarf from around my neck before abandoning it on a cream sofa and then, taking my hand in his, led me through a door into a warm sitting room where champagne stood on an antique table, cooling in an ice bucket.

'Oh, what a heavenly room.' I looked round in wonder, taking in the cream and red embroidered curtains and the cream Knowle sofas, their sides lassoed together with expensive-looking scarlet tassels. An open fire burned in the grate, sending warmth out together with a heady scent of pine. 'Oh,' I exclaimed again. 'Is he all right?' Flat out on the rug, to one side of the fire, was a huge dog, his head lying between his paws, of which the front left was heavily bandaged. He opened his eyes and wagged his tail slightly but it all seemed too much effort for him and he closed them once more.

'He had an operation this morning to remove a growth from his lower leg. He's getting on and I'm not sure he'll survive this… not sure what I'll do without him really.' Xavier pulled a face and I could see he was upset.

'Oh,' I said, accepting a glass of the champagne. 'I hadn't thought of you as an animal lover.'

Xavier smiled. 'Oh?'

'I suppose I have this idea of you as a city slicker, you know, working in industry, not really interested in the countryside, or animals…' I trailed off lamely.

'Come here.' Xavier smiled again and I went cold, thinking: I need to tell him, I've got to tell him what I know but, instead of pulling me into his arms as I'd anticipated, he drew back the heavy curtains and opened the French window revealed there.

'Oh, wow!' I exclaimed, stepping out onto a patio. The whole of Xavier's backyard was fields. 'I wasn't expecting that. What a view. There are no other houses for miles.' The moon, risen higher in the ten minutes or so since I'd first seen it, was illuminating the vista in front of me, outlining woods, trees and acres of rolling fields in a marked silhouette.

'It's a shame I'm going to have to sell up.'

'What? Why?' I looked at Xavier, shocked.

'Come inside, you're cold.' He took my hand and led me back to the sitting room, pulling the heavy curtains against the chilly evening. He bent down to check on the dog, stroking his head and fondling his ears. 'You OK, Trevor?'

'*Trevor?*' Despite my nerves at finding the right moment to tell Xavier what I was going to *have* to tell him, as well as dismay that he was thinking of selling up, I giggled. 'You can't call a dog *Trevor*. Uncles are called Trevor, next-door neighbours are called Trevor, vicars are called Trevor…' I laughed again.

'The Rev. Trev?' We both laughed this time.

'So, what are you talking about? Selling up?' I frowned up at him. God, he was gorgeous. That dark hair and those brown eyes. But you can't kiss your brother, I told myself. I took a good look. Did he have my nose? Were those my ears? I looked more closely. His top lip was just the same as mine. Shit.

'What?' Xavier was amused. 'You look like you're checking me out? Do I pass muster?'

I dropped my eyes, embarrassed and then raised them again as he came to sit down on the sofa with me. 'Packing up?' I repeated.

'Well,' he said, almost cheerfully. 'I'm having nothing more to do with the Bamforth Estate's plans.'

'What?' I looked at Xavier incredulously.

'I've told my dad: I want no more part of it. I don't want to see these beautiful fields concreted over. I never did. I needed my share of the money to keep Ophelia happy.'

'Bloody hell, I bet that went down well with your dad?'

'Like a lead balloon. I've been with him most of the day, trying to get him to drop quite a few of the plans. There's some land that *can* be built on to provide more housing: land no one would object to being developed.'

'And did he go with that?' I asked hopefully.

Xavier shook his head. 'Nope.'

'Right, OK...' I stared at him, desperate to smooth back a lock of hair that had fallen onto his forehead. I sat on my hands. 'But why do you need to sell up?'

'I'll need to pay a settlement to Ophelia. That's what happens when you divorce. Dad won't help me now I've pulled out on him. I'll be surprised if there's a job waiting for me on Monday.' He smiled and bent to kiss me, but I jumped up.

'Er, Xavier, strange question, but did your dad go to university?'

Xavier laughed. 'Sorry?'

'Your dad, did he go to university?'

'Yes, Bristol.'

'And he studied?'

'Maths: my dad's a brilliant mathematician. He could probably have been a professor of maths if *his* dad hadn't wanted him to come back to help run the company...' He frowned. 'Why?'

I closed my eyes and took a deep breath. 'Xavier, there's something I have to tell you...'

Twenty minutes later Xavier had bundled Trevor and me into his rather upmarket little two-seater and, despite my protestations that we talk a little more about what

I'd just revealed, we were heading for his father's (our father's?) place twenty minutes' drive away.

'Sorry about the lack of space – I daren't leave Trevor by himself. The vet said I had to keep an eye on him at all times.'

I tried to speak, which is a bit difficult with one hundred and twenty pounds of stoned Irish Wolfhound laid across one's middle. 'This isn't fair on your mum.'

'Mum's not here. She's in Paris with Grandmère. I left her there; she's staying for another couple of weeks.'

'OK, but you can't just turn up with me and expect your father to listen to some garbled tale about something he got up to forty years ago,' I argued.

'Why not? Of course I can. We need to get this sorted, Cassie. Come on, it's highly unlikely that you're his daughter. And my sister? Never. It's too ridiculous. No wonder you were having a good look at me. We don't look a bit alike. I've dark hair and brown eyes. You've blonde hair and blue eyes.'

'Yes, like your dad...' I shifted Trevor's head onto my left shoulder so I could have another look at Xavier's mouth. 'Our mouths are almost identical.'

'You mean we have two lips apiece?' Xavier said crossly. 'Look, I'm dark because my mother is very dark. You probably take after your real father – this Rowan guy your mum was sleeping with.'

'I told you, Paula says Rowan had red hair and brown eyes.'

Xavier, impatiently tapping the steering wheel as we were brought to a halt at temporary red lights, frowned. 'A strange combination of features, don't you think?'

'Possibly, but why would my mother have made it up?'

'*I* don't know.'

'Oh, come on, Xavier, no one could make this up.'

He took my hand with his free one. 'I'm sorry, Cassie, it's just… it's just… Cassie, I don't want to lose you.' He turned back to the road, indicating a right turn. 'I've fallen in love with you. There I've said it now. I'm sorry, that's the last thing you want to hear.'

'Actually, it's the *one* thing I want to hear.' I felt my heart lurch and there was a silence as we both realised we'd crossed a line.

'So, have you come back to tell me you've changed your mind?' Edward Bamforth, glass of whisky in hand, came out from a room off the huge blue-carpeted, oak-panelled hallway as soon as he heard the front door open. 'Oh, Mrs Beresford…?' He looked at me in obvious surprise, but led the way back into the sitting room he'd just exited and held up the bottle of whisky. 'Can I get you both a drink? There's wine in the fridge, if you'd rather?'

'Dad, I think you're going to need that drink. I wouldn't mind one too. Cassie?'

Once Xavier had made Trevor comfortable by the fire, he set off for the kitchen to find the wine.

'He loves that dog,' Edward smiled at me. 'Always been the one for poorly creatures, even when he was a little boy. Should have been a vet really.'

I smiled back, stroking Trevor's silky ears, not having a clue what to say to this man. I took a surreptitious look at him from underneath my eyelashes as he poured himself more whisky before adding dry ginger. Hmm, Edward Bamforth certainly had the same sort of mouth as Xavier and me and his eyes were a vivid blue like mine.

'My father used to have a fit if he saw anyone adding anything but water to whisky,' Edward said as he realised he was under close scrutiny. 'Was *your* father the same?'

Oh, well done, Edward Bamforth. Ten out of ten for getting your lines spot on.

'I never knew my father, Mr Bamforth. He never even knew he'd got my mother pregnant.'

He laughed, slightly embarrassed. 'Well, these things happen.' He looked up with obvious relief as Xavier came back with wine and two glasses.

'Right, Dad.' Xavier sat opposite his father and leaned forward. 'Do you remember forty years ago?'

'Xavier, I have all on to remember yesterday, I've so much on my mind at the moment.' Edward laughed and looked across at me.

'Dad, this is important. Summer 1976. The incredibly hot one. Everyone remembers that summer apparently? And you went off to Paris and met Mum?'

'Well, yes, of course I remember that…' He laughed again. 'As I'm sure you're aware, you were the result of that trip to Paris.'

'OK, yes. So, before you went, do you remember meeting someone in the garden?'

'Meeting someone in the garden?' Edward frowned. 'What, like the gardener or the postman?'

Xavier sighed. 'No, a young girl about your own age, that you shared a joint with?'

Edward looked slightly embarrassed. 'Gracious, you're going back a long time. That's in the days when I did have an occasional smoke...' He trailed off and stared at Xavier.

'Look, Cassie's mother was in your garden one night back in 1976. She'd had a picnic and then got talking to you...' Xavier was embarrassed now. It's not an easy thing to ask your father if he remembers having sex with some floozie who just happened to be floating round the garden. '... and you ended up... well, put it this way, you weren't pruning the roses.'

Edward said nothing for what seemed ages, but was probably only a few seconds. He looked from Xavier, to me and then back to Xavier. 'Yes, I remember.'

'Well, Dad, in a nutshell, Cassie thinks you're possibly her father.'

'What?' Edward downed his drink and set the glass on the table. 'I'm not sure what you're implying here.'

'Dad, come on, the implication is very straightforward. That girl – Paula – is Cassie's mum. Now, Paula did have a boyfriend; she'd been with him for several months, so more than likely *he* is Cassie's father...'

'Much more likely.' Edward stared long and hard at me, taking in every one of my features as I had done previously with both Xavier and himself.

'The thing is, Mr Bamforth, Mum's boyfriend, Rowan, who I'd always been led to believe was my father, had red hair and brown eyes.'

'Right. OK.'

'And my son, Tom, is really good at maths...'

Edward actually laughed out loud at that. 'So, because your son knows his three times table, that makes him my grandson, does it? Is that what you're trying to say, Mrs Beresford?'

'The way things are going, it looks like he'll be offered a place at Cambridge to study Pure Maths and Further Maths.'

That shut him up, but only for a few seconds. 'Can I ask why now? Why have you come to tell me all this now?' Edward looked at both of us in turn.

'Because, Dad, I've fallen in love with Cassie.' Xavier took my hand.

'Oh, Xavier.' Edward was obviously exasperated. 'You've only just fallen *out* of love with your wife. Mind you, congratulations on that one. You know how I felt about *her*.'

'Dad, will you listen? It's obviously not bloody congratulations if Cassie is my half-sister!' Xavier shouted his frustration and Trevor opened one eye in surprise. I patted the dog, who sighed and whimpered before settling once again.

'Well, it's obvious, isn't it?' Edward frowned. 'A DNA test will sort it. That will tell us the truth.'

30

You Do Bewitch Me...

'I met someone when I was in Mexico.'

'We gathered.' Clare laughed. 'You slid down the wall? The text?'

'Oh gosh, yes, I forgot I sent that to you and Fi.'

'Love and lust do that to you: you forget *who* you've told *what*.' Fi poured wine and helped herself to a handful of crisps. 'So, fire away. We want to know all about it.'

'Actually, Mark texted me as soon as I got to Mexico.'

'Did he?' We were sitting in The Jolly Sailor down in Westenbury village the following Tuesday evening and Clare and Fi both looked up from their drinks. 'What did *he* want?'

I shrugged. 'Very strange, really. He said he wished he were there with me.'

'The pillock. Typical philanderer,' Fi sniffed disparagingly. 'Wanting what they've let go the minute they feel you've lost interest in them. I blame his mother…'

'I didn't know you knew Mark's mother?' I looked at her in surprise.

'No, I don't. Never met the woman except at your wedding and, being horribly pissed from the kick off, I can't remember much about that. But somewhere along the line she'll have spoilt him and made him think he's terribly important and should be allowed to have anything that anyone else has.'

Clare and I laughed. 'Amateur psychologist now, are you?'

'Just common sense, really,' she said airily. 'OK. Who did you meet? Does he live near enough that you can see him again? And, more importantly, did you have sex with him and was he any good?'

'Fiona,' Clare tutted, giving her a warning glance.

'Oh, don't go all sensible and grown up on me, Clare, just because *you've* given up shagging around for domestic bliss. Just wait until Rageh starts *hovering* and you've discovered *your* pelvic floor is a pulverised trampoline. You'll be the *first* to want other people's juicy details as a distraction.'

'Xavier Bamforth.'

'What about Xavier Bamforth?' Clare and Fi looked at me.

'It was Xavier Bamforth. It *is* Xavier Bamforth…'

'What's Xavier Bamforth?' Fiona looked aghast.

'Xavier Bamforth was in my hotel in Mexico and I've fallen in love with him and he feels the same way.'

'Well, how lovely, sweetie,' Clare kissed me. 'My friend Sal knows him. She says he's very gorgeous, very fanciable…'

'Yes, and very much part of the Bamforth Estate bastards. You're not serious, Cassie?' Fiona wasn't happy.

''Fraid so,' I tried to smile. 'Unfortunately… unfortunately…' Tears welled up and I scrabbled for a tissue.

'Oh God, he's married?'

I shook my head, then nodded, remembering that he *was* still married.

'Which one? Yes or no?' Fi was baffled.

'Yes. Married. But not *with* her. Unfortunately…'

'What?' Clare and Fi asked in unison.

I blew my nose. 'Unfortunately, he's probably my brother as well.'

'Right,' Fiona said, half an hour later, 'you'll need a hair from Edward Bamforth's head. Which if I remember rightly, from eyeballing him at the village hall meeting, might be a bit difficult seeing as how he's as bald as a coot.'

'Oh, yes,' Clare enthused. 'It's like in that novel – you know – *The Rosie Project*. When the guy needs to get DNA, he has to get a hair with a *bulb* on it.'

'A bulb?' Fiona frowned. 'To plant it and grow more hair, you mean?'

Clare tutted. 'Do stop talking inane rubbish, Fi—'

'It's all being done at the moment,' I interrupted. 'Edward, Paula and I have all sent off samples of cells for testing. The results will be back by the end of the week.'

'And Paula agreed to giving a sample, too?' Clare asked.

'Why wouldn't she? She's as eager to know as I am. I know she's still hoping that Rowan, the long-lost love of her life, will prove to be my dad.'

'And did Paula meet up with Edward?' Fi asked eagerly. 'Gosh, I bet that was strange after all these years.'

'No, not at all. We all just rooted around in our mouths for cell samples, popped them into the plastic tube and then sent them off to one of the recommended companies that sorts paternity DNA testing. So soon I'll know if I've finally gained a father and, in doing so, lost the man I've really, really fallen in love with.'

'Well, Cassie,' Fiona sniffed, 'look on the bright side: if Edward Bamforth *is* your father he might just leave you a shed-load in his will...'

When Xavier and I – and Trevor – had finally left Edward's house on the Saturday evening we didn't know quite what to do. The idea of making our way back to Xavier's house and eating the lovingly prepared food as if nothing was amiss seemed almost irreligious. But we did it anyway.

As we walked up the path to Xavier's front door, I stumbled slightly and he grabbed hold of me, breaking my fall. We stood in the moonlight staring into each other's eyes and he held me. And didn't stop holding me.

'Come on,' he sighed eventually, 'let's go in and eat.' Xavier unlocked the door and led me through to a ravishing kitchen, all creams and blond wood, totally modern and functional and, if my whole body hadn't been crying out for Xavier's touch, I'd have been in kitchen envy. A large wooden table, laid for two with beautiful cut glass and silver cutlery, stood at one end of the room. It was a perfect kitchen.

'I think it'll probably be spoilt now,' he frowned, opening the oven and sniffing its contents.

'Smells heavenly,' I smiled, although I wasn't sure I'd be able to eat anything.

'Come on, we need to eat something.' He smiled. 'There's not much *else* we can do.'

'So,' I said, through a mouthful of fragrant lamb and couscous, 'you have a sister?'

'Yes, Amelie.'

'Well, do I look like *her*? Could *we* be sisters?'

'Amelie is a mixture of Mum and Dad. She has dark hair like Mum and me, but Dad's blue eyes. So, no, I can't say you do look a great deal like her.'

'Well, that's good then, isn't it? If we were sisters we should look a bit alike, don't you think?' I was clutching at straws, anything for Xavier not to be my brother.

'She's a lot taller than you, but then my mother is very tall.'

'And elegant, I bet, being French?'

Xavier smiled. 'Very. She was only young when she got pregnant with me – even younger than Dad. My mates used to come home from school with me and just gawp at her. I can see what Dad saw in her. Not sure what she saw in Dad, to be honest.'

'Oh, that's not fair. He's an attractive man – or I bet he was when he was younger.'

'You'll have to ask your mum,' Xavier said pointedly, and carried on eating.

We ate the couscous and Mediterranean-type salad together with the lamb that, despite Xavier's misgivings over the time it had spent in the oven, was fragrant and tender.

'So, where did you learn to cook?' I asked.

'Mum. She's a brilliant cook. She taught me all she knew, particularly about French cuisine.'

Lordy, was there no end to this woman's repertoire? Gorgeous, tall, elegant and a brilliant cook into the bargain? Poor old Paula, with her lentil soup and cauliflower curry, wouldn't have stood a chance if she'd decided to put herself into the running forty years ago.

'I'm going to drive you home,' Xavier said after we'd drunk coffee and, in front of the fire, nibbled at cheese, much of which went into a now more alert Trevor. 'Look, Cassie, just wait a week and then we'll know. It'll be fine, I know it will.'

'I've only had the one drink at your dad's,' I said. 'I'll be fine to drive. In fact, I'll go and pick up Freya from Paula's; I did sort of abandon her this evening.'

'I thought you had a hot date?' Freya looked up from applying another layer of black to her nails.

'Hot date? Who told you that?'

'Mum, I'm not daft. You've been wafting around with a soppy look on your face like some love-sick duck ever since you got home from Mexico.'

'Love-sick *duck*?' I laughed in spite of myself.

'Yeah, you know. Singing to yourself, staring into space with a daft smile on your face; picking at your food like when Dad went. Mooning all over the place.'

'Mooning? Isn't that when you show your bare backside to a crowd?'

Freya considered for a moment as she waved her nails to dry them. 'Hmm, possibly. Mooching, then. I thought it was supposed to be adolescents like me who mooched around and locked themselves into their room and wrote poetry?'

'I've not been writing poetry,' I protested.

'Bet you've been reading it, though. I saw my English textbook was well thumbed at old Michael Drayton:

You do bewitch me; O, that I could fly
From my self you, or from your own self I.'

I laughed again. 'You do talk rubbish.'

'Anyway,' Freya went on, 'good on you. If Dad can put it about, I don't see why you can't—'

'Stop right there. No one is *putting it about*.'

'Anyway, he's been texting me quite a bit.'

'Who has?'

She looked at me. 'Dad. Dad's been texting me again.'

'Oh?'

'Wanting to meet me for lunch, pick me up from school, come and watch my next match…'

'Darling, you should meet him. He's your father and he loves you. You know that. My argument with your father is just that – mine. Your sense of loyalty to me is really appreciated, Freya, but I'd be much happier if you and Tom began to have some sort of relationship with him again.'

Freya shrugged. 'Maybe. But I don't want to see him with Auntie Tina. That would be, like, so gross. Weird.'

'I can understand that, darling, but your dad has been trying to see you for weeks now. I think you should ring him. You know, *you* actually make the move to arrange to meet up with him. Granny Mavis says he's pretty upset how you and Tom have not wanted to have anything to do with him.'

Freya reddened slightly. 'But you were so upset about it all, Mum. I was as well. It's not easy seeing you crying most days, you know. He did a terrible thing and… and actually it's all a bit embarrassing.'

'Embarrassing?' I smiled at Freya. 'Why embarrassing?'

'Well, you know, what he's been up to. What do I say to him? "Hi Dad, how's it all going with you and Auntie Tina?"'

'No, of course you don't,' I laughed. 'You talk about what you'd have talked about before he went. So, ring him, please. For me? Now, where's Paula?' I went on.

'Meditating. You haven't asked where Tom is.' She looked at me from under her black heavy fringe.

'Tom's seventeen, Freya. He has a key.'

'It's a bit bloody much when your brother cops off with the main attraction.'

'And has he?'

'Well, he was down at Clementine's for a while – everyone wanted to know where *you'd* slipped off to, you know – but then he disappeared.'

'Oh?'

'Tom's happy, Mum,' Freya said, examining her nails. 'And he hasn't been for a while.'

'But I'm bound to worry about Tom, Freya. About, well you know...'

'About the fact that he appears to be gay?'

'I'm not sure I should be having this conversation with you, Freya.'

'Oh, Mum, don't be so, so... old.' Freya tutted and then sighed. 'Mum, I've had long talks with Tom about this, you know.'

'Really?' I stared at Freya. 'And Tom's confided in you?' I felt quite miffed that Tom felt able to talk to Freya but hadn't really opened up to me apart from when he'd walked me down to Clementine's restaurant in the dark.

'Well you're a different generation. You're his mother, what do you expect? I bet if he was into *girls* he wouldn't be chatting to his mum about them. Don't worry about him. He talks to me and he's always on the phone to Jenny. She's his best friend, and she's great with him. I think you should try to stop worrying about Tom. He has been finding it hard, but now that it's more out in the open, and he's met Harry...' Freya shrugged. 'It'll be fine.'

'But that all worries me more,' I sighed. 'So, is Harry

Kennedy gay, then? I mean, if he is and Tom starts hanging round with him, Tom's going to find himself in the papers, discussed everywhere he goes... I don't want his studies being interrupted.'

'Come on, Mum, *nothing* will come between Tom and his algebra. Anyway, it's only Harry Kennedy. He was at school with us. He just happens to have won *The X Factor*. I think it's brilliant.'

'Yes, you would.' I smiled slightly at her. Freya was right. I just had to go with the flow.

'So now *he's* sorted, *you* appear to be sorted...' Freya paused, '... it just needs me to ring Dad and arrange to meet up with him – oh and be chosen for the Under 16 Yorkshire Netball squad next week – and we're *all* sorted.'

31

And the Results Are in…

Because we'd been told the results would take a week to come back, I wasn't expecting the white envelope that would alter the course of my life to be there that Thursday evening, on my return from school. Tom, home earlier than me from college, had picked up the post and carefully – as was his wont – left the couple of envelopes addressed to me: a tax bill, information about Nectar points, and the test results neatly propped up against the salt and pepper pot.

I ripped open the envelope and feverishly scanned the single sheet of paper.

… by comparing the DNA profiles of the child and the mother, it is possible to establish the common factors between them. The child's factors not found in the mother's profile must therefore come from the biological father. An alleged father is excluded as the biological father if factors found on his DNA profile are not shared with the child's. However, if the alleged father's profile shares common factors with the child's then he is not excluded as the true biological father. A statistical analysis is then carried out to calculate the probability of paternity…

And? And? I skimmed over the explanatory paragraph until I found what I was looking for.

… As such, we can confirm the paternity link as being positive…

That was it, then. Edward Bamforth was my father. In the crudest, most basic of terms, one of his sperm – obviously the Usain Bolt of spermatozoa – had snuck past Rowan's less athletic specimens and scored a hit.

Bull's eye.

One hundred and eighty.

'You all right, Mrs Heads?' Deimante, promoted to Little Acorns' cleaning staff and dinner lady team, as well as continuing her career as its Traffic Organisation Consultant, was giving my desk a good polish when I arrived in my office the next morning. 'You looks a bit knackereds.'

I shook my head, not wanting to get into conversation with her.

'A bits sads maybes? Is Mrs Adams bullying yous? She try to bully me, but I shakes my lollipops at her. "Don't sinks, Mrs Adams," I says to her, "don't you sinks just because I poor lollipops girl you sinks I am down from yous. I now Sanitation Consultant and Educational Nourishment Officer as well as lollipops girl. And one days I shall be back here as teacher…"'

I turned to look at Deimante, surprised. 'Oh?'

'I aims to be teacher one day,' she said seriously, dusting my chair. 'I doing English at night school.'

'Oh, well done,' I said, smiling.

'Mrs Heads, I have lot of respects for yous, but please don't patronise me. I not a ninny. I have degree in Astrophysics from Aleksandras Stulginskis University in Lithuania...'

That floored me. 'Gosh, I didn't realise, I'm sorry...'

Deimante sniffed. 'As I say, I not a ninny.' She flicked her duster along the bookcase and then grinned at me. 'I just bollocks at learning English.'

'Edward Bamforth is here, Cassandra.' Jean frowned, running her finger down the diary. 'He's not made an appointment. Shall I tell him you're busy? And you are, you know. You've Mr and Mrs O'Farrell, prospective parents, to show round in twenty minutes as well as the rep from Pinkington Books, who's *already* here and setting up in the library.'

I shook my head. 'Just give me a minute, Jean, and then ask him to come through. Would you mind awfully making some coffee for us? Sorry, I know you're busy yourself.'

'There's no "I" in team,' she smiled. 'Life doesn't give you things you can't handle...'

Bloody well depends on what life gives you, I thought sourly, but managed a rictus smile back at her.

I combed my hair and checked my lipstick and then buzzed Edward through.

'You've had the letter?' he asked, sitting down opposite me.

I nodded, not sure what to say. What does one say to one's newly acquired father? 'So, do I call you *Dad*?' I asked, and then flushed, embarrassed at the inanity of my words.

'Look, Cassandra, I'm not entirely unhappy about all this...'

'You're not?' Well, I bloody well am, I thought.

'I love both my children and I'd have been over the moon to have had more. But Brigitte put her foot down: two were plenty she said.' He smiled at me and, again, I searched his features for my own. 'I don't have grandchildren. Xavier's been led a merry dance over the years with that wife of his, and Amelie, who's been living in New York for the last ten years, appears far too interested in her career to have them. Who knows? Hopefully she'll change her mind...' He smiled again and leant forward. 'I'd love to meet your son at some point. He sounds like a boy after my own heart.'

'Jean's bringing us some coffee,' I said. I felt totally disorientated, while Edward seemed excited almost. He smiled again and then, obviously realising my unease, stopped smiling.

'I'm sorry, Cassandra, you do know you can't carry on any sort of, er, *relationship* with Xavier?'

I nodded numbly.

'I'm really sorry. You seemed well suited, and you got him away from that money-grabbing wife of his.'

'Sugar?' What was the matter with me? Why couldn't I speak properly?

'Thank you, no. Cassandra, I'd like to think you and I can get to know each other. When Amelie is home, I'd love you to meet her. She is your sister, after all.'

My mouth and vocal cords started to behave themselves. 'But what about your wife?'

'It can't be helped,' he said cheerfully. 'Once she returns from Paris, next week, I'm just going to have to confess. It was all such a long time ago, after all. And,' he paused and looked straight at me, 'maybe now, you and your family will back off a bit with your objections to the building plans and development?'

'What?' I just stared at him.

'I mean,' he added hastily, 'now we're all family, we should be on the same side, don't you think?'

'Sorry?' I appeared to have lost my ability to speak once more.

'It might be in your interests to work *with* us. It can't be easy bringing up two teenagers single-handed. Cambridge won't be cheap, you know...'

'Are you bribing me, Mr Bamforth?' I glared at him.

He gave a short laugh, obviously embarrassed. 'That's a bit strong, don't you think? And do you think we can get rid of the *Mr Bamforth* now?'

'So, let me get this straight. You want me to call you *Daddy* and go hand in glove with you and your plans to concrete over the fields?'

'What I would really like is for you to talk to Xavier. You obviously have quite a bit of influence over him. If *you* won't come on board – and I can quite understand that you have what you see as the best interests of the school and your grandfather to think about – at least talk to Xav and suggest he comes back in with us.'

When I didn't say anything, he said, 'Look, Cassandra, I don't want to fall out with you, especially now I've just found you. I genuinely would like to get to know you and your children. You're my flesh and blood, for heaven's sake. But, at the end of the day, you're standing in the way of progress. Don't be a Luddite. You could be head of a huge junior department of a wonderful new academy school. And...' he paused, '... your grandfather is ninety-odd. He's not going to be around for ever.' He stopped talking and stood, placing his mug carefully on the desk as Jean knocked and popped her head round the door to say my prospective parents were waiting. 'Cassandra, I genuinely feel I've gained something with suddenly finding I have another daughter, but I don't want to lose my son at the same time.' He picked up his briefcase and headed for the door. 'If I can't persuade *you* to think again *re* the planning, I'd really appreciate you helping me to get Xavier back on board.'

I held out my hand. 'Thank you for coming, Mr Bamforth. All I can say is, *I'm not my brother's keeper*.' I opened the door for him. 'Jean will show you out.'

Just landed. Meet me after work. The Arlington Arms out on the Midhope Road. Five p.m.?

As soon as I'd ripped open the letter the previous evening and read its pernicious contents, I'd locked myself in the bathroom, not wanting Tom or Freya to get wind of what was going on, and rung Xavier. I knew he was in Copenhagen; we'd both assumed he'd be back in the country by the time the DNA results arrived.

There had been silence from his end of the phone and then he'd sighed deeply, obviously taking in the news. 'Oh God, Cassie, no. I don't believe it. Could there be a mistake? Shall we try another company? You know, make sure...'

'Xavier, there's no point. I'm your sister. You're my brother...' I'd begun to weep down the phone.

'Don't, Cassie, don't cry,' he'd pleaded from his hotel room in Copenhagen. 'Look, I'll change my flight and be back tomorrow afternoon instead of Saturday morning. I'll ring you as soon as I'm back.'

So here I was, driving through the rain and the Friday teatime traffic on a miserable November afternoon to seal my fate. It was already nearly five and I had to pick Freya up in less than an hour. I put my foot down, accelerating out into the fast lane and prayed there were no traffic cops around.

Xavier was sitting in one corner of the deserted bar and I understood why he'd chosen this place. Halfway between both his house and mine, it obviously wasn't either the most salubrious, or popular, of drinking holes. He was nursing a glass of wine but hadn't made much headway with it and stood as soon as he saw me, coming over and putting his arms round me. I leant against him, feeling the warmth of him, wanting to stay there. Knowing I couldn't.

'Do you want a drink? I don't recommend the wine,' Xavier whispered in my ear attempting humour. 'I reckon the landlord's just trodden the grapes himself.'

I glanced over at the paunchy bartender who was sat, alone, on the customer side of the bar, dirty-stockinged feet up on a stool as he watched some sports channel on the huge overhead TV.

'I'll just have a Coke. I've to drive over to pick Freya up from school in twenty minutes.'

Once we sat down, Xavier held my hand, 'I'm sorry,' he said. 'I don't know what to suggest…'

'There is nothing to suggest. I suppose we were lucky that Paula arrived at my place the other day before we, you know…' I trailed off.

Xav smiled and then frowned.

'So, Xavier, your dad came to see me this morning.'

'Already?'

'Almost waiting at the school gate with the lollipop lady.'

'And?'

'Wants to welcome me into your family.'

'I don't think I can do this whole family thing. I think I need to keep away from you.' Xavier was serious.

I just looked at him.

'There's no other way, Cassie, you know that.'

I nodded numbly.

'I never thought I could feel anything like this for another woman,' Xavier whispered, holding me close as we made to say goodbye in the car park. 'I know I've only known you a while, Cassie, but you have my heart. I can't lose you. I don't know what to do…'

His arms were wrapped tightly round me and I had to gently unpeel myself. 'I have to go: Freya will be waiting. Are you OK?'

He nodded but couldn't speak and, instead, kissed the top of my head. 'I'll call you,' he said, and with that I unlocked the car door, fastened my seat belt and drove off. I didn't look back.

Freya had invited her mate Gabby home for the night – she had asked at breakfast and, my head full of more important things, I'd totally forgotten. As there was little in the fridge apart from the rather suspicious-looking remains of a two-day-old spag bol to tempt two famished teens, I suggested they have a takeaway of their choice. Pleased, they grabbed the various takeaway menus from the kitchen notice board and were soon on the phone, my bankcard to hand, ordering ridiculous amounts of food.

When Tom and Harry Kennedy appeared at the sitting-room door, Gabby went white and then scarlet.

'See,' Freya crowed, elbowing Gabby in the ribs. 'You didn't believe me, did you? How many poppadoms, Harry...?'

I went to see Paula.

I loved it that my kids were happy and sociable but their euphoric banter did nothing to make me feel any better and I decided to leave them to it.

The minute Paula saw me at the door she came over and put her arms round me, holding me while I wept.

'I'm sorry it wasn't Rowan,' I sniffed.

Paula laughed. 'Well, I did hope he was a part of you, but I suspected a long time ago that he wasn't. I don't remember Rowan ever being at all tidy. I'm certainly not, and your nan and granddad weren't overly so. It had to come from somewhere.'

I didn't like to remind her that I was convinced my obsession with orderliness was a directly proportionate reaction to her *disorderliness*; her ability to have two days' washing-up still in the sink while she meditated or went picking elderberries for her wine, or her total disregard for the unironed pile of washing sitting for three days on the kitchen table while she ate her meals around it.

'I envy you, actually,' I smiled. 'It must be wonderful to not feel the necessity to make your bed as soon as you get out of it; not to bother unpacking your suitcase when you go on holiday; not to—'

'"Life's too short to stuff a mushroom",' Paula interrupted.

'Actually, you're probably right, and this sense of needing order in my life more than likely *is* genetic.' I thought back to Edward's sitting room. It had been immaculately tidy, cushions standing to attention, the two sofas equidistant from the Persian rug in the middle of the floor. I laughed shortly. 'So, that wily sperm that won the race was carrying Edward's blue eyes, blond hair, an astounding ability with maths and a bent for tidiness.' I shook my head at the thought. 'Amazing.'

'One thing about all this, Cass,' Paula smiled, almost shyly.

'Hmm?'

'Do you think it's brought us two a little closer?' She looked at me hopefully.

'I'm sorry,' I said. 'Really sorry. There have been times when I haven't always appreciated you.' I felt a little embarrassed. Mum and I didn't normally have these types of conversations. 'I have sometimes cut you out of my life a bit, haven't I?'

Paula smiled. 'Yes, but I'm more to blame. I was a pretty crap mother. Too idealistic, wanting to go and do other things, *get involved* with other things.'

'You were very young. You could have not had me. But you did.'

'And thank goodness I listened to your granddad and didn't have a termination.' Paula shivered slightly. 'Let's not talk about it. All I will say, Cassandra Moonbeam, is that you are the best thing that ever happened to me.' She smiled, but her lip trembled.

I leant over, kissed her cheek and hugged her.

'Cheeky thing, Edward Bamforth, asking you to stop the protests,' Paula called ten minutes later from the kitchen as she made tea. 'What he should have said was, "Now you're my daughter and a part of the Bamforth family, we'll of course withdraw all the plans from the planning department and leave everything as it is..."'

I smiled. 'Ha! Pigs might fly.'

I felt comfortable sitting there with my mother. I curled up in my old chair, remembering other good times she and I had spent together: planting seeds in Norman's Meadow, her teaching me how to bake bread; a train ride to the seaside at Scarborough.

'Did you never meet anyone else, Mum?' I asked, looking across at her as we sat companionably together in front of the fire.

'I had my moments,' she smiled, 'but you were far too precious to me to put you through the trauma of being part of a new family. After a while, I just didn't bother. You get out of the habit. Having said that…'

I looked at her. 'What? Have you met someone?'

'Yes,' she said, shyly. 'Early days, but I'll let you meet him soon.'

32

The Bully Is Sent Home From School...

Although still only the third week in November, Christmas had arrived at Little Acorns with a bang. Nativity rehearsals were already underway and many an angel, bored with sitting waiting for her big moment, was seen picking her nose while trying to adjust her wings, or poking a tea-towel-attired shepherd with her broken halo.

I missed and longed for Xavier dreadfully, but was determined not to slide back into the anxious depressed state that had characterised my first few weeks as acting head teacher and, instead, put all my energies into either running the school or being with the kids or my mother. Mum and I were the closest we'd been for years as we spent time with Granddad and Freya, discussing the NMLA's next moves. Refusing to allow wonderful – but heart-breaking – pictures of Xavier and myself on the beach in Mexico to intrude, I got on with my life: holding meetings, covering classes, speaking to parents and helping Deimante with her English language work.

Things with Karen Adams came to a head one morning after not one, but two, parents had rung me to complain about her. Their children were frightened of her, they said. She picked on them and didn't explain lessons properly to them. While I assumed the two mothers had chatted beforehand, and made a joint decision to ring me and air their grievances, two complaints in one day was not good and at lunchtime I asked her to come and see me.

Since I'd ambushed Karen in my office after drinking Deimante's *gira,* weeks ago now, we'd kept each other at a safe distance, avoiding each other where possible and being icily polite when not. I'd never really worked out where her dislike for me had sprung from, and accepted she was just one of those women whose lack of self-esteem manifests itself in cynicism and unpleasantness in order to belittle those she felt were getting out of line.

I didn't mince my words. 'Karen, I've had two separate phone calls within ten minutes from parents of children in your class.'

'Oh?' She folded her arms, immediately on the defensive.

'Maisie Lewis's mum and Daisy Ford's mum.'

'Troublemakers, the pair of them.'

'Who? The mums, or the girls themselves?'

Karen didn't say anything, just did her usual eyebrow raising and tutted.

'Both mums said the same thing: their girls are not happy at school any more. They've not been since they came into your class. Any idea why? Did you realise there was some problem?'

'Oh, they're just full of themselves, those two. Want to be top of the class, always want to finish first, want to be form captain, want to be this, want to be that…'

'Surely we should be encouraging that?' When Karen just glared at me again I said, 'You seem not to like the kids who are bright and confident. Would you say that's a fair assessment?'

Karen sniffed and said, 'Certain kids need putting in their place or they end up running the class. You know that.'

'Well, I know there are always children who think they're better than others. They can make life quite unpleasant for those who're not as talented as they are, maybe.'

'Exactly.'

I frowned. 'But I wouldn't have thought either Daisy or Maisie come into that category. I've always found them charming, bright, helpful.'

'Full of themselves,' Karen muttered, but she refused to look at me or say any more.

'Do you enjoy your job, Karen?'

'*Enjoy it?*' Karen stared at me. 'I don't believe anyone can *enjoy* teaching these days.'

'I do.'

'Yes, well, you've found yourself in a very nice position, haven't you?'

Something clicked. 'Did *you* apply for the deputy headship here, Karen?'

'Well, of course I did. I should have been given it, never mind had to apply for it. I've been here over ten years.'

'So that's why you resent *me* being here?'

'Mrs Theobold was a brilliant head teacher. *She* would have soon sent complaining parents packing.'

'But she didn't give you an interview for the deputy's job?'

'Well, yes, I applied and was interviewed along with all the other applicants. But she gave the job to you. New blood and all that...' Karen gave a little sniff. 'And then you and David Henderson got together and offered Debs Stringer the acting deputy headship.'

'But, Karen, we asked for applications in writing. Debs was the only one who applied. You had the chance to apply like everyone else.'

'I shouldn't have had to *apply*,' she snarled. 'It should have been *given* to me. I am the most senior teacher here.'

'Karen, you know as well as I do, it doesn't happen like that. I think we're getting off the point here...'

I looked at her and was just going to get back to Daisy and Maisie when Karen sniffed again and then again. She fished a hanky from the sleeve of her cardigan and made to stand up, tears streaming down her face.

'Karen, sit down. You can't go back to the classroom like this.'

'I've had enough,' she sobbed. 'I've had enough of it all...'

'What? Enough of what?' I passed the box of tissues that always sat on my desk and she took a handful, burying her face into their white softness.

'You wouldn't understand,' she eventually managed to say.

'Try me.'

'Drugs,' she started sobbing again.

'You're on *drugs*?'

'No, not *me*,' she tutted crossly, wiping her eyes. 'Gareth.'

'Gareth?'

'My son. He's twenty-five. He's a heroin addict.'

'I'm really sorry.'

'Why should *you* be sorry? With your smart kids, over at the grammar school… What would *you* know?' Karen glared at me and blew her nose loudly.

'There's always *something* with one's kids…'

'My husband has thrown him out. I don't know where he is. He was stealing from us… and I don't know why I'm telling *you* all this but John's business has gone down the pan…'

'John?'

'My husband. He's a builder. He was hoping to get the Bamforth Estates job…'

'If it goes ahead,' I murmured.

'Yes, and you're doing your damnedest to make sure it doesn't. John needs that contract. We're going to have to sell the house otherwise.'

'I'm really sorry, Karen.'

'And… and…'

Oh, heavens. Was there more?

'And I'm frightened...' She buried her face once more into a fresh supply of tissues.

'What of?'

'A lump. I've found a lump in my... you know...'

'Your breast?'

'Hmm.'

'Right, OK, Karen, you're going to go home now. I'll take your class this afternoon. Ring for an emergency appointment at your GP; don't be fobbed off. Say you need to see someone today. I'll speak to Maisie's mum and Daisy's mum and tell them you and I have had a chat and I'll have a chat with the girls themselves, too.'

Karen looked at me, tried to say something, but ended up in tears once more.

'You've got a lot on your plate, Karen,' I said. 'Go and see if you can at least sort some of it with your GP this afternoon.'

'OK. Thank you. And, I'm, you know, I'm... sorry...' She suddenly thrust out her hand towards me.

It seemed very strange, her standing there, hand held out stiffly and I wasn't quite sure what to do with it. I wanted to say, 'Don't be daft, Karen, you don't have to shake my hand.' But instead I took it and she shook mine briefly without looking at me, picked up her bag and headed for the door.

I had a lovely afternoon with Karen's class of eight-year-olds. I missed being actually at the chalk face, and her kids were a particularly nice bunch, enthusiastic and friendly, and we ended the afternoon singing a rather lively and raucous rendition of 'The one-eyed, one-horned, flying, purple person-eater'. Well, it was Friday afternoon and it *had* been a long week.

The house seemed cold and unloved when I finally got home around six. Both kids were out with friends, and I considered ringing Paula and asking if she fancied joining me for my usual cheese on toast and glass of red wine. Get used to being on your own, I scolded myself.

I pulled off my work clothes, donned an old tracksuit and set to, cleaning the house, stripping beds and cleaning loos and basins. Tom's room was immaculate: not a thing out of place. Freya's was a jumble sale.

The housework helped a little and, once I'd stuck a load of washing in the machine, I ran a bath, lit a candle I'd brought back from Mexico and poured myself a glass of red wine. I slid beneath the scented water, breathed in the combined scents of cinnamon and honeysuckle from the candle and sipped my wine. I closed my eyes and almost immediately found myself crying, tears running down my face and joining the bathwater. Maybe I should ring Julian and Ritchie and have a good weep down the phone to them. No, nobody loves a cry baby on a Friday evening. Paula? No, she'd gone for a curry with her new friend. Clare? No, too loved up with Rageh. Fi would make me laugh and bring me round, I reckoned, but then I remembered it was her wedding anniversary. My new dad? Hardly. Samaritans? A big possibility.

Xavier?

I wanted Xavier.

I needed to see him. He *was* my brother, for heaven's sake. I'd always wanted a brother.

I jumped out of the bath, dried myself, pulled on jeans, sweater and trainers and half an hour later was sitting outside his house in the car in the pouring rain. Lights were on in the downstairs windows and the curtains were drawn. Oh God, what if Ophelia were there? In a panic, I was about to put the car into reverse when his door opened and Xavier stood there, hair rumpled and feet bare.

I opened the car door, got out and he came towards me.

'You've no shoes on,' I said.

'Cassie…' He took me in his arms, stroking my hair.

'I can't bear not to see you. Look, you're my brother. There's no reason not to see you… I've always wanted a brother…' Rain was running down my face and I wiped it away with my hand. 'We don't have to… you know…'

Xavier pulled me inside into the warmth of the house and then held me at arm's length so he could look into my face. 'Cassie, do you really think I can be with you, in a room with you, without wanting to…? I can't do this, Cassie. I'm so sorry…'

I looked over his shoulder. 'Is Ophelia back? Is that it?' I asked, looking round the room for signs of female belongings: a pair of shoes, a scarf, a handbag maybe.

He shook his head, stroking my face, wiping the tears and rain away. 'No, of course she isn't. As far as I know she's in London or possibly South Africa. I really have no idea and I really, really don't care. Cassie, I can't do this, I can't be your brother. Do you want me to drive back with you? Make sure you get back OK?'

I shook my head numbly and walked back to the car.

Freya turned from buttering crumpets as I pushed open the kitchen door.

She peered at me. 'Are you OK? Where've you been? You were supposed to pick me up from Gabby's. Her dad had to drop me off.'

She took a bite of her crumpet, indicating, with a nod of her head, upstairs. 'And, er, I'm not sure how to tell you this, Mum, but I think you'll find Dad's back, too.'

33

But Does He 'Ave Your 'Eart...?

At least Mark had had the decency to leave his cases downstairs in the hall even though he'd had the temerity to take himself up to our bedroom. I found him sitting on the edge of the bed, head in his hands, the very picture of sorrow and remorseful regret.

'What are *you* doing here?'

'I'm so sorry, Cass, I'm so sorry.' Mark raised his head but was unable to meet my eyes. 'I want to come home.'

'Looks like you are home,' I snapped. 'Why?'

'I love you. I love you and the kids.'

'So, has Tina thrown you out?'

'No, no, not at all. It was my decision to come home.'

'Oh, so is she going to be knocking on my door – *my* door, Mark – demanding you back?'

'No, she knows I've come back...'

I just looked at him, this husband of mine, this weak

man who'd deceived me for so long, who'd made such a fool of me. I didn't care, I realised. I really didn't care what he did.

'Whatever,' I muttered, sounding like a thirteen-year-old who'd been told she was grounded. 'Do what you want. I really don't care anymore.'

'So, is it OK then?' Mark made to take my hand but I shrugged him off.

OK? Mark had been messing around with my best friend for two years, he'd been gone for almost four months and then suddenly decides he wants to come back to us. And the pillock wanted to know if it was OK? I just looked at him, this man that I'd loved and had my children with, this man that I'd made a home with.

'OK for us to try again, I mean. For the sake of the children, Cass?' he pleaded, trying to take my hand again. 'I know I've let you down…'

'*Let me down*? Forgetting to take the bins out is *letting me down*. Not remembering my favourite chocolate biscuits on a shopping trip to Tesco is *letting me down*. Deceiving me for two years with my best friend and then leaving me on the eve of my starting a brand-new job is *not* fucking well *letting me down*.' I glared at him as my rant finally ran out of breath.

He looked up at me with puppy-dog eyes and managed to squeeze out a small tear.

I watched it move down his face and fizzle out somewhere around his nose. God, he couldn't even produce proper tears. 'Actually, Mark, it really *isn't* OK.'

'But it can be, Cass, I promise. I can make it all better. Just give me time. Trust me…' Mark stood up, trying to take me in his arms.

Trust him? I almost laughed at that. 'I suggest you go to your mum's, if you've nowhere else to go tonight. I really don't want you here.'

'But I don't want to go to my mother's…' Mark's eyes narrowed and I saw, perhaps for the first time, the spoilt little boy who'd always wanted, and usually managed, to get his own way. He folded his arms and put his head to one side. 'So, it's true then?'

'What's true?'

'You're seeing someone.'

'And where have you heard that little snippet of gossip?'

'Well, that didn't take you long, did it?' Mark almost sneered.

'Mark, I want you to go. I don't care where you go, but I don't want you here.'

Mark's voice went back to its former pleading. 'Cass, come on, you can't throw almost twenty years down the drain for some holiday romance… And it is all over with Tina, honestly it is. I've come back to *you*.'

'OK, that's it. I want you to go back down those stairs the way you came up them, take your cases and go. Really, Mark, go.'

'So, what's Xavier Bamforth got then, besides a ton of money and a very gorgeous wife? You do *know* he's married?'

'Mark, I'm assuming Clare told Tina about me and Xavier Bamforth…' When he didn't say anything, I just shook my head. 'Yes, well, what Clare wouldn't have said, because she doesn't actually *know*, is that Xavier...' I stopped myself. This had nothing to do with anyone but Xavier and me.

'Xavier is what?' Mark narrowed his eyes again.

'Nothing. Mark, I'm not with Xavier Bamforth...' Just saying the words out loud made me want to cry. But knowing I couldn't have Xavier, and never could have, didn't make me want to have Mark instead. Just the opposite in fact '... And, do you know, you did me a big favour going off and leaving me. I actually quite like myself now. I'm not sure I ever really did before.'

'But, Cass, I...' Mark was wheedling again. '*I* like you, I *love* you.'

'Please, Mark, go. I really, really don't want you here.'

An hour after Mark had left, banging the door behind him, I was halfway through a bottle of red and trying to summon up the energy to clear up the mess in the kitchen when Mark's mum, Mavis, appeared on the doorstep, rain-mate covering her newly set hair. She'd obviously spent the afternoon at the hairdresser's as she did every Friday.

'I thought it best I actually come round, Cassandra, rather than try to phone you.' Mavis shook her rain-mate at me like a wet dog. 'It's tipping it down out there. It's not a night to be driving, you know.' She looked at me accusingly as if it were my fault she'd had to come out.

'I suppose Mark sent you?'

'Well, you did throw him out into the street, Cassandra. This is still his home, you know.'

'I think he gave up that right when he started sleeping with my best friend. Two years, Mavis...'

'Oh, I'm sure it wouldn't have been that long,' Mavis sniffed. 'Things always seem worse than they actually are. Now, do you not think it's time you forgave him? You know, forgive and forget, start again?'

I looked at my mother-in-law and shook my head. I was feeling a bit woozy from the alcohol. 'I'm sorry, Mavis. It wouldn't work. You see, well, the thing is, I'm actually in love with someone else.'

Mavis stared at me, a red flush creeping up her neck and face. 'In love?' she stuttered. 'In love? Who with?'

'It really doesn't matter who with,' I said, tears rolling down my cheeks. 'It's all over now and I can't have him...'

'Well, you kept that quiet, lady.' She glared at me. 'Married, I suppose?'

'It's irrelevant.'

'So, let Mark come back then,' she said eagerly. 'You've both done wrong, so you're quits. Forgive each other.'

'No, Mavis, at the moment, no.'

Mavis narrowed her eyes. 'Well, if not for you, for Tom's sake.'

'Tom?'

'Well, hasn't he turned queer? Mark said—'

'Queer? Oh, for heaven's sake, Mavis...'

'If his father were back, a manly influence, then he'd soon start to forget these ridiculous notions of being...

gay.' She almost spat the word. '*Gay* in my day meant happy, jolly, not, not… well, you know.'

'Mavis, I'm going to ask you to go home now,' I said slowly, summoning all my strength to speak calmly when I really wanted to yell. 'I'm not taking Mark back…'

When Mavis opened her mouth to remonstrate, I held up my hand like Deimante in lollipop lady mode. 'I mean it, Mavis, go. Go back to Mark, let him stay with you, feed him some nice steak and kidney and a big slice of Battenburg.'

Without another word, I almost manhandled her to the front door, locked up and went upstairs to bed.

It snowed in that first week of December, huge wet clumps that left rivers of grey slush in the playground too slippery for the kids to play out on. If I'd had my way I'd have had the lot of them outside in their coats, hats and wellies, enjoying the fresh air and making futile attempts to build snowmen. But this was today, not some playground of latter years where children were allowed to slip, slide and fall on their backsides without Ofsted investigating or parents ringing in to complain that their precious offspring had arrived home with wet socks or tights.

The Friday lunchtime, after a full week of wet playtimes, had been particularly trying. Deimante, obviously fed up to the back teeth with a couple of spoiled kids who daily turned their noses up at the lunch choice, had turned on them telling them, 'Eats, you eats this lovely grubs,' before slapping huge spoonfuls of watery cabbage onto their plates and, in doing so, reducing the recipients to tears.

There'd been bumped heads, fallings-out, fights and a whole queue of kids standing waiting outside my office for various misdemeanours. I'd had enough. With twenty minutes still to go until the end of the Key Stage 2 lunch break, I instructed the lunchtime supervisors to round up the whole junior school and bring the kids into the hall. They trooped in expecting a bollocking, but instead of the little ones at the front and the Year 6 children slouching against the wall at the back – which every eleven-year-old saw as his or her rite of passage – I teamed up each older child with a much younger one, slotted in my special CD, turned up the volume to high and we were off.

We started with Pharrell Williams' 'Happy' – and I defy anyone, nine or ninety, not to just *have* to move to that – and went through Maroon 5's 'Moves Like Jagger', Wham!'s 'Wake Me Up Before You Go Go' and Michael Jackson's 'Thriller', finishing with that chap – I never know his name – singing 'Gangnam Style.'

We were all, including Grace and Deimante – who on hearing the music belting out had come into the hall and joined in – bouncing and boogying like there was no tomorrow, sweaty and totally exhausted. With five minutes to go until the end of lunch break, I brought the kids to a standstill and sat them down, legs crossed, arms folded, eyes closed and took them through some calming deep breathing with the dire warning that I would be visiting every single class during the afternoon's lessons.

They were to be calm and productive or *I* would want to know why.

'That were right good, Miss,' Chelsea Simpson, the most formidable member of Year 6, beamed as the children led off, in silence, to their respective classrooms.

I smiled back, pleased. 'Good, I'm glad you enjoyed it, Chelsea.'

'Yeah, it were almost as good as when we had sex with Mrs Stevenson in the dining room.'

I looked in total horror at Grace, who was at my side helping supervise the last of the children out of the hall.

'Sex education,' Grace giggled when she saw my face. 'If you remember, I stood in for Debs when she was off and had to teach Year 6 in the dining room because all the electricity was off in their classroom.'

'Jesus, Grace, I thought I was going to have to call in the police.'

'I should go and cool down, if I were you,' Grace laughed, following her class back to their classroom. 'You look a bit hot under the collar.'

Never mind hot under the collar: dressed for the snow in black polo-necked sweater, woolly tights and boots, I was hot everywhere, sweating from boogying on down with one hundred and twenty, seven to eleven-year-olds. Thankful that I had no appointments or visitors that afternoon and that my teaching commitment was down to appearing, unannounced, on inspection of behaviour duty, I tried to run a comb through my sweating hair and flapped my armpits in an attempt to cool down a bit. I longed to take off my woollen jumper and discard my boots and tights but knew, if David Henderson or any other of the governors put in a surprise appearance, it wouldn't look too good. Smiling at the thought of greeting David Henderson in my greying Marks and Sparks bra, I settled at my desk to go through the day's mail.

Jean rang through after ten minutes. 'Mrs Beresford, there's Mr Bamforth to see you.'

My heart went into overdrive. Which Bamforth? Xavier? But he had made it perfectly clear he was staying out of the way. Anyway, it was obviously Edward Bamforth. He was notorious for dropping in unannounced, bent on hassling me to see his point of view over the fields and the idea of a new Trust school.

I opened my office door. There was no sign of Edward *or* Xavier. A tall dark-haired woman sat in the chair outside Jean's reception office. I racked my brains: did I have an appointment with a mother I'd forgotten about and, if so, why hadn't Jean rung her through?

'Ah, Mrs Beresford?' The woman stood, looking me up and down with such close scrutiny I began to feel embarrassed. Was I still such a sweaty mess? I put a hand to my hair, running my fingers through it in order to achieve some semblance of authority rather than the obvious scarecrow. 'You look rather hot.'

'Yes, I've been dancing,' I smiled. 'Trying to exhaust a hundred cooped-up kids before afternoon lessons... Oh, is it snowing again?'

The woman brushed leather-clad fingers across the shoulders of her very elegant camel trench coat. 'Just a little.'

'I'm sorry, do you have an appointment? I didn't catch your name? It's just that Jean, our secretary, told me someone else was waiting…' I glanced through the open door of reception. 'Jean, I thought you said Mr Bamforth was here?'

'*Mrs* Bamforth,' Jean said knowingly, raising her eyebrows at me.

'*Mrs* Bamforth? Oh…' I was momentarily lost for words. The woman stood. 'Brigitte Bamforth.' She held out a gloved hand. She spoke perfect English apart from an occasional vowel inflection that gave away that she was French-born. 'I do 'ope this isn't inconvenient, Mrs Beresford?' She glanced across at Jean, who was taking it all in while on the pretext of sorting through the box of lost property outside her office. 'Can we speak somewhere private?'

'I'm so sorry,' I said, once we were sitting in my office. 'I really thought Jean said *Mr* Bamforth. I was expecting your husband.'

'Or my son?' She looked across at me with her very dark eyes and I reddened, feeling as though I were being judged. I did hope she wasn't here to make a fuss, demanding to know where Paula lived. 'Mrs Beresford, I know all about you. I know you are my husband's love child. I also know—'

There was a knock on the door and, before I could switch on the red *Engaged* light, seven-year-old Ibrahim Assaf had opened the door and come straight in.

'Mrs Beresford,' he said tearfully, 'Miss Crawford said I had to come straight to you to tell you.' Great fat tears rolled down his face.

'Tell me what, Ibrahim?'

'I said that word.'

'Which word?' I glanced across at Brigitte Bamforth, who was looking amused.

'You know, *that* word... It begins with F...'

'Right, OK, Ibrahim. You can see I've a visitor here...'

'... And I were working right hard like you said we had to. I'd even got on to doing the maths extension problem, and that's *really* hard.'

'Right, OK...'

'... And Miss Crawford patted me on my head and said, "I bet that were hard, Ibrahim, well done." And I said, "It was, Miss, it were *fucking* hard..." It just popped out, Mrs Beresford. I were concentrating so hard on it, it just popped out. You won't tell me dad, will you?'

'Ibrahim, I want you to go back to Miss Crawford. Tell her I've seen you, I've had a word and I know that that *very* rude word will never *pop* out again, either here or at home. And if it does, if it *does*, Ibrahim, your dad will be *popping* into my office quicker than you can do that extension problem.'

Ibrahim wiped his face with his sleeve. 'I promise, Miss.'

'Sorry about that,' I apologised as the door closed behind Ibrahim, and I immediately switched the green *Come In* light to red.

Brigitte smiled for the first time. She was a very beautiful woman and I could see why Edward had fallen for her on his trip to Paris: she must have been stunning in her twenties. 'Oh, don't worry. I always wanted to be a teacher...' She stopped smiling and was instantly serious once more. 'Mrs Beresford, I was with Xavier last night. I've only just returned from staying with my mother in Paris. Xavier is in a bit of a state...' She sighed. 'It is very difficult when you fall in love but you know you cannot be with that person for whatever reason...'

'Ophelia?' I asked, praying she meant me.

'Ophelia?' She glared at me. '*Non, non*. Not Ophelia. I'm very glad she appears to be out of his life. You must know 'e's in love with you?'

'Well, yes...'

She stared at me. 'I need to know. Do you feel the same about Xavier?'

'Well, yes, but—'

'Never mind the buts, Mrs Beresford. Do you love my son?'

'Yes, but—' Did this woman not realise the problem?

'Does 'e 'ave *your* 'eart?' Brigitte leaned forward and took my hand, her accent becoming more pronounced in her earnestness to know whether I was serious about Xavier or not.

'Yes,' I said, wanting to cry. ''E 'as *my* 'eart.'

Brigitte sighed and sat back in her chair but never once took those dark eyes from my face. 'I was eighteen, Cassandra – may I call you Cassandra?'

I nodded.

'I know what it's like to be in love. When I was eighteen I fell in love with my father's friend.'

'Your *father's* friend?' I stared at her. 'Gosh, he must have been quite a bit older than you?'

''E was. I was eighteen and 'e was forty-five and 'e was about to be recommended to the Executive...'

'The Executive?' I wasn't particularly up on the French political system but I knew it was something to do with being in government. 'The *French* Executive?'

'But of course. Which other Executive?' Brigitte tutted. 'Monsieur Barre, the prime minister back in 1976, was in the process of recommending 'im to the Executive and President Giscard d'Estaing. You know, from the National Assembly?' She frowned. 'Unfortunately, as well as being my father's best friend and in a very delicate political situation, 'e also had a wife and three children.'

'That must have been hard for you.' I smiled in sympathy.

'It was. In the words of your little friend, it was "fucking hard". Fucking impossible actually.' She smiled at what she'd just said and then went on, 'If I'd revealed that I was pregnant, at eighteen, to a married minister in the government, it would have ruined his career.'

'You were pregnant? Goodness, that could have brought down the government.' I was pretty hazy about French politics but could imagine the sensation if, for example, Tony Blair or David Cameron was revealed to have got his best mate's teenaged daughter pregnant just as they were heading for Downing Street.

'Correct.'

'So?' I asked. 'What? You had a termination?'

'This was 1976,' she said, never taking her eyes off me. 'And France. We weren't quite as liberal-thinking as England back then. In fact, a certain Marie-Louise Giraud was actually sent to the guillotine as late as 1943 for having an abortion. Termination was not adopted permanently in France until 1979...'

'So?' I felt my heart begin to pound. I *knew* where she was going with all this.

'So, I slept with Edward Bamforth when he came to stay at my parents' house, knowing I was pregnant with another man's child...'

I felt a strange buzzing in my ears and broke out into a sweat at what Brigitte had just said.

'Cassandra, I have never revealed to anyone, even to my sister whom I adore, what I'm now telling you. This is why I need to know that you love Xavier – that you want to be with him – because if you *don't*, I will leave here and my secret goes not only out of this room with me, but...' Brigitte gave a Gallic shrug and stared intently at me, '... but also to my *grave*.'

'How can you be sure Xavier isn't Edward's son?' I asked. God, here we go again, I thought.

'But I've explained to you. I knew I was a couple of weeks pregnant when Edward came to stay with us. It was very easy... Xavier was a couple of weeks premature, shall we say?'

I breathed deeply. 'And you've told Xavier all this? You've told him Edward isn't his father?'

Brigitte tutted once more. '*Non, non.* Absolutely not. I've just told you, I've never revealed this to anyone until now. I spent all last evening with my son while 'e poured out 'is 'eart to me. I love Xavier more than anything in the world. I will do this for 'im, but only if you love 'im. If you don't love 'im then I don't need to tell my secret. You see?'

I saw.

Shit, poor Edward. Within a couple of weeks, he'd gained a daughter and lost a son. Enough to make anyone question their relationships. 'Let me get this straight,' I said carefully. 'Just so I can be sure...'

'Xav is *not* your brother.'

'So, we can be together?' A great cacophony of bells was ringing; fireworks were going off in myriad colours in my head.

'Only if you love 'im enough. If it is at all 'alf 'earted then I must ask you to forget that I ever came 'ere this afternoon. By giving you Xavier you 'ave to see that 'e will lose his father. He can't 'ave both. It is in your 'ands, Cassandra.'

'Mrs Bamforth,' I pleaded, 'what do *you* want me to do?'

She shrugged. 'Edward and I don't spend all our time together. I stay in Paris a lot at my mother's 'ouse. I love Paris; I never really love Midhope. If, by telling Edward that Xav isn't his son and that I 'ave deceived 'im all these years, my 'usband and I fall apart then that must be so. I shall go and live with my mother in Paris permanently and 'ope that Xav forgives me.' Brigitte looked at me intently. 'You know, it's only been a few weeks with you and my son. You need to be sure the relationship is strong

and stable before you put the cat amongst the pigeons.'
She smiled.

I nodded, unable to speak.

Brigitte stood up, scrutinised my face carefully and then, kissing me on both cheeks, walked out without a backwards glance from my office.

34

Is That Jesus, or Maybe Beyoncé?

Clare, Fiona and I had planned a walk for the following day.

We've not been together, just the three of us, for weeks, Clare had texted us both earlier in the week.

Get your walking boots out and we'll head for the moors.

'I don't want to be accused of being one of those women who, the minute they have a new relationship, abandon their women friends in order to be there solely for their new man,' Clare announced, hopping around in stockinged feet by the boot of her car as she changed long black leather boots for a sturdy pair of walking ones.

'You mean Rageh is at the hospital?' Fi asked drily. 'I can't imagine you giving up a chance to spend a whole Saturday with him in order to tramp over the moors with us.' She adjusted the bright pink woolly hat atop her head and pulled on a pair of gloves. 'God, it's cold. Wouldn't we be better just going for coffee somewhere?'

'For your information, I've left Rageh tucked up in bed,' Clare said loftily. 'As I said, my friendships are important to me. You…' she poked Fi in the ribs through her padded jacket '… are important to me. Come on, we'll walk up over the moors and round Robinwood Reservoir.'

The rain, sleet and wet snow that had continued to fall throughout the working week had finally petered out, leaving one of those fantastically cold but crisp days where the sun has deigned not only to put in an appearance, but is determined to be a total show-off. Even while I donned sunglasses, the cold scoured my cheeks like a Brillo pad and our breath smoked in the freezing air. My hands, in their gloves, were numb and I slapped them together in an effort to bring some life back into them.

I was tired, having spent much of the previous night unable to sleep. I'd swung from total euphoria, hugging myself with excitement and happiness as I lay in bed, knowing that Xavier was no blood relation whatsoever to me, to total anxiety that I held the key to opening the biggest and wormiest can of invertebrates I'd ever come across. By opening that can I was going to shatter Edward's relationship with both his wife and his supposed son.

'Are you OK?' Fi took my arm as we set off from the car park. 'Careful,' she warned as I skidded slightly, bumping into her. 'Watch your step; all that slushy snow has turned to ice.'

'You've been very quiet all the way here.' Clare walked quickly to catch us up after locking her car. 'Come on, fill us in with the latest. Is Mark still badgering you?'

'Badgering me?' I laughed. 'Sounds a bit rude, does that: oh, hang on, that's *rogering*, isn't it?' I laughed again. 'God, can you believe two months ago I'd have been in heaven if Mark were rogering... or *badgering* me.'

'So how do you feel about him now?' Fi asked.

'He just seems a bit pathetic. Weak and spoilt. Did he always seem like this? I don't know...'

'And Xavier? Is he still sticking to the rules and not contacting you? That must be so hard, Cassie.' Clare patted my arm as we strode out against the cold.

I nodded. And then, unable not to, stopped walking, bringing us all to a halt. 'I've got to tell you two or I'll burst. I've just got to tell *someone*...'

'Ooh, what?' Fi was excited.

'Look, I shouldn't... it's not my secret. Do you absolutely *promise* that what I'm going to tell you will not go any further than we three? Even Matt and Rageh musn't know.'

'Blimey, what is it?' Fi took my arm once again as I set off walking, unable to keep still. 'Oh, I know, you've murdered Tina and buried her somewhere. That's why Mark came back: no one to have sex with or wash his socks.'

I laughed. 'No, according to Mark he came back because he wanted to: realised he loved me after all...'

Clare snorted. 'Sorry, Cassie, and I wouldn't have told you this if I knew you were going to take him back. Tina *told* him to leave. Seems that the excitement of an affair soon loses its thrill once all the exciting subterfuge and illicit meetings become legal. There's only so many times you can step over your lover's dirty socks and pants left on the bedroom floor. Mark, apparently, was under the assumption they would be picked up, washed, ironed and back in his drawer by the sock and pants fairy.'

''Fraid that was me,' I said guiltily. 'I couldn't stand mess, you see. I had to pick them up otherwise we'd have been stepping over them all week. I tell you something – there's no way I would *ever* do it again for any man.'

'Yes, well, Tina didn't put up with it,' Clare finished.

'Look, can we get off Mark's dirty pants and on to the *secret*?' Fi was impatient.

'OK, so you two promise? I mean, it's not my secret to tell and it's *really* not fair that you know what I'm going to tell you and the people involved don't—'

'For fuck's sake, Cassie, just spit it out.' Fi took one arm and Clare my other, and, while I knew I shouldn't, I related, verbatim, Brigitte's visit to my office the previous afternoon.

'But, that's brilliant,' Fi said, hugging me. 'I don't see the problem. What the hell are you doing here, with us, when you could be with Xavier?'

'Oh, come on, Fi…' Clare stopped walking and pulled out a hip flask. 'Hang on a minute, have a slurp of this brandy to keep us going.' She handed us the flask in turn, and the mellow liquid radiated warmth as we swallowed.

'I understand totally Cassie's dilemma. By telling Xavier this secret that's been kept for forty years, she'd be lighting the blue touch paper for an absolute implosion. I don't see how you *can* tell him, Cassie.'

'And I don't see how you *can't*.' Fi was adamant. 'He made her slide down the wall, for heaven's sake. The first man to ever do that. She *has* to tell him.'

'Last night, in bed, I thought of you and Rageh, Clare,' I said, 'and how you refused to see him because his happiness was more important than your own. You refused to upset the apple cart...'

'For God's sake,' Fi snorted. 'We've had *upset apple carts, cans of worms, cats and bloody pigeons*. Just let the shit hit the f- - -ing fan and have done with it.'

'I think, Cassie,' Clare said calmly, 'you have to decide which Xavier himself would rather. Would he rather continue thinking that Edward is his real father? Or would he rather have you? It really is as simple as that.'

And so I did nothing.

I'd not seen Xavier since the evening I'd gone round to his house and he'd told me in no uncertain terms he couldn't be my brother. Surely, if he felt the same about me as I did about him, he'd have wanted to see me if only to be my brother? I felt he'd made the decision for me.

I filled every waking moment with my family's needs: seeing Mum, visiting Granddad and making sure that my kids didn't miss out from being in a single-parent family. I put ridiculous time and effort into Little Acorns in order to prove that I was the right person for the headship once the permanent post was advertised. Which, according to David Henderson, would probably be after Christmas.

But I really filled my head with school stuff in order not to leave any room in there for Xavier. I *couldn't* allow him there. Pictures of Xavier on the beach; Xavier holding my head as I was ill on the boat; Xavier with his warm mouth on my neck in my kitchen. They all had to be extinguished.

The countdown to the final week of term started with Little Acorns' Nursery and Reception Nativity which, I knew from past experience, would go down a treat as parents and grannies assembled to see their little darlings on stage for the first time.

''Oo's this 'ere then?' George Sanderson, one of the local farmer's sons, executed his lines in a broad Yorkshire accent.

'It's my baby,' Mary, aka four-year-old Molly Dixon, simpered, showing her dolly to the audience.

'Wot's 'is name then?' George asked, accentuating every word in a wooden monotone.

'Beyoncé,' Mary said proudly, holding up a swaddled Jesus.

'Is it 'eck,' George said loudly, frowning and looking offstage for reassurance that he'd got the right name. 'It's *Jesus*...'

'It's Beyoncé,' Mary reiterated once again.

'It i'nt, is it, Mrs Beaumont?' George looked offstage, beyond the curtains once more. 'It's Jesus, i'nt it?'

'It's my dolly, Beyoncé, George,' Mary said soothingly. 'But we're pretending she's Jesus, just for today.'

Two Kings made their appearance, walking slowly towards Jesus, a.k.a. Beyoncé. From my seat with the governors on the front row, I peered towards the stage curtains: weren't three Kings the norm? The third, five-year-old Noah Pogson, bored with waiting to come on in majestic triumph, had experimented with putting his foot on the bottom of the stage curtain and twisted round. And round and round until he was trussed up in the curtain like a Christmas turkey. It took two nursery nurses to spin him in reverse and push him on stage, giggling and slightly drunk with the excitement, to join his more regal mates.

'I must remember to put that in next year's risk assessment,' I whispered, grinning at a laughing David Henderson.

Karen Adams was on sick leave. While the lump in her breast was not malignant, thank goodness, she'd apparently broken down in her GP's surgery, unable to move from her chair until her husband was sent for. Stress was diagnosed, and Karen told to take an immediate and, it turned out, extended leave. Little Acorns was a much happier place without her.

So, I filled my days and, exhausted, fell into bed and deep, dreamless sleep. When Harry Kennedy was back in

Midhope from recording in London, he would turn up at the house in his Mini to see Tom. Harry had, according to Freya, who knew about these things, been totally open with the press about his sexuality from the start. It didn't appear to put off the village teenage girls, who hung around our garden waiting for autographs. They even asked Tom for his and, grinning, he signed his name with a flourish on their pieces of paper and Second Coming posters. I worried for Tom, of course I did. What mother of a seventeen-year-old, in love for the first time – or second, I reminded myself, remembering the boy in the Blue Ball – didn't?

I was concerned that living in a small rural village might be difficult for him and he could find himself alienated at his new sixth-form college. I needn't have worried. We were terribly lucky that this particular establishment, one of the best in the country and situated down in Midhope town centre, with kids travelling in by train from Manchester as well as Leeds and Bradford, was exceptionally right-on with regards to its students' personal and social welfare and particularly its stance on LGBT issues. While maths was still Tom's number-one love, he was now allocating time in his life for more personal matters and had even put himself forward for election to the Student Welfare Committee at college. I had chatted to Tom's tutor and been assured and reassured that, whilst the college was always open for chats and even counselling sessions with regards a student's sexuality, kids today were, on the whole, far more confident about expressing their sexuality, with other students accepting as normal their choice of orientation.

I became very friendly with Nicola, Harry's mother, a divorcee, and together we had mutual worry sessions over a bottle of wine.

Mark had moved in with his mother but would arrive unannounced at the house several times a week. I'd often come home late from school or a prolonged meeting to find Freya and Mark sitting at the kitchen table sharing a bowl of pasta and pesto, the only dish in either of their respective culinary repertoires.

'He is trying, Mum,' Freya announced one evening just before the end of term. 'He really wants to come back, you know…'

Biting back the obvious retort that yes, her father *was* bloody trying, I said, 'Look, Freya, I'm glad, really glad, that you appear to have a relationship with your father once more. I certainly wouldn't deny either of you that.' I just hoped Tom would come round, too, but that didn't seem to be on the cards at the moment. Tom was too caught up in his own new and exciting life to be overly concerned with his father's. 'But,' I went on, 'you have to understand that *I've* changed over the past four months. I'm sorry, but it's just not on, having your father back here on a permanent basis.'

Freya had actually grinned. 'Fair enough; just be his friend rather than his wife.' She hesitated. 'I can see why you fancy that Xavier Bamforth.' She looked up at me through her emo fringe, which seemed to get longer and darker on a daily basis. 'Mum, I know…'

'Know what?' My heart lurched at the mention of his name.

'That you had a bit of a fling with him in Mexico... and that he's your *brother.* Bloody hell, Mum, how come it's turned out that Edward Bamforth – the biggest enemy of the NMLA – is my granddad?' She grinned again. 'But I can see *why* you fancied Xavier. He's pretty hot... Gosh,' she went on excitedly, 'I suppose he's my *Uncle* Xavier. Our very first real uncle. Do you not think he and Edward Bamforth will stop all this planning now? Now that we're related?' Then she stopped smiling as she saw my eyes fill with tears. She came and put her arms round me. 'Oh, Mum, I'm sorry. You really did fancy him, didn't you? And you can't have him.'

Freya thrust the roll of kitchen paper in my direction and I tried to smile. 'Paula told you, I suppose?' I'd kill her when I saw her.

'Of course she did. She's worried about you, Mum.' She frowned. 'Mind you, I don't think she really wants you and Dad to get back together either. Paula says you've become a strong independent woman with your own views.'

The Saturday before Christmas – I was determined to make an effort for the kids' sake and had invited not only Paula and Granddad Norman for Christmas lunch, as usual, but also Nicola and Harry Kennedy as well as Clare and Rageh – so I made some mince pies and decided to take a batch round to Granddad.

He was irritable when I arrived. 'What's that you've got there, lass?' he asked suspiciously as I placed the plastic box on his kitchen table.

'Mince pies. I thought we'd get into the Christmas spirit.'

'Aye, well, I don't like mince pies: the pastry gets stuck behind me plate. And I don't like Christmas. Any road, I reckon I won't be around by Christmas.'

'Oh? Are you going anywhere nice?' I asked, playing along. 'Do you want a lift to the station?'

'I reckon I'll be singing wi' bloody angels by Christmas.'

'Well, then, as it's only two days to Christmas, you'd better come to All Hallows Church carol service with me tomorrow. Get some practice in before you meet them. St Peter won't let just anyone in, you know.'

Granddad grunted but refused to get out of his chair.

'Come on, you miserable old so-and-so. Get your coat on and we'll have a wander around Norman's Meadow. You need some fresh air.'

'I can't be bothered, our Sandra. If they're going to build on me field I'd rather not be here.'

'Here, get your coat on.' I pulled it down from its usual place on the back of the door and threw him his flat cap.

Granddad grunted again, but stood up, planted his cap firmly on his head and reached for his stick beside his chair. 'There's nowt to see at this time of year, anyhow. Miserable bloody time of year...'

'God, Granddad, if I was fed up before, I'm almost suicidal now.'

He looked at me sharply. 'What's up wi' you? That husband of yours still not come back, then?'

'He wants to, but I don't want him back. I'm perfectly fine by myself.'

He nodded approvingly. 'Yes, you're a lot like your mother... an independent, strong woman... Get off me arm, Sandra, I'm perfectly capable of walking meself. Anyone'd think I were on me last legs...'

The damp, foggy weather was enough to make us turn back before we'd started, but I opened the gate at the top of Granddad's garden and we were immediately into the meadow. A combination of autumn grazing by the local farmer's cows, followed by a flock of sheep, now gazing balefully at us through orange satanic eyes, had rendered the meadow unpromising, keeping the glory of what would come by the spring and summer well hidden.

We walked slowly round, keeping to the meadow's perimeter, Granddad poking his stick crossly at the wall wherever stones had parted company from the main structure. 'So, have you heard owt about the planning then? Has t'council agreed to it?'

'Any day, I should think,' I said. 'The Bamforths had the plans into Midhope Council long before we knew anything about it...' I stopped talking as three figures appeared to our left, their backs away from us as they stood, leaning against the wall, looking across to the fields beyond.

'Who's that over there, then?' Granddad waved his walking stick in their direction, peering through the mist at the two men and one woman who continued to stand, unaware of our presence, deep in conversation.

I stopped walking, my heart pounding, pulse racing. We needed to turn around; go right back the way we'd just come. I took Granddad's arm but, as if he knew he was under scrutiny, the man in the middle suddenly turned his head, looking right at me.

Xavier.

35

Here Comes the Llama Farmer...

Later, much later, when Edward and Brigitte had driven off together in Edward's huge four-wheel drive, wheels spinning in the muddy ruts, tail-lights red eyes in the deepening fog of the late December afternoon, Xavier stood in Granddad's kitchen, a mug of strong tea in his hand.

'Cassie,' he said, drawing me to him. For what seemed like minutes, neither of us spoke but he stroked my head as both my arms went around him. His black woollen jacket felt rough beneath my fingers, his breath warm against my face.

Granddad had fallen asleep over his tea, his mince pie consumed with relish once he knew his precious meadow was, for the moment, anyway, safe from development.

'I can't believe you decided not to tell me what Mum had told you,' Xavier said, holding me away from him and staring into my face with his beautiful brown eyes. 'How could you *not* tell me?'

'How *could* I, Xavier? Knowing that it would mean you would suddenly know your father *wasn't* your father. It wasn't *my* secret to tell. You must see that.' I scanned his face. Did he see?

Instead of speaking, Xavier stroked my hair. Neither of us said a word for a good minute, happy just to be in each other's arms. And then Xavier said, 'Dad knew the planning wasn't going well, you know.' He smiled. 'He's pretty astute: all along he's known it was a long shot he'd get planning for the three thousand houses, and he certainly wasn't bothered about the damned dry ski slope. That was just a sort of present to the village.'

'A present?' I tutted, crossly. 'Some bloody present.'

'He really wanted you and David Henderson on his side with the promise of a new school.' Xavier smiled again. 'But you fought him off.'

'I really don't think Midhope Council would have taken much heed of what *I* wanted,' I said, frowning.

'Well, you know David Henderson is pretty influential round here. And I'm sure Paula and Freya's protest in the meadow showed them what they were going to be up against. Once they had Harry Kennedy and *Look North* on board as well…' Xavier smiled as he broke off, kissing my forehead softly. 'Anyway, one of dad's friends on the council rang him yesterday afternoon to warn him. Dad knew Planning would be making a decision fairly soon but thought it would be after Christmas, but apparently Planning had been discussing it all day yesterday. All isn't lost for him. He'll be given permission to build on quite a few of the fields, and a couple of brown sites that no one will object to – even welcome, I would imagine – but nowhere near anything like he originally wanted. And it certainly won't affect Norman's Meadow or Little Acorns. There'll be an official turning-down of planning consent but not until the new year.'

'So, let me get this right, once your dad knew of the decision – unofficially, of course – he rang you and you went round?'

'Yes.'

'And your mum just came out with it? There and then?'

'Well, not quite. She'd obviously been building up to it for a few days. She did assume that once she told you, you'd be straight round to tell me. She's been on eggshells for days. And then she suddenly realised how unfair she'd been, asking *you* to make the decision to either keep or tell *her* secret. She also knew that losing you was the tipping point and I was off...'

'Off? Off where?' I stared at him. How could I bear it if he was going to leave, now that I'd found him again?

'South America.' Xavier was serious as he studied my reaction to his leaving.

'South America? You're going to South America?' I felt as though I'd been hit in the stomach and totally winded.

'Not if you don't want me to.'

'Jesus, Xavier, need you ask?'

'Mum knew I was serious about going. I've been mooting the idea for years. She knew the one thing that would make me stay now was you and, seeing *you* hadn't told me her secret – well, there was no alternative but to sit Dad and me down and tell us both herself.'

'But how did your poor dad react? Hang on, *my* dad...' I suddenly felt a bit protective towards him. 'Jesus, it's not news you really want to hear, is it?'

'Well, he went incredibly quiet for a few minutes. Didn't say a word. And then totally lost it, shouting and throwing things. Then he went into his snug and threw a few more things, drank half a bottle of whisky and then, because he can't stand any untidiness, came and cleared it all up.'

'And then?'

'And then he fell into a drunken sleep while Mum cried her eyes out and told me the full story. She was ready to pack her bags and go. Thought Dad would tell her to go.'

'So, what happened then?'

'Once he surfaced, with an incredible hangover, and found Mum in their bedroom packing her things, he broke down. He's actually quite a sensitive man, you know. I mean, he appears to be a hard-nosed businessman but underneath he's a bit of a pussycat...'

'The poor man,' I said.

'I'm not sure what he said to her – I obviously wasn't listening at the door – but she unpacked her things and they had a cup of tea...'

'Just like that? A cup of tea after all that?'

'They've had forty years of pretty happy marriage. Mum might not have loved him at the start, but I tell you now, she really does love him and certainly didn't want to have to leave.'

'And what about you? How do you feel knowing your dad *isn't* your dad?'

Xavier tutted and for a moment looked cross. 'Of course he's my dad. Just because some other guy got there first...' He tutted again. 'My dad *is* my dad. Always has been and always will be. My real dad, if you like, is... is just a sperm donor.'

Xavier became serious. 'And you know, Dad really wants to get to know *you* a lot better. You are his *real* daughter, after all.'

'Really?' I said delightedly. 'He wants to have a relationship with me?' I didn't say anything for a few seconds as I mulled this over. And then I said, 'Your mum adores you, doesn't she?' I smiled, thinking of the tall elegant woman I'd first met a couple of weeks ago.

'She's a mum. Think how you feel about Tom and Freya.'

I smiled again, picturing my own gorgeous kids, but then frowned, remembering what he'd said about South America. 'But why South America? Not more frigatebird hunting?'

Xavier laughed. 'Alpacas.'

'Alpacas?' I couldn't for the moment think what an alpaca was.

'Like llamas, but prettier. I've always loved them and I'm going to invest in and farm them.'

'In South America?' My heart seemed to nosedive once more.

'That was the plan. The biggest farms are in Chile and Bolivia and it would be a sight warmer there than here.'

'Oh. But you said that *was* the plan...?' I looked at him hopefully.

He smiled. 'That's why we were up here today, having a good look round: Dad's showing an interest, too. There are forty acres adjoining Norman's Meadow – don't worry, that field won't be included – which I'm going to turn over to farming alpacas. As your friend, Matthew the farmer, said at the meeting the other month, we need to farm the land. Need to diversify if necessary.'

'*You* are? You're going to be a *farmer*?' I stared at him in delight.

'So, Mrs Beresford, do you think you could love a *llama farmer*?' Xavier took my hand and held it to his face and I sank into him, kissing his open mouth while he responded slowly and sensuously, holding my face with both his hands.

'Jesus,' Xavier muttered into my hair. 'We need to get out of here...'

'Oy, lad, none of that mucky stuff in my house and with my granddaughter.' Granddad opened one eye. 'Any more of them mince pies going, love? I reckon I might just make it to Christmas after all...'

Acknowledgements

A big thank you to Jane Sargent, head teacher at All Hallows' C of E Primary School, Almondbury, who talked me through the process of, and implications for, a school becoming part of a Trust.

Thanks as always to my agent Anne Williams at KHLA Literary Agency and also to my editor Hannah Smith and the team at Aria, Head of Zeus, for their invaluable help and expertise with this book.

About Julie Houston

JULIE HOUSTON is the author of *The One Saving Grace*, *Goodness, Grace and Me* and *Looking for Lucy*. *A Village Affair* is a Kindle Top 5 general bestseller. She is married, with two children and a mad cockerpoo and, like her heroine, lives in a West Yorkshire village. She is also a teacher and a magistrate.

Hello from Aria

We hope you enjoyed this book! If you did let us know,
we'd love to hear from you.

We are Aria, a dynamic digital-first fiction imprint from
award-winning independent publishers Head of Zeus.
At heart, we're committed to publishing fantastic
commercial fiction – from romance and sagas to crime,
thrillers and historical fiction. Visit us online and discover
a community of like-minded fiction fans!

We're also on the look out for tomorrow's superstar
authors. So, if you're a budding writer looking for
a publisher, we'd love to hear from you.
You can submit your book online at ariafiction.com/
we-want-read-your-book

You can find us at:
Email: aria@headofzeus.com
Website: www.ariafiction.com
Submissions: www.ariafiction.com/
we-want-read-your-book

🄵 @ariafiction
🐦 @Aria_Fiction
📷 @ariafiction